JACKED UP

Elle Aycart

Editor: Rory Olsen
Cover Artist: Sofichinski Designs

This book is a work of fiction. While reference might be made to actual historical events or existing locations, the names, characters, places and incidents are either the product of the author's imagination or are used fictitiously, and any resemblance to actual persons, living or dead, business establishments, events, or locales is entirely coincidental.

Warning
This book contains sexually explicit scenes and adult language and may be considered offensive to some readers. Elle Aycart's books are for sale to adults ONLY, as defined by the laws of the country in which you made your purchase. Please store your files wisely, where they cannot be accessed by under-aged readers.

DEDICATION

To my mother, who passed away unexpectedly twenty days before this book was released. You were as beautifully stunning as stunningly complicated. I hope you finally found in heaven the peace you so desperately sought on earth.

PROLOGUE

Thinking with his dick was going to get Jack killed.

The guys he was dealing with wouldn't hesitate to reach down his throat, rip his balls off, and make a Colombian necktie with them at the slightest hint of weakness. Or deception. Heck, just for the sheer fun of it. No big reason needed.

Too damn bad Jack couldn't help himself. A cocked gun shoved to his head wouldn't change shit.

He logged in to his e-mail account, the one he was supposed to ignore, hands fucking sweaty. His heart leaped, lodging in his throat. Yeah, there it was. Unopened mail. From her.

He should have deleted this address the second she'd gotten her pretty, meddling little hands on it. Definitely before taking the new assignment. At the very least forget its existence. There was a reason for breaking all ties. Ties were dangerous, but here he was, literally unable to go a handful of days without checking that damn account. His only lifeline to the outside world. To her.

Yo, Borg, I thought I'd give you the immense honor of my company, even if you clearly don't deserve it. It's Christmas. No one should be alone on Christmas. Not even rude, insensitive assholes.

Such a smart-ass. He could see her in his mind's eye. All sass, throwing attitude left and right. That glossy dark hair cascading down around her shoulders, framing her killer, hourglass body, those big, bottomless black eyes narrowed at him, challenging him. Pissing him off and giving him the biggest hard-on of his life at the same time. Elle Cooper, the bane of his existence.

Is it snowing where you are? I hope you get a white Christmas.

1

Jack looked around him. He was in a helicopter in the middle of a jungle in buttfuck nowhere, supervising a weapons run, and the only thing coming from the sky was a permanent horde of vicious mosquitos he'd long ago stopped caring about. Nope, no white Christmas for him. Not any other kind either.

Wherever you are, I'm sure you've booby-trapped the chimney, hell, the whole place, and Santa won't be able to drop by to leave you anything without risking his life in the process, so I've sent you a present. A cyberpresent, as I'm positive you would have to kill me if you were to give me an address.

He clicked on the attachment and something exploded on the screen.

A Christmas card for badasses, it read, with Santa parachuting down sporting commando clothes and an Uzi.

Jack cracked a smile, the muscles of his face complaining at the rare gesture.

He hadn't seen her since James's wedding in August, yet her image was as fresh in his mind as if she were standing in front of him. All he had to do was close his eyes and there she was with him, in full 3-D and surround sound, exuding sex appeal and attitude and the most potent pheromones he'd ever experienced and against which he didn't seem to have defenses.

He should have stayed away from her at the wedding, but with him being best man and her maid of honor, it had been virtually impossible, especially when the bride and groom had insisted on them dancing. Against his better judgment he'd acceded, and now the feel of her luscious curves were imprinted in his hands. In his brain really. Her sweet scent too. He'd avoided touching her for a reason and this, his pathetic, juvenile behavior while undercover, in the face of mortal danger, was exactly why.

He'd remained grim and silent during their dance, clenching his teeth, trying to block the sensory bombardment, but it had been too late. And she'd known it. She'd smiled that teasing smile of hers. So fucking beautiful. And so fucking aggravating.

He'd been under for five months, monitoring the flow of illegal weapons to the rebels and watching those motherfuckers use the assault rifles and rocket launchers on civilians and peacekeepers. Five of the shittiest, most miserable months of his entire existence—which was saying a lot, seeing as he'd had pretty crappy assignments before; the only points of light were her wiseass e-mails. He'd gotten a zillion—well, ninety-three to be exact. For a guy who only got encrypted messages—a couple a month, tops, ninety-three were a shitload. Some of them were barely a line. A "Yo, Borg, sweet dreams, wherever you are." Others were pages long.

His brain had ordered him ad nauseam to block her address. End of issue. No more spam. No more Elle intruding into his personal space, forcing him to interact with the real world. Ha! Like there was a chance in hell his body would follow through on that executive decision. He'd reread her messages many times. Knew them by heart. The sarcastic cracks too. He couldn't get enough of her. Even when she just talked about her day, he'd greedily read every word, soaking them in. What was said, and what wasn't.

Checking the sender's details, he realized she'd written to him in the wee hours. Again. What the hell was she doing up at that time, on a regular Tuesday? And that was not an exception; it was the norm. Elle was a party girl. Always shit to do. Places to go. Men to entice. Not that she had to put too much effort into it; they trailed after her like lovesick puppies, ready to lick her toes and worship at her altar for just a smile. She was the kind of woman for whom necks snapped whenever she entered a room, and when she left it, there wasn't a single guy not following her gorgeous behind. The kind of woman one could look at but should never touch. You touch her, you get burned. Jack was too old and jaded for that kind of crap. The aftermath of such a rollercoaster would be a killer. He'd rather get shot in the stomach and be left to die, thank you very much. Less painful.

He repeated that to himself but continued reading.

As you can see from the pictures, all is good here. We had a full house for Christmas. I was supposed to work but Aunt Maggie swore she'd hunt me down if I didn't show up. Mr. Bowen came from Florida. Christy's mom from L.A. All the Bowens and their women were there. Lots of fun. It would have been funnier with you, of course, barrel of laughs that you are. Life and soul of the party, really.

Right. *She* was the life and soul of the party. Of any party. She just had to smile to be the center of attention. Hell, all she had to do was show up.

He glanced at the second attachment. Pictures probably. Elle always sent him photos, which he normally refused to look at, stashing them in a file in the cloud. It was bad enough this idiocy he had going on; no need to go the whole nine yards. But today he needed too much. In three minutes it would be his birthday. Thirty-six and shit to show for it. No wife, no kids. A half-decent day at work was one he survived unscathed while dealing with crazy fanatics. He was so wound up he couldn't contain himself, and, gut churning, he opened the file where he'd gathered everything she'd sent.

One look and his throat clogged. Fuck, she always knew what he needed. There were shots of Alden and the Bowens, all laughing. Barbecues. Birthday parties. The newest were from Christmas Eve. Max with his hands on the pregnant belly of his new lady friend, the one Elle had talked to Jack about. The one prone to weird accidents. It seemed like the last Bowen had already bit the dust, willingly, with a big, sappy smile on his face. Jack's chest tightened. Love and family and friends, the very things he was missing the most.

He reached into his pocket and took an antacid. His stomach had been bulletproof. Until Elle. Now he had a fucking hole the size of Texas, or so he thought. He was still in denial and refusing to go to the doc, living under the illusion that whenever his exposure to her ended, the ulcer would disappear.

He chewed the tablet, ignoring the chalky taste, and continued with his foolish task. Rosita's was featured very prominently too. Not so much Elle, who was always the one behind the camera. She was only in a couple of shots. In one she was showing her tongue and making a face. In the other she was laughing, hugging James and her sister Tate.

At that moment an e-mail appeared in his inbox from Party Girl. He looked at the time stamp: 00:01, rather early for her.

Without thinking, he clicked on it.

Happy birthday, Borg!!

Don't look so surprised; you know I'm very resourceful. It wasn't easy, let me tell you, to get it out of James. It was a slip, long time ago, but I have a great memory. He never said your actual age so don't freak on me, big boy, your secret is safe.

I would have never pegged you for a Capricorn though. I thought you'd be a Scorpio; after all, most dangerous sociopaths are born in November...

Then again, being a goat suits you too.

Wherever you are, whatever you are doing, I hope you have a fabulous day. You would have a much better time with us, but you can't have everything in life, can you?

No, he couldn't. Learned that long ago.

Don't have much time now, too busy at Rosita's. Just wanted to be the first to congratulate you on your birthday—or your assembly day—however your kind of people are made.
I'll write to you later.

This time, the attachment was a video. Before he realized how stupid it would be, he opened it, and his heart tumbled the second he heard her laugh. Someone, Tate by the sound of it, was filming her and Elle was joking with her. Then, as she stood under the mistletoe, she threw an air-kiss to the camera and winked an eye. His chest clenched so fucking hard his lungs burned from the lack of air.

Jack stared at the image greedily, like it was air and he was a drowning man.

Which he was. Drowning in filth and lies and human misery. Dealing with the worst of the worst, risking a Colombian necktie and God only knew what else for just a peek at Elle's words and a world he didn't belong to. His chest in a fist. His cock fucking hard.

He slapped the laptop closed, pissed at himself. This was no place to lower his guard. He was surrounded by scum. He ought to behave accordingly and stop daydreaming about the only woman in the world he couldn't allow himself to have.

* * * *

Two months later, Boston
Elle looked around the hospital chapel. It couldn't be denied; Bowen men were extremely original when it came to weddings. First it had been James with that romantic midnight ceremony in the backyard, a thousand small lights illuminating the garden. Then Cole had pledged himself to Christy surrounded by aliens in Las Vegas. Elle hadn't been there, but she had irrefutable proof of it at Rosita's, framed, in a central position on the wall of fame.

And now Max had gathered a bunch of trigger-happy preppers on one side and some stick-up-their-ass socialites on the other and

5

was getting hitched in a hospital chapel, before taking his woman and his newly born daughter home with him. A last-minute, simple ceremony. After what had happened, Elle couldn't blame Max for not wanting to waste a second. Staring death straight in the eye— even worse, watching the woman you love almost be killed—would do that to you.

The brothers were talking while waiting for the bride, Mr. Bowen by their side, standing proud. Once he'd finished fussing over Tate, James joined them.

Elle walked to where Tate was sitting. "How are you doing, sis?"

"Can't wait to be able to tie my own shoes again," Tate grumbled, looking at her distended belly. "And to get James off my back."

Right. Like she needed to tie her own shoes with James around. "Come on, he treats you like a queen. He worries."

Tate smiled softly, glancing at her husband. "I know."

Elle still couldn't get used to the image of her prim and proper little sister married to the tattooed-up-to-his-ears, possessive James Bowen. And yet she couldn't think of a better husband for her.

"How's Rosita's?" Tate asked.

"Still standing." Man, her sister had been away from the restaurant for a couple of days and she was already fretting. If it were up to her, she'd be there this last month of pregnancy, but the doctor had ordered her to rest and James wasn't taking any chances.

"Mom offered to come to help," Tate insisted. "We can call her. She'd be here in a flash, and you wouldn't be alone in that big house."

Elle shook her head. She could manage. Her mom liked it in Florida, where there weren't so many reminders of her deceased husband and son, and being with Ron was good for her. "Rosita's will survive. And I like my space."

Tate didn't believe her, not for a second. "Why don't you rent it and with the money pay for a place of your own. You know, somewhere not so full of..."

Memories. That was the word Tate was probably working toward.

"I'm fine there," Elle assured her.

Before Tate could reply, Annie walked in with the baby in her arms, her mother by her side. Max darted to them right away, face beaming with love.

Elle had known from the very beginning that Annie was going to be the one for Max. He'd had that look in his eyes, the same one James and Cole had when they looked at their wives.

"Let's get this show rolling," Max said after the priest arrived.

As they took their places, Elle scanned the premises. No sign of Jack. He was still doing whatever commando shit he'd been doing since summer, but she'd sent him an e-mail with the info about the wedding a couple of days ago, hoping he'd read it on time.

Suddenly the doors opened and a big black shadow stepped in. The air she didn't know she'd been holding came out in a *whoosh*. Jack. She didn't need the man to remove the hood to recognize him. The massive force field around him gave him away. When he revealed his face though, she froze. His demeanor had always been severe, but now he did look like a cyborg. Deep, soulless eyes. Sharper features. Skinnier, if the massive tank he still was could be called that.

Elle approached him and stood next to him. "So you do read my e-mails," she whispered, her gaze never leaving the priest. "You're just too rude to answer them."

She didn't need a response from him, because one, she knew he was that rude and two, there was no doubt he'd read her e-mails. And thank God for that; otherwise Max and Annie wouldn't be here getting married, and their story would have ended very differently. Just the thought of it made her sick.

"Quiet, pet," he answered back. She couldn't see it, but she felt his smile in his voice.

Pet. How she got that demeaning and patronizing nickname from him, she had no clue. He'd barely talked to her the entire time they'd known each other; just grunts and scowls. Then James had gotten hurt last summer and had been admitted to the hospital, scaring the living shit out of everyone, her included. When Elle had tried to leave in order to go open Rosita's, Jack had blocked the door, snatched the car keys away from her, and not only forbade her to drive but called her pet. Worse still, when she replied that she didn't recall giving him permission to call her pet, the asshole dared to say "I don't recall giving you permission to talk at all, pet" with that frigging arrogant tone of his, the one that gave her those embarrassing shivers. Modern women shouldn't get shivers at being ordered around in that tone. So politically incorrect, dammit.

And the asshole was immune to her. She got her way with everyone but him, who aggravated the living hell out of her by ignoring her. And the more he ignored her, the more she felt like pissing him off. A vicious, rather enjoyable circle.

She stood by his side, their hands brushing during the service, feeling the tension rolling off him. The darkness too. He was in a bad place. Not caring that he might rebuff her, she slid her hand into his and gave it a tight squeeze. He needed that, whether he would admit it or not. He froze for a second, and to her surprise, when she tried to end the embrace, he didn't let her, holding her hand tighter.

They didn't exchange a word during the ceremony. Elle didn't move a hair, afraid it would break the spell and Jack would remember he was a badass, in no need whatsoever of comfort. He *was* a badass, true, but whatever he was involved in was eating at him. He was tense and grim. Worn out, although he was standing stoically and would probably rather die than admit it. He needed the comfort, the human touch, even if it was just a small gesture, and damn if she wasn't going to give it to him.

After Max and Annie were presented as husband and wife, everyone rushed to congratulate them.

Jack released his grip on her, and Elle moved to kiss the newlyweds.

When she turned around, Jack had already disappeared.

CHAPTER ONE

One and a half months later, Alden

Jack adjusted his tie, feeling uncomfortable as all fuck. The service at the chapel had been bad, but the mingling and the chitchatting at the reception was much worse. That it was a very informal one, barbecue-style, at James's, didn't make matters better. The other way around, actually. It made them chattier. He'd rather eat glass.

He couldn't wait to get the hell out of there.

"What have I ever done to you to deserve this?" Jack muttered to James.

He hadn't been back in the States forty-eight hours and he was already in Alden, neck-deep in babies, parties, and marital bliss. Under normal circumstances, this family fest would have been hard. In his present state, it was unbearable. He was still too raw inside. All he wanted was to be alone, drink himself unconscious, and zonk out for at least a week.

"Come on, man. You know I love you," James said, laughing.

"Thank God. I don't want to know what you would do to me if you hated me."

Being back among normal people doing normal stuff was fucking hard. Not life-affirming. Just uncomfortable and pointless. Making him feel disconnected and more of an outsider. The small talk, the smiles. His stomach roiled at it all, but James was a persistent son of a bitch who had refused to see reason.

"You could have declined to be my son's godfather."

"And I would have if you'd told me who the godmother was," Jack grumbled.

James chuckled. "No, you wouldn't."

True. Refusing wouldn't have been an option for Jack. Whatever James would ask of him, he would do, no questions asked. And the motherfucker knew it.

"And I didn't lie to you about the godmother," James continued with a smirk. "You never asked. You must be losing your touch."

True again. It was all this happy-happy, love-is-in-the-air, pink-marshmallow gooeyness around Jack that was melting his brain.

Alden and the Bowens were bad for his mental health.

"I told you I wasn't up for this."

"And that's exactly why you need to be here," James stated. "You need to be reminded of the good things in life. Get a haircut. Shave and go get laid."

"Whatever." Like it was that easy to unplug. He'd scrubbed himself bloody, but the stench of misery still stuck to him. It was difficult to wash away.

At that moment, one of the main reasons for his piss-poor mood tapped him on the shoulder.

"Come on, T-800," Party Girl said from behind him. "The photographer wants a picture of Jonah with his godparents. I tried to convince him that the godfather is not really photogenic and might break the camera with his growls and shitty disposition, but he wants to risk it, professional that he is."

Without waiting for a response, she briskly walked away.

James clapped him on the back. "As I said, the good things in life."

"T-800?" That was a new one.

"Infiltration unit. Model 101, series 800," James whispered. Then, probably realizing that meant nothing to Jack, added, "The dumbest of all terminators?"

It figured.

He'd been told many times he came across as threatening and unapproachable, that everyone was intimidated by him. He liked it that way. The less human interaction, the better. But for some surreal reason, "everyone" didn't include her.

He hadn't known Elle was the godmother although he should

have imagined James would pull a stunt like this. Not that Jonah was unlucky to have her in his corner. On the contrary; she was fierce and protective. Damn abrasive and infuriating, also. And yet when he closed his eyes, she was the only woman his mind invariably conjured up.

"Come on," she called, turning around and wiggling her index finger at him. "Keep up."

Right.

He followed her, trying very hard but failing not to notice her hourglass figure and the hypnotic sway of her hips. That gorgeous ass. The way her long, glossy dark hair seemed to float down her back. And that smell. Fuck, that smell always shot straight to his cock, never mind how inappropriate the moment was.

The photographer wanted several pictures of them in different locations, but Jonah took pity on Jack and decided to start fussing, so the ordeal was cut short, ending while they were sitting on the porch swing. He would have stood up and left if he could have, but his legs weren't obeying him. Besides, the way out of there was through a horde of giggling, happy people, all nice and friendly. Oblivious to the darkness in the world. Wanting to know why he looked so gloomy and trying to cheer him up.

With Elle cooing at him, Jonah calmed down pretty fast, and Jack found himself staring at both of them. He never felt disconnected or like an outsider while being around Elle. He was pissed at himself and bothered beyond belief, and amused and aggrieved all at the same time, but never disconnected.

She turned to him, smiled, and he got the full impact, like a eighteen-wheeler slamming against his chest. Olive skin. Delicate features; sultry, extremely kissable lips. Killer body. Too bad every inch of her radiated that belligerent disposition of hers, the one that made his cock so fucking hard he couldn't breathe. He'd hoped her effect on him would have worn off, but no dice. She was even more beautiful, which should have been impossible, because she was stunning to begin with.

He could still remember the first time he'd seen her, at Rosita's. She'd looked at him with her black eyes full of attitude, and the world had tilted on its axis. He'd tried to realign it, but so far he'd had no luck whatsoever. With her around, everything was a mess— which he hated—but without her nothing felt right. Go figure.

"So you finally resurfaced. You sticking around, or is this just another of your quickies?"

He all but choked. "What?"

"In and out in a flash. Now we see you, now we don't, like Max's wedding."

Max's wedding, another of his lapses in judgment a bit over a month ago. He'd flown into Boston and then driven for two hours to make sure he didn't have a tail, arriving just in time to see the couple walk down the aisle.

Going there had been his first mistake. Allowing Elle to touch him had been his second, and even far more dangerous. Standing there, silently holding hands, had been the most peaceful he'd felt for months.

Whatever Elle had seen in his eyes must have been pretty bad, because she hadn't said anything, but after that she'd started writing to him daily and sending him more pictures than ever.

"Done. For the most part." Infiltrating the illegal arms trade to uncover the source of weapons flowing to scumbags all over the world had been gruesome. They managed to close down several routes without getting his cover blown, but there were always loose ends to be tied up.

"Where were you?" He didn't answer but she didn't seem to take it personally. "Got it. State secret." She gave him a once-over, and without allowing him time to react, brushed his beard with her fingertips, the unexpected caress sending a jolt through his body and zapping his brain. "You look different. Scruffy. I like it."

Jack pulled away and ran his hand through his shaggy hair, trying not to think about how good her touch had felt. "Don't get used to it."

"Oh, I wouldn't dream of it," she said with a laugh.

Before he could censor himself, his dumb mouth opened. "Where is Kai?"

She studied him with big inquisitive eyes, the corner of her mouth tilted up in amusement. "Where's the blonde?"

Blonde? Ah, that babysitting job he'd been guilt-tripped into during James's wedding. Gorgeous woman, no two ways about it, but Jack hadn't even noticed her. Elle was all he had seen. Her and her date, Kai, grinning like a fool, his hand on the small of Elle's back.

He'd wanted so badly to chop off that hand. The whole arm, actually.

"Forgot her tied to your bed?" Elle continued. "That's the problem with gagging your dates; they can't scream and one forgets they are there."

"You speaking from experience, pet?"

"No one would ever forget I'm in their bed."

He looked into her eyes. No, of course not. Any man with blood in his veins would kill for that memory. Instead, he answered, "I bet. You're that obnoxious."

She didn't take offense, tapping condescendingly on his chest. "Not the right word, buddy. But I'll forgive you. Everyone knows T-800s have limited vocabulary. Besides, this must be overwhelming for you. Wifeys and babies all over the place."

He shrugged. "I don't have a problem with that." Which, under normal circumstances, was true.

"Really? I thought you'd be another of those commitment-phobic guys."

"No."

That seemed to surprise her. "You want to marry?"

"Sure. I just would never marry someone like you," he said, his tone hard.

Now was when she would smack his face and leave in a huff. Lord knew it wouldn't be the first.

Elle burst into laughter. "You're so full of yourself. What makes you think I would marry you? You aren't husband material. You are…fucking material." She whispered the last two words, covering Jonah's barely month-old ears, as if the baby could understand. "At best. And that remains to be seen. You might not be good at that either. Not that I have the slightest interest in finding out."

"You are lying, pet," he blurted out.

Her expression was deceptively sweet. "Do not call me pet."

"Do not lie, pet."

"I'm not. Given up on bad boys, sweetie. And you are as bad as they come."

Then she stood up and, still chuckling, walked away from him, leaving him stunned and with the mother of all hard-ons tenting his pants.

In spite of everything, he felt a smile breaking over his face.

Yep, he needed to get the fuck out of Alden and away from her. Pronto. Before what little mind he had left melted.

CHAPTER TWO

One week later, Florida

"Don't worry, Marlene," Elle said into the cell phone as she walked through the airport dressed in her old uniform. "No one noticed I'm not you."

"Not even the guards?" her friend asked from the other end of the line.

"Especially not the guards. You know how they are." A smile, a soft glance, and a bigger-than-usual sway of her hips, and no one looked at her airport ID. Why would they? They knew her. She'd worked at the Miami airport for a year after moving to the Eternal Sun Resort to keep an eye on her mom. Whoever knew her didn't look at her ID, and whoever didn't know her didn't realize she wasn't Marlene. "Relax, everything is under control."

Elle had done as they'd agreed: she'd borrowed Marlene's ID card, signed in with it, and taken her shift while her friend was driving back from visiting her sister in North Carolina.

"Thanks, Elle, you saved my life. Damn Joshua. I don't know why he wouldn't let me change shifts with another flight coordinator. What did it matter to him who dispatched flights as long as someone did it?"

Stick-up-his-ass Joshua was a shitty, slimy boss. It didn't help that he had a crush on Marlene and she hadn't accepted his advances. Asking him to give her an extra day off for the trip had been a no-go. So was getting him to approve a shift change, even if it was no skin off his nose.

"I just was at the office picking up the documents for the first two flights, and he wasn't there. Donald was, but he won't say a word. He's on vacation after today, so he won't see Joshua," Elle explained as she opened the door of the car assigned to her and turned on the engine. "As a matter of fact, he thought I was you at first. Oh, and so you know, my head hurts from these damn braids. Couldn't you wear something more comfy? I have this unstoppable need to scratch my scalp."

Marlene was a hairdo junky. She currently braided the left side of her hair tight to her scalp, and so did Elle.

"The itch will go away. Then it will feel weird when you take them out. I'm sorry I'm ruining your break. You came for three days. The last thing I wanted was to make you work while you are down here."

"No sweat. I love catching up with the guys. Besides, your corporate flights are a walk in the park compared with my two-hundred-passenger tourist ones." Or maybe it was the Boston weather that made everyone cranky, because in Florida even the regular flights were a piece of cake. "And I'm not on vacation; I'm just arranging some paperwork for my mom while she's on a cruise with Ron." If anyone should be grateful, it was Elle. She hated taking time off, and running her mom's errands hadn't taken as long as she'd expected. "Are we still on for tonight?"

"You bet," Marlene answered. "The old gang together. We'll burn up the streets!"

Elle laughed. Yep, Marlene was a hot package.

"Good. I gotta go," Elle said. "I'm in the car. Or I'll be late."

Elle couldn't see her friend's face, but she was sure she was grimacing. "Please don't wreck the car during my shift."

"It wasn't my fault. The driver of the pushback wasn't watching."

"Maybe he didn't see you since you were driving like a maniac?"

Elle chuckled. "Okay, maybe I was a bit over the speed limit. But don't worry, I'll stick to the rules now that I'm you."

After they said good-bye, she drove to the parking spot assigned for her first flight. The plane was already there, and the fuel she'd ordered was being pumped into it.

She walked on the tarmac toward the private jet. It was early in the morning, but the sun was blinding so she put on sunglasses and hurried on. Man, she'd forgotten how hot it was in Florida, even in

April.

Her cell beeped. A message.

Girlie, Mr. Asshole will be flying from Logan in two days. You'll be back in Boston?

Mr. Asshole had gotten a restraining order on her when she'd called him out on his shit, so it was her moral duty to be there every time he planned to fly. To bother him and delay him and generally speaking pester him. The arrogant twit always asked for special treatment, so his name came up on their lists beforehand, allowing Elle to be ready for him.

Sign me in for that shift she texted back.

Whatever shift it was, she would make it work, and she would be there.

He thought the world revolved around him because he was worth more than the Queen of England. Elle didn't have an issue with rich people, but she despised entitled assholes.

As she finished supervising the catering, the passengers arrived. Three men. She quickly glanced at the documentation. Joaquín Maldonado was listed as the owner of the jet and the one who had handled the red tape and scheduled the flight to Cuba. Two of the men looked like security detail, from the way they moved and scanned the surroundings, so the one in the middle had to be Mr. Maldonado.

"Good morning, Mr. Maldonado. Everything is on schedule. We don't expect any delays today."

"Good," he said, and without a second glance, headed for the plane.

The security detail stayed behind, near the stairs.

"Marlene Cabrera," one of the guys said, looking at her ID. *"Bonito nombre para una bonita chica."*

A pretty name for a pretty girl, she thought he said.

She nodded, but remained silent. And that was why studying Spanish would have been a better choice than Italian, especially considering how big the Spanish-speaking community was in Florida. Marlene's parents were Cuban, and she spoke Spanish fluently. The two girls did look similar, and the hairdo and sunglasses helped, but Elle couldn't fake the language skill.

Fortunately, he didn't ask anything more. He turned to the other man and continued their chat in Spanish too fast for her to understand. After the pilot arrived, Elle handed him the preflight briefing documentation. They were all set to go when a big black car stopped near the one from the airline. The driver opened the back door and a man in his late sixties or early seventies, dressed in a suit, stepped out.

"Last-minute passenger," one of the bodyguards told her while his boss and the newcomer shook hands. "Now we are ready for takeoff."

Well, they might be ready for takeoff, but she wasn't. The newcomer wasn't on her passenger manifest. There were only three passengers on it. Mr. Maldonado and the security detail. Elle checked her watch. When dealing with last-minute changes, they were supposed to drive back and print an updated copy, but only for big things. This was small potatoes. Besides, going back to the office, never mind how fast she drove, would risk losing their assigned slot, and that would not only piss the passengers off, but it would mean changing all the flight documentation, weather report included. Too many waves that would raise questions for poor Marlene afterward.

She sprinted up the stairs and to the cabin.

"All in order?" the captain asked.

"Yes. Let me add something." She reached for the passenger manifest and wrote "+1pax" to it. "There. All ready. Have a safe flight, Captain."

They took care of takeoff procedures and she watched the plane fly away.

Okay, one flight dispatched. Four to go.

* * * *

Elle walked across the grass at the Eternal Sun Resort, more than tipsy, wobbly even though her heels were in her hand, when she noticed the two grandmas sitting in the garden of the common area.

"Look who's doing the walk of shame," Violet said, smiling.

Elle reached them and plopped into a chair. "It's not the walk of shame unless you've spent the night with someone. Besides, it's five o'clock. Too early for the walk of shame."

Violet glanced at her companion and they both chuckled. "In our time, anything after ten was the walk of shame. Heck, the death march of your reputation."

"Mine died long ago," Elle said.

"Nonsense, dear," Violet answered, patting her on her hand. "All of us here know you're golden."

Mrs. Nicholson nodded too.

Elle loved these two grandmas. She'd gotten to know them pretty well during her time at the Resort. "Not sleeping tonight?"

"Old people don't sleep. Not when they're supposed to, anyway. And you? Still having trouble with it?"

Elle shrugged. "Getting better," she lied, not that she was fooling anyone.

Mrs. Nicholson poured her a glass of iced tea. "Here. Did you have a nice time?"

"Yes, but I forgot how hard they party down here. I'm dead. And drunk." Not dead or drunk enough as to be able to sleep, though. Not yet. "So, what are we watching?"

"Same old, same old."

The three of them had spent many a night awake, watching the local TV channel these grandmas loved; the one that ran local news and forensic police shows.

"Great handiwork," Mrs. Nicholson complimented Violet, pointing at Elle's braids. "You still have the touch."

Violet nodded. "Yes, fifty years working as a hairdresser. No arthritis, no cataracts can stop me. Muscle memory. Ingrained forever. When I die, you'd better hire a fantastic hairdresser for me. I have the names of a couple in the top drawer of my dresser. Don't cut any corners, or I'll come back and haunt you forever at night."

Mrs. Nicholson turned her wrinkly eyes to Elle, a smile on her thin lips. "Like now, then."

Violet waved her friend off. "So, dear, tell us, how come you're coming back alone? Men should be fighting to walk you home."

"I'd rather pay the cab fare. Less trouble. And you just want to snoop around my dates."

"You can't blame us. Seeing you beat the shit out of that rude man was the most fun I've had in a long while."

Elle smiled at the memory. It had happened soon after moving to the Eternal Sun. Leave it to her to meet the state's biggest son of a bitch on the very first day. It never failed. She was a magnet for asshole bad boys who believed the sun rose and set between their testicles. On the flip side, no matter how tough they pretended to be, their balls were as susceptible to knee kicks as anybody else's. "I'm much tamer nowadays."

"You seeing anyone?"

At the shake of her head, both grandmas frowned. "How are things going with that young man from James's wedding? The big, scary one who scowled at you as if he was going to eat you."

Elle chuckled. "Jack. And 'as if he was going to murder me' would be more accurate. He hates me."

Mrs. Nicholson and Violet looked at each other and then both said, "Nah."

That would mean so much more if the lovable grannies weren't legally blind.

"I haven't seen much of him since then. He's been busy."

His presence at Jonah's christening had been a surprise. That he'd been his rude self hadn't.

She'd also stopped sending him e-mails because he wasn't undercover anymore. After all, she'd just wanted to keep him up to date. At least, that's what she'd told herself to justify writing to him. Be that as it may, it had become such a habit she didn't realize how much she enjoyed it until she decided not to write anymore. Going cold turkey had been damn hard. She missed it, even though he hadn't answered, not even once.

"So you are not seeing each other?" Mrs. Nicholson asked, interrupting her thoughts. "His loss. Have I ever told you about my grandson?"

Elle laughed. Only one or two million times. Playing at matchmaking was the official sport at the Eternal Sun Resort. James had complained about it often enough, but he had no clue how bad it got, especially when you lived with the crazy seniors as she had for a year.

"Rita, your grandson is no match for Elle. She would eat him alive. I don't mean any disrespect, dear." Violet hurried to appease them both. "He is a sweetheart, but Elle needs…"

Elle looked at her, waiting for the grandma to finish. It would be good to know what she needed, seeing as she had no frigging clue herself.

"Fire. Backbone. Someone solid as a rock who wouldn't budge no matter how hard she pushed. Our Elle is a fighter."

Elle smiled. She wasn't a fighter. One needed to be strong to be a fighter. She wasn't; she was a runner. A classy one who did it with a smile, but a runner nevertheless. She'd proved that again and again after the death of her father and her brother. Before that too. Her default response was to fly; never stand her ground and fight, especially if that meant facing unpleasantness and feelings she didn't want to revisit.

"We miss you around here. Your workshops were the best. No one has taken up Zumba for seniors since you left. We got an instructor that treated us like deaf, dumb mummies."

"I miss you guys too." In spite of the sad circumstances surrounding her mother and Elle's move to Florida, she'd loved it down here. It had provided her a permanent source of escape; comings and goings all day long. A hectic job at the airport. Endless student parties. And she'd needed it so badly.

"You still organizing the Zumba class tomorrow?"

"Sure I am."

"Great. I'm taking my husband along," Mrs. Nicholson said. "I finally convinced him."

As they were talking, she noticed that the TV program had been interrupted and a picture of a man was on the screen.

"Who's that?"

"They've been broadcasting about it the whole night. Dick Aalto, the politician, has been found dead."

"What do you mean 'dead'?" Elle turned on the volume on the TV, staring, stunned, at the picture of the man she'd seen boarding the corporate jet this morning.

"Squashed into the pavement, flat as a pancake," Violet said and made a very descriptive sound. "In the Florida Keys. Almost gave a heart attack to the couple who ran over him with the car. Squashed and run over. Poor fella. They don't know how long he'd been there in the middle of the road because that's one of those backwater places, hardly no traffic. Police suspect he was thrown from an airplane but they can't find his name in any passenger manifests."

Of course they couldn't, and they wouldn't, because she hadn't written down his name. *Oh God.* She sobered up right away.

"Lately he's been making a lot of noise about illegal immigrants and the need to tighten and restrict entry into the US. He has the port all but paralyzed. An old-school loony Republican, if you don't mind me saying," Violet added. "As if this whole country wasn't based on immigrants searching for a better future to begin with."

Mrs. Nicholson started talking, but Elle wasn't listening. She had to speak with Marlene. They had to call the cops.

She grabbed her cell and dialed Marlene's number. She'd left her at her place before asking the cab driver to take her to the Eternal Sun. There was a good chance she was still awake.

The phone rang but no one was picking up. Finally, someone did.

"Marlene?"

"Who is this?" a male voice asked in response.

"A friend of Marlene's. Who are you, and why are you answering her phone?"

"I'm Detective Sheehan from the Miami police. I'm afraid something terrible has happened to Ms. Cabrera."

CHAPTER THREE

"Protective custody? Are you serious?" Elle asked, gaping at the detective sitting in front of her.

"Dead serious. You don't know who this guy is and what he's capable of."

No, she hadn't known who Joaquín Maldonado was. Now she did. Apparently, he was the biggest, most powerful narco this side of the Milky Way.

"Look at this," the detective, Hensen, continued, pushing a picture toward her. It was the pilot of the morning flight. "Dead. Apparent heart attack." Then he put another picture on the table. "This is Dick Aalto's driver. Dead. Apparent hit and run. And Marlene Cabrera," he finished, showing her a shot of her friend lying on the floor of her condo in a pool of blood. "Dead. Apparent home invasion. Oh and let's not forget this one," he said, tapping at what looked like...she wasn't sure what. "Dick Aalto, a bit worse for wear as you can see. Apparently fell from a plane."

Elle's head hurt, and she was in a daze.

After speaking with the police on the phone, she'd rushed to her friend's to find the place cordoned off. A home invasion gone wrong, they'd told her. A case of wrong place, wrong time.

"Did something special happen tonight? Something that stood out of the ordinary? Some guy showing too much interest?" the police officer had asked Elle while taking her statement.

No, nothing out of the ordinary. Not in the evening anyway. Not sure it had anything to do with it, she'd explained about her— that is, Marlene's—morning flight and Dick Aalto boarding it with a guy named Maldonado, and the officer had turned white. He'd gotten on the radio and soon after that four plainclothes cops had flanked her and unceremoniously escorted her to the police station. That had been hours ago.

Elle looked at the pictures in front of her on the table, trying to avoid Marlene's, feeling totally overwhelmed. "This is insane."

"Let's go over what happened one more time," the detective insisted.

She threw her arms over her head. They'd gone through it a million times. "I told you. Dick Aalto showed up at the last minute. He boarded the plane with Maldonado and two of his bodyguards and they flew away. End of story."

"Are you one hundred percent sure this man is the one you saw with Aalto?" Hensen asked, jabbing at a mug shot of Maldonado.

"Yes and yes. Totally sure. I still don't see the need for protective custody, though."

"These are the people that saw Aalto getting into Maldonado's plane. All of them dead on the same day. What do you think is the chance this is accidental and unrelated? What do you think will happen to you when Maldonado and his goons discover there's a witness they haven't dealt with?"

Good question. Elle gulped. "You have my statement. Can't you arrest him?"

"Your word might not be enough. We need hard evidence."

"I don't understand the problem. You already know who was with Aalto when he was thrown from the plane. Three passengers. Maldonado and two men that looked like his security detail. I don't remember their names, but they are on the passenger manifest at the airline's office. Isn't this info enough to, I don't know, get an order to search the plane? Check the cameras at the airport? I watch *CSI*. I'm sure you can find some physical evidence that Aalto was on that plane and build your case. You don't need me."

"The plane is not in the US now. According to our information, Maldonado is coming back tomorrow. You can bet your sweet ass that plane is going to be pristine. We'll try to find other evidence to link Aalto to that plane, but at the moment you are it for us. Not to mention the little detail that our star witness was committing a major felony. Juries and judges do not take kindly to witnesses who break the law."

And they were back at the point Hensen had been hammering

for hours already: the fact that apparently she'd broken a thousand laws and breached national security by taking Marlene's shift, and now she belonged on the FBI's most wanted list.

On top of that, they wanted her to go into protective custody. She wasn't sure if it was the hangover or the shock. Probably both, but nothing made any sense.

There was a knock on the door, and a woman with a police badge on the waist of her pants entered and approached Hensen. Since being escorted to the station, she'd been kept incommunicado, and hadn't seen a single police uniform. Just suits. She spoke in his ear, and Elle couldn't make out what was being said.

"We found Marlene Cabrera's killer," Hensen informed her once they were alone again. "Dead. Overdose. A small-time criminal and junkie. His fingerprints were all over the crime scene. He apparently forgot he was left-handed and injected himself in the wrong arm."

"What does that mean?" Elle asked, confused. She'd been awake since God only knew when. She felt nauseated, and her head was spinning.

"It means that someone helped him overdose. Whoever gave him the job to eliminate Marlene Cabrera was tying up loose ends. People are dropping dead left and right, and you're our only witness."

"I can't go into protective custody." She would go insane locked in some stinking apartment. Unable to sleep. Unable to escape into work. Besides, she couldn't disappear. Tate was recovering from giving birth and she had her hands full with the baby. Elle needed to pull her own weight and take care of Rosita's. "Maldonado doesn't know I exist; he thinks I was...Marlene." Her voice cracked at the mention of her friend, but she fought to regain composure. Crying would get her nowhere and she couldn't afford to break down. "I'm leaving for Boston today. Nobody would think to search for a person they don't know exists. When the time comes to testify, I'll fly back."

"And who ensures that, sweetheart?"

She stared at him, offended. "I give you my word."

The man let out a bark, not a speck of humor in it. "I told you, your word ain't good around here, and protective custody is the least of your problems, lady. Dead people do not testify."

"Can I have a break?" Elle asked, overwhelmed. "I need some air. And coffee." Her adrenaline was crashing. In other circumstances, she would have tried to charm her way out of this, and she still might, but at the moment she was too exhausted to even think, let alone pull any kind of stunt that required the use of brain cells.

"We are not done yet."

"I want out of here," Elle demanded, standing up and heading for the door. The walls were closing on her, her lungs too. "You can't keep me here. And you can't force me to go into protective custody."

The detective got in her face. "You're in deep shit. You broke the law and you'll do as we say or so help me God— "

Suddenly the door burst open.

Elle turned to the menacing man dashing in. Dark hair, beard. Piercing, ice-cold blue eyes. Her jaw dropped. *Oh my God.* "Jack?"

He didn't address her. He stepped in between her and the detective and growled, "Back the fuck off." He didn't scream, but the threat in his voice was so evident Hensen staggered back before regaining his ability to speak.

"She's in big trouble and—"

"I said back the fuck off. I won't repeat it a third time. You put a finger on her again, you lose it."

* * * *

Jack watched through the two-way mirror as Elle lay curled up in the chair of the interrogation room, finally asleep, after running herself ragged, pacing up and down for a long while.

"Who is she to you?" Mullen, the FBI agent in charge asked, after approaching.

Jack pondered his response. The bane of his existence? A pain in the ass? The woman responsible for his permanent hard-on and his permanent bad mood?

"My godson's aunt," he answered finally. The last person he'd thought he'd find in that interrogation room. As soon as Mullen had informed him that they had a witness tying Maldonado to a murder, Jack had rushed from Puerto Rico to Miami, ready to squeeze that witness mercilessly and use him to get the drug lord. Until he'd seen who the witness was. Then all his protective instincts had kicked in. That Elle had thrown herself at him and hugged him tight, hiding her face in the crook of his neck, trembling, hadn't helped a bit.

"Can you vouch for her? That what she's telling is true?"

"Yes," he said resolutely, not having to think about it. Whatever Elle was, she wasn't a liar. And that little trick of switching IDs had Elle written all over it.

Leave it to her to come to Florida for a couple of days, do some dumb shit, cross paths with the likes of Maldonado, who'd just recently moved to the US, and end up with all the three-letter security agencies in the country and then some, fighting to claim jurisdiction over her.

It seemed that the case was going to be turned over the Feds, which was a stroke of luck, because Mullen and his men owed him.

"What the fuck was Maldonado doing in a plane to Cuba with a tight-ass politician like Aalto?"

"My guess? Maldonado was taking Aalto on a friendly trip to share a cigar and talk business. Something happened and the friendly trip was cut short. Aalto's latest proposal was to tighten travel restrictions and drastically limit tourist visas, which Maldonado's men depend upon to come and go from the US. Maldonado's infrastructure would have suffered. He was probably trying to influence Aalto, get him to lighten up."

"Why throw Aalto off a plane?" Jack asked. "It doesn't make sense. There are easier ways to get someone to disappear." Not that making the politician disappear made much sense either way. Killing a high-profile public figure was never a good move. Especially if you wanted to sway his decisions.

Mullen shrugged. "It was probably unplanned. Strong winds yesterday. Maybe they miscalculated and thought the body would fall into the sea, never to be found again. You know Maldonado's got a temper."

Even though Elle was asleep, Jack could see the reflex movement under her lids. She looked exhausted, but jumpy too. With her hands under her face, she snuggled into the chair as if she were cold. Of course she'd get arrested wearing nothing but a tight dress just slightly bigger than a fucking bandage and smelling like a distillery.

Hensen stopped next to them, his greedy gaze on the two-way mirror. "She's out of options. I say we use her as bait to draw

Maldonado out. Fine piece of ass like that, she wouldn't have problems—"

Jack turned to him, blocking Hensen's view of Elle and crossing his arms over his chest, then stared straight into the guy's eye.

"You don't talk to her. You don't look at her, and you sure as fuck don't use her for anything, especially not bait."

"Who put you in charge?" the asshole demanded.

Jack smiled predatorily. "Way above your paygrade. And clearance. When it comes to Maldonado, you do as I say."

"Or?"

"You'll be the next one skydiving from a plane."

"Jack, for fuck's sake," Mullen growled, stepping in between the two men.

That was the good part of not being under the direct command of the FBI, DEA, CIA, or NSA. Jack didn't have to obey anyone there. And they knew it.

"Hensen, leave us," Mullen ordered, then turned to Jack after the detective walked away. "And you, calm the fuck down, will you?"

Jack didn't look at the special agent, his gaze back on Elle. "I'm calm."

"You know that under the National Defense Authorization Act we can keep her for as long as we want? And Hensen's idea of using her as bait has its merit. We spread rumors about a witness, drop her name, and we just sit back and wait for Maldonado's goons to appear. Or better yet, we put a microphone on her, make her contact Maldonado to blackmail him, and get him to admit his involvement in the killings. Risky, but she would have to go along with it, seeing as she's facing major jail time for the airport stunt."

"No fucking way."

He knew what happened to bait. Bait was expendable, and they never came to good ends. At best, Elle would have to enter the witness protection program. If she was refusing protective custody, he didn't want to think how she would react to that. "You owe me a lot of favors, and I'm calling this one in. You find a way of arresting Maldonado that doesn't involve her life going down the drain."

The detective's lips thinned. "Jack, you, more than anyone, know how difficult it is to pin anything on this guy. Maldonado is extremely dangerous. This is a once-in-a-lifetime opportunity—"

"Not up for discussion. You won't use her as bait. You keep her name under wraps. I don't want anyone outside the investigation to know about her existence. Use her info to build your case. She didn't have to tell you squat about Aalto boarding her plane, yet she did, even knowing it was going to mean trouble for her. You cut her some slack." He'd wanted to get Maldonado for years; more now that the scumbag had relocated to Florida, but all the witnesses had the nasty habit of ending up dead. He wasn't risking it.

"Let's start with finding a link between Maldonado and Aalto." Maldonado was a well-known narco and Aalto an old-school Republican obsessed with kicking out illegal aliens and cutting back on immigration and foreign import of goods. Why would Aalto agree to a meeting?

"So far we haven't found one. His secretary knew nothing about the trip and there wasn't a single reference on his agenda."

No shit. Trips to Cuba for a cigar were off the record, which explained why Aalto had been sneaking around at the airport and no one at his office knew about it. Or maybe they did, but considering their political views, they weren't going to admit to Aalto traveling to Cuba, much less in company of a well-known criminal.

"Someone at his office must have known. Men like Aalto and Maldonado do not talk without intermediaries. What about the bodyguards? What do we have on them?"

"Emiliano Ramírez and Jonathan Escudero."

"Isn't Ramírez Maldonado's cousin?"

Mullen nodded. "Escudero has a niece with a drug habit and a rap sheet. As soon as he's back on American soil, we'll turn up the heat on him; let's see if we can get him to snitch on his boss."

Jack didn't know which kind of trouble the niece was in, but it sure had to be a shitload of it for her uncle to risk crossing Maldonado.

"Get your men to pick up the girl. That should encourage Escudero to talk. What about the autopsy?" Maybe they'd get lucky and the coroner would find something.

Mullen cocked his left eyebrow. "Don't get your hopes up. They had to scrape the body off the pavement with a shovel. After a car had run over it."

Jesus Christ.

"We can't let her walk out of here," Mullen insisted. "Protective custody is the best solution."

"I'll watch over her."

"Maldonado has long-reaching arms. He'll find her in Boston."

"Not if he doesn't know she exists. Did you make every trace of her disappear in the reports?"

Mullen nodded. "The officer that first interrogated her at the scene was a rookie and got so nervous when she mentioned Maldonado that he didn't fill out the paperwork. And we have restricted the access to her. No one knows about her."

"Keep it that way until she has to testify."

Jack just hoped Mullen found a way to get Maldonado that didn't involve her taking the stand. Testifying against him was a sure death sentence. That, or enter the witness protection program and look over her shoulder forever.

Mullen stared at him, undecided.

"I will not back down on this."

After a long, tense second, Mullen sighed. "Get her out of here and to Boston before I change my mind." Shaking his head, he walked away. Then he stopped and turned around. "And, Jack? I hope you know what you're doing."

Jack hoped the same.

He opened the door and moved toward her quietly. Careful not to wake her, he took off his jacket and covered her up.

Fat chance. At the slight contact she jerked and blinked twice at him, disoriented. "You're here. I thought I'd been having a nightmare."

"Seriously, pet, what the fuck? You come to Florida for a short visit and you have to cross one of the worse criminals in the state?"

"How did you know? You stalking me?"

As if.

She gestured outside. "Did they send you in to arrest me?"

He ignored her snarky question. She'd find out soon enough that he was nobody's errand boy. "Do you have any fucking idea how illegal what you did is?"

He could see his harsh tone was making her confrontational, but there was nothing he could do about it. She made him tense in the best of circumstances. Fucking tense. And this wasn't anywhere near the best of circumstances.

"Which part, exactly?" Elle asked. "Because everyone around

here seems to forget I came forward and helped them with Aalto's murder."

"You entered an international airport with a false ID. What were you thinking?"

She pursed her lips. "I beg your pardon; the ID wasn't false. It wasn't mine, which is a different matter. Be more precise when you scold me."

Always the last word. Fucking attitude.

It looked like she'd gotten some rest, because the part with her hugging him tight and keeping her mouth shut was over.

"Impersonating someone else and entering an airport and its restricted areas under false pretenses and with someone else's ID is a federal offense. Ten to fifteen in a maximum-security prison. Is that precise enough for you?"

"You lecturing me about obeying the law? That's rich, coming from someone who does what you do for a living."

And more deflecting. She was worse than Ronnie. "Don't fuck with me, pet."

"Don't call me pet." Elle held his stare defiantly but in the end gave up. "Marlene's sister was getting married. Their relationship had always been rocky. She didn't want to miss the wedding and her jackass boss wouldn't give her the day off. This was an emergency."

Her eyes went somber at the mention of her friend. Her lips trembled as she spoke. "I need to call her family. Find out when's the funeral. I need to—"

"Family's been notified and you're not going to the funeral. Too risky. We have to leave Florida ASAP."

She lifted her eyebrows. "We? What do you mean we?"

"It's me or protective custody. You choose." Although there wasn't much choice to make, because if she went the protective-custody route, which he doubted very much, he would be supervising that too.

His behavior sure as hell hadn't ingratiated him with Hensen, but he hoped he'd made his position clear. Anything to do with Elle would have to go through him first.

And God help Hensen if he tried to intimidate her again or upset her in any way.

His words must have sunk in, for she was shaking her head. "No, no, no, no," she chanted, trying to stand up. He grabbed her by her arms. "There must be another—"

"This is fucking serious, pet. And fucking dangerous. Hensen is an asshole, but he's right about one thing: you're in a world of trouble, and the only way you're walking out of here and going back to Boston to something resembling a normal life is with me watching your back. Mullen and his team will try to build a case and get solid evidence. In the meantime, I will make sure nothing happens to you." And would pull her into hiding the second he thought she was in danger or if the investigation had been compromised. Not that he was going to tell her this last part. She would freak out.

"You watching my back is a very bad idea," she said. "We'll drive each other crazy."

No shit. He couldn't agree more.

She'd been driving him crazy since the first day they met. Close proximity was only going to make matters worse.

"And what are we going to say about why you're with me? I don't want anyone in Boston to find out about this."

"Good luck with that, pet. By now the whole Eternal Sun knows you've been at the police station for over twenty-four hours." As a matter of fact, there were two grandmothers in the lobby being very vocal about getting to see Elle. "That means everyone close to you in Boston knows. The Bowens too." He hadn't gotten any phone calls yet, but those were coming, he was sure.

Elle grimaced. "They will get overprotective. I can't handle that."

"I'll take care of them. I'll get them off your back."

Her snort was dry. "And who's going to get you off my back?"

"Until this situation is resolved, no one. And I do not have the patience all the males around you have. I won't treat you with kid gloves. You will do what I say when I say it. Stay where I put you."

"Or?"

"You don't want to find out."

"You don't intimidate me," she said, looking him straight in the face.

"Good. I hate when women start trembling and sobbing. Too messy. Let's go pack your things and get moving. Now." He stood up, waiting for her to follow suit.

She sighed. "That tone is not going to go down well with me,

Borg."

"Which tone?"

"The obey-me-or-else tone, the one that demands servitude. Doing things on command is not a skill I've acquired or have any interest in acquiring," she explained, but nevertheless she got up and headed for the door.

He trailed her, surprised as all fuck that she was actually obeying. Obviously, she was still in shock. It wouldn't last, he knew, but he'd take any reprieve he could get.

CHAPTER FOUR

One of the advantages of having Jack shadowing her was the wide berth that everyone gave them, even at the Eternal Sun. She hadn't seen that rambunctious bunch that restrained since…ever, really.

"What's taking so long?" Jack asked, barging into her bedroom after inspecting the whole apartment, bodyguard-style. He scanned the bags scattered all around, the vein at his temple pulsing. "How the fuck can you have so much shit? You only came for a couple of days."

"It's not for me," Elle said, piling the bags into several already overstuffed suitcases and then sitting on one to attempt to zip it. "They are filled with things for Jonah and Lizzie. We should be grateful that this crowd watches shopping channels and bought vacuum bags. Otherwise, we would have three times this much."

Getting out of the police station had done a world of good for her. She was still freaked out, but at least now she could breathe and think more clearly. And she had things to do. She did much better with things to do.

Marcel, one of the Eternal Sun instructors, knocked on the door. "Sweetheart, they're waiting for you. You coming?"

Elle smiled. "I'll be there in five." At Jack's fulminating glare, Elle explained after Marcel left, "Zumba class for seniors. Just half an hour and we'll be done."

He crossed his arms over his chest. "We do not have time for Zumba classes."

"Too bad, because I promised."

"Don't give a shit."

Elle inhaled deeply. She wanted to disappear from Florida too, but she wasn't going to let Mullen, Maldonado, or Jack mess her life up more than they already had. But picking a fight with The Borg wouldn't improve matters. "It's just half an hour. You heard what Hensen said. Maldonado is not in the US, and even if he was, I doubt he would have any business in a senior community, watching grannies dance."

"Unnecessary risks are not acceptable."

She looked into the ceiling, praying for patience. "Listen, I truly appreciate you getting me out of the police station, don't misunderstand me, but don't you think you're exaggerating?"

"No. I told you. It's me or protective custody. Or jail."

"Jeez, can I have a minute to think about it? Because jail isn't sounding so bad anymore."

"Smart-ass," she thought she heard him grumble.

She hurried to the common area, where her faithful crowd was already gathered. Violet and Rita were in first row, with Mr. Nicholson standing by his wife, not looking that thrilled. "Okay, folks. Ready to shake it?" she asked, jumping to the stage and then connecting her cell to the sound system. "We'll start with merengue. Get our hips loose."

After that came a little of salsa and a rather mild version of reggaeton.

She could see Jack glowering at her, losing his patience. Tough shit. She'd promised a senior Zumba class and she wasn't going to disappoint them. Besides, contrary to popular belief, old people had sharp memories.

"Now we get a partner," she said, while Marcel approached.

Apparently seeing Marcel bumping hips with her was too much for him, because Jack stalked toward her, then suddenly she was airborne and perched over his shoulder; all she could see was Jack's ass.

"You are done. I told you we didn't have time for this," he growled, compounding the fiasco by slapping her behind while she thrashed.

As she was being carried away she lifted her gaze in time to see Mr. Nicholson shaking his head at his wife and lifting his hands up in surrender. "Sorry, there's no way I can do that."

* * * *

"You're shitting me," Jack grumbled, glaring at Elle clawing the armrest of her seat on the plane. "You scared of flying?"

She shook her head. "No." At his incredulous look she added, "A bit."

"A bit?" Her nails were digging into the leather and she looked fucking tense.

"Okay. A lot. I'm scared shitless about flying. Most people who work in an airport are. Scared, I mean. We see too much."

Damn reassuring.

On the plus side, she was talking to him again after his stunt. On second thought, scratch that; it wasn't a plus, it was a minus.

The fasten seat belt sign hadn't gone off yet when one of the flight attendants brought Elle a double Scotch. "Paul sends his regards. He asked me to keep you stocked."

Elle took the glass and emptied it. "Thanks. Tell him I'll try to behave."

As the flight attendant walked away, Elle turned to Jack. "Paul is the pilot. Old friend."

"Why would he want to keep you drunk? What did you do to him?" He could think of a number of possibilities and none of them were good.

Her eyes fired up. "I didn't do anything. I got a bit nervous once. He knows flying rattles me."

"Don't worry," the older lady sitting behind them said, leaning forward and patting Elle's shoulder. "We won't crash. I have it on good faith that we will be hijacked."

Elle stiffened.

For the love of God. "Lady…" Jack grumbled.

But she ignored the acrimony in his tone and continued, "My grandson told me flying is the safest way to travel, and that more planes are hijacked than crash. Then again, forty-five percent of the hijacked planes end up crashing too."

"Forty-five percent? That's damn specific."

"Andy's a statistics postgrad. He's worked out some kind of system, according to which the next aviation incident has to be hijacking. He also said that, statistically speaking, it's more probable that it happens in Eastern Asia, but he hasn't taken into account the fact that I'm a magnet for bad luck. You should ask my late husband," she added, shivering. "Anyway, there's no doubt in my mind this is the flight getting hijacked. I've already spotted several men that look mighty suspicious to me. I'm Eve, by the way."

Elle turned to her. "Nice to meet you. I'm Elle. You are very relaxed, considering."

She shrugged. "It's the blue pill Andy gave me."

Fantastic. He was surrounded by crazy women. One on her way to getting drunk, the other doped up to her ears.

This was going to be a memorable flight.

"Don't worry. Jack here is an air marshal," Elle whispered, gesturing to him. "He'll stop the hijackers. Right, Jack?"

He shot Elle a reproving look. The last thing he wanted was to humor some nutty lady, but he realized that all that nonsense had made Elle forget about her own fears and her nails were not buried in the armrests anymore, so he nodded curtly.

Eve leaned toward Jack and whispered, "Can I see your gun? I've never seen one in real life."

From the corner of his eye, he noticed Elle smiling. "And you won't."

"We don't want to scare the general public," Elle interjected in a whisper.

"Oh. Of course," she answered.

In between the crazy talk and the constant flow of Scotch, soon Elle was more relaxed.

"So, Borg, what's your plan once we're in Boston? Assuming we can make it there without killing each other, that is," she added, turning her beautiful eyes to him. Man, black eyes. He hadn't known those existed. So mesmerizing.

"We lay low. You put in for vacation time. Cancel whatever classes you have, if any. At the first sign that something is wrong, I'll pull you out and into hiding."

She narrowed her gaze belligerently. "Shouldn't I have some say? What about reaching a mutually satisfactory compromise?"

Fuck that. "You agree with me. That's how we reach a mutually satisfactory compromise."

She pursed her lips, and murmured in Italian, *"Nel mondo dei sogni, bello."* In your dreams, buddy.

He didn't know Italian, but he was fluent in Spanish, so he got the idea.

"And I still believe your best bet is to disappear for a while," he pressed on, ignoring her words.

"Can't. Tate needs me."

"Tate needs a live sister."

"You're being dramatic."

"I think that too," the crazy lady whispered, leaning toward them again. "Men tend to dramatize a lot. Now if you excuse me, the bathroom calls."

"I have a cabin in the middle of nowhere," Jack continued after the woman had left. "That's your safest bet. You have to disappear."

"Listen, I truly appreciate you getting me out of the police station, and I'm going to do my best not to murder you in your sleep, but get this through your thick skull: there's no way in hell I'm disappearing."

"Not asking for your opinion. Or your permission."

"That's kidnapping," she whispered, irate, going nose-to-nose with him.

Such a perfect, cute little nose.

And that he was thinking about that and getting a hard-on while a confrontational woman was facing him off, he didn't understand.

"Only if I get caught. And I don't get caught."

"Don't even think about it. I will fight you every step of the way if you try to pull a stunt like that on me. If it seems like I'm not being cooperative now, you have no clue what you'll have on your hands then."

"An irrational female. The same as now," he answered.

She sipped more Scotch, muttering something very unflattering.

"Give me a good reason why you can't disappear. One that makes sense."

The alcohol came to his rescue, because Elle dropped her gaze and fidgeted. "I failed my sister when our father and Jonah died. I ran and dumped everything onto her. The restaurant, my mother. Emma, Jonah's girlfriend. All of it. I owe it to her to take care of everything now. She had a rough time with delivery and the baby is a handful. Even with James helping her twenty-four seven."

Fuck. Guilt. Guilt was a powerful motivator. So was death, though.

He grabbed her chin and tipped her head up to meet his stare. "I can't guarantee your safety out in the open, pet."

"I'm not in danger. Not yet anyway. I might not be asked to

testify. They'll get the plane, link it to Aalto, and the feds can make those bodyguards sing, right?" His expression probably wasn't that reassuring, for she added, faltering, "What do you think my odds are?"

"If they crack the case without you, great. If not, not so good, I'm afraid." Testifying would mean having to look over her shoulder forever. Maldonado was that dangerous and bloodthirsty. Jail wouldn't stop him. And standing up to him would mean witness protection. Jack kept that to himself. She hadn't realized it by herself, and he wasn't too keen on upsetting her more than necessary.

"No good deed goes unpunished, right?" She smiled sadly.

He didn't answer. Her good deed had been fucking illegal, but yeah, he could understand the sentiment.

"You didn't tell me what you were doing at the police station," Elle said after a long pause.

"No, I didn't."

She shook her head, laughing softly. "And you won't."

No, he wouldn't.

At that moment, the crazy lady, Eve, came back from the bathroom.

"Dear, could I change seats with you?" she asked the woman sitting beside Jack. "I have some things to discuss with this gentleman."

"Sure, no problem."

Damn, damn, damn.

"There are two suspicious men in row thirty-two," Eve said to him. "I think we should—"

The flight attendant approaching, a third Scotch in her hand, interrupted her. "Here you go."

"No," he said, before Elle could grab the glass or even say anything. "She's had enough."

"I could use a little sip," Eve chimed in, holding out her hand.

In any other circumstances, he would have kept his mouth shut and let the chips fall where they may, but he found himself saying, "I don't think the Scotch would go with the blue pill."

Eve waved him off. "It's just an itty bitty pill. How bad can that be?"

Famous last words. Especially when the person taking the itty bitty blue pill was already paranoid enough.

The flight attendant handed her the drink and then turned to him. "Can I get anything for you, sir?"

He shook his head. "Not thirsty."

"Something to snack on?"

He shook his head again. "Not hungry."

"Be sure to let me know if you need anything at all," she replied with a smile, then left.

Elle jabbed him with her elbow. "Dummy, she wasn't talking about drinks or food. She was checking you out, and what she was offering was herself."

"She's right," Eve mumbled after downing her Scotch. "Even I noticed it and I'm a bit…absent."

Absent. Sure.

"Not my type," he replied curtly, hoping the conversation would end there.

Fat chance.

Elle turned her inquisitive eyes toward him. "What's your type? And what's not to like about her? She's a gorgeous blonde, much like the one you brought to James's wedding. Smaller rack but stunning nevertheless."

"That blonde from James's wedding was a babysitting job I got stuck with. Pretty much like now," he growled.

She let out a giggle. "Boy you're rude. Good I'm a bit buzzed or I would be frigging offended. Now answer, what's your type? You said that you wanted to get married. A guy as task-orientated as you must already have a list of attributes your future bride requires."

It looked like this crowd was not going to let it go, so he opted for the shorter way to end this conversation. "I want a traditional wife, whose priority would be our children and me. I want a homemaker, not a career type." Or anything closely resembling the irresponsible, party-crazy woman he'd had at home while growing up. He wanted his kids to have a mother greeting them with a smile and a plate of cookies when they came home from school. A present, involved mom.

"You mean one of those women who bake their own bread and sew their own underwear?"

"I don't care about the underwear but, yeah, I'd like my wife baking our own bread. Growing our own produce. I'm an old-fashioned guy."

Elle looked at Eve and both burst into laughter. "You should ask Violet if any of her friends are available at the Eternal Sun. If that fails, you can always try Amish communities."

Ha-ha.

The flight was three hours, but it felt like thirty.

He recalled his eleven-month stint in Afghanistan more fondly. And that had gone faster.

When they started descending, they hit a pocket of air, and the whole plane rattled and jumped.

The captain's voice came over the speaker, announcing turbulence due to strong winds.

Great. Bumpy landing on top of everything else.

"Shit," Elle mumbled as the plane trembled. All the relaxation and chatter were gone. She was tense, clawing the armrests again.

"They've taken the plane," Eve whispered almost in tears. "The captain is just trying to keep us calm."

"I neutralized them," Jack muttered against his better judgment.

"What?"

"When I went to the bathroom. I neutralized the hijackers," he lied shamelessly. "I have them tied down and gagged at the end of the cabin. Nothing to worry about."

He caught Elle's smile, and for some reason he felt ten feet tall. And that her smile mattered to him one way or the other pissed him off to no end.

Eve sighed. "I guess that means that my grandson's system was wrong and we're just crashing."

Yep. No good deed went unpunished.

The flight attendants were hurrying around, picking up the drinks that the passengers were holding in their hands. Well, the glasses, because the liquid had already gone flying all over. One cart got loose and went careening down the aisle, scaring the living shit out of everyone.

With the landing maneuvers and the opening flaps, the sounds grew exponentially louder while the plane bounced up and down and swung sideways.

Elle was frozen in place.

Jack grabbed her hand and shrugged at the question in her gaze. "Look at it this way. If we crash, by holding on to me you ensure you drag me down with you."

"Fair enough," she said with a wavering smile.

The turbulence became worse and everything started shaking,

so Elle clutched his hand. Hard. Man, for such a tiny woman, she was strong.

Then Eve latched on to his free hand. She was terrified so he tried to smile reassuringly. He was so out of practice comforting people that it probably came out as a grotesque grimace, but she didn't seem to mind because she didn't release him.

"I…I think I'm going to be sick," she said.

Getting better and better. Jack looked up.

Jesus fucking Christ. Let the plane crash and put him out of his misery.

* * * *

While driving to Elle's place, Jack heard his cell ringing. He threw a glance at it. James. Since turning the device on after landing, he'd done nothing but get calls from him, and some colorful messages too.

"Yo," he said, answering.

"Finally. You already in Boston?" James asked.

"Yeah, we landed a while ago."

And thank God for that. He'd been in controlled airplane crashes. He'd parachuted from shitty planes with even shittier parachutes into enemy territory. Crawled miles with a broken leg. He'd repeat any of those experiences—heck, all of them together, in a blink of an eye—if that meant deleting the one he'd had today.

"The grandmas from the Eternal Sun called, saying that some Terminator-looking guy had come to pick Elle up and was escorting her back to Boston. I figured it was you. What gives?" James asked, interrupting his thoughts.

"Nothing."

James didn't believe him. Not even for a second. Jack knew him well enough to read his friend's silence.

"Elle with you?" James asked.

"I left her at her house to rest a bit. Now I'm going to her." He'd had to pick up some of his stuff and Elle had told him she needed to sleep. She'd been running on fumes, so he'd driven her home and ordered her to wait for him and open to no one.

She hadn't seemed to be too happy about it, but she'd saluted him mockingly and hadn't challenged him.

James's tone was concerned. "How much trouble is she in?"

"She saw something she shouldn't have seen while doing some dumb shit she shouldn't have been doing. Nothing you should worry about. I'm on it." James wanted answers, but Jack couldn't give them to him. The Bowens would freak out, get in Elle's face, and try forcing her into hiding…which was actually what Jack thought she should do, but she'd trusted him. He knew how important it was for her to stay and do right by her sister and the restaurant, and for some unfathomable reason, he wanted to give that to her.

"What the hell is going on?" James asked as Jack parked in front of her place and got out of the car. "You've been running away from Elle since ever. What do you mean you're 'on it'?"

He walked to the door and rang the doorbell, but there was no answer.

"James, I have to go." As he rang the bell again, he disconnected the call.

Nothing.

Shit, fuck. After glancing discreetly around, he picked the lock.

The place was totally silent. And empty.

Not even twenty-four hours and she'd ditched him already.

CHAPTER FIVE

"Thanks for the ride, sweetie," Elle told Barney while she jumped off the pushback and blew him a kiss. She got into her car, drove as fast as she could to the office, left all the documents from her last flight, and rushed on foot to the check-in counters. It was at moments like this she missed her sneakers the most. Who said airline agents had to wear pencil skirts and heels? Someone who had never worked at an airport, obviously.

"Here you are," Louise called when Elle approached the counter. "I was worried you wouldn't make it on time."

"Please, girlie. I haven't missed him even once in the last year," she answered and started typing on their reservation system. "Not going to start now."

Elle had managed to switch her flight-coordinating duties for supervising the check-in for this intercontinental, so all was good.

She still couldn't believe that Jack had fallen for the old I'm-tired-going-to-sleep trick. Maybe the trauma of being puked on by Eve had had something to do with it.

"You sure there won't be any trace?" Louise asked, watching over Elle's shoulder.

"No trace. You don't work around these programs for ten years without picking up a few cheats of your own."

Elle did her magic and then helped Louise with check-in procedures, making fast work of the line.

Suddenly, she noticed Louise had stilled and was gulping. "Umm, Elle?"

Following Louise's scared eyes, Elle turned around and saw Jack, looking frigging pissed off, his bulging arms crossed over his broad chest. Fuming.

Damn, that was the risk of being at the counter. Open access to the public.

That would have never happened on the tarmac. And there she had other means of escaping.

Before she could get a single word out, he grabbed her arm and pulled her away.

"You've been bugging the shit out of me for over half a year with inconsequential e-mails, and when you find yourself in trouble you decide to ditch me?" he growled.

"How did you find me?"

"Check your purse."

Her jaw dropped. "Oh. My. God. You put a bug in my purse? Do you know what kind of privacy invasion that is?"

Apparently he didn't consider it such a big deal, because he snorted.

He dragged her to a far corner, and then he got in her face, his expression menacing. "What the fuck were you thinking? Is it all a big fucking joke to you?"

"Of course not."

"Then what the hell are you doing? What part of 'stay home until I get back' didn't you get?" he snarled.

"I had to go to work. I have a life, you know?"

He obviously didn't think so. "You had to stay home, sleeping like we agreed. Or what do you think, that I don't have anything else to do than chase you around Boston? You unhappy with this arrangement? Because I'm not bouncing from happiness either. There are a million places I'd rather be than here, stuck with you."

That did it. She wasn't going to take any more of that shit. "We agreed? In what frigging universe did that happen? I agreed to nothing! You just ordered me around and expected me to comply. I told you I don't do shit on command!" she yelled at him, going up on her tiptoes and jabbing at his chest with her finger.

"Shut it and listen to me," Jack ordered menacingly, but she was too far gone to stop now.

"No way in hell! We agreed? Ha! That's so rich. As if I had a chance to get a word in. You've done nothing but shoot orders at me and now you think you can come to my work and start bullying me? Well, let me tell you, mister, I won't—"

"Quiet, pet," he interrupted her, the cords at either side of his neck standing out. The guy looked bigger and scarier by the second, but she didn't let it intimidate her.

"Oh, and newsflash, buddy! There are a million places I'd rather be too, hell included, than with you. I'm sorry being stuck with me is such a burden, that you find me so repulsive and unbearable that you can't stand being around me, but don't worry. I liberate you from it! Beat it and don't let the door hit your ass on your—"

Suddenly Jack cupped her neck and brought her to him, pressing their lips together.

Surprised, Elle froze. God, for such a hard man, he had soft lips.

"Finally," he said after releasing her mouth.

Then it dawned on her. Talk about adding insult to injury. "You kissed me to shut me up? How dare you—"

But she couldn't continue because he took her mouth again, and this time he didn't just press his lips against hers. This time he forced his way in, kissing her deep and hard. Thoroughly. His stubble rubbing her skin. And suddenly she wasn't clutching his arms trying to get him off but holding on to him for dear life.

His speech skills were limited, true, but when it came to kissing, he sure knew what to do with his mouth.

When he released her, she was dazzled and her lips felt puffy and on fire. He was so close that she could feel his breath on her, cooling her. His ice-blue eyes were ablaze.

They stayed silent for a long second, their harsh breathing the only thing she could hear even though they were in a packed airport.

"You drive me insane," he growled, his voice gravelly, his gaze never leaving hers.

"Same here, buddy. And so you know, I'm not okay with you kissing me to shut me up."

"Tough shit. Try to be less annoying and don't fight me. Talk less and listen more."

Man, he needed manners. If she went on a rant, he would kiss her again, which she wasn't too much against, but it would defeat the purpose.

"We need to leave, pet. You're going into your supervisor's office and putting in for holiday time. Now." His tone brooked no argument, yet it wasn't as cut-and-dried as before.

"Do you have a clue how notoriously understaffed airlines are? I need to file dozens of forms to ask for personal days, let alone a vacation."

"Get family leave. You need a family crisis for that. I say this constitute a crisis."

She looked at him. Yes, he did constitute a crisis. A major one. "I can't leave right now. I need to wait for the asshole who put a restraining order on me."

The corner of his mouth tilted in a rare half smile that was gone in an instant. "What did you do? E-mail him to death too? Cyberstalk him with inconsequential e-mails?"

How sweet. He knew how to crack a joke. "Nope. I reserve that rare honor for you. And those e-mails were not inconsequential," she found herself blurting out, her voice barely there as she finished the sentence.

He didn't answer, his eyes like laser beams going through her.

"Getting time off is not a good idea. If I drop all the stuff I normally do, people around me will notice there's something wrong." Not to mention she would go ballistic if she wasn't busy. She would never be able to sleep again. "And not only that, but how the hell are we going to explain your presence? What are we going to tell the Bowens?"

She didn't want them involved in any manner. James and Max had two small babies. Christy was pregnant. Their hands were full without having to worry about her or babysit her. And they would the instant they found out about the whole Maldonado situation.

"I'll tell them we hooked up."

The absurdity of that statement made her burst into laughter. "And who would believe that?"

"Does it look like I can't play the part?" he asked, pressing her flush against him.

Well, if that hard thing poking from below his waist was anything to go by, then no, he had no problem playing the part. But that was beside the point.

She couldn't deny Jack pushed all her buttons, getting her hot and bothered with just a look. The problem was, whenever she was around him she felt trapped between wanting to kiss him and wanting to beat the shit out of him.

And she'd given up on bad boys.

"What about me being repulsive and unbearable? A burden?"

"'Repulsive and unbearable' were your words, not mine, pet. And you are a burden, but not in the sense you think."

"What do you mean?" A burden was a burden; no two ways about it.

He shook his head, looking pissed off again, and put space between them. "Forget it."

Once she wasn't in his force field, she regained her bearings and realized Louise was waving at her from behind the check-in counter. Oh crap.

"I need to go. The passenger I told you about is arriving."

"I let you go take care of this, and in exchange you're putting in for time off. Otherwise you're going nowhere."

She narrowed her eyes. "You'd *let me*?"

He didn't correct his words, remaining silent, his face inscrutable, his grip on her shoulders unshakable. Yeah, apparently he'd meant exactly what he'd said.

Damn, Elle wanted to hash this out now, but she couldn't miss Aston Biggs. She had the moral duty to make his life as miserable as humanly possible, so she nodded curtly.

She had lots of accumulated extra hours, and with Tate out of Rosita's, the workload at the restaurant was going to double. Maybe getting some time off at the airport wasn't such a bad idea after all.

He released her and she hurried to the counter, Jack at her heels.

"What did this guy do to you?"

"To me? Nothing."

Aston Biggs, famous Internet mogul, had thrown his weight around and used his name and influence with her supervisor to get a last-minute seat on a transatlantic flight that had been totally booked. Because of him, there was a domino effect of bumped passengers, and a woman who had a confirmed seat was left out. She hadn't made it on time and her son had died alone in a hospital after an accident. All so that asshole could go have lunch in Paris or whatever it was pricks like him did there.

Elle hadn't been working when that had happened, but she'd been there when the woman had been waiting for the next flight and had gotten the news of her son passing away.

She hadn't been able to say her good-byes, so it had been Elle's mission ever since to be at all his flights to stomp all over his rights.

"I hate bullies, and he's the worse kind," she answered. "The kind who can't take what he himself dishes out. All talk, no walk. Because of him, someone missed something that she can't ever get back." And she knew very well what she was talking about.

"Why did he put a restraining order on you?"

"The guy has no sense of humor," she muttered as they reached the counter.

Louise's eyes were still wide. She gave Jack a once-over and whispered, "Elle, who is this?"

"Borg, Louise. Louise, Borg," she introduced them.

"Oh. Good idea to get a bodyguard. Perfect intimidation technique. You never know when Biggs will snap."

Elle hadn't thought of it that way, but Louise was right. Not that Elle needed someone fighting her battles.

As always, Aston Biggs was fashionably late. He believed people of his stature weren't supposed to be kept waiting, much less with commoners. His time was too valuable.

The little weasel scrunched his nose at the sight of her. "You. I don't want her tending to my business," he said to Louise.

Elle smiled widely and took a step away from the counter. She'd already *tended* to his business; she was there just to observe.

"I'm on this flight. Business class." Even though it was an intercontinental flight, the bastard didn't present any documentation. No passport. No e-ticket. As if everyone should know him.

"And you are?" Louise asked.

"Mr. Biggs. Aston Biggs, of course," he spat, obviously not pleased.

Louise tapped on the keyboard. "Hmm, I'm sorry Mr. Biggs, but according to our system, you booked a seat in coach."

"Impossible. I do not fly coach."

He was today. Last row. Closest to the bathroom. Constant flow of people. Least legroom, loudest seats on the whole plane. Flanked by the two most robust passengers she'd found, whom she'd awarded several thousand bonus miles for the aggravation to have to put up with Biggs for eight hours.

"Sorry, sir. Nothing I can do. Check-in is all but closed. The business-class seats are taken, the boarding passes printed and handed out. If you would have come in earlier, maybe we could have—"

"I want your supervisor here. Now."

"That would be me," Elle said, her voice sugary. "You will have to take this up with your travel agent when you get back."

"I want *her* supervisor," Biggs yelled at Louise.

"We are very sorry for the misunderstanding, but there's nothing he can do either. Boarding has started and unless you hurry to the gate, you'll miss the plane," Louise explained, handing him the boarding pass.

He ignored her and, after turning to Elle, took a step forward. "All this is your fault. You conniving little bi—"

She would have had no trouble beating the shit out of him; after all, she had the right to defend herself and the restraining order had expired, but before he could reach her, Jack intercepted him.

"You heard the lady. Get moving."

Biggs wasn't used to being talked to in that manner or addressed by someone looking like Jack, because he stammered a bit before answering. "And you are…?"

"Assaulting an airline agent is a very serious offense. I suggest you rethink it."

"I have unfinished business with her."

"No. Your business is finished. Get moving," Jack repeated. His back was in front of her, so she couldn't see his eyes, but she could guess by the tone of his voice his expression must have been frightening.

Biggs recoiled, huffed. "You're lucky I'm in a hurry, because this is not the end. I *will* have your job," he threatened Elle as he grabbed the boarding pass and left.

"Have a nice flight," she said, waving at him, and then whispered to Jack, "Wait till he sees the seat I picked out for him. This is a trip he won't forget anytime soon."

Jack shook his head. "Why didn't you tip off the police he was smuggling drugs?"

"Already did that once. He got arrested and his ass probed. I try to mix it up," she answered, winking at him. "You know, to keep it entertaining."

Louise laughed. "You're diabolical."

Just evening the odds.

"When you get off? You could come for a beer. The Borg too," Louise said.

"She's off already," Jack answered for Elle and then turned to her. "No beer. Now let's go to your office."

"You could wait here."

"Not a chance in hell," he said with a snort. "You're not ditching me again."

Damn. He'd read her. Although she was sure the security checks wouldn't have stopped Jack from charging in to drag her ass out. Then again, him chasing her on the tarmac would have been a sight to behold.

She gestured for him to follow her. She might as well get it over with, because this was a battle she wasn't winning. "Let the record reflect that I'm doing this just to humor you and to avoid a scene. I'll arrange some time off, if you agree to get off my back with my other activities. Oh, and if Biggs is back, I will be back too. Non-negotiable."

"This is not a democracy. We already had a deal in place. A deal I didn't need to make. Don't tempt your luck."

She rolled her eyes. How generous of him.

The second she got to her locker, she was so debugging her bag.

As she walked into her boss's office, she heard Jack say, "And get it in writing."

God. This…partnership of theirs was going to end up very badly. Murderously so.

* * * *

"We're taking my truck," Jack said, staring at Elle's ride. There was no way he was getting into that slick, tiny sports car.

"Why?"

He looked at himself and then at the car, which barely reached his waist, and cocked his eyebrow. "Why do you think? Not to mention it's fucking girlie."

She patted the hood of the car. "Don't listen to him, René, you're very masculine. The Borg is being mean on purpose."

René. Of course she'd named it. So fucking Elle. And that sports car was so her too. A hot little package. A tease.

He'd observed while she'd smiled at her boss and managed to get time off without any notice whatsoever. The supervisor had given her five personal days so she could go right away and had agreed to file the paperwork for family leave with the human resources department. All that at an airline famous for being notoriously understaffed on the best of days. Elle got absolutely whatever she wanted from men, which Jack couldn't stand. She'd played with that Biggs too. By the look of it, he was a complete asshole but that didn't take away from the fact that she was putting him through the wringer. Toying with him. Just for fun.

Too bad Jack didn't seem to remember that when she was close and her scent was all over him, filling his nostrils and driving him mad with lust.

"We could take separate cars," she suggested.

Right.

"Come on, my truck is over there." He would get René later on. When they made it to his ride, she whistled. "Cool. Can I drive?"

"Nope. As long as I'm around, I'm driving and you're riding shotgun. And that's the best of the scenarios, because if you piss me off too badly, you'll be sitting in the back." Or on the roof. On second thought, forget the roof. She'd actually enjoy that.

"Spoilsport."

"Besides," he continued, "you drive like a homicidal maniac."

"I do not."

Jack shook his head, ignoring her. "Can't understand how they let you drive at the airport."

"I had to pass an exam to get my airport driver's license."

Which she probably got by smiling and fluttering her eyelashes. His expression might have been too evident, for she added, "And I passed it fair and square. I may drive a bit fast, but we flight dispatchers are busy people. We have places to go, planes to get to."

"People to run over," Jack muttered as the engine roared on their way out of the parking lot.

She chuckled, not taking offense. "That too."

"Next time that fucker Biggs is going to fly, you should put him in a boarding bus and play Mad Max with him."

"I might."

"You are making that bastard's life miserable just for fun."

"I have my reasons."

"Which are?"

"None of your concern. About today's schedule," she said,

changing the subject. "I need to go to Rosita's to supervise prep, but before that, there's somewhere I need to be at six o'clock."

"Where?"

"At the square in front of the train station."

"Why?"

"I'm meeting somebody, but it will be just five minutes. You can go home and wait for me there. Or head to Rosita's."

"Let me make something perfectly clear to you, pet. Wherever you're going, I'm going with you, or you aren't going at all. Pick."

"Okay," she grumbled while her cell chimed and she read the message. "Don't say I didn't give you any options."

He frowned, but she didn't seem forthcoming and Jack welcomed the silence. Being around Elle was so exhausting. She was always talking about something or on her phone and on the go. He was sure he'd spoken more the past twenty-four hours than in the last month.

"Damn, I got a run in my pantyhose. This job is a killer on hosiery," she said. "Don't look."

Fantastic. That was the equivalent of saying "don't think about a pink elephant."

From the corner of his eye, he saw her squirming in her seat. "What are you doing?"

"Taking my pantyhose off. I can't go around with a run on them as big as a freaking highway, can I?"

Crap. Shit. That was exactly what he needed. Elle lifting her hips, pulling her pencil skirt up, and shimmying out of her stockings. As if his poor dick wasn't in enough pain already.

He kept his eyes on the road, his jaw clenched, his knuckles white from clutching the wheel.

Being undercover always played a number on his libido, but one look at Elle and he was standing at full salute, ready to go—dying to go, actually—his cock throbbing and reminding him he'd gotten no action in almost a year.

"Done," he heard her say.

Jack threw a glance her way. Yep, her gorgeous, tanned legs were bare and she was straightening her skirt. She dumped the tightly bunched pantyhose into her purse. Then she rummaged around, grabbed something, and after opening the window, threw it away.

A small, black, button-shaped thing. His bug. He turned to her.

"I saw that."

She held his gaze, amused, not the least sorry. "Oops. It slipped."

Cheeky, his pet.

Her cell beeped and she started texting again. In between texting, she reached for the radio and flipped the channels until she found one with something that sounded like music from the fifties.

"Yeah, *Grease*," she said, and began singing "tell me more, tell me more, did you get very far," while typing something on her cell. Jesus Christ, talk about multitasking.

They hit traffic on their way downtown, arriving with just a few minutes to spare. By then, Elle was tapping her knee nervously, her phone beeping constantly. Getting on Jack's last nerve.

"We're here; now what?" he asked, parking.

"We're on the wrong side. We have to be at the corner of Fifth and Palmer." She jumped out of the car and rushed ahead, dodging people.

"Slow down," he growled, catching up with her.

"I'm going to be late. I should have driven. You're frigging slow. A yellow light means speed up, not slow down."

Sure. If it had been up to her, they would have run half the red lights.

That he was an excellent getaway driver, he kept to himself. "Risking one's life when it's not absolutely necessary is unacceptable."

She didn't hear him, or if she did, she totally ignored him and kept blabbing, trying unsuccessfully to make headway. "Next time we're taking René. I told you the I-15 was no good."

Jack grabbed her by her belt loop, bringing her to an abrupt halt and turning her around.

"Jack, what the hell are—"

He took her mouth, hard. "Calm down. Shut up and follow me."

She narrowed her eyes at him, her luscious lips shiny from him ravishing them. "This is becoming a habit already," she muttered as he navigated the crowd much more efficiently. "Very unflattering."

No shit. Very unflattering—not for her, but for him. He didn't seem to be able to stop kissing her. Twenty-four hours and he was already breaking all sorts of rules. No physical contact, the most important, had gone out the window. As if he didn't have trouble enough keeping it down when she was around.

He got her to the corner where she was supposed to meet God fucking knew who as the train-station clock struck six o'clock.

"Now what?"

"Now we cross the street," she stated.

What the fuck? They'd just come from that direction.

She was toying with him.

"Pet," he growled, "I will not be played—"

But he couldn't continue because the light turned green, and when people started crossing, loud music blasted from speakers whose location he wasn't able to pinpoint.

We're your Weather Girls

Suddenly, everyone around him burst into dance, Elle included.

Fuck. He was in the middle of a flash mob. Talk about going unnoticed.

Of course Elle would be in a flash mob. Why wouldn't she engage in one of the most useless activities in the world?

He moved a bit aside, as the dancers got it on, their choreography very elaborate and coordinated as the song went on about raining men and umbrellas and God knew what else more.

People were exiting their cars and other surprised passersby were clapping their hands to the rhythm of the song, all of them singing along.

Jack felt like he was in a fucking movie. He would have been more comfortable in the middle of a bombardment.

… every specimen! … rough and tough and strong and mean…

At those last words, Elle searched Jack's eyes, their gazes colliding.

She had that irritating smirk on her face. Daring him. And then she winked at him.

Jesus, she was gorgeous. With those expressive eyes and that long dark hair. The hourglass figure, the boobs, the ass. The long legs. The cheekiness.

And that uniform. With that ridiculous yellow scarf around her neck and that skintight, formfitting short jacket. The skirt riding high on her thighs while she danced. Sexiest stewardess he'd ever seen.

Jack reached for the antacids in his pocket. Man, now that he was with her twenty-four seven, his ulcer was acting up and he was running out of pills.

He stood there, spellbound, soaking her in. Every one of her movements. It didn't help that she seemed to be dancing just for him. Oozing sex appeal and that in-your-face disposition of hers, the one that made his cock so hard he could hardly breathe.

She was all that he would ever want in a woman. Except for that attitude of hers. That would ruin everything. It would drive him crazy. He could never trust her, and she would never be happy staying in, making a home for him. Her priority would always be her work. Her agenda. And he was playing with fire. She affected him just by being close to him. Not good.

She must have noticed his frown, because she gestured at him and pouted. And the more he frowned the more she pouted until she just burst into laughter, never breaking a step.

When the music ended, the flash mob dispersed as fast as it had formed. Traffic was still stopped, passersby clapping and whistling.

Elle walked up to him. "Now let's go, Borg. I'm expected at Rosita's. We are a bit late, but I'll change out of this uniform and into the one for Rosita's in the car."

He reached for his pills. Man, he was so fucked.

CHAPTER SIX

"Two-minute sprint. Rev up to one-oh-five."

Joaquín Maldonado huffed, watching the small screen on the stationary bike, stuck on 85 rpm.

"Come on, come on. Abdomen hard," Lars, his personal trainer said. "Keep pedaling. Piece of cake."

Piece of cake twenty years and twenty pounds ago.

There was a knock on the door and Nico, Maldonado's right hand, walked in. "You wanted to see me?" he asked over the loud music.

Maldonado nodded and motioned for Lars to leave.

"Slow down but don't stop pedaling or get off the bike. Your heartbeat would spike," he warned. "You need to continue pumping oxygenated blood into your legs."

Like he could get off by himself with all the wires Lars had strapped on him to monitor his heart, and those damn shoes that locked into the pedals.

"When you recover from the cycling, we'll do some weights."

Damn Swede, fucking worse than the Gestapo.

"One of these days I'm going to shoot him. Let's see how he recovers from that," Maldonado grumbled after Lars left.

Nico smiled, but didn't say anything.

"Kill please that damn music," Maldonado ordered, wiping the sweat from his forehead. "It's driving me nuts."

Nico turned it off. "Death metal. It's a Scandinavian thing."

Who the fuck thought pedaling to death metal was a good idea? That shit didn't even have a rhythm. Salsa, bachata, mambo; that was something one could pedal to.

Wouldn't it be ironic that after relocating to Florida for security reasons—mainly to avoid getting shot by any of the thousand hired guns of rival cartels—he'd die here of a heart attack, at the hands of this vigorexic asshole?

"We have a problem. Police got a search warrant and have impounded the jet."

Nico stilled. "The jet is clean. I personally supervised it."

"I'm sure it is. What worries me is the why. Was everything taken care of?"

By everything he meant everyone. Nico didn't need explanations.

"I was told so by your men. Pilot, driver, the chick at the airport. The middlemen were disposed of too. Everyone who could have tied Aalto to the jet is gone."

"Well, those morons missed someone. My sources tell me the police have a witness linking me to Aalto's murder."

"Do we have a name for that witness?"

Maldonado shook his head. "You know what to do." That witness could not be allowed to live; Maldonado had enough headaches as it was without this new threat.

Nico nodded.

Damn Aalto and inflight snacks.

He'd planned to make the politician see reason. If the old fart couldn't be swayed with money, then he'd resort to blackmail and show him all the footage he had on his kinky extramarital escapades. Convince him how beneficial it would be to forget about his latest proposal and support a less radical path. Unblock the port. Then the bastard had choked on the olive he was eating when Maldonado had shown him the pictures.

"Let me, boss, I got this," Emiliano had said as the man was turning blue.

He'd yanked him up and attempted to Heimlich the shit out of the politician. Which he did, managing to break his neck in the process.

Old people broke so damn easily. Especially when the Heimlich maneuver was done wrong and the poor bastard was shaken like a rag. In Emiliano's defense, he did get the olive out of Aalto's throat.

Pity they had miscalculated and his body hadn't hit the Atlantic

Ocean. He would have been lost forever. But no, another mistake in a long line of mistakes.

"Nico?" he called as the man was walking toward the door. "I want this handled fast and quietly."

"Of course. I'll take care of it myself," the Russian answered.

Maldonado had always followed his instincts, and getting Nico to work for him had been a jackpot.

If he'd been on the plane, things would have gone differently, and they wouldn't be in their current predicament. But he'd been supervising the labs and dealing with shit back home while Maldonado was left with incompetent imbeciles who not only snuffed the only hope of resolving their logistical issues but were incapable of cleaning up their own messes.

He should have listened to his gut feeling and shot Emiliano when they were just kids. Family brought nothing but trouble.

"What about the last shipment?"

"Still stuck in the port. Paperwork hasn't come through yet. Controls have tightened."

Damn. Counting the one the police intercepted at open sea, that was the second shipment they'd lost in ten days. "Business is suffering. We need to deliver the product and get paid for it." They couldn't afford more losses. He was beginning to be strapped for cash. Suppliers had to be paid. Funding that never-ending territory war back at home wasn't cheap. "Payment is overdue. I can try buying some extra time but this situation better resolve quickly."

They needed to find more effective ways to move the product. Especially now that Aalto was gone and with him the possibility of using the old bastard's kinkiness to Maldonado's advantage.

Maybe his successor would be more agreeable. Thank God there were so many ready to take Aalto's place. Politicians were like cockroaches: they were never in short supply.

* * * *

It was two in the morning and Elle was sitting in his truck, humming and swaying to the music on the radio. More of that fifties-sounding, great-balls-of-fire shit. All after her stint in the police station, the red-eye from hell, working her shift at the airport, hurrying around Boston for a flash mob, and being at Rosita's over seven hours playing the perfect hostess. Jack was dead on his feet just from keeping up with her and she was fresh as a rose, humming and swaying. At two a.-fucking-m.

"Well, thanks for the ride. You going now, right?" she asked as he parked in front of her house, in a quiet residential area on the outskirts of Boston.

"Wrong. I'm staying here," Jack said, gesturing toward the house.

Elle frowned. "You could plant another bug on me. I promise not to get rid of it. Them, if you want." She lifted her arms, like a martyr. "Wire me. I surrender."

"My place is across town."

"And now that we're on the subject, where's your place?" she asked. "I would love to go take a look."

"We are not on the subject."

"Don't tell me you already have a wife and a couple of kids there." He held her scrutinizing gaze and kept quiet until she spoke again. "Either way, you can't stay at my house. Don't you have anything else to do than stalk me? What about that biker bar of yours? Aren't you needed there now that you're back from doing whatever it was you were doing in Florida?"

"I was saving your ass in Florida. And I'm not stalking you. I'm watching over you."

"There seems to be a very fine line between stalking and watching over."

"I don't understand fine lines, pet."

She snorted. "No shit."

"You're a good one to talk."

"I do understand about fine lines," she said, a saccharine smile on her face. "I just don't give a damn."

He stared at her for a long while. "If I have to stay in the car, I will. In a residential area like this, all the neighbors will see me and call the cops, and probably your mom and sister as well, but we can play it that way if you want."

He'd noticed how she'd avoided answering Rosita's phone. She was trying to dodge someone and his money was on Tate.

Elle caved. "Okay, come in if you must. The house is big enough that we don't have to see each other. But keep in mind I'm doing you a favor. If my neighbor Mrs. Copernicus spots you, and she will, she'll bring a thermos and sit with you. They take neighborhood watch very seriously around here. And they are very nosy and chatty."

Fuck, no, please.

He'd had enough of that at Rosita's. Thank God people seemed to understand he didn't want to socialize and left him be. Not before bothering the shit out of him for a while though.

He gestured to the pink house. "Copernicus is that one, right?"

"Yes. Why?"

Because when he'd picked the lock to get in earlier that day, he'd bumped into her on his way out. He'd been swearing and looking mighty pissed, but the lady hadn't even blinked. She'd smiled, handed him a plate full of cookies, and informed him that she'd seen him and Elle arriving and that the Coopers left a spare key under the second flowerpot from the right. No need to break and enter, she'd added.

"Met her already," he answered curtly. "Cookies on the table. The spare key under the flowerpot I confiscated."

"Oh, how romantic. You've barely kissed me, and we're already exchanging keys."

As if. She was getting the key to his place like fucking never.

He hoped his glare spoke volumes, but Elle didn't seem to mind or care. She threw him an air-kiss and, smiling, opened the front door.

After dumping her stuff on the table and taking one cookie, Elle headed for the kitchen, opened the freezer, and took out a gallon of ice cream.

At fucking two thirty.

"Midnight snack. You want?"

He shook his head. How she could be hungry when they'd eaten a feast at Rosita's once the last diner had left, it was beyond him.

She sat on the sofa, tucked her legs under her ass, turned on the TV, and began scooping ice cream.

At fucking two thirty.

Jack frowned. "You're not tired?"

"Not yet." She waved around. "I'll give you the grand tour later, but basically what you see is what you get. You can park your things in the guest room upstairs. It used to be Jonah's, so no fear of frilly anything."

"You live alone?" he asked, looking around the huge Victorian house.

"Most of the time. Whenever Mom is back from Florida, she stays at Ron's. She seems uncomfortable being here with him. She blushes." Ron was Tate and Elle's mother's boyfriend. Nice quiet guy if Jack remembered correctly from James's wedding.

What wasn't clear to him was why Elle lived in the family home, surrounded by what must be painful memories. Then again, this was a perfectly good house. No reason to go empty forever.

"No Bowen wall of fame here?"

"Still shocked about that pic, right?" Elle asked, chuckling.

Fuck, yeah, he was.

Rosita's was full of pictures, ranging from very old, beginning-of-the-twentieth-century shots of Italian immigrants to the US to recent ones, featuring the Bowens prominently. Jack had been standing in front of that particular photo for a long while, not sure what he was seeing. "What is that?"

Elle had walked to him and giggled. "That's Cole's wedding. The centerpiece of my Bowen collection. Such a pity I wasn't there to take more shots."

"Where the heck—"

"Las Vegas. During a *Star Trek* convention."

That at least had explained the aliens. Amazing that Cole had allowed Elle to hang it. Things must have changed a lot since the last time he'd seen the oldest of the Bowens.

Jack wasn't sure yet whether to be amused or horrified.

"The marker on James and Tate's wedding picture; your handiwork, right?" he asked.

"How did you guess?"

Side by side with Cole's *Star Trek* wedding photo from hell there had been one of James and Tate's wedding party. Jack's face had been covered with black marker and someone had written "top secret" near it.

"I figured you would want to protect your identity," she continued, scooping more ice cream and then licking the spoon. As if staring at her at Rosita's swaying her ass hadn't been bad enough, or trying not to watch as she changed out of her airport uniform in his truck, now he had a ringside view of her gorgeous mouth playing with her food. "I guess getting new fake passports and changing names must be a drag. And cost a mint. I have a close-up the photographer took of us while dancing at the wedding reception. I personally think we look amazing, but I can't hang a picture with half of it crossed over with marker. I'm waiting for you to be a normal civilian so that your face can be publicly revealed."

She was making fun of him. As always. People gave him a wide berth. Grown men had trouble holding his stare and this tiny woman was laughing at him.

"Why don't you have a man?" he blurted, suddenly irritated.

"I do have plenty of those."

"No, you don't. You have half-assed, no-balls, no-dicks, wet-behind-the-ears kids with barely any stubble who worship at your feet and agree with you about everything. I meant a real man looking out for you. Getting in your face when it's needed." Which, as far as he could see, was all the fucking time.

"Oh, they have balls. And there's nothing wrong with their dicks, I can assure you. Besides, I don't need a man getting in my face."

He begged to differ, but that conversation was a lost cause if he ever saw one.

"And that?" he asked, gesturing to the sentence on the kitchen door. *Believe in the impossible*, it read. He'd noticed inspirational stickers on every door he'd seen so far.

She shrugged. "Good to remember."

For the first time the entire night, Elle seemed down. He'd been praying for her to stop blabbing and be quiet, but now that she was, it didn't sit well with him.

"So what other moronic activities you take part in that I need to be aware of?"

Her eyes brightened. Her lips quirked up. Yeah, much better. "I keep busy. But don't worry, we aren't having another flash mob until the next month."

Oh, he wasn't worried. Much.

"You need to cancel all that shit." No more running around for stupid flash mobs. "And get rid of those braids," he added, pointing at her head. "I don't like them."

She let out a soft snort. "Let's see what I can do. And about my schedule, I'll keep to just the bare necessities. Swear."

She lifted her hand, those angelic eyes and that damn smirk on her face not boding well with him. He felt his ulcer acting up. He'd dealt with lowlifes and criminals all his life and not a glitch. He'd met her and gotten a fucking ulcer.

He reached into his pocket and took another antacid. Mullen needed to get his ass in gear and catch Maldonado soon, or Jack's insides would burst into flames.

"There's no food in your kitchen."

"There's ice cream."

"What I said. No food."

She threw a glance at him and asked, "You were joking in the plane, right?"

He pondered for a second. "Yeah, I didn't neutralize any hijackers."

"I didn't mean that," she said, between giggles. "I meant what you said about wanting a Pilgrim as a wife."

"Nope. Totally serious."

"You're in the wrong century. Heck, the wrong millennium."

"I don't think so."

"Why a bread-baking wife?" she asked, narrowing her eyes. "Is it because you can't cook? Because that's why God created takeout. You just stick the menus on the fridge door, have a phone handy, and you're set."

"Of course I can cook." Rather well, actually. Nothing fancy or gourmet, but he could create an edible meal from almost anything. He'd had lots of experience. He'd grown up on that. "Did I tell you already I prefer my women silent?"

Elle broke into laughter. "I prefer my men with a working brain. We can't always win, can we?"

Smart-ass. Beautiful, sexy, exasperating smart-ass.

He caved. "I want someone that will have my children, and whose priority would be taking care of her family. Not someone who just wants to have fun and run around, flaunting herself and probably cheating on me the second I step out the door."

He knew before he closed his mouth that he'd spoken too much.

Elle smiled, realizing that too. "Ahh, so that's why you said you didn't want someone like me. Because you think I flaunt myself and cheat? You think I'm a whore."

"I didn't use that word."

"Didn't have to, Borg. You're spot-on about one thing, though. I'm anything but silent. In bed or out of it. Not that you'll ever get to experience the 'in' part. The other, all the screaming and yelling I do outside, I'm going to give you plenty. I suggest you save yourself a world of pain and aggravation and take on another super-secret assignment and disappear."

"I don't think so, pet," he growled, planting his feet onto the sofa table and looking at the ceiling. "Despite whatever you need to believe, you are a witness to a crime, and Maldonado plays in the big leagues. He will not hesitate to cut your throat. The second I think your cover is blown, I'm pulling you out and into hiding. And I don't want to hear a word from you."

Silence.

Oh, miracle.

Jack turned toward her and to his utter surprise found her sleeping. No wonder she hadn't given him one of her clever comebacks. Even when she fell asleep, she always had the last word.

Her head was bent at an awkward angle, the spoon still dangling from her hand. Almost three. So this was why she always wrote to him at those ungodly hours.

He disposed of the ice cream. He was going to throw a quilt over her and leave her there, but before he even realized what he was doing, he was lifting her in his arms and heading upstairs. She was a flight risk after all, and having her sleep so close to the front door was stupid.

The first room he tried was Tate's. The next one was definitely Elle's. Bold, in-your-face, messy place. Bed unmade, clothes stacked on the chair. More of those inspirational sentences on the walls. Yep, Elle's.

Life is short.
Break the rules.
Forgive quickly.
Kiss slowly.

Undressing her would make it more difficult for her to bail unnoticed and would piss her off immensely in the morning, but there was no way he could survive that. No way whatsoever.

He put her to bed, tucked her in, and made himself walk away.

He left his duffel bag in the guest room, the one that had been her brother's. James had told him that Tate and Elle's dad and older brother had died in a car accident almost a year before he'd met Tate. Drunk driver. Elle never spoke of it, not with him anyway.

No frills. No mess. Perfectly clean room. But instead of staying there he found himself heading to hers. He watched Elle for a long second, and before he could order his legs not to move, he was getting into her bed.

Jesus Christ, not even forty-eight hours around this woman and he was already in her bed. Unable to walk away, not even to the next room. His mind in turmoil, his dick hard as stone. His ulcer killing him. He repeated to himself that if he kept his arms around her, she couldn't ditch him. This was just an extra precaution. Nothing to do with him at all.

Then she turned to him in her sleep, snuggling and burying herself into him, nuzzling her face on his chest, throwing her leg over him. She took a small, deep breath and went soft in his arms.

This was going to be a long night. A very long, very painful night.

* * * *

I'm calling you exactly two seconds after I send this message. If you don't pick up, I'm taking the car and heading your way. Haven't slept much and I'm cranky as hell. I suggest YOU ANSWER OR ELSE.

Elle had barely finished reading the message when her phone rang.

She'd been avoiding her sister and her calls since yesterday, so she knew this was coming. Better get it over fast.

"Hi, sis," she greeted Tate. "I see your hormones are still raging."

"Finally!" came from the other side of the line.

"I sent you a message yesterday to tell you everything was okay."

Tate snorted. "Sure everything is okay. Just peachy. You spent over twenty-four hours in a police station after one of your coworkers was murdered and you came back escorted by none other than Jack."

"We happened to run into each other in Florida. That's all."

"Save it. I talked to Paige."

Damn. Paige, Rosita's maître d', was a tough cookie, but she had nothing on Elle's little sister even when she was calm. A hormone-ridden, sleep-deprived Tate? A steamroller.

"She said you showed up at Rosita's with Jack and left with him after dinner," Tate continued. "What's going on?"

Elle decided to try Jack's explanation. "We hooked up."

A snort of incredulity. "Try again."

"What? You don't believe we could hook up? I have my charms."

Elle was not self-absorbed, but she had eyes in her head and she knew how men looked at her.

"Yes, you have plenty of charms, but Jack is impervious to them, remember? Besides, any hookup between you two would end up on the five o'clock news. The second the sex was over, maybe even before that, you would be ready to shoot each other."

That was not that flattering. But it was probably true.

"Paige said Jack was scary-looking. More than usual."

Damn Borg. He'd kissed her twice at the airport and once before the flash mob, but at Rosita's he'd kept his distance. Of course no one was going to buy they were hooked up if he looked at her as if he was going to kill her. Although in all honesty, he did look like he was going to kill her while kissing her too.

Elle let out a loud breath. She might as well admit defeat and give Tate something. If not the truth, then something close enough. "Jack is keeping an eye on me. He was at the police station when I was there giving my statement about Marlene. I had spent the whole night partying with her and the cops wanted to know more about it." Which was not a lie per se. The cops had been interested in that. Until she'd told them about their little identity-fraud trick. "I was upset and in shock and he got worried. The case is not closed yet so he insisted on watching my back. He's staying at the house."

Silence. Then disbelief. "Jack is staying at the house?"

"In Jonah's bedroom," Elle felt the need to clarify.

Or so she'd thought. She'd totally zonked out on the sofa and woken up alone in her bed. Tucked in but dressed. With the faint recollection of hard arms around her and an even harder chest behind her, unbending, keeping her trapped and weirdly safe during the night. And her pillow smelled like Jack. Then again, to her everything smelled like Jack by now. He took up so much space. He walked into a room and the space grew smaller, as if he'd sucked in the light and the air around, all the attention going to him.

Be that as it may, she'd woken up incredibly hot and bothered.

Her pussy wet and throbbing. Her nipples hard, her clit engorged and pulsing. Needing to come so badly she'd had to go to the shower to relieve herself. She'd been without sex for months and hadn't really missed it. Then she spent one measly night under the same roof with testosterone-ridden Jack and she was finger fucking herself in the bathroom like there was no tomorrow, legs barely holding her as she came, hoping real hard the sound of the shower's running water would muffle her moans.

"Where is he now?" Tate asked.

"Not sure. I think he's in the kitchen." When she'd gone downstairs he was coming in with his hands full of groceries. He'd growled a "Not a thing to eat here, pet" and stomped down the hall.

"I don't eat breakfast," she'd whispered more to herself than him.

At least not this early in the day, anyway.

"Now you do," he'd growled back, not even turning to her.

How he'd heard her, she had no clue, but she hoped he'd heard the screw-you that came after that.

She was actually waiting for him to burst into the bathroom at any moment and drag her out to eat protein shakes or some shit like that.

There was a long silence before Tate spoke again. "You're lying to me. There's more to it than Jack watching over you."

Elle put on her poker face. And her poker voice too. "What makes you think I'm lying?"

"Have you forgotten who you're talking to? And I know Jack. You're back in Boston. He would be running in the opposite direction if you were safe, not watching over you. Much less staying in the same house as you."

Her sister was absolutely right.

More silence.

"Are you going to tell me the truth anytime soon, or do I have to come and beat it out of you? I'll remind you, hormonal women do not go to jail. It's called justified temporary insanity. Now spill, sis."

CHAPTER SEVEN

Jack stood up the moment Elle left her advisor's office. Thank God. About time.

As an undercover operative, one of his strengths was infiltrating all sorts of environments, but on a university campus he was out of his depth. So many brats around, he was getting a fucking headache.

"Aren't you too old for school?" And for all these schmucks salivating around her? A lesser man would have been struck dead by her fulminating glare but he shrugged it off.

"No one is too old for school, dummy. I took several detours, restless soul that I am."

Pain-in-the-ass soul, if they asked him. "How many detours?"

She took a bite of the ice cream she'd bought. Well, technically she hadn't bought it, because as she'd tried to pay, the kid working the stand had smiled and refused her money. He'd still been dazzled when Jack had grabbed cash from his pocket and shoved it in the kid's hand, daring him not to take it.

"Let's see. There was that sabbatical after college; then the time I spent in San Francisco before the Eternal Sun Resort and transferring to school to Florida. Hi, John," she greeted the guy who crossed their path waving at her. "Then the couple of semesters I took off to get my physiotherapy degree. And—"

"You a physiotherapist?"

"Not a licensed one; I didn't show up for the last exam. I didn't need it. I already knew all I had to. And by then I was into teaching

English for foreigners, so I jumped into that. It's a great way to travel the world and earn money."

That explained why she was twenty-eight and just finishing her studies. Because she wasn't able to keep on track even if her life depended on it.

"Was that before the snake-charming studies or after becoming a bounty hunter?"

She threw him another dirty look. "No, it was before the class on lifeguarding if you must know. No snake charming, but the bounty hunting is interesting. I'll look into that. You can never have too many hobbies."

Yes, one could, obviously.

"And what are we studying now?" he asked mockingly.

"Astronomy."

That stopped him dead in his tracks. Astrology, sure. Astronomy? Never in a million years would he have guessed. That explained all the geeks around though.

If she was dangerous enough working at an airport, he didn't want to know what she could do at NASA.

When the irony of it dawned on him, he felt his lips quirking up.

"What?" she asked impatiently.

"I remembered your fear of flying. I hope you aren't planning on any deep-space exploring."

"Very funny, Borg. I'll call Eve and get some of her blue pills."

"Hi, Elle," another schmuck interrupted, waving at her.

"Hi, sweetie," she answered, offering him a smile. Jack turned to her and she shrugged and whispered, "Can't remember his name, but he makes to-die-for daiquiris. And knows all the names of the pulsars."

"Are you acquainted with every-fucking-body here?" Which was amazing, considering all her extracurricular activities and how much time she actually spent away.

"I'm friendly and talk to people, not like others."

"I'm friendly enough," Jack muttered.

"Sure, for a bloodthirsty, inarticulate terminator you are," she said, going in the direction opposite from where the car was parked.

"Now what?"

"A short stop."

"A detour to learn how to restore old buildings?"

"Ha-ha. I agreed to get a mani with the girls. It's just here around the corner."

"I don't think so," Jack growled, but his cell rang, and when he saw that the caller was Mullen, he decided that fighting with Elle had to wait.

"Jack here," he said, answering the call while she sprinted to the beauty salon. "Any news?"

"Maldonado is back in the US. We subpoenaed all the videos from the airport. We've placed Aalto at the airport, but not near Maldonado's jet, which, by the way, was spotless."

No surprise there. The second he realized the body had been found, he must have started covering his bases. Major criminals didn't make it that long without taking precautions.

"We're going through Aalto's computers with a fine-tooth comb, but so far we haven't found anything."

"Using Elle is not an option," Jack warned, already foreseeing where Mullen was heading.

"You know she would want to testify. Bring her friend's killer to justice."

"Please spare me the bullshit. What about the two bodyguards? Have you turned the heat up on them?"

"Escudero and his niece have disappeared."

If Elle would be more agreeable, Jack would consider leaving her under someone else's watch and go to Florida himself to sort that mess out. He was not a cop, so he didn't have to play by the same rules; he would get results much faster. Too bad Elle would eat her keeper alive. She'd smile and bat her eyelashes, and the poor devil would be doing her bidding in no time.

He knew firsthand; he was waiting outside a beauty salon. How fucked up was that? He hadn't done shit like that since Ronnie.

"And the autopsy? Any leads there?"

"No bullets recovered if that's what you are asking. They couldn't find any injury inconsistent with plunging twelve thousand feet at a hundred twenty-five miles per hour. There wasn't a single bone unbroken."

Fuck.

"Oh and Copeland?" Mullen said from the other side of the line, taking Jack out of his musing. "The NSA is sniffing around, extremely interested in getting Maldonado. So far the FBI is coordinating the whole operation, but if they decide to take over, we will have to hand the whole investigation to them."

That wouldn't happen. Jack would make sure of it. Having the NSA involved would mean more people knowing about Elle. Unacceptable.

After disconnecting the call, he took a deep breath and entered the beauty salon.

"You have a back exit in there?" he asked the befuddled girl behind the counter, who shook her head. "Windows that open into the street?" Another head shake.

He didn't get why those questions always left people flabbergasted. First thing he did when entering a place was study the layout. Entrance and exit points. Shit happened no matter what, but there was no excuse for letting it surprise you.

Satisfied with the clerk's answer, he nodded and sat down. No risk of Elle disappearing. Not that he hadn't covered her with bugs, because he had—one could never be too safe when dealing with such a nutcase—but he didn't want to let her out of his sight. He'd been in this business long enough to know things could go south in a second, so he opened a magazine and tried to forget he was reading fucking *Cosmopolitan*, in a beauty salon, with women around him whispering and gesturing.

He'd gotten his hands on Elle's agenda—that is, he'd studied the humongous calendar on the fridge door, where apparently she kept track of her crazy schedule and marked all her appointments—and apart from university in the morning, Italian classes early in the afternoon, and then Rosita's, she'd had nothing else planned. That improvised stop in the middle of her schedule came out of the blue.

He wasn't sure how many *Cosmopolitans* it took before Elle was standing in front of him, with all of her hair braided. Not just the left side as she had before.

"*Andiamo, il professore di italiano mi aspetta!*" Let's go, the Italian teacher is waiting for me.

He studied her, frowning. She was beautiful, those big eyes of hers even bigger and her delicate features more gorgeous and accentuated without anything in the way, but he loved her thick long hair flowing around her. Man, he should have been paying more attention to what she'd been doing. No wonder she'd chosen the styling chair farthest away from him.

"What?" she asked innocently, lifting her hands to him, fluttering her eyelashes. "Don't like my nails?"

Long, bloodred, decorated nails. Fucking sexy.

Not the problem. Not at all.

He cupped her neck and took her mouth, deep and hard. She tasted so damn good. That he didn't kiss her to shut her up was lurking in the recesses of his mind but he did his damnedest to ignore it.

"I don't think you heard me correctly yesterday; I said the braids had to go," he growled against her lips.

She smirked. "Oh, I heard you, believe me. I heard you loud and clear."

* * * *

"Wow, you're smashing." Paige greeted them with a whistle at Rosita's. She looked at Jack, then back to Elle. "I take it he doesn't like it, does he?"

Nope, he didn't seem to like it. Then again, he'd kissed the living wits out of her, before *and* after the Italian teacher, so it was anyone's guess. She wasn't too crazy about the new hairdo either, especially how tight her scalp felt and how badly she wanted to scratch it, but his expression every time he glared at her was worth all that discomfort and more.

'Those braids have to go." Who the hell did he think he was? She didn't take orders, much less ones issued with that tone of master of the universe.

"I have a bone to pick with you, lady," Elle said to Paige. "You've been blabbing to a certain very hormonal sister. I thought you had my back."

Paige grimaced. "So sorry. She's scary. She forced it out of me. Who knew brand-new moms became such Godzillas?"

Elle laughed. Didn't she know. She had always been an overbearingly responsible little sister. Always ready to lecture her. Heck, Tate had become a very successful corporate secretary mere months after graduating from college. Elle herself had been partying and missed her own graduation.

Never mind how stubborn and straitlaced her sister had been, Rosita's was still theirs thanks to her, not to Elle. Tate had stuck with it come hell or high water and restored it to the successful family restaurant it had been when Jonah and their dad were alive, and had gotten a fantastic team in the kitchen and outside. Paige, for example, with her choke collars and piercings and Goth makeup, was the best maître d' Rosita's had ever had.

Elle, instead, had done what she always did: run. Such a frigging irony that now that she wanted to stay, everyone wanted her to go.

"Checking around, pet. Don't go anywhere," he growled, then walked to the back.

"Pet?" Paige asked in a whisper.

Elle rolled her eyes. "He's delusional, but I'm humoring him."

"Is he going to be here on a permanent basis? I thought yesterday was an exception."

Elle shrugged. "Honestly? I don't know."

"He is so…intense."

Tell her about it. She couldn't pinpoint what it was about him, but boy it got her motor running. That severe demeanor, those icy-blue eyes. That gravelly voice. No man had ever gotten that primal reaction from her. Crazy attraction none withstanding, she knew there could never be anything between them. They would drive each other insane. But that was just as well, because she was not looking for love or a relationship. Heck, she wasn't even sure sex was a good idea. Every time he kissed her, her damn heart stopped and her core flooded. Such raw passion. Such intensity, in the kiss and in the hand restraining her. She didn't like being held in place, being told what to do, and that was all he did. He was a rock and she would never get him to move. And yet, for all her sound reasoning she couldn't deny she wanted him, badly.

Shaking those thoughts, Elle got on with prepping, and soon they were welcoming the first patrons.

The evening started calmly, but it soon took a turn for the worse.

The second Elle saw Cole, James, and Max marching into Rosita's, their faces stern, she knew she was in trouble. Tate had given her up. She'd seen that same expression on Jonah's face many times and it always meant trouble.

"My bro-in-law and his lovely entourage," she greeted with a smile. "What brings you here at this ungodly hour? Got the hankering for some Italian?"

The three of them stopped in front of her, James and Cole with their arms crossed over their chests. Max leaned on a table, more relaxed, but serious nonetheless.

Nope, no hankering for some Italian.

They were there to ride her Italian ass, she could tell.

Jack could too. He glared at her. "You told them."

"No, I didn't. Momzilla did."

"Who?" Jack and James asked at the same time.

"Your wife," she told James and then turned to Jack. "I had to tell her. There were only so many times I could dodge her."

Elle had explained to Tate what was going on. Well, a decaf, light version of it, keeping out names and as many gruesome details as possible. By the end of it Tate had been cursing like a sailor. Elle had sworn Tate into silence. Ha.

"Believe her. Resistance is futile," Max said. "I love Tate to pieces, but she's terrifying these days."

"The only reason she isn't here is because Jonah is sleeping, for once, and she doesn't want to wake him up, so you got us," James explained. "Much better for you."

"I told her not to worry and not to tell you. Jack has everything covered."

"No offense, man," James said to Jack, "I trust you with my life and with hers, but she's too visible here. She needs to lay low. Head out of town."

Jack didn't say anything, although she knew he totally agreed with her brother-in-law.

"Christy has a friend in LA who went to Europe for a month," Cole began. "Her place is on the beach. That's perfect for you."

Elle smiled innocently. "What, Europe?"

"L.A. Although Europe could be good too," Cole said, turning to James. "What was the name of the small town you were in for your honeymoon?"

"Lucera. No one would look for her there."

Max shook his head. "An American woman in a tiny Italian village with someone looking like Jack is anything but inconspicuous."

No shit.

"The cabin in St. John is a no-go. Too obvious," James added.

"We could send her to Redwaters with Annie's mother," Max suggested. "That town is full of crazy doomsday preppers armed to their teeth. Although with those resources Elle is very capable of starting World War III."

"Guys, no—"

"Right. L.A. is it then," Cole stated, ignoring her. "I'll get the tickets for tomorrow. It's short notice, but I'm sure I can organize some time off."

"No," she repeated, but no one was listening.

"I'll drive her to pick up her stuff, then to Alden," James said. "I know Tate wants to see her before she leaves."

"I said no," Elle screamed to get their attention.

The three Bowen men stopped talking and turned to her.

Bad idea. Too much attention.

"No? What do you mean no?" Cole asked. "You don't get a no."

Like hell she didn't. "I'm not going anywhere. I have things to do here. Thanks for your concern but butt out."

"Elle, for once in your life stop being difficult and do as you're told," Cole growled, exasperated. "This is no joke. We're trying to protect you, and we can't do it if you're here."

"Last time I checked I was an adult."

"Maybe you should start behaving like one," James suggested.

They were crowding her, using their size to intimidate her. All of them too big and taking up too much space. She wouldn't be surprised if they snatched her and she woke up in Utah, in the middle of nowhere. With Jack's blessings, of course.

To her utter surprise, Jack stood between them. "Cut it out and back off. All of you."

Watching Jack and Cole stand toe-to-toe was nerve-racking. They looked like two tanks on a collision course.

The oldest Bowen frowned. "You, if anyone, should agree with us. Why are you taking her side?"

Yeah, why? Elle would have asked, but she couldn't find her voice.

"She wants to stay, she's staying," Jack said. "She's an adult. We can't kidnap her."

Elle's eyebrows shot to the sky. Really? Because that was exactly what he'd threatened her with a couple of days ago on their way back from Florida.

"Things run smoother if we don't have a hostile hostage in our hands," Jack finished.

Max snorted. "Good luck, because Elle is the definition of hostile hostage."

"Guys, I appreciate the concern, I really do, but you're wasting your breath and my time. There's nothing you can say Jack hasn't already said. We agreed we'll reconsider the situation the second he believes there's danger, but until then I'm staying and that's final. Now, if you want dinner, you're more than welcome; otherwise it's bye-bye."

"I knew she would win," James muttered.

"By the way," she said to him, "have you already updated Jack on the family addition?"

"What family addition?" Jack asked, frowning.

Nope. They hadn't.

"We inherited an old locker and a new sister," Max chimed in.

* * * *

Nico was settled in the Irish pub where Marlene's wake was taking place. That Marlene had been Cuban and most of the assistants were too didn't seem to matter one bit to this crowd that were toasting her with whiskey. Typical Florida. A total mesh of people and cultures. He knew; his sorry Russian ass had been working for a Colombian since what seemed like for-fucking-ever.

He really hoped this little incursion would bring some results, because he'd cast a wide net but nothing had panned out. He'd followed all the possible leads, checked on the pilot and Aalto's driver. From what he'd discovered so far, neither of them had talked, texted, or e-mailed about Maldonado or the trip. The police were keeping the witness's name and whereabouts well under wraps, and none of his contacts knew squat.

The wake had gone on for a while, but he'd started working the crowd just recently, after enough alcohol had flowed to muffle uncomfortable questions like "Who the hell are you?"

He'd gone through the group of frat boys from her school, the airport personnel, her family and friends, being as inconspicuous as possible.

He approached an African American woman who seemed to be a bit tipsy. Sad and tipsy, the perfect combination to loosen a woman's tongue. And blur her memory.

"For Marlene," he said lifting his glass.

She followed suit and took a sip. "I'm sorry, I don't know you."

"A friend from the neighborhood."

"Ah…yeah," she said, dabbing her reddened eyes.

"So horrible," he mumbled, repeating what he'd heard a thousand times tonight.

The lady nodded. At least this one was not trying to score with him. How people thought a wake was a good place to pick up partners was beyond him.

"We worked together at the airport."

Damn. He'd already snooped around the airport crowd and gotten nothing.

As he was already moving to leave, she said, almost to herself, "I still can't believe it. I worked a shift with her two days before it happened. In the morning she was driving back to Florida after spending the weekend with her sister and that night she was dead." Her voice broke at the last word.

Nico stilled. If Marlene had been driving back to Florida in the morning, who had dispatched the flight?

* * * *

The day had been hectic, but not as much as the previous one, so Jack wasn't the least surprised when Elle came downstairs in the wee hours in her pajamas, fetched her ice cream, turned on the TV, put her feet on top of the table, and opened her laptop.

Jesus, how many things did she need to have going on in order to calm down and fall asleep?

Jack walked to the TV and turned it off. Before she complained he sat on the sofa by her side and said, "I mounted a security alarm on the door and the windows. Just in case you're thinking about going out for a spin."

She laughed. "Why?"

"I think it's self-explanatory," he said, taking a pill and flushing it down with a sip of water.

"What's that?"

"Antacid. You're giving me a ulcer."

"It's not me. It's eating at one a.m. It takes some getting used to."

"Says the lady gorging on ice cream. You should be five hundred pounds, gulping down food the way you do."

Elle shrugged. "Fast metabolism."

Yeah, and running herself ragged every day.

"Besides, tomorrow I have gym," she added. "I'll train an extra half hour."

Which brought him to his next question, no matter how badly he dreaded the answer. "What's in store tomorrow?"

"Gym, classes, work. The usual."

Fuck him. The usual was a killer.

"What? Too much for you?" she asked, reading him perfectly. "Because I'll remind you I was up on my feet all evening while you were sitting with the Bowens having dinner."

True. She'd been running all over tending to patrons and still had had the time and energy to visit with the Bowens as they'd been telling him about the freaky news of their lost sister.

Elle studied him for a long second before she spoke again. "You didn't answer when Cole asked why you were taking my side."

No, he hadn't answered and he wouldn't now. The truth of the matter was he hadn't liked seeing Elle pushed against the wall. Sassy little thing that she was, the Bowens didn't understand that she thought too much of them to give them her wrath.

Pity she didn't have the same issue with Jack.

"You could have gotten rid of me today very easily, yet you didn't. You like having me around; admit it," she said with a smirk.

He dodged her statement. "You like pissing me off; admit it."

"Wrong, Borg. I looove pissing you off."

It figured.

She pondered for a second, then added, "I think it's that don't-fuck-with-me vibe of yours. It makes me, you know, want to fuck with you."

His cock stood at full attention at the way her eyes danced with laughter and her lips quirked up. Such a tease.

"You don't want to fuck with me, pet."

"But I do."

"You can't take me on. I like my women tied up. Ball-gagged. Blindfolded. Plug up their asses. Pussy spread open for me to fuck it however I want. If I take the gag off, it's to fuck their mouths."

He was going for shock effect, not that he was exaggerating much. That didn't shock her. She just whistled. "Wow. No wonder you forget they're in your bed. How do they communicate? What about the safe word? Do you give them a pad and they use their fingertips to Morse it to you?" She imitated Morse-code-like sounds and added, mimicking a robot, "Tap. Taptaptap. Please scratch my nose. Dying here."

In spite of himself, he smiled. "You are a smart-ass."

"Thanks, I do my best. You didn't admit you like having me around," she pressed on, changing the subject.

"Because I don't." He hated having her around. Hated what she did to him, how easily she got his attention. How he couldn't think straight whenever she was near him. How he couldn't shock her into compliance.

"You're a shitty liar, Borg." In a swift movement, she straddled him. "Hasn't anyone told you you're handsome when you smile?"

He curtly shook his head, frozen as he was with sensory overload.

"They are probably distracted by the growls and the ice-cold stares."

"And you aren't?"

"They don't bother me."

No shit. They rolled off her back. Nothing seemed to faze her.

"I think they're damn sexy. Can I ask you something?" Before he nodded, she was already talking, her hands flat on his chest. "Why do you kiss me all the time?"

Her sweet mouth was so close to his he could smell the tiramisu gelato she'd been eating. Vanilla with a little kick from the coffee, just like her. Tamping down the need to ravish her lips, he answered matter-of-factly, "To shut you up. And I wouldn't say it's all the time. Just when strictly necessary."

"So all I need to do to get you to kiss me is chatter?"

Actually, all she had to do was look at him. Hell, breathing was enough.

That he kept to himself. It was already bad enough that his dick was jumping up and down from excitement, pounding against the zipper, trying to break through his jeans.

She felt it too, he could tell. It was in the smugness in her eyes. "Not interested," she said, unstraddling him, a cocky smile on her lips. "I know you think I'm borderline slutty, but I'm not. I'm searching for the one. And you so are not."

She strode to the TV and turned it on.

Suddenly, Jack jackknifed, and crowding her, turned it off, gripping her waist when she tried to swirl around.

"Really?" he growled in her ear.

"Really what?" she whispered, attempting to hide her surprise.

"You're not interested? That's why you sway around me half-naked, your nipples hard as stones? Why you sit on my cock?"

"I'm not the one sneaking into your bed at night. Or kissing you all the time."

"No, you're the one jacking off in the shower." Her intake of breath was loud and sharp. She tried again to turn but he tightened the hold he had on her. "No. Keep still."

Her voice was husky and so fucking sexy. "Why?"

"Because I say so." And because his cock was hard enough pressed against her ass. Didn't need any more visual stimuli.

She snorted, her tone incredulous. "Is that supposed to work on me?"

"Oh, but it works on you," he said and kissed her throat, feeling her body tremble. "You know what your problem is, pet? You go for men who are used to wearing the pants, but you tell them what pants to wear. They cave in; you win and then lose interest. You can't tell me which pants to wear. I don't work that way."

"Don't say. You into quilts?"

Such a smart-ass, his pet. He cupped her pussy, ripping a whimper out of her. "I'm into fucking. Stuffing yourself with ice cream will give you a sugar rush and ultimately put you out." He increased the pressure on her core. "I can do the same much faster."

It took a second before she could find her voice. "How much faster? Faster is not always better, Borg. Do you have files on female anatomy? You know what you're doing?"

Yep, a smart-ass through and through.

He moved his hand up to her belly and then delved under her panties. Oh fuck, she was bare. Soft, smooth, bare pussy. He caressed her slit. "You bet I know what I'm doing." Sex he could manage. Sex he understood, how to make a woman's body melt with pleasure. Besides, the more distracted they were by coming, the less inclined they were to want to talk. Or berate him for his lack of social skills. Sex was up his alley; the rest was just a jumbled mess that got him nowhere but into trouble.

He circled her clit, spreading her juices. "Twice I've stopped myself from reaching for you and giving you what you were aching for. You were dripping wet all over me in bed, rubbing against me. Moaning in your sleep. So fucking ready to come. By the way, you are fucking sexy jacking off. Were you thinking of me?"

"You saw me in the shower," she all but whispered.

"You need to learn to close the doors, pet. And come in silence."

She was trembling. Creaming his hand. "And yet you didn't..."

"Barge in?" he finished her sentence. "No. I wasn't invited to the party."

Elle cleared her throat. "And now you are?"

"Now you're awake and pressing against me, panting, not telling me to stop, so yeah... Now I'm invited to the party."

Her voice was unsure for the first time. "Jack, this might not be the greatest idea."

He slid one finger inside her, her inner flesh clamping around him. Sweet Jesus. So fucking tight.

"Jack—"

He wrapped his other arm around her, supporting her and keeping her trapped. "You haven't been fucked that much, have you?" Elle was such a tease. So brazen, so in-your-face, but it was a big, false facade.

She licked her dry lips. "Why do you say that?"

"You're fucking tight, pet. You can't be giving it up too often."

At his words, he felt her pussy contract around him. Her spine straightened, her whole stance radiating offense.

"You're wrong. I fuck everything that moves, the bigger and the rougher the better, and once a year, for Christmas, I get a vaginal reconstruction and start all over again."

He chuckled softly. Fuck but she was funny.

"And let me tell you," she continued, her voice choppy, her body slowly yielding to his invasion. "If you're one of those shitheads who only wants to break into untried, tight holes to then move to the next one once it has been 'stretched,' you should know that one, I'm not a virgin, and two, the tightest holes in this earth are in men's asses. Maybe you should move into fucking those."

"Not interested in men or virgins. Too high-maintenance and easily attached."

"Men or virgins?" She was trying to resist the pleasure. Trying not to give in. It was in the slight trembling of her voice. In the fluttering of her pussy.

"What I meant is you're a cheat. Not at all the experienced

minx you pretend to be."

"No, I haven't been fucked that much, as you so romantically put it. My choice."

He slid a second finger inside her, making it only to the first knuckle, and felt as the breath that she was taking caught in her throat, her core tensing further around him. "I know, pet," he whispered in her ear, pressing his palm against her clit. "Any man with half a working brain would sell his soul for a taste of this pussy."

He knew because he was ready to part with his soul, his brain, and half his vital organs for a chance to feel her coming around his fingers.

"Jack…" Her body tightened. Her core too. She was so close.

"Like this. Give it to me." He penetrated her to the second knuckle. "Come for me."

She leaned her head on his shoulder, arching her back and rubbing herself against his hand, climaxing long and sweet, her needy whimpers reverberating through his body, his cock jerking like a motherfucker.

When she started coming down, he spread her legs further with his thigh. He wanted her so badly he couldn't even remember his own name, let alone why this was a shitty idea.

"You're so small. This is going to be a tight fit, but you can take me." He yanked her pants down and unbuttoned his jeans. His cock sprang out, at the ready, the juices dripping from her sweet pussy fucking hot as he nudged the crown against her folds. "Brace yourself on the mantel."

That seemed to snap her out of it, and she turned around, defiantly, her chest rising and falling rapidly.

"I don't think so. If you want to fuck me, you'll have to do it looking me in the face. Or can't you?"

He took a step back. No, he couldn't. He couldn't look at her while his cock was inside her. Heck, he couldn't even kiss her. He would lose himself in her. In her sweetness. In her fire. In what she did to him. And he would never find his way out. Not in one piece anyway. And he was too fucking old and jaded to be shipwrecked.

"You're scared of me," she whispered, realization and hurt flashing through her eyes.

"Not scared of you," he said, tucking his painfully hard cock in and zipping up.

Scared of her? Please, he was fucking terrified, thank you very much.

"Then what? You can't perform without all your...hardware to keep me under control? You don't want me? Because your dick says otherwise."

"My dick is not in charge here," he spat out, and without looking back, he walked away.

CHAPTER EIGHT

"Stop touching my radio," Jack ordered, his hands gripping the wheel, his eyes never veering from the road. "Stay still for a fucking second, woman; we're almost there."

"That would not have happened if we'd taken René," she said, continuing to flip the stations until she finally found one playing *Grease* songs. "My car is tuned already."

Jack grumbled something back, but Elle didn't catch it. And it was just as well, because he hadn't said anything worth listening to the whole day.

From the corner of her eye, she studied him. For some reason, Jack was looking mighty pissed, which didn't make a lick of sense to her. After all, she'd been the one left standing with her pants around her ankles, still trembling from her orgasm, watching dumbfounded as the asshole zipped up and walked away, his face carved in stone, as if two seconds before that he hadn't had his fingers inside her and his hard dick tucked against her behind. Not to mention he'd been the instigator of the whole situation. Yes, she'd straddled him on the sofa, but she'd unstraddled him and told him she wasn't interested. He'd been the one cornering her.

Leaving her badly wounded female pride aside, she had to admit not going all the way had been the right thing to do. Sex with Jack would complicate their fragile arrangement to an impossible extreme. He was overbearing enough as a babysitter; she didn't want to know how he behaved when he thought he had more say because he was fucking her. And fucking her would be all that he would do. There would be no making love. His severe demeanor and the contemptuous way he looked at her ensured that.

"You going to train at the same time or you plan to stand beside me in the dancing room, stalking my every move? It's an all-female dance class, but I'm sure we can accommodate you. Teach you the steps and include you in the choreography."

A grunt was his only answer. He hadn't said two sentences to her today. Grunts and growls had been about it.

She'd been pissed too after the way he'd walked out on her. She'd felt cheap and rejected and, well, hurt. Jack wanted her, but he couldn't stand the fact that he wanted her, like she was some kind of shameful weakness of his. Her plan had been to read him the riot act in the morning, but she realized there was no need. Jack was punishing himself enough for the both of them.

"Not sure you'll be any good at dancing though," she added while Jack parked in front of the gym. "One needs certain flexibility, and you seem a bit stiff, if you know what I mean."

He threw her a murderous look and got out of the car. Stiff? Ha! Every single muscle in his body was strained by the looks of it. She was afraid at any second he would sprain something.

Good. He deserved that and so much more.

They entered the gym in silence. He didn't ask what kind of dancing class and she didn't tell. She wasn't going to be the one spoiling the surprise.

Jack walked to the practice room with her and glanced around. She rolled her eyes. A frigging miracle he hadn't insisted on entering the dressing room too. Paranoid ass. Which kind of self-respecting Miami mobster with more money than God would be seen in a suburban Boston gym with violet walls and carpool housewives? Please.

"Sure you don't want to stay?" she taunted him. "The girls would enjoy a man dancing with us for a change."

He threw another murderous glance her way and, without saying anything, left the practice room and walked to the weight machines nearby.

"Who's that?" one of the women whispered to her.

Judging by his language and social skills, the missing link between humans and monkeys.

"A friend of my brother-in-law."

"He is hot," she said giving Jack another once-over.

Sure he was hot; a hot pain in the butt. And he brought out the worst in her. The belligerent side. The Elle that didn't want to submit, never mind how much her body was dying to give in. Exhausting, really.

The rest of the ladies started pouring in and soon the teacher, Dolores, trotted in and got the music going. "You ready to twerk?"

Everyone cheered.

Elle reached for the door and locked it.

She appreciated what he had done for her. What he was still doing, never mind how disgusting it obviously was for him to stick around her, but he exasperated her. It was his black-and-white, unbending attitude. His arrogant superiority. His my-way-or-the-highway. That air about him that demanded obedience.

"Five, six, seven. Let's shake those booties, ladies," Dolores screamed as hip-hop blasted from the speakers. She loved loud music and flashy lights. Part of the sexy experience, she always said.

Before the first song was over, Jack was at the door, trying to open it. Elle could pinpoint with maddening accuracy the second it dawned on him that it was locked because his icy-cold eyes flashed with fury.

She turned to him and with an I-told-you-so smile, waved at him. She would have thrown an air-kiss his way, but she wasn't sure the glass door would hold if he rammed it, so she refrained.

Dolores was a stickler for punctuality—a fact that had landed Elle in trouble many times—and hated people coming late or interrupting, so she ignored Jack, which suited Elle just fine.

Through the glass she watched as he reached for his pocket and took one of those antacids he seemed to gobble nonstop. He might have looked tense before, but now it was much worse. The vein at his temple was about to burst and he was grinding his teeth.

Screw him. His fault.

For a whole hour, Jack stood in front of the glass walls, his arms crossed, his eyes spitting fire while Elle did her damnedest to make him pay.

He was sweating more than she was, especially when she did the floor movements. She could swear his muscles had increased in size, his silhouette big and ominous. The few men who dared to brave Jack's threatening demeanor didn't even get close enough to see too much. Jack made sure of it.

Once the class was over and the girls started marching out, she expected Jack to rush inside but he didn't. He waited for her, immobile, his expression inscrutable.

She walked past him, trying to hide her smug expression, but failed miserably. "I saw you at the door. Would you have wanted to join us after all?"

He remained quiet, but it cost him a hell of a lot, she could tell. His knuckles were white, his jaw about to split.

They walked to the truck in silence. The engine roared to life.

"Don't you fucking ever lock a door on me."

She lifted her eyebrow, dying to tell him he was dreaming, but she refrained and went back to fiddling with the radio.

* * * *

"Can I tempt you? I make a mean mojito and you look like you need one," Paige said, the bottle of white rum in her hands.

Jack didn't need a mojito; he needed a whole bunch of them, but he shook his head. He'd seen the results of Paige's mojitos many times. Besides, he was still supposed to drive. Elle had some sort of unplug session or low-key jam or whatever the fuck she'd called it after working at Rosita's.

If this was what Elle understood by keeping things to a minimum, he didn't dare speculate what her normal day was like. Crazy running from one place to another until she crumpled exhausted into bed, he bet.

Not that she wasn't enjoying putting him through the wringer, because she so obviously was. Like the twerking shit this morning. Man, oh man, that had been fucking torture.

"Hard day?" Paige asked with a smirk. "Wednesday is twerking day."

She was trying not to laugh.

"If it is any consolation, she goes out of her way to bug you. Most guys only get indifference. Or mild interest at best. You must be doing something right."

How sick was it that Paige's statement felt good?

It was past twelve and the last customer had left five minutes ago, so when the front door opened, Jack turned immediately.

In came an almost seven-foot, two-hundred-fifty-pound Japanese American guy with Yakuza-looking tattoos coming out of the T-shirt collar and peeking from the leather jacket sleeve.

Kai.

"What are you doing here?" Jack asked in a growl.

"Came for Elle. Is she around?"

"She went upstairs to get ready," Paige offered.

"Right. I'll wait."

Fantastic; this day couldn't get better.

Kai and Jack went back a long way, but there was no love lost between them. They had their brushes when both had been young and stupid and Kai was doing something much more dangerous than tattooing people. And far more illegal.

He admired how Kai had managed to change his life and extricate himself from his family, but that didn't mean he liked Kai. He didn't. And that he had had some kind of relationship with Elle, or maybe still had, didn't help matters in the slightest.

Paige noticed the tension in the air and without even trying to make small talk, she got busy clearing the counter. Clever girl.

"Okay, I'm ready."

Elle came from the back looking like Jack's wet dream come true except for those annoying braids running along her scalp, now up on a bun. One a.m. and dressed to kill with some sort of vintage dress that gave her a pinup vibe. As if staring at her in her sexy-as-fuck Rosita's uniform hadn't been bad enough. Or the twerking shit he'd been forced to endure, with Elle clad in tight, barely there shorts. Although by now anything on her made his cock hurt.

"Hi, Kai," she said walking straight to him and hugging him. "What are you doing here? Weren't we meeting at the club?"

"Hello, beautiful. I thought I'd pass by to pick you up."

"Oh, great. Let's go then." She turned to Jack and whispered, "You see? Beautiful, not pet. Beautiful. That's how you treat a woman."

"I heard, pet," he answered curtly.

Kai motioned toward Jack. "I didn't know you already had a date."

"Him, you mean? Not a date."

He hated the camaraderie between Kai and Elle. Totally fucking hated it.

"You in trouble of some kind?" Kai asked, looking at him and then at Elle. The motherfucker had always been very perceptive.

"We hooked up," Jack stated, taking her by her neck and silencing her with a kiss he'd been dying to give to her for the whole day. Once he released her mouth, he stared at her, daring Elle to deny his statement.

"Such a joker my Borg," she said, patting his cheek harder than necessary. "You don't like parties. You could stay and I go with Kai. I'm sure I'll be perfectly safe with him."

"I don't think so," he answered. "Let's get moving."

The faster they got there, the faster it would be over.

Elle pursed her lips but addressed Paige, "Can you take care of closing up?"

"Sure. Go have fun."

"Great," Elle said heading to the door.

She was breathtaking from the front. From the back she was even better, the dress hugging all her curves. Fuck, she had a great ass, and fuck, she knew how to move it. Just the right amount of sashay to look classy and sexy. Jack was an ass man through and through. Unfortunately, so was Kai, who was glancing at it appreciatively.

Elle reached the door and held it open. "Gentlemen."

Jack grabbed the coat from her arm and wrapped it around her. "Go," he ordered, holding the door himself.

"Cute hairdo," Kai complimented her on their way to the car.

Elle turned to Jack, her eyebrows lifted, a conceited expression on her face. "Isn't it? I thought so too."

"I'm parked there," Kai said, pointing to the right. "See you at the club."

"I can ride with Kai," Elle said to Jack. "He doesn't mind me fiddling with his radio."

"Get in, pet," he growled, unlocking the doors with the remote. He didn't want her fiddling with anything of Kai's. Not a single thing. Not even the damn radio.

Jack gritted his teeth and kept quiet during the ride.

When they made it to the bar, the parking lot was full. Not good.

After entering the establishment, his fears were confirmed. The place was packed. As in to the brim with rockabillies.

"This is what you understand by low-key?" he demanded, holding her by the arm. "We're going home."

For the first time today, Elle looked panicked. "Jack, this is important to me. My brother Jonah loved this band. I haven't missed one of their jam sessions for two years. I can't start now."

Fuck, fuck, fuck.

He could deal with sassy and belligerent Elle without batting an eyelash. But vulnerable Elle he was not ready to handle. It tugged at the wrong part of his body. At his heart.

If he'd learned anything in the last fifteen years in the field, it was that thinking with his cock would get him killed. Thinking with his heart would get him killed even faster.

"Half an hour," he grumbled against his better judgment. Crowded, enclosed spaces like this one were a security nightmare.

Once they hit the main floor, he had to reassess his first impression; it wasn't a security nightmare but an all-around clusterfuck that, judging by the level of alcohol flowing around, had been going on for a while.

Elle shrugged off her coat and he realized that some shiny white inscriptions and flowing lines had appeared on her body. Fuck him, she had UV tattoos, the ones that only were visible under black light. Fantastic, like she wasn't visible enough.

"Elle!" someone from a big group sitting at the counter yelled, waving at them. Kai was already there.

It took a while to get to them, because she seemed to know everyone.

"Hi, guys," she greeted when they reached them.

Jack got introduced to a bunch of people as Borg and then Elle proceeded to ignore him.

"Going to dance," she said, leaving her beer on the counter.

He watched the crowded dance floor. "No dancing, pet."

He knew the second he said it that it was a mistake. Right on the money. She smiled at him deviously and sashayed to the dance floor.

Fuming, he watched Elle dancing. Watched as all the men around were eating her with their eyes. And who could blame them? She was so fucking sexy, those white inscriptions and lines on her legs playing off her dark dress, seeming to flow as she moved.

Then the music changed to a slow song and Kai approached her. Fuck no.

"Step aside," Jack found himself growling.

Kai lifted his hands and let out an amused smirk, stepping back while Jack took her in his arms, holding her harder than need be.

"I thought you said no dancing."

He loomed over her and fought to get the words out from between his clenched teeth. "What the fuck are you doing? Do you want me to kill every man in this place?"

"Why would you?"

"Because all of them are looking at you and fantasizing about fucking you."

"And? What is it to you? You walked away from me yesterday, remember?"

Before he could assess the wisdom of speaking the truth, he blurted it. "I find it fucking difficult not to think of you as mine."

Surprise left her speechless for a second, but then her expression twisted in anger. "Start learning then, buddy, because I am not yours and it was your choice. Live with it. Besides, if fucking from behind is all you can offer, any woman will do. We are all alike from the back. I told you I'm sorry you're stuck with me and this is such a burden you can't even look at me, but—"

He grabbed her by the arms, their noses almost touching, and growled low. "You think I can't even look at you? I want you so fucking badly I can't even breathe."

She faced off with him, going on her tiptoes. "Well, I hope your ninja training includes holding your breath for long periods. Or let me ask at the counter, they might have an iron lung somewhere. Either way you said your dick is not in charge here, so order it back to its cave and don't waste my time." And wrenching away from him, she took a step back.

"You dancing, doll?" a guy that had been eying Elle asked.

She turned to Jack. "Doll. Not pet. Doll." Then she smiled at that mofo and answered, "Sure, I'd love to."

That was it. That belligerent Elle he could deal with without remorse.

He yanked her away from that asshole and threw her over his shoulder. The crowd might have thought it was staged because they started to cheer.

"Jack! What are you doing?" she screamed, fighting to get free.

He gripped her even harder. "Quiet, pet."

"Let me go," Elle yelled, hitting his ass. She tried to incorporate herself so he dipped her even lower. *"Bastardo! Lasciami andare!"*

She could call him whatever she wanted. Curse and scream and thrash. He was not letting her go.

He marched to the truck and put her down, trapping her

between the door and him. She was spitting mad, those gorgeous black eyes of hers flashing fire.

Her breathing was labored, her chest falling and rising rapidly over her wide neckline. She was magnificent.

For a couple of seconds they were both silent, staring at each other.

Her voice was deceptively low and it trembled with fury. "Do not presume you can manhandle me because you got inside me. That doesn't give you any rights."

"Wrong, pet. It does. You're mine. This is mine," he growled, cupping her pussy with one hand while holding her neck with the other, forcing them face-to-face, breathing into each other's mouths.

It was a risky move; he wouldn't put it past her to bite him, but she didn't.

"Sorry, Borg. Pussy is not a detachable body part. It comes along with the smart-ass tongue and the snarky attitude. Oh and this face, the one you can't stand to watch, remember? It's a package one takes or leaves. It was your choice to leave it."

He cut her off, kissing her ravenously. Then he fisted her bun and locked eyes with her. "Look at me. I know it's a package. And I'm taking it. I tried to stay away from you. I tried to make this easier." Now it was too late. He couldn't help himself. He was going to give into it and the hell with the consequences. "You kept pushing and pushing. Taunting me. Now you got my full attention." He lifted her, rested her back against the truck and worked his way in between her legs, bunching her dress up.

"I do not want your attention anymore," she said, but she was holding him tight.

"Too bad, pet, because you're getting it." He shoved his hand under her panties. "And you do want it. You're already wet for me."

She didn't move. Didn't answer anything. She was furious and excited, he could tell, and he was so far gone that if she turned him down now his cock was going to fall into pieces. But she didn't reject him. She took his mouth as hard as he always did hers. Harder.

The kiss got fucking hot, fucking fast. Like everything with her.

"Let's go home."

She shook her head, sinking her hands in his hair. "Here.

Now." Her breath was heavy, her tone defiant.

"I don't have condoms, pet." He should have known he couldn't make it a couple of days around Elle without needing protection, but moron that he was, he thought he would be able to resist her. "And we're in a public parking lot."

"It's deserted, Borg," she whispered, pressing herself against him.

Yes, there was no one around. Still.

"Not up for the challenge?"

He grabbed her hands and immobilized them over her head. "I haven't had sex for almost a year and I've been dying to fuck you for twice as long, since the first time I laid eyes on you. You can't ask me to pull out, because I won't. The second I get inside you, I'll be coming."

"I'm protected."

She was killing him.

He held her challenging stare. "So that we're clear: if I fuck you here I'm going to fill you with my cum." Something he hadn't done ever before but couldn't wait to do now. Nuts.

She nodded. "Now."

He couldn't deny her anything. Which pissed him off to no end, but his cock had a mind of its own. Heck, his whole body.

He unzipped, yanked her panties aside, and pressed against her core, breaching her tight opening. Her teeth sank into his shoulder, a ragged cry escaping her.

Fuck, she was so hot. And so fucking small. He was going to hell for this. She needed more foreplay if he was going to get more than the crown of his cock inside her, but he was so crazed by the sensory overload he wasn't sure he could hold still.

Praying for a control there wasn't a snowball's chance in hell he could maintain, he pushed down his need and thrust a bit deeper, when suddenly her grip on him got even tighter. "Jack, oh God, I'm coming..."

He took her mouth and swallowed her cries as she exploded all over his cock, her pussy clutching him like a vise, locked in a powerful contraction. Robbing him of breath and the last shred of sanity. He surged all the way in, the straight barbell ladder he had at the base of his cock slamming against her clit, the contact with the metal ripping a whimper out of her and sending her over again. Jesus fucking Christ, she was flooring him. Wrapped around him, quivering. So hot. So tight. He managed to plunge into her several times but soon after that he lost it, and with a roar he let himself go, filling her with his cum.

CHAPTER NINE

Jack didn't utter a single word on the way home, back to throwing murderous glances her way, which, considering his cum was all over her pussy, felt weird to say the least. A couple of jokes came to mind, but she opted for keeping them to herself. God forbid she give him a coronary.

After making it home, Elle headed for the bathroom; a bit of space would do them good.

She stripped and entered the shower, wondering what had come over her in that parking lot. That kind of heavy-handed, Neanderthal behavior from a guy normally enraged her, earning him a kick in the balls instead of a free pass to fuck her, which was exactly what Jack got. She had no explanation for it; the man revved her motor to unprecedented heights and she'd needed him so badly. And boy did he deliver. Him and that big pierced cock of his.

Elle took her sweet time, soaping up and soothing her muscles under the water, then rinsing. She reached for a towel and when she opened the shower curtain, she saw Jack there, leaning on the wall.

"Enjoy the show?" she asked, stepping out of the cubicle. The curtain only let a shadow through, but still.

He ignored her question, although he must have appreciated it if the huge erection tenting his jeans was anything to go by. "You know what this is, right?"

She glanced around. "Hmm, a bathroom?"

He grunted, not a speck of humor in his hard tone. "You understand this has no future, right? This is just sex and that's all that it ever will be."

Arrogant ass. "Don't overestimate yourself, Borg. Who says I want more? I know what you are. You're fucking material."

"Good, we understand each other. When the Maldonado situation is resolved, we part ways."

"Depending on your skills, we might part ways earlier. I can't help it if you fall for me though, wonderful girl that I am. Oh, I know, I know"—she waved him off—"I don't bake bread or sew my own underwear. I'm sooo going to hell."

He was searching for the one, but she was too, and Jack was so far away from it, it wasn't even funny.

He strode toward her, his glance traveling over her and stopping on her legs. "What were those inscriptions and lines?"

What? Ah, the UV tattoos.

"You'll have to get me into another club if you want to see them again. Maybe if you hadn't dragged me out of there, you would have had more time to inspect them. Oh, and by the way, now that we're on the subject, you don't want to end up with my boot up your ass, you don't manhandle me," she added. "Ever."

"You don't want me throwing you over my shoulder, maybe you should consider behaving." His tone was clipped and matter-of-fact.

"I foresee a painful relationship ahead of us." He frowned at the word "relationship," so she corrected, "Fling, hookup. Whatever you want to call it. If you'd sleep lighter, I can sign a waiver."

He caressed her skin. "UV tattoos always leave some scarring. Yours are unnoticeable."

"How do you know about UV tattoos?"

Jack shrugged. "Someone close to me is interested in them."

She waited for him to elaborate, but of course he didn't. "I got mine done by the best."

At her words, his expression grew severe. "What is Kai to you?"

"Hmm, none of your business?"

Jack got in her face. "Wrong, pet. When I walk out you can go back to doing what you want, but as long as I'm fucking you, I'm the only one who touches you, are we clear?"

"Clear." She resented the implication. He considered her an

untrustworthy, shifty floozy and couldn't be more wrong, but she didn't want to get into it now.

"And you'll do as I say."

"Not so clear, buddy."

Yep, definitely a painful relationship ahead of them. Correction; ahead of him, because as far as she was concerned, she was going to have a blast.

"And talking about body alterations, that piercing of yours caught me by surprise. I would never have thought you were pierced. Care to explain?"

True to form, The Borg didn't bother to answer, just studied her.

"What?" she finally asked, impatient.

"Nothing. Wondering if I can fuck that attitude out of you."

She smirked. "I doubt it very much, but you can try."

"I plan to. Believe me, I plan to."

He brought her to him and kissed her, hard and deep. The towel fell to the floor and a shiver ran across her as she felt his calloused hands on her sensitized skin. She crawled up his body, wrapping her legs around his hips, the rough denim against her core and the soft shirt against her nipples playing havoc with her senses. The kiss got more desperate, his cock throbbing against her, his hands cupping her ass.

"Bed. Now," he growled.

"I think your speech processor is failing you, sunshine. Maybe it got corrupted when you overheated?"

"Smart-ass." He carried her to her bedroom, where he put her down on the bed.

Without taking his eyes off her, he made quick work of his clothes. He kneeled in front of her and unceremoniously lifted her legs up and wide.

"How many times can you get off in one session?"

In spite of her disadvantageous situation, she flaunted some attitude at him. She couldn't let him intimidate her or he would walk all over her. "I don't know, Jack, how talented are you?"

He cocked his eyebrow. "I recall someone coming around my cock explosively before I was totally in."

True, but that might have had more to do with her than with him or his skills. After all, she had a lot of sexual frustration pent up since a certain asshole moved in with her.

He caressed her open folds and a whimper escaped her. For such a hard man, his touch was so soft. "You couldn't wait to have me inside you."

She couldn't help egging him. "Of course I couldn't. With your fickle personality I wasn't risking you changing your mind by the time we made it home. You would have gotten all proper and uptight on me again."

A devilish smile flashed on his face. "I might have been a bit slow on the uptake, but don't be mistaken, I'm in charge here. And I'm never proper."

Yeah, she'd gotten the idea while he'd been pounding into her in that deserted parking lot, her hands restrained over her head. Although in all honesty, she was still baffled that she'd managed to make him lose control. She would have bet good money he would never have gone for public, unprotected sex.

He trailed the tips of his fingers along her folds, caressing her entrance and then her clit, making her jump as he spread her moisture. "I didn't give you what you deserved outside the club. You didn't get any foreplay and yet you took me."

He leaned over and put his mouth on her open core, taking a deep swipe.

She jerked at the rough contact, but he tightened his grip.

"Fucking sweet, pet. You washed me off. You don't taste like me."

She cleared her throat. "You would have wanted to eat me out covered with your semen?"

"No, I wouldn't. I'd rather lick your juices, but I like your pussy dripping with my cum. Let's remedy this. As soon as you spill on my tongue, I'll fuck you and fill you up again. Take you so hard you'll be sore for a week."

She wasn't sure if it was the image in her brain that his words created, or his breath slamming against her core, but a jolt of pleasure tore through her. Still, she had to provoke him. Had to. It was ingrained in her. "Promises, promises. You should talk less and go down to business, Borg. Before I fall asleep on you."

That look on his face, so male, so sure of himself, shot straight to her clit, making her core convulse.

He ate her out the same way he kissed, hard and deep and thoroughly. No mercy. Raking his teeth on her sensitive folds, licking every inch of her, tonguing her entrance and sucking her clit. Making her so hot she could barely stand it.

"Oh God." She lifted her hips and pushed herself against him, her hands grabbing the bars of the headboard and using it for leverage while Jack worked her ruthlessly until the pleasure was too overwhelming and she went over.

She was still orgasming when he flipped her on her stomach and raised her hips.

So that was the price for oral. She tried to rise up. "Jack. Face-to-face."

"I know you are not too crazy about this position, but I will make it work for you." And before she could say anything, he pushed inside her, knocking the wind out of her. "Like this, I can get so deep you'll feel every inch of me."

He was not kidding. God, he was huge; even after coming in his mouth and being soft and ready, it was a tight fit. He moved slow but relentlessly until he was buried balls-deep in her and his cock was nudging her womb. She was going to complain that very instant, but she couldn't find her voice, busy as she was moaning.

"Fucking perfect, pet," he said, dipping his hand and touching her clit while she fisted the sheets, groaning into them. "You will come for me."

She shook her head defiantly. If she could stop trembling it would have been more convincing.

Jack chuckled softly. Full of arrogance. "Yes you will, I can already feel your pussy gripping me greedily, trying to suck me in deeper. Your clit is throbbing. You will come for me in this position. In any position I choose. Milk my cock and make me blow."

He fucked her hard and fast, her whole body shaking with his powerful thrusts, but when she was about to orgasm, he stopped and hauled her upright to her knees, her back against his chest. "Do not come." He stayed still, pulsing inside her, and moved his hand to her clit, rubbing it gently. "Not yet, pet."

What? Jesus, could the guy make up his mind?

"Coming or not coming on command is not a skill I've acquired." Actually, anything on command was a no-go with her.

"You'll acquire it with me," he said, immobilizing her hips so that she couldn't force his hand. "And no more twerking."

She spoke in choppy pants. "Twerking is great for strengthening the pelvis muscles. I'd rather avoid the future possibility of peeing on myself when I sneeze, if it's all the same to you."

"And I'd rather avoid the possibility of ending up in prison for beating the shit out of the guys coming on to you. You want to twerk, twerk for me, pet. Like now. Try to buck me off."

He pushed her back down and resumed pounding into her. She tried dislodging him, but the more she thrashed, the stronger his clutch and the hotter she got, until she was trembling and about to come and then the bastard stopped again.

He lifted her upper body to his again and fisting her braids, pulled her head to the side, trailing kisses on her neck. "Get rid of the braids, pet. I want to sink my fingers in your hair. I want it all over me as I fuck you."

She was shaking, but she got the words out as steady as possible. "Magic word?"

"Wiseass."

"Wrong."

"You take them out, I'll make it worth your while."

It wasn't a "please," but it was close enough. Not that she could think about it when all the nerve endings of her body were on fire. "I might be more agreeable if you, I don't know, let me frigging come?"

He had the balls to let out a bark similar to a laugh. "Not yet," he repeated.

"Stop fucking me so good then." Her belligerent side urged her to disobey, but there was another part of her that wanted to please him and prove that she could control herself.

"Huge payoff if you do."

God only knew how, she managed to suppress her burning urge to climax.

"That's my girl," he said as he caressed her gently. Then he pushed her down and went back at pounding into her.

"Jack…" she choked out. Her whole body was quaking; she needed so badly to come she was almost hurting.

He buried himself deep inside her and lifted her torso to him, his hand on her pussy, the other one wrapped around her breasts. "You're wrong." This time he didn't stop moving. As he was talking, he jackhammered into her, his arms keeping her trapped. "All women do not look the same from behind. I know exactly who I'm fucking. Your scent is all over me. Your taste. Your fire."

She flung her head back. God, she wasn't going to be able to stop this time. She reached to him, hugging him.

"Your pussy is killing me. Squeezing me like a vise."

He redoubled the speed, his plunging hard and devilishly hitting all her sweet spots while he rubbed her pulsing clit in tight circles and she dissolved in his arms, letting the wave sweep over her, unable to delay it anymore.

In the midst of her haze she heard him growling as he gave in to his own release and shot inside her.

After regaining consciousness, Elle realized Jack had rolled onto his back. God, she wasn't sure if she'd climaxed or had a stroke. A stroke probably. Although she doubted there was any kind of stroke in the world that left you tingly all over and floating in neverland, extremely happy and satisfied.

She turned to Jack and studied him, trailing her fingers over his warm skin. She'd known he was fit, but man, he was magnificent. Thick veins running along starkly defined muscles, not an ounce of fat anywhere. Not an ounce of softness either. And not a single tattoo.

She lifted her gaze to his and found his eyes trained on her, his face inscrutable as always. He hadn't been too open to letting her touch him, and with her holding to the headboard for dear life while he was eating her out or pounding in her from behind, she hadn't had that many chances, either.

"I can't believe you don't have tattoos." Clean skin, so weird. Considering how strongly she was attracted to him and how nuts she always went for tattooed bad boys, she'd figured he would be inked.

"I heard you have a thing for assholes with tattoos," Jack said.

"Yeah, well, I sometimes have a thing for just assholes," Elle answered, pointedly looking at him.

Her whole life she'd gravitated toward tattooed bad boys, but Jack wasn't a bad boy. He didn't go around flaunting attitude, pretending to be a tough guy because he had tattoos or a bike. Those were wannabes; Jack, she had the feeling, was the real deal. He didn't need to show off or mouth off in front of anyone. The other way around: one stare, one word, and the job was done. He had an aura of authority very few people could pull off and even fewer could withstand without crumbling. Compared with her past experiences, Jack was in a class all his own.

Tattoos he didn't have, but his body was full of marks and angry scars. "What's this?"

She didn't expect an answer, but surprise, surprise, she got it. "Knife wound. Bosnia."

"And this?" she ventured, tempting her luck further.

"Shrapnel. Afghanistan."

She moved unto the next one. He answered before she asked.

"Bullet. Sierra Leone."

There was a very similar scar on his lower abdomen. "This a bullet too?"

He shook his head. "Bayonet. Colombia."

Jesus Christ, the guy was a road map to the world conflicts of the last two decades, but he wouldn't take any pity from her, so she went for light.

"You need to have a word with your travel agent, Borg."

He let out a dry snort.

Several weird scars on his arm and chest got her attention. They were round and looked old. "And these?"

"Cigarette burns. My mother."

She froze. The marks were by far the smallest and the least life-threatening, yet they were the most horrifying of all. Jack must have been a kid; she couldn't envision anyone doing that to Jack as an adult, much less as many times as the circles on his body indicated.

She tried very hard not to let what she was feeling show, but she failed miserably, because his expression hardened.

He got out of bed, a scowl on his face, and turning his back on her, headed for the bathroom. And then she saw it.

Oh. My. God.

At her sharp intake of air he swirled and stared at her. "What? Did my shitty childhood put you off?"

She shook her head. "Your back…"

It was completely tattooed. A fallen angel of some sort covered it, not an inch uninked.

His expression relaxed as it dawned on him what she was referring to. "Right. You see, asshole with tattoos here. You didn't stray too far from your path."

* * * *

102

Jack watched Elle sleep, tense as a fucking bow.

She was resting on her side, her head on the pillow, her hands under her cheek. Man, she looked so sweet sleeping. So…agreeable. And why the fuck was he staring at her instead of sleeping, or better yet, why was he still in her room, he had no clue. It seemed he was incapable of making himself walk away from her, even after fucking her senseless.

It was the lack of shut-eye that was compromising his thought-processing and decision-making skills. He recalled getting more z's during his last deployment in Afghanistan than these past days with Elle. Her rhythm was inhuman. Of course, if he used the little time he had left for sleep for fucking her, it wasn't going to help matters. Not that he could do anything about it. Now that the doors were open, he wasn't going to keep his hands off her. The need to get his fill and fuck her out of his system was too powerful.

Elle opened her eyes, a big smile on her sleepy face. "Something to say to me?"

He didn't answer, just swept his thumb over her lips, propped on his elbow. "Why did you let me fuck you bareback?"

She laughed. "Good morning to you too."

"Answer me. That was fucking dumb. I could have all sorts of diseases." He didn't; he got himself checked religiously twice per year, but she didn't know that.

"You're a stickler for security. The kind of man who would laminate his own dick. If anyone in this world is clean, it's you. I'd bet my life on it."

Which she actually had done.

"The million-dollar question here is, sunshine," she continued unfazed by his hard tone, "why did you fuck *me* bareback? I could have all sorts of diseases. I might not be clean. I'm a reckless loose bullet."

Good question. A tantrum from her and she'd had him losing his goddamned mind in a parking lot, eating from her hand like a fucking teenager, forgetting about everything. He knew Elle was reckless, but stupid she wasn't. She was clean.

And now that he'd gotten to take her without protection, there was no way in hell he was going to suit up.

"Nothing else to tell me?" she asked after a long pause. "Not too skilled at morning-afters, are you?"

Nope, he wasn't. He always went to the shower and suggested

to the lady that she be gone by the time he came out, if they were in his apartment, which was very seldom. More often than not he would have his sexual encounters in hotels or in their places. Easier to leave. Less messy. Now? Now he couldn't make a single muscle flex to move away from Elle. Mental.

"Okay, let me help you with that. What about, 'Elle, my princess, you kicked ass. You blew my mind. You are the most beautiful woman in the world and the sexiest. Last night was the best, sweetheart.'"

"Do you need all those words to let me fuck you again, pet?"

To his utter surprise, she laughed. "Nope, Borg."

"Good." He wasn't much of a pillow talker.

He rolled them onto their sides and lifted her thigh over his, palming her ass proprietarily and delving lower.

"How sore are you?"

He caressed her sweet pussy, her folds puffy from the night, but she didn't flinch; she rocked against his hand. "Not sore enough."

At her words, his cock jerked. Man, such a tease. His kind of tease.

"Any more UV tattoos your dress covered?"

She smiled coyly. "Women do not reveal their secrets."

He was going to get his hands on a black light. In a place where he could strip her.

She reached for his cock and palmed him. "I thought piercings were not allowed in the military."

"And they aren't."

"So there's a rebel streak on you."

He didn't answer and slid a finger in her, then moved some of her lube to her ass.

"No," she said, tensing.

He stopped. "I'm not used to that word."

"Get used to it. Anal sex is not my thing."

"Have you given it up for anybody?"

She shook her head. "No and don't get your hopes up because I won't. I'm not comfortable with the idea. Contrary to what men seem to believe, the route to a woman's heart isn't through her ass."

"You mean you don't trust your lovers to give you what you need."

She snorted. "And who says I need hemorrhoids?"

He would not give her hemorrhoids. Far from it. He would make her come explosively, but he would never take something that wasn't offered freely. "Understood. Ass's off-limits. Anything else I should know?"

She pondered for a second. "Yes. I like my orange juice without pulp."

* * * *

From the SUV, Nico watched the heavyset woman playing with the toddler in the front yard.

"Not her," he muttered.

He'd hacked the company providing the IT services for the airline, and once he'd gotten the list of the people who had worked that morning shift, it had been a question of matching names with license pictures and comparing them to Marlene's. There had been twenty-six women, of which only three could have passed for her. After some snooping around, he'd discarded two of them, and now, seeing Vivian Stone huffing and puffing under the blasting heat, trying to keep up with the kiddo, he discarded her too.

She might have been able to pass for Marlene some years back, when the picture on her driver's license had been taken, but she was one of those ladies who married, had kids, and exploded, her ass expanding faster than the family's credit line. No way did she dispatch their flight. Besides, she was safe and sound at home, taking care of her offspring, not under police surveillance.

"You don't say," the man sitting shotgun spat in disgust. "Jesus, when a toddler can outrun you, it's time to take matters into you own hands and get your ass to Weight Watchers or Jenny Craig or major liposuction or whatever shit women do these days to stay slim. In between Photoshop and chicks using old pics, Carlitos Junior ain't coming out to play until I see the bitch live and real."

Nico didn't answer, wishing Carlos would shut up. He didn't have time for brainless idiots, and getting stuck with this moron rubbed him the wrong way.

"Stop smoking and roll the window up," he snarled instead.

They were in the middle of a motherfucking heat wave and he was cranky as hell. The smell of tobacco wasn't making things better.

"*Tranquilo*, Russian," Carlos said with a chuckle, throwing the smoke through the window. "Take it easy. You don't have that problem back home, right?" Nico thought he was talking about the heat, but Carlos pointed at Vivian. "Asses the size of aircraft carriers, I mean. Don't get me wrong, amigo, Russia is probably as fucked-up a place as any and I'm in no hurry to freeze my balls off, but your women, perfect porcelain dolls. All primed up always."

Nico didn't bother answering. "This is a waste of time," he muttered.

"We could always have a little chat with Vivian. Work her a bit. Find out if the bitch knows something. And this is a nice neighborhood; they might have expensive stuff. Besides, I like the sound that comes from fat flab. It's like punching a jelly ball."

And this was why he preferred to work alone.

Nico looked at the man, whose eyes were already shimmering with sick excitement. Jeez, that was the worst kind of thug: dumb and bloodthirsty.

Incompetent, ineffective bunch of shitheads. They'd managed to kill the very person they needed alive and then compounded the mistake by eliminating the wrong witness.

Annoyed, Nico started the engine.

"You're no fun, Russian. Now what?"

At this point there was only one option left: track down the shift's supervisor and ask who the fuck had dispatched Maldonado's flight. Which he'd hoped to avoid, more than anything because Donald Solis, as luck would have it, was on vacation. In fucking Hawaii.

He drove into traffic, almost running a red light. Shit, he couldn't think in this heat wave. He didn't get how people could live like this, constantly sweating. The sun frying their brains. He'd take freezing temperatures any day over this. Cool kept you sharp, in movement. No wonder these assholes never got shit done and their tempers exploded at the smallest setback.

"Sure we can't take a short detour to play with that fats—"

Carlos didn't finish the word because Nico had smashed his face on the dashboard.

Then he cranked up the AC. Much, much better.

CHAPTER TEN

"Stop staring at my sister-in-law's boobs," James said to Jack. "You're going to break blood vessels in both eyeballs. I don't dare to guess what's happening to your other more Southern pair of balls. Strangled blue, right?"

"I'm staring at your son."

James let out a bark. "Right. Try again."

Jonah was laughing and gurgling, looking happy as all fuck, lying on Elle's chest and nuzzling her tits. Lucky kid. Jack would be happy as all fuck too in his position. Had been, just several hours ago. Elle's shirt was getting ruined with so much dribble, but she didn't mind. She continued kissing and caressing the baby while she talked to Tate, both of them sprawled on lounge chairs.

"You're sleeping with her," James stated.

Jack didn't answer, but apparently his friend didn't need confirmation.

"Don't bother denying it. I can see it in the way you look at her."

"How do I look at her?" As far as he was concerned, he was scowling like always. Because she drove him crazy, like always.

"Proprietarily. Like she's yours."

She was. For the time being at least.

"I knew this was going to happen if you spent any time together," James continued. "The only reason it hasn't happened earlier is because you avoided her like the plague."

"She is a pest," he muttered. A sexy, extremely fuckable, and devilishly attractive pest, but a pest nonetheless. That he wasn't in a hurry to shake her was what surprised him the most.

As if she felt his gaze on her, she turned to him and winked. Fuck, she was beautiful. More so now that she'd lost the braids.

"You were in luck, buddy," she'd said as she'd came out of the beauty salon the day before, her thick hair free again. *"The braids were too tight and itchy. If I had liked them, there's no way I would have given them up for you."*

He was sure about it. Heck, she probably had put up with them longer than she would have if he'd kept his trap shut.

"Has she tried to ditch you again?" James asked, taking him out of his reveries.

"Not recently, no." Then again, he hadn't given her many opportunities. He spent the day trailing her, and the night between her legs. "She does a million things a day." Even on Mondays, when Rosita's was closed, she organized a boot camp in her backyard for the women of her neighborhood. Where she got the energy, he had no idea.

"What happens when this situation is over?" James asked. "When you're not forced to spend time with her?"

"I'll walk."

James's expression went hard. "Jack—"

"She knows," he cut James off, already guessing what he was getting at. "I've been very clear about this and she agrees. Believe me, she doesn't want me around anymore than I do."

Fucking her was mind-blowing, and he couldn't deny enjoying her wiseass comments and their back and forth outside the bedroom, but he was thirty-six. It was time to stop jerking around and plan for the future. Elle wasn't his future and he wasn't hers. She needed an easygoing, laid-back guy that would let her do her thing. He needed a dedicated woman. They would drive each other insane. Love didn't grow out of conflict. Sexual chemistry did. And building your future on your dick's whims was a very shaky foundation.

"I don't want her hurt," James warned. "You're my son's godfather and I love you like a brother, but if you break her heart, you'll have me to answer to."

"I would never hurt her." He was not at risk of breaking her heart because her heart was not on the table. She'd made that clear too. They were two consenting adults having the best sex of their lives. His life, at least. Although she hadn't seemed unhappy at all this morning, when he'd taken her in the shower and she'd come twice, screaming and scratching his back.

"Who did Elle cross in Florida?" James asked. "She never gave any names to Tate."

Jack pretended he didn't hear him. "What about the search for your lost sister. Any news on that front?"

"Elle is much better at deflecting than you." James scowled him. "No, so far we've gotten no leads. Now answer; who did she cross in Florida?"

"Maldonado."

James stilled. "Maldonado? Joaquín Maldonado?" Jack nodded and James cursed. "Maldonado is not a small-time crook like she told Tate. He's a…"

"Monster," Jack finished.

Jack explained what had really happened in Florida and James turned white as a fucking sheet. "Fuck, fuck, fuck."

Yep he could say that again. "Mullen's on the case."

"And? Have they found a way to arrest Maldonado?"

Jack shook his head. "Plane was clean and other than several appearances of Aalto in the airport cameras, they got nothing that would tie him to Maldonado." The bodyguards were a no-go. The one who had a niece with drug problems seemed to have disappeared. The niece too.

Whoever in the deceased politician's office was aware of his connection with Maldonado was not talking, and their computers didn't hold any leads.

Jack knew how this shit worked. Maldonado was very powerful with influential friends. Big pockets, even bigger connections. He could buy anyone he wanted and cover his own tracks. Surround himself with so many lawyers, it would take a century to peel through them to reach the bastard. Not to mention his underground, ruthless, extremely illegal ways. After all, one didn't become the most feared narco in South America by being a softie.

To nail Maldonado was going to require much more direct action than the police could provide. They would need Jack down there. They had to figure out the connection between Aalto and Maldonado or Elle didn't stand a chance.

"Why are you letting Elle get her way? You need to lay low. Stay under the grid."

"Elle doesn't want to leave and dump the restaurant on your wife."

"Fuck that," James cursed again. "Paige, Tim, and me can deal with Rosita's. Does she understand the danger she is in?"

Jack didn't answer.

The truth was Elle didn't have the slightest clue of the danger she was in. The second Maldonado found out she was alive, there would be a bounty on her head so big she would have to look over her shoulder for the rest of her life. Which, if Maldonado had anything to say about it, was going to be damn short. Should she testify and the DA managed to put him away, the bounty on her head would be even higher. Imprisoned, spiteful narcos had long memories and lots of free time. Bad combination.

If the police couldn't catch Maldonado without Elle and insisted in involving her, Jack would take matters into his own hands. He was walking out on her, but he wasn't going to let a single hair on her precious head be harmed.

* * * *

Maldonado was sitting on the terrace of the exclusive spa when he saw Nico walking in his direction. "You here for some relaxation?" he asked as the Russian reached him.

"The person your men thought dispatched your flight, didn't. Somebody impersonated her."

Fantastic. So those idiots snuffed the wrong chick. "Who did then?"

"Don't know yet, but I intend to find out. I'm off to Hawaii."

Thank God Nico was taking care of this personally, because Maldonado was going to start shooting his own people if there were more fuckups. The morons better pray real hard to Jesús Malverde, the patron-saint of drug dealers. Not for protection from the DEA, but from him.

A waitress approached them. "Anything I could bring you today, Mr. Maldonado? We have this new recovery drink."

He shook his head, watching while the man at the neighboring table drank one of those murky protein shakes and spoke into his earpiece.

Man, Americans were so freaky. Even Latinos had been

Americanized and were doing the weirdest things.

His country might be considered third world, but Maldonado preferred the way of conducting business down there. While hunting, or enjoying a good, bloody barbecue. Drinking in a country club. Not in Florida. Here they spent all their time in a gym doing yoga, saluting the sun and shit like that. But when in Rome, right? So after moving to Miami Maldonado had joined the most exclusive gym and spa in the state and started conducting business Florida-style. Heck, he'd even hired that buttard Lars to keep him in shape, but he drew the line at those murky protein shakes. So fake everything. But he wasn't the one going to judge folks taking a preference for powdery stuff, was he?

Joining that gym had been most profitable. Not so much health-wise, for networking, it had been invaluable.

After giving him an approving once-over, the waitress offered a shake to Nico, but he refused.

The Russian was in top shape, though Maldonado never saw him using the spa facilities. Or training with the ultramodern machinery there. Not the style of the enforcer.

Nico's phone beeped. After reading the message, his expression tightened.

"What? More trouble?"

"Another shipment has been lost. Intercepted upon arrival."

Not to mention they still had one stuck in an all but paralyzed port.

Maldonado let out a curse in between clenched teeth.

Lately, everything was going to hell. And it didn't seem to be improving in the immediate future. The whole mess with Aalto. The mysterious witness at large. Back home he was having trouble with the police and the other cartels. Nico would be the one to send to take care of that, but Maldonado was forced to see his best asset off to Hawaii on a wild goose chase because an old fart didn't know that when he couldn't swallow an olive it was time to retire. Oh, and he couldn't forget the morons who'd dumped a body over the ocean and had it land on an island. And then made the wrong witness disappear.

"Any news on Jacobson? Any vices we could exploit?" Maldonado asked, trying to breathe through the murderous thoughts.

Nico shook his head. "Nothing so far."

Jacobson, the politician who'd replaced Aalto, had even a tougher line on immigration than his predecessor. What was worse, he was squeaky clean, and no matter how hard they tried, they hadn't been able to dig up any dirt on him.

He was a fanatically religious man with an equally enthusiastic wife. No vices. No extramarital affairs. No kinks. The asshole was a frigging saint. Give him a decade and all that enthusiasm would go down the drain. He would be taking bribes, doing drugs, and fucking whores by the dozens, but they didn't have a decade.

"We can talk to him," Nico suggested. "Convince him of the error of his ways."

True. Intimidation worked as well as blackmail, but fanatics tended to love to end up like martyrs. No time for that kind of shit. He'd try other venues. It would take some time and would require him traveling and kissing some ass, which he was not too keen on doing, but he reckoned it'd be worth it.

As Nico stood up to leave, Maldonado said, "By the way, I saw Carlos. What happened to his face?"

Nico didn't even flinch. "I work alone. And heat makes me cranky."

It was best that the Russian worked alone then, or he was going to disfigure half his men.

* * * *

"Why is your bodyguard-slash-private-terminator staring at you as if he wants to eat you alive?"

Elle smiled at her inquisitive sister. "Probably because he does. Starting with biting my head off."

"Nah," Tate said, "I think he means to start eating much lower."

Elle covered her nephew's tiny ears and feigned shock. "Who are you and what have you done with my straitlaced sister?"

"Please. Your straitlaced sister, lover of soft-mannered, politically correct metrosexuals, married James Bowen. She's gone."

That was true. And this new Tate was so much fun. Motherhood really became her. James became her.

"Are you still pretending to be together, or are you fucking him for real?" Tate asked.

"Let's just say we decided it would be mutually beneficial to find a way to work out the sexual tension between us before it went *kaboom*."

"And?"

Elle chuckled. "What do you mean 'and'? We are working it off." Although it didn't help. The more they went at it, the more electrified the air around them got.

At that moment, Jack walked to them and nodded to Tate, then turned to Elle. "Pet, wrap it up. There's somewhere I have to pass by on the way home."

"Two minutes, Borg."

He cupped her neck and took her mouth. "You have one," he said and strode away.

"I see getting into bed with him hasn't made him more laid-back," Tate whispered.

No, it hadn't. Jack was as intense as always. More even.

And God help her she liked him. His intensity and grouchiness too. He didn't speak much but he had a very sharp sense of humor, which she loved. Even if it came at her expense.

"You taking him to Jonah and Lizzie's party this weekend?" Tate asked while they both got up from the loungers. Jonah didn't seem to like being moved because he started to fuss.

"Have to," she replied, rocking the baby in her arms. "He's made it very clear that he goes where I go or I don't go at all."

Tate lifted her eyebrow. "And you haven't chewed his head off yet?"

"I tried, but he's like a tank, sis. Immovable." Nothing veered him from his path.

"I told you he wasn't like your other boyfriends."

No shit. He was like nobody she'd ever met. Not that she knew that much about him, but what she knew, wow. She hadn't recuperated yet from the revelation about the burn marks on his body. And worse yet, the dismissiveness in his tone when he spoke of them.

"Let me get James," Tate said and went into the house. The second she left, Jonah started crying.

As Elle reached the truck where Jack was already waiting, she remembered her bag and handed the baby to Jack. "Just a sec. I forgot my stuff."

She strutted inside and bumped into James and Tate in the

hallway. Her sister was carrying Elle's bag.

Elle looked at them and suddenly her chest clenched. She didn't even dare to speculate what would happen if she had to testify against Maldonado. Witness protection program, probably. Which meant severing all ties with her family. Forever. Now that she'd started manning up and showing up for her life and she'd be cut off from everybody. Her mom, Tate, her nephew, the Bowens. Rosita's.

Panic rising inside her, she pushed that thought away. No, no, no. One crisis at the time, please.

She took a deep breath and plastered a smile on her face. "Thanks. I almost forgot. I have the things for my next flash mob in here."

"Do not aggravate him," James warned her, looking more serious than usual. "And for the love of God, do as he says. This is his area of expertise."

Elle hugged her brother-in-law. "Don't worry. I'll return him to you safe and sound. I promise."

"It's not him I'm worried about, you nutcase," James muttered.

They walked out of the house, and she noticed right away Jack was holding a quiet baby in his arms. He was talking to Jonah. Smiling at him, his huge hand cupping his tiny head, his thumb caressing his cheek. The giant was not fond of big displays of affection; he always greeted people with a curt nod—if he greeted them at all, because minimum physical contact seemed to be his mantra—yet he looked so comfortable with the baby.

James took Jonah and after saying their good-byes, Jack and Elle got in the truck.

"You're great with kids," Jack said.

"Of course I am. Kids are very smart. They sense awesomeness," she said, wiggling her eyebrows. "You are not bad yourself. You got him to stop fussing."

Jack shrugged, his gaze on the road. "I had experience."

In true Jack form, he dropped that bomb but didn't explain further.

"Well, I do love kids," she continued. "I plan to have a bunch of them."

He narrowed his eyes, looking surprised. "You want to have children?"

His skeptical tone rubbed her the wrong way. "Of course I

want kids, sunshine. And before you ask, sorry, but I'm a firm believer in modern diapers and child vaccinations. Along with electricity, indoor plumbing, and cars. Oh, and when I say I plan to have a bunch of kids, I mean three, not eighteen."

"I'm not against modern conveniences."

"Your future Amish wife will. Never been in one, but considering your size, good luck surviving a buggy ride. On the plus side, it will be your speed."

A smile flashed across his face. "I never said I want an Amish wife. I said I want a woman whose priority would be her family. I don't have anything against her working."

"As long as she's devoted to you and satisfied with that kind of life."

"I plan to be devoted to her too. And keep her plenty satisfied."

"Keep her chained to the foot of your bed, you mean." Pregnant and barefoot too.

He turned to her, his expression intense. "However I have her in the bed, tied or otherwise, I can fucking guarantee she'll be satisfied."

That last part she believed. She could still feel him inside her, making her come like crazy. But she wasn't about to admit that. "So, where are we going?" she asked, attempting to distract herself.

"I need to check some things at V-2."

"V-2?"

"My bar."

Oh hell, yes!

The bar she had been dying to check out for ages.

"Okay, if you must." She tried playing it cool, afraid he would change his mind and drop her off home first. Then again, he'd been the one insisting they were attached at the hip. About time she got to enjoy the perks.

After driving for a while, Jack parked in front of a bar on the outskirts of Boston, a humongous row of bikes by the front door.

"So here it is, your famous place," she said. "James never told me the name."

She would bet big money Jack had sworn her brother-in-law into silence under threat of severe torture and beheading.

"James values his balls. It'll be five minutes. Wait for me in the truck," he ordered and got out.

Yeah, right. In his dreams.

Elle wasn't letting the chance pass her by.

She tried the door. Surprise, surprise, it was unlocked. Not her fault if Jack still lived in la-la land and thought that she was obeying him.

As soon as he disappeared from sight, Elle sprinted to the bouncer, who let her in right away.

It took her a second for her eyes to become accustomed to the darkness. V-2 was much bigger than it seemed outside. A watering hole with loud music and even louder patrons, rather popular by the looks of it.

She spotted Jack talking with a man behind the bar, so she moved in the opposite direction, meshing with the crowd. Hopefully that would buy her enough time to snoop around.

"First visit, right?"

She looked into the direction those words had come from and saw a big guy. Her kind of guy: leather pants, muscle shirt, long hair, sexy beard, tattoos up his arms. Thick rings on his fingers. A bike probably waiting outside.

She nodded.

"I figured. A face like yours, I would have remembered. Can I buy you a drink?"

"Thanks, but I don't have that kind of time."

She turned around and crashed into a big chest.

"What the fuck are you doing here? I told you to wait in the truck."

Jack's voice. Jack's chest.

Damn, that had been fast.

She lifted her gaze to find his eyes spitting fire. He was pissed.

"What part of 'wait for me in the truck' is unclear to you?"

So many things were wrong with that question and his tone, she didn't know where to start. As she was thinking what to tackle first, she heard a high-pitched squeal.

"Jack!"

A gorgeous woman with red hair, smoky eyes, and long legs came running and threw herself at him, wrapping her arms around him, and began showering him with kisses.

Jack hugged her too, a big smile on his face. "Hi, baby girl. I see you're happy to see me."

The breath Elle was taking froze in her lungs.

"You kidding? I missed you like hell," the woman said in

between kisses and hugs, clinging to him as if she were a monkey while Jack chuckled and returned the embrace.

Elle staggered back. That was why she was supposed to stay outside, to keep her from meeting Jack's other squeeze.

"When are you coming home?" the redhead asked, pouting cutely and smoothing his shirt. "I'm so lonely without you."

CHAPTER ELEVEN

When are you coming home? I'm lonely without you.

Elle hadn't caught his answer, but he'd snorted at the redhead and said something, his tone light and playful, that made her laugh.

She shook her head, trying to wrap her mind around what was going on in front of her damn eyes.

Jack had a woman. Not just a woman, but a frigging sexpot. Feeling sucker punched, Elle took a step back, bumping into the biker dude.

Her throat was dry, but she forced the words out. "Who's she?"

"Veronica Copeland. Owner of this joint. Wildest cat this side of Boston, which makes Jack Copeland the most envied and feared man this side of Boston."

Oh. God. Jack was married? And to a sex bomb whom he called baby girl?

Numbness and disbelief transformed into fury, Elle's blood boiling up in a nanosecond.

She dashed to him and punched him on his arm. "You asshole. How dare you?"

"Who's this?" the redhead asked.

Elle ignored the woman and yelled in his face. "All that shit about searching for an Amish wife and you're already married?"

Kudos to him, he even managed to look surprised. "What?"

The redhead lifted her eyebrows. "You're searching for an

Amish wife? When were you going to tell me?"

"Yeah, baby girl," Elle continued, putting emphasis on *baby girl*, "and for your information, he isn't home with you because he's at my place, busy screwing me!"

Baby girl turned to Jack, her eyes big as plates. "You're busy screwing her?"

"Not discussing that," Jack answered and addressed Elle. "What do you think is going on here?"

God, would he still have the balls to deny what she just saw with her own eyes? "So you were not smooching with this...bombshell?"

"Aw, thanks. You kick ass too." The bombshell stuck her hand out to Elle. "Nice to meet you. You're the first person he's busy screwing whom I get to meet. Very exciting."

"Ronnie," Jack growled.

Elle couldn't believe her ears. This Ronnie was nuts. "This doesn't bother you?"

She pondered for a second. "I must admit I'm a bit grossed out, but I'll live."

Drunk. The bombshell was drunk. Or high. Heck, drunk *and* high. Or they had a very liberal marriage. Amish wife, her ass.

"Veronica, you are not helping," Jack said in a warning tone Elle knew far too well. It infuriated her even more.

The redhead smirked. "And who says I want to help, hubby?"

"Enough. You," Jack said to her, "go back to the office, where you're supposed to be, not behind the bar serving drinks. And you," he said to Elle, "go back to the truck. This is not the time or the place for this conversation."

She punched him again but the ass didn't budge an inch. "You don't get to order me around. And this is the perfect time and place for this conversation."

The bombshell leaned toward him and mumbled something that sounded very much like "I like her. And you don't get to order me around either."

His voice was calm. "Yes, I do get to order you around. Both of you. This is not what you think, pet."

Pet. The balls of this man had to be cast iron.

"Don't you even. And don't pretend she isn't your wife. He told me," she said gesturing at the biker.

Jack zeroed on him and the big guy lifted his arms, taking a step back, shaking his head.

She stood on her tiptoes and jabbed at Jack's chest, facing off. "I. Do. Not. Screw. Married. Men. "

By now half the joint was staring at them, but she didn't care.

"When we're done," Elle said, imitating his baritone, "you can go back to doing as you want, but until then I'm the only one who fucks you. Forgot to mention the little wife at home? Two-timing, two-faced *figlio di puttana*. You said you had no one, that no one was waiting for you."

Veronica slapped him on the chest. "What do you mean you said you had no one? You didn't tell her about me?"

Then something dawned on Elle. "Oh my God. You have kids too, don't you? That's why you said you had experience. And why you were so good with Jonah."

"You mean with her?" Jack had the nerve to ask while pointing at Ronnie who frowned, looking confused.

"What?" A pause, and then it clicked in her head, for she grimaced. "Oh, you think he and I have children? Eew, no. No kids for us."

"Kick his ass to the curb," Elle told her. "Don't believe a word the bastard says. He's stepped out on you with me, he will do it again."

Ronnie nodded. "He is a pain in the butt; I give you that, but I'm kind of attached to the bastard. Plus he's my landlord too."

"You are the pain in the butt," Jack muttered to her. "*My* butt."

"Don't use that tone with your wife." Elle came to her defense. "It's a miracle she hasn't murdered you in your sleep already."

"Sooo true," Ronnie said, assenting. "I'd be open to sharing him. What do you think?"

Nuts. This chick was nuts. "Keep him. I don't want him. We are done, Borg. As a matter of fact, I'm going to take you up on your offer," she said to Biker Dude. "A drink and some R&R would do me good."

"No you won't." Jack shot a glance at Biker Dude that made him stagger.

Fantastic, the toughest-looking guy in the place was scared of Jack.

Biker Dude glanced at her, then at Jack, and took another step back, lifting again his hands. "Sorry, man. Didn't know she was with you."

That was it. Elle exploded. "I'm not with him. I don't share—"
She opened her mouth, but Jack grabbed her and suddenly his tongue was deep in her throat. She thrashed, unable to wrench away from him until he finished thoroughly kissing her and lightened the pressure in the back of her head.

"Don't you dare touch me again. Go back to your—"

"Sister, pet," he whispered against her lips, a smirk on his face. "Ronnie is my baby sister."

* * * *

Jack watched, amused, as Elle fumed and cursed in the truck.

"Why are you so pissed at me?" After all, he was the one who had been yelled at, jabbed, and punched.

"Why? Because you let me make a fool of myself, that's why. You didn't correct me."

"You didn't let me talk, pet."

"Ha! Since when has that stopped you? 'Elle, meet my sister'. How difficult is that?" she screamed, jabbing him with her finger again. "Or you could have mentioned it on our way there. You were having too much fun while I made an ass out of myself and insulted your sister and advertised to everyone you were fucking me."

He grabbed her hand. She looked furious now, her expression thunderous. Man, she was magnificent. "I wouldn't worry about Ronnie. She doesn't offend easily. When it comes to other people, it's good they know I'm fucking you. No misunderstandings."

"You...you..." She seemed to have trouble finding the right words. "Ass!" she finally said, punching him on the arm.

"You want a chance to beat the shit out of me? Not these little annoying jabs and slaps. I mean sock me for real."

She snorted. "Where do I sign?"

Jack took a sharp left. "Come on. I know how to work this off." She was so wound up, there was no way she was going to be able to sleep. He had a better plan.

"Where are you taking me?"

"You'll see."

They were close by, so in two minutes they arrived.

"A gym?" she said looking around as he killed the engine.

Jack nodded, opening the front door. "I come here to train. I keep unusual hours, so the owner gave me the keys."

"What about training at Haddican's in Alden? Like all the Bowens?"

Sure. In Alden, with the OGs and the strippers and now the mega-famous rock band Amantis and their crew. Right. He dragged her to the boxing ring. "Get the gloves. You want to hit me? Hit me."

"Don't think I won't."

"Oh, I know you will," he said, in a tone that would grate on her nerves. "Try, I mean. Hopefully you can do better than those annoying finger jabs of yours."

She stomped to the boxing ring, dropped her jacket and pulled off her sweater. Clad in a T-shirt, she grabbed the gloves. "I'm so going to kick your ass."

Jack took the paddles.

"No gloves for you?" she asked.

"Not in the business of hitting little girls. Do your worst."

"Not a little girl," she grunted and threw a punch that wasn't half bad.

"You're good," he said, dodging a leg kick.

"This is nothing. Wait till I warm up," she stated, dancing around him, her arms in perfect defensive position.

She warmed up pretty fast, because in no time she was throwing punches and leg kicks and body blows that didn't faze him because of his training. Wearing a cup would have been a good idea, though. She was that mad.

"What is all this about, pet? Why are you so angry?"

"I don't know shit about you," she spat out, the fury in her words followed by a killer hook. "You could have been married with children for all I knew. I had no clue you had a sister. Don't know where you live. What you do for a living. Basic frigging stuff."

"What do you want to know? Ask."

"And you'll tell me?" she asked, her eyes incredulous.

"Probably not, but go ahead and give it a shot."

"*Vai a cagare.*"

Go to hell. Well, a more colorful way of saying it but the sentiment was clear.

He dodged a jab. "And you know what I do for a living. I run a bar."

"Liar. You don't spend any time whatsoever in the bar. I was talking about when you disappear and James freaks out."

"I'm a free agent."

"What does that mean?" she asked, bobbing and weaving.

"Whatever you want it to mean, pet. Where I live I won't tell. Basic preservation. Although, if you agree to go there blindfolded and not peek through the windows, maybe I would reconsider." Then again, she couldn't be trusted, so no.

She was aiming her punches too low for his comfort. Yet he couldn't stop egging her on. "One thing I'll tell you; you need to learn to stay where I put you."

Her derisive snort was accompanied with a side kick. "And you need to take your meds, *coglione.*"

His Spanish was good enough to understand her Italian. And she was not flattering him. Not in the least.

"Cazzo." Dick.

"You're beautiful when you're angry."

"Vaffanculo, arrogante." Up yours, smart-ass.

"And fucking sexy, pet."

"Stronzo."

This insult he didn't know.

"What?"

"Ass!" Hit. "Hole!" Hit.

Any person without his sharp reflexes would have been decked.

"I think I'll give you a mouthpiece." She wouldn't be able to talk. Although he loved her talking.

"Just try it."

The AC was off and they were both sweating. Elle's T-shirt was wet and clinging to her chest, her nipples tenting the material, more so with every ragged breath.

She was a sight to behold. The right amount of muscles and curves. Big boobs. Long, powerful, sexy legs. Gorgeous, mouthwatering ass. In-your-face, catch-me-if-you-can attitude.

Jack hated superfit women. Or even worse, skinny as hell. All those bones sticking him. He liked to have somewhere to grab, and Elle had plenty in the right places.

"This time we'll do it this way; we'll blow off steam fighting. Next time I'll fuck you until you can't move. Same workout, more pleasure."

She snorted. "Dream on. There won't be next time. I'm done

with you. You're too high-maintenance."

"I say when we are done and we are not. Not by a long shot. You've been taunting me for months. Years, pet. Now that you got my undivided attention, you can't say you don't want it. You can't back down. I won't allow you to. You've been asking for it. For me. This is what you get: me. I'll tie you down and fuck you so thoroughly you will be limp by the time I'm done with you."

And ruined for anybody else. The thought of her with another man made his blood boil, so he shook his head. He had to let that go. Whatever she did once he was gone was not his business. Not. His. Business.

If he repeated it long enough, maybe he'd believe it too.

"Bastardo despota."

Despotic bastard. Good one.

"Prepotente." Punch. *"Troglodita."* Punch.

Jack smiled. "I think I'm going to have a little talk with your Italian teacher."

More leg kicks. She was extremely good.

"Where did you learn to fight?"

"None of your business," she said breathing hard and brushing with her forearm the damp locks of hair that got stuck on her face. "You don't tell me about yourself, I won't tell about myself either."

"I should have figured you would be great at fighting. Fighting is like fucking, and you're fantastic at that."

She smiled sarcastically. "That makes one of us."

Smart-ass.

"You need to fight. Fight me all you want; you won't win. It will just make you hotter for me. Wetter. I can take on whatever it is you will dish at me and not budge an inch."

"Not budge an inch," she repeated mockingly. "Is that supposed to be a turn-on? Because it is not."

Liar. He threw the paddles to the canvas and, cupping her neck, brought her to him and took her mouth, his tongue thrusting ruthlessly. Possessively. He needed her so much. Backing her into one corner, he lifted her against the ropes.

"What are you doing?" she asked as he released her lips.

"Fucking you."

"You said next time."

"I lied," he said, dragging his teeth along her throat, nipping and sucking her damp skin. He was taking a huge risk. She was very capable of beating the shit out of him now that he had his hands busy and couldn't protect himself.

She seemed to consider that option for a second, but then said, "Help me with the gloves."

He held her up, pressing his lower body against her, and made quick work of one glove. Once she had one hand free, she took care of the other while he was busy getting rid of her T-shirt. All the pent-up desire that had accumulated sparring was spiraling out of control and he couldn't wait to have her.

"Floor," he growled, lowering them both to the mat and stripping her of her pants, her scent filling his nostrils.

She was wet, the moisture dripping from her smooth pussy lips. She wanted him. Badly. Good, because he was dying to fuck her. But before, he needed her taste on him.

"I love that your pussy is bare. I would have taken care of it myself if it wasn't," he said hoarsely, spreading her legs, watching as her inner folds fluttered.

"You'll get to wax my pussy the day I get to shave your balls with a rusty knife, sunshine." Her breath was labored, her voice choppy, but she gave him attitude. She was creaming for him and giving him attitude. So damn sexy.

"Fuck yourself against my mouth. Show me how much you want me."

"Stop talking and lick me," she ordered.

He loved her fire. Her hand was buried in his hair and she arched her back, lifting her hips to get him deeper.

Not shy, his pet.

He placed his hands on her inner thighs, immobilizing her legs and raked his teeth over her mound, teasing her entrance with his tongue. "Show me your tits."

"Jack—" she let out impatiently.

"If you want head, you'll show me your tits. Play with your nipples. You stop, I stop."

"Control freak," she muttered, but she lifted her bra and staring at him defiantly, pinched the hard tips, her whole body jerking, her pussy contracting.

Fuck, such a turn-on. His woman open for him to do as he pleased, whimpering from need. Drenched. Touching herself.

He ate her out with a desperation that he himself didn't understand, sucking her plushy folds and working her gorgeous clit, using his fingers to stretch her, while she moaned and bucked against his face, stroking her tits, liquid heat flooding her pussy.

He would have loved to make her spill in his mouth and make her beg for him to let her come, but he couldn't pull that stunt off. Couldn't wait a second more, so he yanked his pants down and loomed over her.

He needed to be inside her when she exploded. Deep inside her. Feeling her orgasm in every inch of his cock.

She seemed to agree. Grabbing handfuls of him, she wrapped her arms and legs around him, crying out as he rammed inside her, her taut flesh bathing him in instant heat.

"Fuck me hard," she demanded against his ear. "Make me come."

God, she was his wet dream come true. Her core was extremely tight, but she was taking all of him. And asking for more.

Pressing his hand against her ass, he obliged her and pushed in and out, giving her his cock again and again, so deep inside he could feel her heartbeat.

She gripped his hair and pulled his head up, looking him straight in the eye. "When we're done," she let out in broken pants, withstanding his savage thrusts, "you can go back to doing as you want; until then, I'm the only one who fucks you. I'm the only one who touches you. Are we clear?"

Fuck. Throwing his words back at him while taking his cock. Jack had to grit his teeth not to blow on the spot, especially as she lost it and came, her pussy clutching him so hard it left him without breath.

He needed a bit of distance or she was going to drag him with her. And he didn't want this to finish, not yet.

While she was still orgasming, he got out of the boxing ring and, pulling her by her legs, yanked her to the edge, her ass in midair.

"Hold on to the ropes. This is going to be a rough ride."

And it was. He took her hard while she moaned and thrashed, giving as good as she got, making her explode again before letting go and coming himself.

He wasn't sure how—heck he might have blacked out, but when he floated back to reality, they were both sprawled inside the boxing ring, bathed in sweat. His throat felt raw and he couldn't move. Jesus, having sex with Elle got better and better.

"I know you don't know shit about me, but you need to understand I don't cheat. Ever." He didn't get cheating. Despised cheaters. A man who couldn't pledge himself to a woman and maintain his promise was not a man, but a spineless moron. "If I had a wife, I would sleep every night by her side. I would never stray."

"Good to know," she whispered.

"I have experience with kids because since the day Ronnie was born, I cared for her. There wasn't a responsible adult around, so I learned pretty fast."

They were seven years apart. He'd fed her, clothed her. Read to her and corrected her homework. Looked after her. Taken all the beatings himself to make sure nothing happened to her. Stayed in that hellhole of a home for years and years so that he could protect her, until he'd been old enough and had enough resources to take her with him.

"You grew up together?" Elle asked, surprise and dread and fear marring her face. "In the same place where you got those burns?"

Jack nodded. "I made sure she never got any."

"And your dad?"

"Small-time crook. Not better than the guys that came after, or Ronnie's dad, who bailed out before she was born."

"Bailing out on your pregnant woman. Very classy. A real stand-up dude."

"Hate to defend the scumbag, but I doubt he knew. My mother found out when her water broke. She'd been too high to wonder before."

She closed her eyes, grimacing. "God."

Nope, God had been nowhere to be seen. "Ronnie is all I have."

Elle was quiet for a long time before speaking again. "You ordered me to stay in the truck because you didn't want me to meet her."

"Yeah, I didn't." He didn't want Elle in his life. Didn't want to get used to her. That meant keeping her as far away as possible from his home, his bar, and his sister. And his heart. Especially his heart.

Her smile was sad and resigned. "I'm not used to the man I'm screwing being ashamed of me, but at least you're honest."

"Not ashamed, pet. Not by a long shot."

She needed an explanation; he could see it in her hurt eyes, but he didn't give it to her. It would just make matters worse.

It was very easy to miss things if one got used to having them and caring for them. He couldn't afford that.

"Come on, let's get dressed and go home."

She didn't fight him.

* * * *

Jack parked in front of her place, turned off the engine, and looked at her. She'd been quiet during the ride back, like the rounds of sex and sparring had sucked the energy out of her.

"Do you mind if we sit for a second?" She didn't seem in too much of a hurry to get home, as if she needed a strength she didn't have now to enter that house.

Jack glanced toward the property. "Why do you live here?"

She shrugged. "I have to live somewhere, don't I? Quite a place the V-2," she added, changing the subject. "Rough crowd. It suits you."

His snort was dry. "I wanted a bakery."

"What?"

"I wanted a bakery. A local nice little shop in suburbia, where carpool moms could spend their afternoons eating pastries and drinking lattes. Ronnie was going to run it. I had everything planned, but I had to leave for work, so I left my sister in charge. When I came back Ronnie had opened a biker bar."

Elle broke into laughter. "I like her."

They hadn't had much time to talk, and what little they had, Elle had spent apologizing to Ronnie, but he had no doubt they would get along.

Ignoring how in the open they were, and how unwise this was, Jack reached for her and lifted her onto his lap. He swept his thumb over her luscious lips. "In V-2, you were jealous."

Elle nodded. "I am a very jealous person. You ought to remember that. Especially if you are emotionally attached to your dick and intend to keep it."

"I'd like to keep it, yes."

"Then it should stay in your pants. Or inside me."

He barked out a laugh. So much sass.

"That made me feel ten feet tall," she said, her eyes soft.

"What?"

"That honest-to-God laugh." She caressed his face, as if trying get rid of the frown lines. "You don't always need to be alert. You can relax."

"If you want me to relax, then you should be caressing something else."

She threw her head back and laughed. "I can't believe you want more," she said, gently pressing herself against him. "After the boxing ring?"

Jack didn't need any recovery time whatsoever, not with Elle by his side. "Of this sweet pussy? Absolutely I want more." Always. All the time.

"Next visit to the gym, I'll be on top. I have boxing-ring burn in my back."

"Sorry."

She winked mischievously. "That's all right. They match the scratches on yours."

They stared at each other for a long second.

"I know you don't know shit about me," she whispered his words back at him. "But you need to understand I don't cheat either. Ever. I flirt and I like to party, true, but I'm very aware of where the limits are. No one but the man I'm with touches me."

Jack did know lots about her, but he said nothing, just nodded. Cupping his face, Elle brushed her lips with his, running her tongue along the seam of his mouth before sweetly kissing him.

"You taste like me," she whispered.

"Does it bother you?"

She shook her head. "What surprises me is that it doesn't seem to bother you. Men like you don't strike me as enjoying eating pussy."

"You'd be wrong, then. A man who doesn't go down on his woman is not a man. He's a moron who has no clue what he's missing."

"Amen." She continued kissing him, slowly rubbing against his throbbing erection.

"You have a rather exhibitionist streak in you, pet."

She giggled. "Yep, I'm discovering I have, but you're the one who fucked me in a public gym and just lifted me to your lap."

"Tinted windows."

"Oh, in that case, after you ate my pussy and nailed me in a public gym, maybe it's time I return the favor, and you know, suck your cock and fuck you in the car."

Jesus Christ.

Her little hands reached for his zipper, but she didn't get too far, because from the corner of his eye Jack saw the neighbor walking toward them with a thermos. He hoisted her up and got them out of the truck. "You are not sucking my cock with Mrs. Copernicus looking out the fucking window."

Elle waved at the old lady and whispered to Jack, "I told you they take neighborhood watch very seriously."

Once inside the house, Jack put her down and stared at her.

Under his gaze and with a wiseass smile on her face, she undressed and knelt in front of him, nuzzling his hard-on over his pants, those sweet little breaths of hers slamming against his cock.

He'd dreamed about this for-fucking-ever. Not sure he could survive it though.

She didn't give him much choice, because before he could even gather his thoughts, she'd unzipped him and was licking his cock.

No matter how many times he'd dreamed about this, it didn't even come close to the reality of having Elle at his feet, giving him head, her hands working his shaft while her mouth devilishly worked the crown, raking her teeth over his slit before taking him deep into her throat.

He was dressed and standing. She was naked, sucking his cock on her knees while he held her head, yet she was the one with all the power. And she knew it.

He forced her to let go of him and stand up.

"Hey!" she complained. "I was enjoying that."

"I want to come inside you."

"You would have," she teased, making his erection jump even more.

What she could do to him with just words should be illegal. It probably was too. "Offer yourself to me."

She walked toward the table, sat on it, and slowly parted her legs, her fingers holding her pussy opened for him to see.

"You're dripping wet," he growled.

"Sucking you turned me on. Are you coming over, or do I have to take care of myself?" she asked mischievously, sliding two fingers inside her, shivering at the pleasure.

"I take care of my woman," he said, walking to her, pulling her fingers out of her pussy, and licking them. Then he spread her wide, nudging the head of his cock against her swollen folds. At the contact, her entrance spasmed visibly. "You want me."

She nodded.

"Watch us."

She did, her eyes glassy, her lips red and puffy from giving him head, her pussy slowly yielding to him. They fit perfectly. As small as she was, she wasn't fragile. She took all of him and when he pulled out, she whimpered in protest, her core clenching, unwilling to let go.

"I love how you feel." She reached for his cock while he was withdrawing from her and caressed him, raking her nails over his engorged veins. "Inside me and down my throat."

He did too. Much more than he should. Much more than he was ready to admit.

He'd been the one ordering her to watch as he took her, but he hadn't counted on the growing intimacy swirling around them, pressing at his chest, not letting him breathe. He plunged inside her, his piercing slamming against her clit, ripping a ragged moan out of her. Without giving her time to react, he set a hard tempo and proceeded to fuck the hell out of her while she grabbed the table, trying to withstand the onslaught, unable to keep the eye contact or talk anymore.

Now he could breathe again.

* * * *

Nico scanned the gay bar and found his target, seemingly alone. Perfect.

He'd gone through all possible scenarios while tracing Aalto's steps that fateful day. Who he might have met, who he might have spoken with. Dead ends, all of them. Hopefully this was going to bear fruit. It better, seeing all the trouble he was going to. Tracking this backpacking crowd all over the island.

Nico reached the counter and flagged the waiter. "A beer, please. And another of whatever he's drinking," he said smiling at the man standing beside him, who gave Nico a once-over and liked what he saw, if the way his eyes sparkled was anything to go by.

"Gin and tonic. Thanks. I'm Donald, by the way. Don."

Nico knew. Donald Solis. Supervisor at the airline poor Marlene Cabrera had worked for.

"You alone, Don?"

"Not anymore."

It always surprised Nico how easy it was to pick up men. Those morons didn't seem to have any self-preservation instincts whatsoever. Actually, every person, man or woman, seemed to go brain-dead while on vacation.

It took him a total of thirty-five minutes to get Don to leave the joint with him. Like stealing candy from a baby, really.

It took him another fifteen more to get Donald to give Elle Cooper up.

CHAPTER TWELVE

Elle couldn't tear her eyes from Jack, too enthralled to even fiddle with the truck radio, despite how satisfying it was to bug him. Her terminator was a sight to behold. Gorgeous in regular clothes, in a tuxedo he was breathtaking. He'd been dolled up at her sister's wedding, but then Elle and Jack didn't have an intimate relationship. She hadn't seen him naked. Hadn't felt his hands over her, his cock pushing inside her, his body straining and his face feral as he single-mindedly fucked her. With all those memories and that sensory input fresh in her mind, Jack's primal nature contained inside those proper clothes revved her up like nothing before had.

"We're here," he muttered, turning off the motor in front of the posh hotel where the gathering organized by Patricia Vaughan was to take place.

Jack was not pleased with this party, but they hadn't been able to get out of it. Patricia Vaughan, Annie's grandmother, wanted to present her great-granddaughter into society and as Jonah had been born several weeks after Lizzie, he had been included too. Elle and Jack, as godparents, had been strongly encouraged to attend.

"Come on, Borg. Let's have some fun."

Before she could open the door, he reached for her and hauled her to his lap. "Let's set some ground rules first."

"Hey, my stockings," she complained. Her gown had a deep slash in one side, so accommodating him between her legs wasn't

133

difficult. Managing not to snag the thin material with his calloused hands was another matter altogether.

"Forget the stockings."

"If you ruin them, I'd have to take them off."

"If you take them off, I'll fuck you."

She broke into laughter. "You'll fuck me either way."

"True, but not here, at this very second."

She flushed, a wave of heat spreading over her. My, what this guy could do to her with just a stern look and a handful of words, delivered with that raspy voice of his, abrading all her senses and utterly scattering her mind. And his scent. So male, so…devoid of metrosexual shit. Just a hint of soap and man. Barely bottled-up raw power.

"You like the idea," he said quietly.

She nodded. It was mind-boggling how sexual she was with him. She had never been prudish when it came to sex, but she was very selective and didn't jump into bed with the first guy who tickled her fancy. Who would have guessed that, now, with her sitting on top of Jack's cock? No restraint whatsoever.

Like the boxing ring. Talk about high-intensity training. Or crazy monkey sex, as people called it. It had left her limp as an overcooked noodle, totally covered in sweat and so high on endorphins, amazing sex, and Jack, it had taken her days to get back to earth.

"It has its merits," she admitted. "I could go without stockings, but your cum dripping down my inner thigh would look kind of conspicuous."

"Tough shit. I won't fuck you with a condom."

She had no intention of humping him now, but that high-handed comment pissed her off. "What? Not ready to part with getting maximum pleasure with your sex? Even if I would ask you to?"

"My cock inside you, it's always maximum pleasure, condom or no condom."

"Then?"

She waited for him to answer but in true Jack form, he didn't elaborated. Ass.

She tried moving away from him, but his grip on her intensified. Control freak.

"About this party," she said, changing the subject. By now she knew when she'd hit a stone wall with Jack. "What are those ground rules of yours?"

"You don't move from my side. Ever."

"Hmmm, can I go to pee on my own, or do I need to bring some sort of bottle?"

His expression softened marginally. "We leave when I say. No befriending strangers. No drawing any attention to yourself." Then he gave her a once-over and frowned. "I told you this dress was a bad idea."

"And I told you this was the least revealing of my gowns. Just suck it up. Your future Amish wife will dress more according to your tastes. I won't. Besides, you are getting it wrong. It's not the dress, you dummy, it's the shoes. The higher the heels, the dirtier the girl, didn't you know that?"

His eyes darkened, but he didn't answer to her jab. "I don't want you doing anything that would make you stand out. More than you already do by looking like…"

"A ho?" she offered, defiantly.

He cupped her face, his expression fierce. "Like the fucking hottest, sexiest, funniest, most aggravatingly beautiful woman I've ever seen."

Judging by his glare, one would assume he was insulting her.

She placed her hands on his chest and, without breaking eye contact, whispered, "Thanks for the compliments."

"They aren't compliments."

Yes they were, even if he obviously couldn't stand it. "The fucking hottest, sexiest, funniest, most aggravatingly beautiful woman you've ever seen will refrain from causing you any trouble or discomfort. In exchange, you have to dance with her."

"That will cause me discomfort. I don't dance."

"You did at James's wedding."

"I was under duress, being the best man and all."

"Consider yourself under duress here too," Elle stated. "I need to assess your abilities. There can never be too many people in a flash mob and the next one is in a couple weeks."

A smile crept across his face. Encircling her neck with his hand, he brought her to him and kissed her long and deep. "In your dreams, pet."

"In your dreams, *gorgeous*? In your dreams, *princess*? In your dreams, *sweetheart*? Don't you think any of these sound better?"

"No."

It figured. Stubborn Neanderthal. "You're so lucky I'm humoring you," she said, attempting to unstraddle him.

"Do we have a deal?" he asked, holding her down and gliding his hard cock over her sensitized pussy.

"About what? I forgot already," she said with a gasp.

"The whole Bowen clan will be there, along with many other guests. You follow my rules, I won't haul you out on my shoulder and I'll make it worth your while later on."

You'll make it worth my while anyway, she almost replied, but at the last second, she kept it in.

She leaned into him and kissed him, making a huge effort to lift herself from his lap. "Yeah, yeah. Calm down, Borg. You'll overheat and lose your speech capabilities again. You need to pass for human now."

Shaking his head, he let her go.

Elle stepped out of the car, straightened her gown, and took the arm he was offering.

"Just so you know, you also look like the hottest, sexiest and most aggravatingly beautiful Borg I've ever seen." And she wasn't the only one who thought so, because all the ladies they crossed paths with as they entered the lobby were eating him with their eyes. "The title of funniest you can't claim, sorry," she finished, winking at him.

Jack shook his head, the flash of a smile warming Elle's insides.

Some of the Bowens were by the door of the ballroom, so they headed their way.

A man approached Jack and Elle, someone looking like a bodyguard on his heels. "Alex, *qué bueno verte por aquí.*"

Jack's expression didn't waver, but she noticed a slight tightening in the arm she was holding. Jack nodded in greeting and let out a torrent of words in what it sounded to Elle like perfect Spanish, shaking the stranger's hand. Okay, so they were friends, but why the hell was this guy calling Jack Alex?

She smiled, hiding her surprise.

Then the man turned to her. "*¿Y esta belleza?*" And this beauty?

Unlike Jack's, his words in Spanish had a heavy American accent.

There was a silent warning in Jack's touch, so Elle continued smiling and waited for his cues.

"This beauty is mine, and I won't make the same mistake twice," Jack answered in a light tone so un-Jack-like it was shocking.

The newcomer broke into laughter and taking Elle's hand, kissed it. "Forgive Alex's rudeness; he's fiercely protective of his dates and I committed the ultimate sin of being more charming than him last time we run into each other. I'm David Exxum."

"Nice to meet you." This Jack was not the Jack she knew. He moved differently, and had a slight Spanish accent when speaking English, a cadence he didn't have before. Unsure what she should or shouldn't say, she opted for keeping her mouth shut and smiled.

"You here for the fund-raising?" David asked, gesturing down the hall, in the opposite direction.

Apparently there were two events in the hotel that evening.

At that moment Tate saw Elle and, flagging her, headed their way.

Jack didn't move, and Elle didn't notice any change in his expression, but James did, because he stopped dead in his tracks and called Tate back.

"Yes, we're here for the fund-raiser. Shall we?" Jack offered, turning his back on the Bowens and walking toward the other ballroom. "Pet, didn't you want to powder your nose? We'll go ahead and wait for you there."

That was her cue to bail.

"Sure, I—"

"Nonsense," David interrupted, taking Elle by the elbow and gently pushing her forward. "The lady is stunning. Any more and she would blind us. And I don't want to miss the opportunity to make such an entrance."

She threw a fast glance backward, toward where Annie's party was. Aunt Maggie had noticed them and was heading their way waving. James rushed behind her, but he wasn't going to be able stop the old lady in time.

"Elle, here," she heard Aunt Maggie call from the other side of the hallway, raising her voice.

"No need to powder my nose," she hurried to say.

There was something in David's touch that gave her the creeps, but hiding her apprehension, Elle smiled reassuringly and walked with him into the crowd, feeling Jack's ominous presence behind her.

* * * *

Fuck. Fuck. Fuck.

Jack kept his face inscrutable as his mind raced. Elle had been quick on the uptake, improvising like a pro, but the last place he wanted her in was that damn fund-raiser with Exxum and his people.

He was dying to rip Exxum's hand off for touching her, but he tamped his fury down. He knew that bastard very well and such move would only spike his interest in her.

The second David let her elbow go to take the flutes of champagne the waiter was offering, Jack reached for Elle and brought her flush to him. She went eagerly, intertwined her fingers with his.

Jack smiled and gave her a kiss under the hollow of her ear. "Follow my cues," he whispered discreetly.

"Can't keep your hands off her, I see," David commented with a laugh. "Not that I fault you. You, my dear, are astonishingly beautiful. What was your name?"

Shit. Before Jack could come up with an answer, Elle said with a smile, "Pet. He had me chipped when I wasn't looking."

David threw his head back and laughed while another waiter approached them with snacks.

"Do try," David encouraged Elle. "I myself took care of ordering the catering from Luxury Delights. Best vegan products available. One hundred percent organic. Eating animals is so cruel and unnecessary."

Right. The asshole couldn't stomach eating an animal but didn't give a rat's ass about all the humans his businesses ruined.

Elle smiled and took a morsel.

David did too. "I don't believe the jails of a nation tell how civilized a country is. It's the way its people treat animals that shows their level of evolution. Having to organize fund-raisers to get animals off the streets already proves we are at the bottom of the barrel."

"Alex, my love," Marissa, one of Exxum's harem, said, reaching for him.

"Hello, sweetheart," Jack greeted, leaning to kiss the woman's face. "As beautiful as ever."

He could feel Elle's stiffness and displeasure. She tried to pull her hand away from him, but he held onto it, keeping their fingers firmly intertwined.

"You need to save me a dance," Marissa said, caressing the lapel of his tux. "Alex is such a good dancer."

"Which reminds me," Exxum interrupted, turning to Elle, "would you do me the immense honor of dancing with me? I know Alex; once he takes someone to the dance floor, he doesn't let go."

Used as he was not to be denied, David was already reaching for Elle when Jack stepped in.

Fuck it. He was getting her out of there.

"*My* pet. She dances with me," he rumbled, pulling her by her hand.

He knew this was a bad move. This would spike the asshole's interest, but he couldn't do anything differently.

Once on the dance floor, he enveloped Elle in his arms, breathing her scent in, trying to calm down. She hugged him and placed her head on the crook of his neck.

"Anything to tell me, *Alex*?"

"You should have gone to powder your nose."

She snorted softly. "Aunt Maggie was about to reach us. There was no time to argue. We didn't have many options. What the hell is going on?"

As much as it pissed him off to admit it, she was right. Another minute and any number of people would have blown his cover to hell and back. David and his people didn't take kindly to undercover operatives. Once his true identity was unveiled, the people closest to him would suffer the consequences. He couldn't risk that. The whole Bowen clan, kiddies included, were there; no fucking way was he having their safety threatened. It was already bad enough that Elle was mixed up in this, with all these unscrupulous bastards pretending to be upstanding gentlemen.

"Who is David Exxum?" she insisted. "And why the hell do you speak Spanish like a native?"

Who was David Exxum? Nobody, just one of the biggest scumbags on the East Coast. Playboy and philanthropist in the public eye. Something much more sinister in private. Too bad the motherfucker was bulletproof, protected by the kind of armor that only money and fame provided.

"I want you out of here. Stat. Excuse yourself. Head for the bathroom and sneak out. Go find James."

She pressed her lips into a tight line, looking aggrieved, probably because he was deflecting her questions, but she didn't comment on that. Good, because he wasn't going to get into an argument with her. "Isn't it going to seem weird if I disappear? I can handle this," she assured him, snuggling against him, caressing his hair, as if they were dancing and murmuring inconsequential things into each other's ears. Just two lovers cuddling. "I might be a pain in the butt and too loud and vocal for your taste, but I know when to keep my mouth shut. You don't have to worry about me screwing up. We dance. Mingle with your…friends and in half an hour I say I'm not feeling well and you take me home."

A lot of shit could go down in half an hour. The hairs at the back of his neck were already prickling as it was, his instincts all yelling at him.

Alex Ayala, his undercover name, was never in Boston. He favored the sun and the south, where he conducted his business as a facilitator. A broker of sorts. Connecting buyers with sellers, all big movers and shakers. Overseeing the deals and offering integral turnkey services. Of all his aliases during the years, this one had been the most effective, enabling him to shut down several big operations without blowing his cover. Jack wasn't about to start fucking up now.

"I'll entertain David and you excuse yourself," he ordered as the song ended. Exxum had been watching them dance, so there was no way to sneak past him. Steeling himself, he walked toward David, keeping Elle's hand tight in his grip.

"Alex, have I introduced you yet to one of our most generous benefactors?"

Jack turned to the newcomer and froze.

Jesus fucking Christ.

"Joaquín Maldonado, this is Alex Ayala and his lovely date," Exxum said.

Jack nodded in greeting and shook Maldonado's hand.

"Alex Ayala, finally. I've heard a lot about you." Then Maldonado addressed Elle, taking her hand and kissing it. "A pleasure. You look vaguely familiar. Have we met before?"

CHAPTER THIRTEEN

Time stood still. Jack could hardly hear a damn word, the way his ears were roaring. He, who had taken part in countless undercover operations, always cool as a cucumber, was about to lose his fucking shit. His gut feeling was to grab Elle and run the hell out of there. Thank God Elle was more rational.

She smiled, not flinching under Maldonado's scrutiny or his touch while his lips brushed her hand. "I have one of those faces."

"Which kind is that?"

"A common one," she answered, not missing a beat.

The bastard's expression lit with a grin. "Oh, I wouldn't call your face or any part of you common."

"Thanks. It's the dim light here," she confided. Jack could tell from the pulse in her wrist that her heart rate was sky-high, but she was joking and pretending to be relaxed. "Makes a woman more mysterious. Smoky. Then you see her in daylight and *kaboom*, you have a heart attack."

Maldonado broke into laughter.

"I'm impressed, Alex. Finally a woman with looks and brains. Where are you seated? I'm sure we can rearrange the setting to include you," Exxum said, throwing a glance to one of his associates, who flagged someone of the staff. "Joaquín is at the same table."

* * * *

Nico parked the car and, taking in a deep breath of cold air, walked toward the hotel where Maldonado was attending a fundraiser for abandoned dogs. What he was doing there, Nico had no clue, because his employer couldn't give two fucks about animals, abandoned or otherwise, much less travel to the other end of the country to spend a whopping ten grand on a vegan diner.

Either way he was glad for the reprieve, short as it might be. Boston was a welcome change of scenery, seeing as how he spent most of his time in the Caribbean or in the jungle overseeing the labs.

Florida was bad enough; Hawaii on top of that had been overkill. Next vacation he had, he was taking his Russian ass to Murmansk.

It was a stroke of luck that Maldonado was in Boston, because as fate would have it, the person they were searching for was from there. After Donald, all he had to do was go online to several professional directories and people-finder apps and *bada bing, bada boom,* in two seconds flat he'd found an Elle Cooper in the BU student directory who resembled Marlene. An Elle Cooper who had been enrolled in UF for a year a while back, and who had worked for the same airline as Marlene. Once sure he had the right girl, it had been a matter of going to Instagram, Facebook, and Twitter. Man, people had no clue what they were doing when they uploaded all of their lives. How exposed they were. How easily they could become prey. He'd get accounts on those social media networking programs as soon as fucking never.

By the time the plane had landed at Logan, he had all the info he needed and more. Where she lived, worked. What she liked and didn't. Her hobbies. Who she socialized with. What she'd had for breakfast, for Christ's sake.

He hadn't needed to do any recon in person. Go through the phone directory, one Elle Cooper at a time and pay each of them a visit, like in the olden days. Nope. The Internet sped everything up, criminal enterprises included.

He entered the hotel, a copy of her driving license in his pocket. Now all he had to do was find Maldonado.

* * * *

Jesus Christ. As if being forced to mingle with Maldonado and

Exxum at a fund-raiser wasn't bad enough, now they were being maneuvered into sharing table with them.

Fuck, no. No way in hell. Before he could make a mess out of things, Elle intervened.

"It would be lovely to dine at your table, but I'm not feeling too well," she hastened to explain. "Alex is taking me home."

"I have the top floor reserved," Exxum insisted. "You could go lie down for a while and then join us here."

"I don't think so," Jack answered curtly. "Gentlemen."

Without giving them a chance to reply, Jack directed her toward the door with a hand on the small of her back, doing his damnedest to keep his stride even and not break into a run.

Fuck. Fuck. Fuck.

What the hell was he doing? Humoring Elle and letting her continue with her life as if nothing had happened? Tagging along happily, his cock at the ready? Lowering his guard and groping her in the car, in the open? Moron. If he had been more alert, he would have noticed the fund-raiser and they wouldn't have been blindsided.

As they made their way to the lobby, Jack saw a blond guy amid the crowd, scanning the premises. That was Nico Grabar, Maldonado's second in command. Almost in front of them. Fuck He hadn't spotted them yet, but it was a matter of a second or two. Jack spun Elle around and kissed her, turning his back to Nico and hovering over Elle, covering her as much as possible.

Nico looked at them and then took a second glance, frowning. Holding his breath, Jack waited for the man to pass.

Once out of the hotel, he ran with Elle to the truck.

"...you listening to me?" Elle's angry words finally computed as he turned the engine on.

Based on her expression, she'd been trying to get his attention for a while.

Well, tough shit. He wasn't listening to her. She messed with his head. Both his heads. And he'd start making decisions with the wrong one. First piece of evidence, this whole clusterfuck.

He was supposed to keep her out of harm's way, and instead, he'd almost delivered her to Maldonado on a silver platter.

"What exactly happened in there? Who the hell are you?"

He wasn't going to answer. The less she knew, the better.

"Why didn't you tell me that Maldonado knew you?" she

demanded. "And what's Maldonado doing in Boston?"

Excellent question. And why he didn't get a heads-up from Mullen, he didn't know. But he was going to find out.

His silence was infuriating her. She was seething; he could see it. And the more her questions went unanswered, the worse it got.

"Who. Is. Alex?" she asked, punctuating every word.

He continued ignoring her while he sped onto the highway, the force throwing her against the window. At least his brain hadn't melted down totally and he still kept a stash of supplies in his truck in case he had to disappear. Good, because he was done playing house. Time to do what he should have done from the very beginning and cut the shit out.

"Where are we going? Talk to me, dammit!" she all but yelled.

He used Bluetooth to call Mullen, who answered in two rings.

"Maldonado is in Boston. We're going under," he barked out before the FBI agent could get a word in.

"We lost him. Last we heard he was on a beach in the Caribbean. He must have flown straight from there to Boston."

"No shit. Now he's downtown, attending a fund-raiser."

"Did he see you?"

Jack's laugh was dry. "See us? We almost had dinner with the asshole."

"Hell. Did he recognize Elle? Let me make a couple of calls. The FBI will have a safe house for you ready in no time."

"No. Not risking another leak. I'm taking her off the radar. You do your goddamned job and arrest this guy."

"We are doing the best we can. It would be much easier if you would let the girl be bait. Wire her up and send her to blackmail him for her silence," he said, obviously not realizing Elle was listening. "The second we have his confession on tape, he's toast. You know that's the fastest avenue."

"I said no," Jack barked, watching as Elle processed Mullen's words.

Outrage sharpened her features. "Jack, what the—"

"I'll contact you later, when we're set up," Jack said, interrupting Elle and hanging up on Mullen.

"You bastard. Why didn't you tell me about that option?" Her eyes were ablaze, boring holes in him. "Didn't I have the right to know?"

"Not an option," he let out in between gritted teeth.

Wiring Elle up and sending her into the wolf's den wouldn't end well. In the unlikely event she managed to get a confession out of Maldonado, she would never live to see it put to good use.

"That's for me to decide, asshole," she yelled.

"No."

"Wrong again! I demand you stop right this frigging instant. I want to know where we are going. Then I'll decide if I go or not."

Tough shit. He floored the accelerator.

* * * *

"So, why are you here?" Exxum asked, after they stepped out on the patio to smoke, his bodyguard by the door. "You come to pay me for that last couple of shipments of guns? Because I've known you for a while now and you don't give a rat's ass about abandoned dogs."

True. He couldn't care less. He'd fought them for scraps in the street.

"I'm still strapped for cash," Maldonado admitted. It wasn't as if he could walk to an ATM machine and withdraw a couple of million dollars to settle the score.

Exxum's lips pressed into a thin line. "Unfortunate what happened to Aalto. Did you have a talk with the witness?"

Maldonado was not too thrilled to have Exxum in his business, but he'd had to give some explanations as to why he needed more time to pay for the guns. "Not yet. Nico is on it. She's under federal protection, but not through the official channels." He would have found her by now if that were the case. Too much paperwork and too many ears. Whoever had her was keeping everyone in the dark.

"Well, I wish you all the luck in the world with that. As for the money you owe me, this is not a good time. I've withstood some heavy losses myself."

Maldonado didn't know any specifics, but several of Exxum's deals had fallen through, the police intercepting the supply lines. Which garnered him a measure of comfort. At least he wasn't the only one going through difficulties.

"So if you've come for financial aid," Exxum continued.

Maldonado shook his head. He wasn't here for handouts. "I came to propose a deal. I have some logistical issues you could help me with. After all, a big part of the humanitarian relief operation is taking care of the logistics."

David Exxum, apart from being a huge advocate of animal rights and doing sports like a nut and eating the weirdest things, was a very influential, respected, well-connected businessman who devoted himself to sending humanitarian relief to countries in need, Maldonado's included. And selling guns to whatever faction needed them. Or both.

His cargo containers went through customs in a much-expedited protocol.

"What's in it for me?" Exxum asked.

"Aside from helping an old business partner?"

Exxum made a scowl. Yeah, Maldonado guessed as much.

"Once the product has cleared customs, my cash-flow problems are gone, which means I can pay you what I owe you. Plus an increase of, let's say, ten percent for the help provided."

Exxum stared at him cockily. "Twenty-five."

Maldonado gritted his teeth, but before he could answer anything, they were interrupted.

"Mr. Maldonado? There's a gentleman outside who wishes to talk to you. Mr. Nico Grabar. He—" Nico was already walking toward them, Exxum's bodyguard moving to intercept him. "You can't—"

"It's okay," Maldonado said, "he's with me. What are you doing in Boston? You already tired of Hawaii?"

Nico greeted Exxum with a nod and waited for the hotel security guy to leave. Then he said, "The person we are searching for is from Boston. Elle Cooper. Closest relatives are a mother and sister. Father and older brother deceased in a car accident over two years ago. The Coopers own Rosita's, a small Italian restaurant on the outskirts of town. She's the one that dispatched your flight. Marlene had a family gathering and they switched IDs."

"So that's the loose end," Maldonado murmured, looking pleased. "Switching IDs. How cleverly stupid of them."

Nico handed Maldonado a copy of Elle's driver's license. "Now we just have to find her."

Maldonado stared at the picture. Son of a bitch. "I think we just did."

CHAPTER FOURTEEN

They were headed up north. At some point Elle had realized yelling at him wasn't going to do squat. He wasn't going to answer or stop, or drive slower for that matter. Jumping out of the truck wasn't an option and even if he stopped for gas and she managed to slip away from him—which she doubted she could because judging by the murderous look in his eyes he would only walk away from her after cuffing her to the wheel—she was dressed in a ball gown and had no money or decent shoes for walking. So she did the only thing she could: cross her arms and give him the silent treatment. Not that it seemed to bother him in the least.

Asshole. Making decisions that concerned her behind her back. And now they were going under, whatever the heck that meant.

After getting off the highway and several hours of driving on secondary roads, she no longer could tell if they were going east or west. Just forest and deserted, crackled asphalt. Until there wasn't even that, just dirt and rocks and deeper forest.

He took a sharp left onto a steep, narrow road, the branches and twigs scraping at the truck until they reached an A-frame cabin in the middle of nowhere.

So that was what going under meant.

He killed the engine, reached in the back, and opened some sort of compartment she hadn't noticed before, grabbed several duffel bags, and gestured for her to get out.

She remained furiously still.

"It gets very cold up here, and there isn't a human being for miles. Move it."

She was angry, granted, but stupid she wasn't, so she followed him.

"What's this place?" she asked, as he unlocked the front door.

"Hunting cabin. Generator should kick in soon." He dropped the bags and produced a flashlight.

She glanced around. No TV. No computer. Heck, no decent sofa either. Two wooden benches flanking a massive table. A fireplace with several O-rings in a wooden beam with some utensils hanging from them, and a mini-kitchen that must have been a century old.

His Pilgrim wife would love to live there, skinning the rabbits he would hunt and cooking over the fireplace, or sewing quilts on the porch, swaying in the rocking chair he would make for her.

"Do we pull water from a well?"

"No. Rain-recycling system. Toilet outside."

Of course.

Jack went to the back and probably did something, because the lights kicked in. Sadly, the place didn't improve one bit; it got worse. Now she knew what Heidi had felt, stepping into her grandpa's cabin for the first time.

"I'll grab some wood," he said, striding for the front door.

"So you know, I don't eat rabbit."

He frowned, turning to her. "What?"

"Nothing," she mumbled.

While he was outside in what she supposed was the woodshed, she inspected her surroundings. Jack had left the duffel bags in the only bedroom, on top of the hardest bed she'd ever tried. Then again, she hadn't been in the Siberian gulag. Maybe they had harder ones.

The celestial sound of a phone buzzing almost stopped her heart. Oh God, there was service. That was her ticket out of the Stone Age.

She rummaged through the bag where the buzz was coming from, trying to ignore all the guns in there. On the flip side, if he refused to let her go, she could shoot him.

Finally, she fished out a satellite phone. She didn't recognize the name on the screen but answered nevertheless.

"Yes?"

"Elle?" said a female voice. "Ronnie here. You guys okay?"

"Define okay."

"What do you mean? Is my brother there?"

"Yes, the ass is out front."

A startled pause and then a soft chuckle. "What has he done?"

"Ha! What hasn't he done would be more accurate. When I finish talking with you, I'm calling 911 and tell them I've been kidnapped by the Unabomber."

Ronnie broke into laughter. "So you are at the cabin."

"Unfortunately. How do you know?"

"I've been there. And Jack sent me an encrypted message, which means he's disappearing."

"Lucky you. I didn't even get three words out of him." It seemed Elle was the only one left in the dark.

She really didn't know squat about this guy. Not a damn thing.

"Jack is not big on giving explanations. But he's damn good."

"I'm not big on being ordered around and ignored. Why haven't you been 'ordered' to hide?"

Ronnie snorted. "You remember V-2's huge bouncer? Jack pays him, and his job is not only to watch the door, believe me. He's on my ass twenty-four seven."

It figured.

"Say," Elle started. "If you've been here, you could come to pick me up."

"Sorry. Couldn't find the place if my life depended on it. And the bodyguard from hell wouldn't take me. Besides, if Jack brought you up there, it means you're in deep trouble. You'd better stay put."

"Sure, what else can a pet do?"

"Pet is good, Elle. Pet is very good," Ronnie answered.

"Meaning?"

"Before I forget; I left a pair of jeans and some toiletries in the chest of drawers," Ronnie said changing the subject.

As cryptic as her brother.

Elle was about to push the issue when Jack came through the door and shot a nasty look her way.

"Wait a second, the ass just came in." Elle handed the phone to Jack. "Your sister."

A couple of nods and "yes," and he hung up. Probably reading her mind, he put the phone on the pocket of his jeans, glaring at her.

"How long do you think you can keep me incommunicado here?"

"As long as it takes," he replied arrogantly.

"So you had the time to stay in contact with Ronnie and talk to Mullen and whatnot but you don't have the smidgen of decency needed to answer my questions, right?"

"I don't give a shit about decency," he grunted, piling the wood near the fireplace. "And you don't need to know."

Didn't that say it all.

She was so angry she turned her back on him while he got the fire started. She wasn't spending any more saliva on this moron.

"You hungry? There are some MREs."

She didn't even dignify this with an answer. She went to the bedroom and slammed the door.

Apparently, Jack didn't speak Woman fluently, because he thought that was an invitation to follow her.

She gathered his duffel bags and shoved them at him. "You take the sofa."

He grabbed them, left them on the floor, and then looked at her defiantly. "No."

"Fine," she retorted, picking up her things. That was, the shoes she'd taken off and her useless, empty minipurse. Such irony; this was the first time she'd left without her own phone. "I'll take the sofa." Or bed of nails. Whatever that was.

Before she could fully comprehend what was happening, she was airborne, and then landed on the bed, Jack between her legs, looming over her.

She was totally overpowered, so she went for dignified and stayed furiously silent. Defiant, while he kissed her ravenously, forcing his way into her mouth, his tongue pushing in.

When he let her up for air, she tried to make her voice sound even. "Not talking to you. You don't need to kiss me to shut me up. I'll appreciate if you'd get off me now."

He didn't budge an inch. Eyes fierce. His expression a snarl. "I tried to stay away from you. I warned you. You didn't stay away. Now you have to face what you find. Own it. You don't get to run when things don't go your way. You knew what you were getting into when you asked me to fuck you."

Pardon? "I didn't ask you to take over my life and nullify me.

Turn me into a wallflower."

"A wallflower doesn't have this effect on me," he said, pressing his erection against her.

She was pissed, but she was turned on, too, so she threw herself into the kiss, pushing for dominance, stuck in a loop of anger and excitement that was swallowing them both.

But dominance with Jack, she wasn't going to have. In spite of all her thrashing and writhing, he managed to pin her down, rip the dress off her, and get naked himself. He rolled them over, putting her on top for about two seconds, before sitting up and forcing her legs around his waist.

"What do you think you're doing? Don't dare take me for granted."

"I don't. I'm taking you, period."

Without preamble, he slid inside her, full of arrogance. The arrogance of a man sure of his lover's welcome. A man who knew his woman trusted him and wanted him. And he was right because she did. It infuriated immensely, but she did. Her body trusted and wanted him, conceited bastard that he was.

"You don't withhold sex from me because you're pissed. You don't go to sleep on the sofa. You don't give me the cold shoulder."

"So what the hell do I do, uh? What?" she spat in broken pants, looking straight into his eyes as he filled her and her core flexed trying to accommodate him.

"We hash it out, pet. Talk."

Now he wanted to talk. Asshole. "You prefer your women silent."

Tightening his embrace, he gripped her locks and forced her to hold his stare. "Talk," he bit out, his huge cock pulsing inside her, the hair of his groin tickling her folds.

Her hands were trembling, even as her nails were sinking into his shoulders.

Her voice came out shaky, a thin thread of almost nothing. "I've been demanding answers from you for hours. You didn't give them to me. I don't want to talk now."

It was a power game. Everything with Jack was a power game. He had the upper hand. He was holding her tight, his chest rubbing her nipples, his cock impaling her, and they were supposed to hash it out? When she couldn't breathe, much less think?

"You truly are a Borg. Made of steel. Nothing affects you. I, on the other hand, can't turn on and off my feelings. Compartmentalizing all."

He opened the hand at the small of her back and pushed her even more flush against him, pressing her aching clit against the cold piercing. She didn't want to respond, but she couldn't stop the shiver running through her, her womb contracting, her pussy clasping around him. He stood still, looking grim, his teeth locked. All his muscles bulging.

He might have been playing power games but he was far from unaffected.

She withstood his glare, doing her damnedest not to whimper. "I am not the kind of woman who needs or wants a man to make decisions for her. If you don't treat me like an equal, you are not worth my time, not even temporarily."

"We are not equal, but I am worth your time." He pushed on before she could show her outrage at that statement. "You are under my protection. I'm in charge of keeping you safe. We are not on equal ground. You have to trust the decisions I make are in your best interest."

"I want to have a say."

"You will. As long as your say agrees with mine."

The gall of the guy. She squeezed her core as tight as possible, almost sending herself over, and watched the vein at his temple pulse, feeling his erection growing even bigger inside her.

"You are in charge of my protection until I get fed up and go to Mullen myself. Or the NSA or the CIA or whoever would be interested in snatching Maldonado. I bet I would have my pick, big narco badass that he is."

He pulled a bit out and then surged in, ripping a surprised gasp out of her. "You want to leave? Go ahead. See how far away you'd get without me. There's a compass on top of the fireplace. Whether you like it or not, you need me."

Suddenly she noticed his finger teasing the rosette of her ass.

"I said I don't like that," she bit out, her body clenching around him, discrediting her words.

"I won't breach it. I'll stay at the door. If you don't come explosively, I will never touch you there again."

Her curt "fuck you" died on her throat as he softly slid in the tip of his finger and massaged her backside, stretching her muscles while he rocked against her, giving her clit all the friction she needed.

"Fucking sweet, pet. You feel like heaven, your pussy wrapped around my cock, your ass flexing around my finger. Trying to suck me in. So hot."

It was too much. Her ass was spasming, her core too. Fighting for breath, she sank her hands into his hair, spellbound by his intense eyes. He was everywhere, in front of her, inside her, enveloping her. So strong, so masterful.

"Come for me," he whispered against her lips. "Now."

She would have loved to disobey him but her body was going solo, imploding into a thousand pieces. Her mind too. All sparkly, bright colors, sending her into a place where there was no room for female pride or outrage. Just pleasure.

Coming down from that high was a long process. When she opened her eyes and saw the satisfied look in Jack's, all the fuzziness from the orgasm disappeared and anger replaced it.

"You can't stop pushing, can you, Jack? Or should I call you Alex?" She tried to wrench away, embarrassed that her body had hijacked her mind. "This is a new low for me; I don't know the name of the man fucking me."

His expression was fierce, he flipped her on the bed and grabbed both of her hands in one of his over her head, immobilizing her. Once he had her pinned down, he got in her face. "You know who's fucking you. The same one who has been fucking you for the last week. Jack. There's no Alex here. This is me. This is real. No pretending. No sugarcoating shit."

"No kidding," she retorted. "Alex looked like a charmer. Educated. Exuding sex appeal. Not a rude ass who takes what he wants."

She tried pulling her arms free, and when she found she couldn't, an unexpected and rather shameful shiver of excitement jolted through her, her pussy contracting.

He loomed over her, their noses touching. He looked feral. "Alex is a lowlife, cynical son of a bitch who would sell his own mother for money. It's all a facade. Using women for his benefit. This is real," he insisted, surging inside her to the hilt. "This is me. And you know me."

All his restraint seemed to have vanished. He thrust into her, keeping a hard rhythm, touching all her sweet spots, and much to her dismay, and while she was trapped by the powerful grip of his hands, he sent her over again before emptying himself in her.

* * * *

Jack lay on the bed, unable to move. He always made the same mistake with Elle.

Whenever he tried to use sex to reassert his position of power, the end result never changed: she always floored him, leaving him shattered.

Her breath was still labored, but she wasn't moving either. Good, because he wouldn't be able to chase her.

With his gaze fixed on the ceiling, he inhaled deeply and started. "Alex Ayala is the fake identity I use when I go undercover. Bulletproof cover with perfect background checks." That multilayered identity had held up under prolonged scrutiny by major warlords and kingpins without a hitch. Until Elle, who'd blown it to hell and back. Fitting, if one took into account how fast she'd blown his head, his peace of mind, and his emotional detachment.

Hanging out with the Bowens had been a dangerous level of exposure for someone like him. Hanging out with Elle, social butterfly that she was, had been suicide.

He felt her gaze on him, but he refused to meet it.

"What does Alex Ayala do?"

"He brokers deals. Arms deals. Human-trafficking deals. Drug deals." Alex Ayala was successful enough to socialize with the likes of Exxum at plush fund-raisers, conducting business on private islands, a great entertainer and charmer of powerful women, but ruthless enough to handle the lowlifes, willing to take risks and supervising the business from the ground level, getting his hands dirty to get ahead. "I've been after Maldonado for years but I haven't been able to pin anything on him. He makes every witness disappear."

"For years? Why the interest?"

"Because I'm the reason Maldonado is who he is. We created him. Cleared his path. Our mission had been to eliminate the head of the Cali cartel. In those days Maldonado had been an up-and-coming lieutenant and we served control of the cartel to him on a platter. We should have killed him when we had the chance, but we didn't. It was a bad call." He'd been considered the lesser evil, but time had proven them wrong. Maldonado had been even more sanguinary and vicious than his predecessors. Playing God had backfired on Jack and his team.

"And Exxum?" she asked softly.

"High-profile philanthropist who rubs elbows with the cream of the crop. Fills his mouth with big words and in the meantime smuggles arms into conflict countries disguised as humanitarian help. Totally untouchable. You did well back there, pet."

"You mean on my back with my legs up?"

He chuckled. "At the gala. When the fucker fished for your name I almost had a heart attack."

"I'm quick on my feet," she said with a shrug. After a pause, she added, "Jack, I will not fight you on the small stuff. On who pays for what, or stupidities like that, but in what matters, I will fight you tooth and nail. Never doubt it."

"What matters?" he asked softly.

"You know very well. I understand the kind of man you are, how you need to make decisions and have control over everything. And I will cut you a lot of slack because of it, but I will not yield to you and lose myself in you. I won't give up my autonomy or my decision-making skills. I will not change myself for you."

"I wouldn't want you to, pet. You need to stay the way you are and it's my job to protect you and make sure you do." He turned to her and tipped her chin up. "You do know me. I have told you things I haven't told anyone. Things very few people know about me. And when you say nothing affects me? You are wrong, pet; you affect me. A shitload. I don't want you to, I actually hated it, but you do. More than you think."

He forced his mouth shut, before he said God only knew what. This was temporary, and it was suicide to want more than sex. Wanting something you couldn't have was a recipe for disaster.

Elle, psychic radar that she was, didn't poke in that direction. "So you are one of the good guys."

Fuck, this direction wasn't much better. "No, I'm not."

She ignored him. "What are you, a member of some elite, ultrasecret special ops force in the military?"

"I'm not in the army any more, pet. I was dishonorably discharged."

Elle looked at him, surprised. "What do you mean dishonorably discharged?"

He hadn't wanted to tell her about it, but he couldn't let her believe he was something he wasn't. "I mean arrested, court-martialed, and dishonorably discharged." From the only place that he'd ever belonged to. The army had been his life; being a Green Beret had defined his existence.

"What? Don't tell me your cock piercing got you discharged."

He would have bet good money he couldn't crack a smile while talking about his dishonorable discharge, but he found himself barking a laugh. "No, you crazy woman."

She studied him for a second, then shook her head. "They made a mistake."

"I haven't told you what happened."

"Doesn't matter. Whatever it was, they made a mistake and it was their loss."

"I disobeyed orders and beat the shit out of a superior."

She shrugged. "Just that? They court-martial people for nothing nowadays. And I'm sure he deserved it."

Yes, he did, but that didn't change the fact that the asshole was his superior. The military tended to take offense at that. It had happened during that same covert operation that had allowed Maldonado's rise. Everything had gone according to plan until the extraction; then it all had gone to hell. That the asshole had freaked out and gotten half their team killed and that Jack had saved the rest by taking charge hadn't mattered either. Rules were rules. And his superior had been well connected. Military family, four generations, while Jack was just a mutt with a short fuse and little to no diplomatic skills.

James had backed him up the whole time. In that fucking jungle and later, during the trial, he'd never faltered.

"Just that?" He repeated her words. "What else do you need?"

"Well, it's not like you killed someone, is it?"

He stilled. "I didn't kill him, if that's what you mean. But I was a soldier for most of my adult life, so drop those rose-colored glasses you watch me through. I've killed many people. I believe most of them deserved it."

"Most of them?" she asked, cocking her eyebrow.

"Some shot at me before I could confirm their backgrounds, so the jury's still out."

That seemed sufficient to her. "Fair enough."

Jack had never cared two shits what other people thought of him, but for some reason, he needed to explain himself to Elle. "The army offered me the opportunity to leave the hellhole where I grew up. Gave me a profession, a roof over my head. Food. A sense of purpose. Not to mention more salary than I needed, which allowed me to take care of Ronnie. Most of our operations were top secret, but I always believed we were working to keep people safe. One mission went FUBAR and my superior cracked under pressure." It was obey orders and see every man in his unit die, or take charge.

"So you kicked his ass."

"After the fact, yes. I never suffer fools gladly." Much less ones that send others to die to cover their own ass. Getting kicked out of the military while that useless piece of shit retained his position had made a huge dent in his belief of the greater good. Nowadays he preferred to choose his causes.

"That must not have won you many friends," she murmured.

"No, it didn't, but it showed me who had my back. James, for example." Jack had been injured, not up to fighting it out if push came to shove, when he started disobeying orders and improvising. James had stood by his side come hell or high water. Up until then, they had not been the greatest of friends, both being the alpha type.

"Ah, now I get it. That's why he can do with you what he wants."

"He doesn't do with me what he wants," he grumbled, not sounding that convincing, even to himself.

"Right. If you're not in the military, then…" Elle asked, interrupting his thoughts.

"You know what a mercenary is?" A private security contractor sounded better. Less…bloody. But he didn't feel like dressing it up for her. Let her start running away from him. It would be doing them a favor, seeing as he was unable to do it.

He'd moved from spec ops to black ops. The government used private contractors for that, and the agency didn't seem to have issues hiring people with tattered backgrounds as long as they got the job done. On the plus side, when he fought for money, priorities changed and he took the jobs he wanted. And obeying orders from superiors was relative, especially when working alone.

"You are a mercenary?" she asked, her eyes round.

"Yes." He'd been one for several years.

"I thought the government didn't hire mercenaries."

"For military operations outside the US they do." They just weren't called mercenaries; they were called private security contractors. Some of them were on a military contract; others were State Department funded. They were not allowed to carry out combat operations, but they frequently did. Getting intel and results was a nasty, ugly business and the government didn't like its men getting their hands dirty. At least not the men who could be linked back to them.

"So that's what a free agent means," she pondered, taking it all in stride.

"I sell my services to the highest bidder." A war whore, was how someone had put it.

She had the balls to snort. "No, you don't."

"You just said you knew nothing about me." And now she was defending him? After he confessed to killing people and being a mercenary? No self-preservation skills on her whatsoever.

"I don't know the particulars, true, but you are not a slime ball. I've met my share of those. You have your code and you're an overbearing Neanderthal, yet in your world money doesn't trump morals. Manners, on the other hand, don't rank that high either."

Jack froze for a second and burst into laughter.

She was right again. He carefully chose the assignments he took. He had more money than he could spend in a lifetime, more than Ronnie could spend either. And manners meant shit to him.

"Why did you stop writing to me?" he blurted out before he could stop himself. "After I came back." Once he'd resurfaced, he hadn't gotten a single message from her.

Her smile was all-knowing. "Aw, don't tell me you missed my e-mails?"

He didn't answer. "Since we're on the subject, why did you write to me at all?"

"You were gone and I thought you could use some sort of connection."

"Now the truth?"

She laughed. "All right. I knew my e-mails would piss you off enough to want to come back in one piece and spank me."

That sounded more like his Elle.

"Then you dropped by for Max's wedding and you looked

so…gone, I realized it was going to take more than a few e-mails to get you back in one piece. So I stepped up the pace."

"A few e-mails? By that point I'd gotten well over a hundred." After that, one popped into his inbox every single day. The constant flow, ironically enough, had kept him sane.

She snuggled against him, leaned her head on his chest and shrugged. "As I said, a few. What were you doing?"

"Trying to shoot down Exxum's extracurricular business. We dismantled some of his infrastructure, but he got away. Why did you stop writing to me, pet?" he insisted after a long pause.

"You came back."

"I didn't spank you."

He couldn't see her face, but he felt her smile. "I'm sure you'll try."

The hectic day had taken its toll, and in spite of everything, she soon began to relax and sound drowsy. "What do you think is Maldonado doing in Boston with Exxum?"

He had no clue, but if Maldonado had known about Elle, they would have never made it out of there as easily as they did.

"You called her 'sweetheart,'" Elle whispered.

"What?"

"Marissa. The woman at the fund-raiser. The one you so shamelessly flirted with. You called her 'sweetheart.'"

He circled her in his arms. "'Sweetheart' means nothing to me. It's not personal. I call all of them 'sweetheart'. Much easier than remembering the names of insubstantial and inconsequential women Alex flirts with."

Elle snorted. "Because 'pet' is so personal."

"Elle Cooper, twenty-eight. Loves chocolate and cheesy music. Smart-ass. Works hard, plays harder. Makes me laugh and hard and angry, all at the same time. Elle fucking Cooper, my pet, the bane of my existence." He took her chin and forced her to look at him. "Pet is very personal. Pet means a hell of a lot to me."

"Watch it. You keep talking like this, I'm going to get attached to you and start believing I do mean something to you."

He didn't answer. What could he say? That she meant the world to him and that regardless of that he was going to leave her?

"Go to sleep," he finally said releasing her chin and hugging her tighter.

"I can't stay here forever. You know that, right?"

No shit. She would implode there, in matter of days. Sooner probably. Elle wasn't the yoga, meditation type. She needed action. He had nothing against keeping her naked in his bed, but they were bound to get hungry and he had shit to attend to.

"Don't worry, I'll come up with a plan."

She harrumphed, but she was obviously too tired to fight him so she kept quiet. Better. Now wasn't the moment to tell her he was going to stash her some place safe while he went after Maldonado.

That they had been allowed to leave the fund-raiser was proof that he didn't know yet, but playing at pretending she could continue with her life was over. And so was his cover as Alex Ayala. Although God knew no law enforcement person in his right mind would have let a witness walk around freely, much less take her to the wolf's den.

Be as it might, Jack was running out of time. He needed to act fast.

"Do you have cleaning supplies here?" she asked, half asleep.

Her question caught him off guard. "Just the basics. Why?"

"Come up with that plan of yours. Fast."

"What?" he asked, not understanding, but she was already under.

CHAPTER FIFTEEN

Jack watched as Elle feverishly swept the porch. She'd started imploding faster than he'd guessed. They'd been at the cabin for a day and she'd already dusted the whole place, three times, cleaned the windows, with vinegar because apparently he didn't have anything effective enough, and dismantled the kitchen to scrub every corner and put it back together. She was running in circles, searching for things to do and ways to keep busy.

Crossing his arms over his chest, he leaned on the doorjamb. Man, she was worse off than he'd thought. He wouldn't be surprised if she started pulling weeds out of the forest. With her determination, she could make a real dent in deforesting the whole state in no time at all.

She must have been reading his mind, or he was broadcasting his thoughts, because she lifted her gaze to him and opened her cute little mouth, ready to give him attitude, when her eyes strayed to the right. She pointed toward the shed with the broomstick.

"Do we have chopped wood?" He nodded but he could have saved himself the effort because she ignored him. "I'll chop some."

"Be my guest."

That would exhaust her faster than sweeping the floors, he hoped.

His phone beeped. A message from Mullen. Damn, the bodyguard and the niece had been found dead. Execution style. Jack had been counting on them for Mullen to build the case. And apparently so had Mullen, because the device started shaking with an incoming call from the agent. Now that that last hope was gone, he was going to turn his attention to Elle.

Pick up, asshole. We need to talk about how to proceed. Bring her in. We need her.

He closed the text. Fuck it. He was not going to let Mullen use Elle.

The angry tone of the phone started again, but he disconnected it. Elle scrutinized him with fathomless black eyes. "Mullen?"

He nodded grudgingly. "He wants me to bring you in."

"And?"

"Not going to happen."

"Do you think we could share that phone?" she asked, picking up a log. "I need access to the Internet to check my e-mails. I did have a life before you forcibly nominated me for next season of *Survivor.*"

"Your life can wait."

"What about Rosita's? I don't want Tate—"

"Rosita's is fine. Tim and Paige have everything under control. James has Tate under control."

Elle snorted. "Momzilla under control?"

"You underestimate James and his persuasive powers."

She pondered for a sec. "You might be right." Then she smiled sweetly at him and batted her eyelashes. "By the way, sweetie…"

"You're so beautiful. Even while plotting."

She even managed to look affronted. So cute. "What do you mean 'plotting'?"

"It's in those gorgeously manipulative eyes, pet."

"In two days there's this event—"

"No."

"It's *El Baile de los Diablos.* They perform—"

"Absolutely not," he interrupted her again. He remembered seeing that pic on the wall of fame at Rosita's, the one of her and Jonah dressed like devils, laughing, holding lit pitchforks at some kind of street event.

"But—"

"Fuck no."

She pressed her lips into a thin line, chagrined. "You understand I have an ax and that this high-handed behavior of yours can get you in trouble?"

"I'll risk it. Besides, if you chop me into pieces, you'll never find your way out of here."

She struck the wood, splinters flying all over. "Unless I call for help."

"And how would you explain my untimely demise? Twenty-five to life is a long time."

Her snort sounded insultingly derisive. "I would go free, believe me. Anyone that knows you would agree with me that offing you was self-defense."

She swung the ax again and more pieces of wood went flying.

No doubt this was going to tire her fast. The question was, was that going to happen before or after losing a couple of fingers?

"We have enough wood," he said after several near misses, and grabbing her by the hand, dragged her inside. "Let's make dinner."

She wrinkled her nose. "Not hungry."

"I'll cook. No MREs."

That seemed to spike her interest. "What exactly will you cook? The kitchen is spotless now. You going to hunt? Because you need to skin the poor devil before bringing it into the cabin. Not that I will eat that. I prefer my meat cut and in vacuum-sealed trays. The fewer similarities with the gruesome reality, the better."

"The kitchen was already spotless, pet. And no hunting." The way she was moving around like a headless chicken, catching anything would be impossible. "Spaghetti carbonara. Sterile enough? It's Italian traditional cuisine."

"It's not traditional Italian," she grumbled, following him to the kitchen. "It was invented during the Second World War. American soldiers stationed in Italy had bacon and eggs as rations, so the Italians came up with that recipe to use those ingredients."

"Your Italian teacher told you that?" At least he was teaching her more than swear words.

She shook her head. "My brother did."

At that, her face changed and went somber. "Tell me about your brother."

"Great guy. Died. End of story." He would have wanted to poke, but she did a total one-eighty. "Not sure how this mercenary shit works, but shouldn't you get paid enough to have a kick-ass cabin with all the amenities in the world?"

"Don't need them. This place is a getaway. Being connected is not getting away."

"Neither is having to relieve yourself in the forest," she

countered and pointed at the supplies he was getting from the pantry. "Or having to put dehydrated egg yolks in the carbonara. I don't dare to speculate what you're using for bacon."

"It's edible and tastes like bacon. Good enough?" She didn't look too convinced. "Besides, it provides all necessary nutrients."

"As far as I'm concerned, there's only two necessary nutrients: chocolate and gelato."

Man, she was worse than a kid.

"Oh, and pasta," she added.

"Well, two out of three isn't bad."

"Two out of three?" she asked, her eyes already shiny with excitement. "Is there sugar here somewhere?"

"Those are empty calories. Useless." He rummaged in his bag and put several protein bars on the table. "These are better and they taste like chocolate."

She opened one, took a whiff, and barked out a laugh. "Sure. In what universe, Borg?"

"Go a couple of days without sugar. This will taste fantastic."

She wrinkled her cute little nose and didn't even dignify that with an answer.

He worked fast and soon dinner was ready. Elle stayed with him during the whole process, chattering nonstop about Rosita's and her job at the airport. He loved to hear her talk. He would love it even better if she would tell him why she couldn't stay still. Why she couldn't stand the silence. Why she couldn't stop talking.

"Let's go to the sofa. I'm sick and tired of the hard benches," Elle said.

The sofa table was too small and low to eat from, so she tucked her legs under her ass and, holding the plate with one hand, dug in right away. Jack sat beside her and, putting his boots over the raggedy table, followed suit.

"Not bad," she said. "I'm impressed."

"Told you. Ronnie's favorite food while growing up."

"You cooked for her?"

He nodded. "We lived off pasta for years. We prepared *spaghetti a la putanesca* all the time."

"So you like slut spaghetti."

Jack laughed. "Slut spaghetti? Some Italian you speak."

"Sounds much better than *pasta a la putanesca*," she retorted, wrinkling her nose.

True. "How come you speak Italian?"

"How come you speak Spanish?" she said in answer.

They stared at each other, defiantly, neither one backing down.

"Yeah, I figured as much," she said finally, her smile resigned. But with a sigh she added, "Jonah was the only one in our family who spoke Italian. With him gone I took it upon myself to make sure that part of our heritage wouldn't get lost."

Her offering tugged at his heart. "He would be damn impressed by the list of insults you know."

"Oh, he was worse, I can assure you," she said with a giggle.

She'd shared, without demanding anything in return, so he gave in. "We lived in the projects. Up until I started school, I thought Spanish was the official language of this country. All our neighbors spoke it and my mother wasn't around much. Whenever she was, talking wasn't one of her priorities. There was this old lady next door, Celia. I learned to talk thanks to her, actually." And to cook and read and write. Anything worth knowing he'd learned from Celia.

"Where's your mother now? Is she…?"

"Dead? Nope. The bitch found Jesus and now goes around speaking in bumper stickers and pretending to be holier-than-thou, turning up her nose at everyone and claiming that God has forgiven her so no one has the right to judge her. Apparently she wasn't at fault because she was sick, and she has nothing to feel ashamed of or apologize for. All her debts are settled."

"Wow. Talk about living in an alternate reality."

Jack let out a dry chuckle. "Tell me about it. She even twisted the Twelve Steps into her liking. Transforming them into Twelve Steps on how to let you off the hook after ruining everybody's life. All she had to do was repent and voilà, the slate is wiped clean and she never broke a plate." Let alone tortured her kids. That her kids didn't want to have anything to do with her was chalked up to Jack and Ronnie's lack of empathy and Christian heart, not to the fact that she'd come back guns blazing, patronizing them, and had dared to question Jack's way of raising Ronnie, who had gone ballistic.

"Do you have any contact?"

Jack shook his head. "Last reunion didn't go too smooth. I would never let her close to the people I loved, but I don't hold a grudge. Ronnie does. And she's very vocal about it."

"What about begging for forgiveness instead of demanding it?" Ronnie had asked their mother.

"The Almighty has already forgiven me."

Ronnie had snorted. *"The Almighty was not the one beaten up and burned and abused."* Then she'd pointed at Jack. *"He's the one you need to beg on your knees for his pardon."*

It had gone south pretty fast from there. Their mother had claimed her conscience was clear for whenever God called her by his side or some preachy shit like that. At that point Jack hadn't been paying too much attention, busy as he'd been keeping Ronnie away from her.

"What makes you think you'll end up by God's side?" Ronnie had sneered as Jack had dragged her away. *"I see you in a much hotter place. Don't forget the bikini."*

Elle seemed to notice he didn't want to talk about that and spared him. "What does your sister think of your mercenary career?"

"What do you think? She runs a biker bar when I specifically ordered her to open a bakery. When she got her driver's license, I bought her a cute, small, sensible car. When I came back from an assignment, she had tricked it out, and nowadays she needs a ladder to get in. In her spare time she drives monster trucks and likes to compete in Monster Jam."

"What do I think?" she repeated, studying him. "I think she doesn't know."

Close enough.

They ate in silence, watching the fire crackle, until Elle addressed him. "Say, would IKEA deliver up here if we draw them a map?"

He couldn't refrain from barking out a laugh. "You're nuts."

She reached for him, swept the corner of his lower lip with her finger, and then licked the bit of cheese from it. "Yeah, yeah, you'll miss me when I'm gone. You'll see. Who will make you laugh?"

His chest tightened. Yes, he was going to miss her. Terribly. That realization was devastating.

* * * *

Paige smiled at the guy approaching the register at Rosita's. He was cute. Nordic features. Tan skin. Blond hair almost bleached white from the sun. Not from spring in Boston, that was for sure. A bit too clean-cut for her taste, too little metal on him, but extremely cute nevertheless.

He'd gotten a drink and had been sitting at a table by the wall of fame, staring at the pictures for a long while now.

Rosita's was a family restaurant. Paige has been working there for well over a year and she could proudly say she knew all their patrons. The Viking stranger, she hadn't seen before. She would have remembered. Her girlie parts would have remembered.

"Could I have another?" he asked, placing the wineglass on the counter and sitting on the bar stool.

She nodded. "I'll bring it to your table."

"Nah, I'd rather stay here with you if you don't mind," he said sheepishly. "I got stood up. A blind date I was forced into by my mother. My pride can't stand being at that table anymore."

Paige laughed at his resigned grimace.

"That'll teach me to come visit my parents," he continued. "Or succumb to their plotting. I'm Nick."

"Paige," she introduced herself, refilling his glass.

"Nice to meet you, Paige. You guys are busy for a regular weekday," he said motioning to the patrons dining. "This is the first family restaurant I've seen with bouncers."

Paige giggled, glancing at Sean and Zack, James's colleagues. "They are not bouncers. They are friends of the owners."

She wasn't sure what had happened, but James had told them yesterday Elle was going to be away for a while. Tate wasn't up for taking on the restaurant, so Paige, Tim, and James were it. Which suited her just fine. She loved working there; she had no problem stepping up to the plate.

Since then, James had been coming in at opening and staying around until Zack or Sean or both would arrive and he could go home to Tate and their son. Cole and Max were constantly dropping by too.

"Good. I've not been to Boston for some time. Wasn't sure if this had turned into gang territory while I was away."

Thank God he hadn't come yesterday. James had turned up with some dude with his face tattooed, Maori style, and with two-hundred-forty-pound, heavily tattooed Mike Haddican.

"Where have you been?" she asked Nick.

"Officially? Working on a sea platform. Unofficially? Escaping my parents. But really, can you blame me?"

Nick was funny. Damn refreshing to meet someone who wasn't intimidated by her looks.

"Love the pictures. You took them?" he asked after a while of chitchatting.

"One of the owners did. Elle Cooper," she replied pointing at a photo with Elle in it.

"Some are shocking. Others are dead scary," he said.

"I know, right?"

"This could be a great venue for my parents' wedding anniversary. Who should I talk to about organizing that? Oh and I'd definitely want this Elle to take the pictures. And to customize them like this one," he added nodding at the shot of James's wedding with Jack's face covered in black. "I have several relatives I don't like."

Paige laughed. "She's taking some time off but I'm sure we can accommodate your parents' party."

"When is she getting back? Their wedding anniversary is in two weeks."

"I don't think she'll make it."

"Such a pity. But I'm looking forward to seeing the new pictures she'll add when she gets back. She seems to keep busy."

Yes, she did. There was something about Elle that called out to people. She'd been away from the restaurant for just a couple of days and almost every diner had asked about her.

He was about to say something, but a patron interrupted and they got sidetracked.

"Would you let me buy you a drink after your shift ends?" he asked once they were alone again.

"So I'm your backup date. Not too fond of playing second chair."

He smirked and threw a glance to the table he'd been sitting at. "You're first chair, honey."

"I don't know," she faltered, finding herself touching her choke collar. She was not in the habit of picking up dates at Rosita's.

His smile was big and unthreatening. "Come on. We could go dancing. What do you say, you in?"

* * * *

Elle was sick and tired of staring at the ceiling.

Soundly asleep, Jack had his arm over her stomach, and she tried disentangling herself without disturbing him. She'd moved maybe an inch when suddenly a powerful leg trapped her.

"Where are you going?"

"Can't sleep. I'm going to the living room for a sec."

He didn't loosen his embrace. "What's wrong?"

"Nothing's wrong. Can I borrow your phone? I swear I won't call anyone. I'll just check my messages."

The silence was deafening. When he finally spoke, his tone was full of disapproval. "That's what you did with your other lovers? Did you leave Kai in your bed and go to your computer to write to me if he didn't exhaust you? And did he let you? Because I won't make that mistake. You're in my bed, you're not leaving it. You'll be too exhausted to even think about it, much less to write to some other guy."

Kai had never been in her bed, but she didn't feel inclined to appease Jack, not while he was back at pretending to be master of the universe. "Fine. Let's fuck. Exhaust me."

"Not yet. I asked what was wrong. I expect an answer."

"Can't sleep. It's not a crime, last time I checked. Oh wait, maybe on Planet Cyborg it is, used as you are to barking orders and being obeyed. But guess what? I'm not one of your soldiers."

She was picking a fight, she knew. If he wouldn't distract her by fucking, they could have a verbal sparring match, right?

He didn't fall for it.

"Stop trying to piss me off and talk to me."

She couldn't contain the snort. "I've been talking all day long. You? Not so much."

"You talk all the time, pet, but you say nothing. It's all babble. Inconsequential. Filler, just to cover up you're hurting inside. I might not talk much, but when I do it's to the point, and, unlike you, I actually say something."

The asshole. She was going to answer but he turned her in his arms and pressed on, his eyes intense on hers. Scrutinizing.

"Can't you stop this crazy life of yours, just for a second, and grieve? Cry? Mourn? You do thousand things a day, balls to the wall, take on everyone's issues and projects until you drop dead of exhaustion into bed. And don't give me bullshit. I know you do. When you don't, you can't sleep. How fucking long are you going to pretend? You can't bury this forever."

She didn't like where this was heading, not at all. "What the hell are you talking about? I do stuff, true, like most people with a minimum of a social life, present hermits notwithstanding. I'm not burying anything."

"Sure, that's why you look like you're on crack all day long, rushing from one place to another. Why you can't sit still. You need to stop running and face reality," he stated.

"That's what I was doing until you waltzed into my life and fucking kidnapped me," she yelled, trying to wrench away. He didn't even move a quarter of an inch.

"Bullshit. You might not physically run out of Boston, showing up every day at Rosita's and being there for your sister, but you're going through the motions, spacing out nonstop. Your body is present; your head and heart aren't. You're always occupying yourself with something not to think or feel."

She swallowed down the intense need to cry. It infuriated that he could see through her so easily. The first year after her dad and brother had died, she'd run. Disappeared for weeks at a time. Traveled to Florida with her mom and spaced out however she could. Then she'd come back to Boston and manned up. Buried all that shit and had gotten on with her life. With Rosita's. With whatever was needed. What else could she do? If she let down the walls she'd erected and allowed herself to feel, she'd get swept away by the flood and might never resurface again.

Then his tone softened. "You have to mourn your dad and your brother, pet. This isn't the way to do it."

"Let me go. I don't want to talk about this." She had better things to do than lying there, visiting memory lane.

"Tough shit. You aren't going anywhere."

"And I don't cry. It's useless. Pointless. It takes too long to put yourself together. Much longer than it takes to fall apart. I can't afford the time or the luxury. I'm too busy."

He snorted, not a speck of humor in his voice. "'Life is short. Break the rules. Forgive quickly. Love slowly'. You surround yourself with all those inspirational quotes but you do the opposite. You kiss fast, never forgive yourself, and never let yourself forget."

"Life is short, so I live fast," she retorted. "And I do break the rules."

"You don't live at all, pet. You exist. And you hide. You

pretend to be careless and free, when in reality you're chained down. Trapped. And you are your own jailer. What are you avoiding thinking about? What, too tough for the fragile little princess to face reality?"

"You know nothing about me," she said, gritting her teeth, which, by the way he was able to press all her buttons, was a big fat lie.

"Why do you stay at your parents' house?" he insisted. "Answer me."

"It's my penance," she yelled, tears finally escaping. "You happy now? It's my penance for killing them! I'm not allowed to forget it." Not even for a second.

This was the first time she'd said those words out loud and no matter how hard she tried not to break down, she couldn't control the waterfall.

Jack didn't even flinch. "You didn't kill your father and brother. A drunk driver did. I read the police report."

"They were there because of me. It was my night to close, but I was too busy partying. My car was in the shop, so I took Dad's and Jonah drove him home. They were not supposed to be anywhere near that intersection. If it wasn't for me, Dad would have been home, and Jonah would have been upstairs cuddled with Emma, his fiancée, pregnant with their unborn baby. And as if that wasn't bad enough, I couldn't be bothered to pick up the phone when Tate and Mom called. Too busy having fun and drinking and whatever the fuck I was doing to rush to the hospital to say good-bye to my dying brother." By the time she did answer, it was too late. "So now I live in the house as a constant reminder and do everything that Jonah used to do." It was the least she could do to right her wrongs. Not that she was doing enough. There would never be enough.

"So that's why Aston Biggs—"

"That asshole took something from Cecilia that she can never have back. He stole her last words to her son. He deserves all the shit I'm dishing on him. All my wrath."

"But that wrath is ultimately directed to yourself, not to him."

As it should be. She couldn't even blame somebody else for not making it to the hospital on time. It had been her. All her.

She wiped her eyes furiously. "Then I took off and dumped everything on Tate, who almost died while I was partying in San

Francisco and Florida, avoiding setting foot in Rosita's." Because being guilty of her dad's and older brother's deaths wasn't bad enough to begin with.

The grandmas at Eternal Sun were wrong. She wasn't golden; she was a fake.

"You did the best you could at the moment. You had to run to survive, but you're stronger now. You don't have to. You can deal with their deaths."

"I'm not so sure," she whispered. It hurt so badly every time she thought about that night. She hated being alone with her mind. Couldn't stand it, actually.

"Give it time."

Right. "Time doesn't heal a damn thing."

"Yes, it does," he insisted. "You're better. You're not running anymore."

"Duh, because you're holding me down."

"And I will keep doing it until you stop wanting to run."

She lifted her eyes to him. "You won't be always here, remember? This is temporary. It comes with a fast-approaching expiration date."

He held her gaze and didn't correct her. For some reason that made her even sadder.

"So you better get over this running-away shit fast. Besides, it doesn't help a fuck. Tried that."

"You also killed half your family?"

He gave her a firm shake. "No, and neither did you, pet. The drunk driver did. You need to forgive yourself."

Too bad she didn't know how to do that.

"So what did you have to run away from?" she asked changing the subject.

Jack gave her an are-you-serious look, and for a second she felt ashamed of her mocking tone. As if the marks all over his body weren't explanatory enough. "Lots of shit went down while in the military, and then later on. On the sleepless nights, we would meet at a diner."

"To talk feelings?"

He snorted. "Fuck no. Sometimes we didn't even talk at all. We sat there, drinking coffee, until dawn. But it helped. You learn to forgive yourself and move forward. You face your fears head on, and the pain. You don't bury them. Cry as much as you have to and yell and get mad at the injustice of it all. Get rid of that anger and despair so that the good memories can take center stage again."

She looked at him and nodded. She would try.

"I'm sure neither your dad nor your brother would have changed places with you."

True. She would give anything, her life included, to have them back, but didn't doubt for a second they wouldn't let her.

Maybe it was the crackling of the fire, or the rhythmic movement of Jack's chest, or the fact that for the first time in two years she was talking about Jonah and her dad, but she found herself relaxing, her mind not racing every time there was silence.

"So now you do all the stuff Jonah used to do."

"Yes."

"The flash mob?" he asked.

"Technically, that was Emma's thing. She dragged Jonah into it, but he sure as hell enjoyed it."

"And the twerking?" His tone was laced with amusement.

She laughed softly, her face on his chest. "Oh, that's all me, baby."

They lay there for a long while, her sprawled over him, listening to his heart, him petting her hair. Both in silence.

"Jack?"

"Mmm?"

"What do you mean you read the police report?"

"Of course I did. That's the sensible thing to do when new people come into your life. Have them investigated."

"You had me investigated?"

He assented. "Thoroughly."

"And?"

"It was as I suspected. All trouble."

"I'm glad," she mumbled, little by little falling asleep.

When she woke up, dawn lit the sky. She lifted her head and found Jack looking at her. After her hissy fit and her crying jag he hadn't let go of her, holding her tight. And funny enough, she didn't feel trapped. She felt great. Lighter than she had in years, even before the accident that truncated everyone's lives.

"I fell asleep."

A smile flashed on his face, softening his otherwise harsh lines. "You did."

Man, her Borg was so handsome with that do-not-fuck-with-me vibe. He was the hardest man she'd ever met, and not only in the physical sense. Jack was the most uncompromising, the most infuriating, and yet there was something about him that soothed her. In spite of all his lord-of-the-manor comments and behavior, he was steady as a rock.

"Thank you," she whispered.

He tucked her hair behind her ear. "This Diablos gathering you want to attend, that's something you used to do with Jonah, right?"

She nodded. "It was our thing, although the last year I bailed on him. Too busy keeping bad company."

He studied her for a long moment and then asked, "How important is it to you?"

* * * *

Elle looked at him, her beautiful eyes shimmering. "Very important, Jack."

"I understand you wanting to honor your brother, but getting killed is not the way, pet. If you need to honor his memory, I'm down with it, but do it by living to the fullest, enjoying every second, not spacing out and going through the motions on automatic. Spacing out delays the pain, but it also delays life and all its joys. Not to mention Maldonado is in Boston."

"Yes, but at a fund-raiser," she insisted. "He doesn't know about me. All of us wear glasses and scarfs, and with the costumes, it's virtually impossible to distinguish who's who. Please—"

He placed a finger over her lips, silencing her. "I'll make you a deal, pet."

"Name it. No sex, though. I don't exchange sex for favors."

"Me neither. I'll get the sex from you anyway." She narrowed her eyes at him but he pushed on. "I'll let you attend the Diablos parade. Afterward, you'll stay where I put you, quietly and without complaint, while I go take care of this Maldonado situation."

"Where exactly do you intend to put me?"

"Someplace safe. You won't give them any trouble and you will wait for me to come fetch you. Agree?"

"Your language is so politically incorrect I don't know where to start. You'll let me? Then come to fetch me?"

He ignored her remarks. Political correctness had never been one of his priorities. "Do we have a deal?"

"You know, in spite of the gruff package, you're sweet," she said cupping his face.

"I'm many things, pet. Sweet is not one of them. Now answer, do we have a deal?"

She saluted him. "Sir, yes, sir."

Smart-ass.

"How do you intend to take care of the situation?"

The only way he could at this point. Taking Maldonado out. Before Elle, bringing the drug lord to justice and making a dent in the trade and the violence of the cartels had been his goal; now that wasn't an option. Elle was his priority and Maldonado was a threat to her as long as he was alive. But he didn't say anything. And she must be starting to know him, because she didn't push it.

"Where does this Baile de Diablos take place?"

"Little Italy. Lots of people. It looks chaotic from the outside, but it's all synchronized."

He was so going to regret this. "Where's your outfit?" She was not getting even a mile close to that event without her gear on to disguise her.

"Rosita's."

"El Baile de Diablos; that's not Italian." That was Spanish for the dance of the devils.

"Probably because it isn't strictly an Italian tradition," Elle admitted sheepishly.

"What?"

"Nowadays it's most spread out over the Mediterranean coast of Spain, in Catalonia to be more precise. Very old tradition dating to Roman times. And you know anything Roman is basically Italian, right? So we sort of claimed it. Besides, some of the founding members of the group did their research and there's some evidence of this tradition in Italy. It just didn't survive to Modern times. And Chinatown was getting ahead with their New Year celebrations and their dragons. Little Italy needed an edge and dancing devils shooting fireworks, having fun and being irreverent is so Italian."

Jack barked out a laugh. Thank God these people didn't decide running in front of the bulls, which the Bowens were so fond of doing in Pamplona, was also a Roman tradition or they would claim it for themselves too and bring it to Little Italy.

"Why didn't you change the name?"

"No need. Spanish language evolved from Latin, and Latin was the language of the Roman Empire. And anything Roman—"

"Is basically Italian," Jack finished with Elle in unison. "You're nuts."

"We keep busy."

"You cold?" he asked, noticing her shivers.

"A bit."

"Come on, let's move closer to the fireplace. Hold on to the blankets," he said hauling her up and taking the whole bundle to the next room and leaving it on the rug.

He turned to stoke the fire and then felt her light touch on his back.

"A fallen angel."

Fallen angel. Demon. Same thing.

"And the cock piercing?" she asked as he lay down beside her. "Does it have some hidden spy capabilities? A cyanide tablet inside one of the balls?"

He chuckled. "Standard issue. No cyanide tablets."

"You lost a bet, then?"

Like he would ever risk his cock in a bet. "Have you ever heard that saying that one guy has one brain, two guys have half, and so on? It's true. The exponential loss of brain cells the more males you get together is a fact. The younger the men, the worse it gets. If you add alcohol in the mix, the neural degeneration snowballs."

She burst into laughter.

"The rule that no-body alterations while inebriated? Not that strict, I'm afraid. My cock is the living proof of it."

All things considered, they had been lucky they didn't get any disease and their cocks hadn't fallen into pieces, because next day they couldn't even remember where they got the piercings done. First and last time he'd ever blacked out.

"Don't tell me Kai is the one who pierced you. Is that the reason why you dislike him so much?"

He shook his head, sobering up. "I dislike him because he had you in his bed."

She stared at him for what it felt like an eternity. "He didn't."

Relief at her statement flooded him. "What about your tattoos?"

"Constellations," she said. "Orion the Great Hunter chasing the

Pleiades, the seven sisters, daughters of the Titan Atlas. On the other leg Scorpio, sent by Artemis, forever chasing Orion."

Orion, the eternal hunter, being eternally hunted. Very fitting.

"Funny description for an astronomer," he said caressing her thigh.

She shrugged. "I could call the Pleiades M45, an open star cluster with middle-aged hot B-type stars in quadrant NQ1, but doesn't have the same ring. Humans always looked at the skies to find their own place. It doesn't hurt to dress it up, right?"

She straddled him and brushed her lips over him. "I think I'm going to take your advice and start to work through the inspirational sentences. Love slowly."

He couldn't stop the chuckle. Of course she would choose to start making a dent in that during the most painful moment for him.

She was not rushing it, caressing him. Taking her time. Then she moved downward and teased his nipples.

"You need to be careful at the Diablos, pet. I can't call Mullen or any backup without risking them trying to get you away from me. You have to do as I say."

She stopped nuzzling his chest and lifted her eyes to him. Her nod surprised him. Then she proceeded to trace his scars.

"What are you doing?"

"Soothing you."

Jack stilled at her words. "I don't need soothing." No one took care of him, ever. He took care of himself.

She ignored him and touched the scars from the cigarette burns with trembling fingers. "Of all the scars, these small ones are the most horrific. No wonder you—"

"What? Turned out to be such a bastard?"

"No. No wonder you are as hard as you are."

"That's on me, pet. What I became. Can't stand losers blaming their childhood and others for their choices and how their lives ended up. They need to grow the fuck up, take responsibility, and own their shit. Make something of themselves."

"Like you did."

"I had motivation. A child to look after."

She cupped his face and looked at him for a long second, the softness in her gaze killing him. "You know, I totally strayed this time. No asshole here."

Tension stiffened his body. "Don't go there, pet. And don't get illusions. I am an asshole."

She snorted and rolled her eyes. "No, you are not."

He felt naked. So fucking naked. He ached for her, for something he had no name for. Every time he touched her, this weight pressed at his chest, because there was not only lust between them; there was something else too. Something bright and warm and precious, glowing more and more with every passing moment. "Do you need me to prove it? Because hey, glad to," he said, standing up. He had to break this intimacy.

Before she could react, he'd hauled her up, taken her hands in one of his, tied her up, and then hooked the ropes to the O-ring in the ceiling.

"That's all you got?" she asked, lifting her chin, defiantly.

Her eyes were shining, her breath coming out in short pants, but she stood proudly.

He grabbed a cloth and blindfolded her.

She stood taller. Prouder. The shadows of the fire reflecting on her body, playing off all the swells and hollows. All her luscious curves. "You don't scare me, so don't even bother with all this macho tripping and power games."

"This is not a game," he said, roughly opening her legs.

"You need to prove you're an asshole? Go ahead, but you don't fool me; you're just deluding yourself. And throwing a tantrum while you're at it."

He walked around her, stopping at her back, and ran a finger from her neck, along her spine, down to her ass, and closed in to whisper in her ear. "Keep talking and you'll earn a ball gag."

She snorted. "Bring it on. You'll have to take it off at some time, won't you?"

"I don't know. Will I?"

"You love my mouth." True. "And my smart-ass remarks." True again. "You keep me gagged, you won't get either."

"You are defenseless. I could take whatever I wanted from you."

"Again with the useless intimidation. Yes, I am defenseless. I'm blindfolded and tied, but only because you're afraid of me. Really, just give it up. You wouldn't take anything that wasn't freely offered."

It floored him. Her confidence in him. How brave she was.

How fucking beautiful. Fire outside. Fire inside.

"Going for the ball gag," he warned, walking around and looking at her face.

"As you wish, but I think you'll want to hear me." She wrapped her legs around him, her hot, wet pussy encasing his cock.

He gripped her hair and pulled her head back, pressing himself against her core. "I say when. I say how."

"Sir, yes, sir. Would now be a good moment for you, sir?"

He'd had many women tied up for him. Not a single one had rocked his world the way Elle did it. Giving herself to him yet never losing her spunk.

"How badly do you want me?"

Her whole body stiffened as she tried to lift herself and force him to penetrate her. "Badly."

He hooked his elbows under her knees, breaking the grip she had on him. "Next time, I'll tie your legs too."

"Promises, promises," she said, a teasing smile on her face.

Uncomfortable with that level of intimacy, he surged balls-deep inside her, slamming against her full force, his mind almost blowing at the intense sensation.

She gasped, clamping around him and he froze, lifting his gaze to her. With the blindfold on, he couldn't read her eyes.

Before he could say anything, she pressed herself against him. "Don't stop. You surprised me, but I liked it. You didn't hurt me."

Jesus fucking Christ. She was perfect for him.

Slowly, he withdrew from her until his crown was just kissing her damp folds. Then, putting all his weight behind his thrust, he plunged to her depths. She cried out, throwing her head back and bowing her body, but not away from him. Toward him.

"More," she let out in a shudder. "Harder."

He could do nothing but oblige. Giving her more, watching, enthralled, as she took all of him until she exploded, her pussy squeezing him so tight he was a split second from coming.

He ground his pelvis over her throbbing clit and took off her blindfold. He needed to watch her, and needed her to watch him.

"You do it for me, pet," he said, trying to hold on to the last shred of control.

Her smirk was all sass as her inner muscles clamped around his erection. "I can tell."

"No. You don't get it. You really do it for me." At all levels.

"Really?" She stilled. "I thought you didn't like abrasive women."

"I don't, but I like you." Which was an understatement if there was ever one. He really, really, liked her. All of her. Even when she was being a pain in his ass and confrontational and giving him hell, which it was most of the time, he found himself with a smile on his lips. When she was being sweet to him and offering him her body, trusting him with it, it just blew his mind. And something else too, because every inch of her tugged at his heart.

She licked her dry lips. "And yet you are going to walk out on me once this situation with Maldonado is over."

"Yes, I will. It's exactly because I like you that I will leave."

She looked puzzled, then hurt, but she covered it fast. "You are going to miss out on a lot, Borg. And I'm not talking only about sex."

Vixen.

He didn't know how to answer to that, so he impaled her again, relishing her ragged moan. From that point on he lost control. He no longer could take the time to push in and out slowly. His rhythm increased, as did the intensity of his plunges. He needed to get deep inside her. Deeper than anybody had ever been. Deeper than anyone would ever be.

His cum was poised at the tip of his cock, ready to blow, his balls so fucking hard they were hurting, but he refused to come. He didn't want this to finish. He wanted to lose himself in her until he couldn't remember why it was such a bad idea to be together.

When Elle started coming again, all the choice was stripped from him. It was like the floodgates had opened and his own need rushed out, unstoppable. Undeniable. Holding himself flush against her, he climaxed, filling her with his seed. Then, before he finished, he took himself in hand and spilled the last cum on her pussy.

"That's the reason why I won't use condoms with you," he said when he could talk again, gliding his cock along her drenched folds. "I want my cum in and on you. I want you to know that as long as you are with me, you belong to me." And he wanted to see it too. He wanted to be able to remember it.

"Cum washes off, Borg. There are other more effective ways of getting a woman to belong to you. Like imprinting yourself in her soul. That doesn't wash off."

* * * *

Nico smiled at the girl behind the register and walked out of Rosita's, picking up his cell. Pretty little thing, this Paige. Dressed and made up for scaring kids during Halloween but pretty nevertheless. And smart. He'd spent the whole evening working her, which hadn't been a burden because she was great company, but he didn't make any headway. She had that sixth sense that nowadays was missing from so many people, the prickle at the neck warning about predators and danger. Nico could spot victims miles away. They moved and talked and behaved in a certain manner. Stank of fear. Like socialized animals that had lost their instincts and were at the mercy of others' whims.

Victims were easy prey; people like Paige weren't. They would put up a fight; it was in her eyes and the way her spine stood straight, radiating self-awareness and security. He'd done his homework before coming to Rosita's and had investigated her. He knew what that choke collar of hers hid. A girl wouldn't get a scar like that and live to tell the tale if she weren't a fighter. And whether she did it unconsciously or not, she'd sensed the danger and ultimately turned him down.

But the visit to the restaurant hadn't been fruitless. He'd learned a shitload of stuff.

Up until now, he hadn't been able to wrap his mind around what the hell Elle Cooper, a witness under federal protection, had been doing in the open at the fund-raiser. And it *had* been Elle Cooper; he'd seen the video footage of the security cameras to confirm it. As far as he'd been able to find out from his contacts in law enforcement, the name of the witness in the Maldonado case was kept secret, her location undisclosed. Not running around Boston attending social events with an alleged high-profile arms dealer. Unless the alleged high-profile arms dealer wasn't an arms dealer at all and she was there by mistake.

He sat in his car and pulled up the copy of the video footage he'd gotten from the security at the hotel, scrolling until he found what he was searching for. There, from the lobby camera, he could see the one with the short Mohawk, the same guy who was in pictures at Rosita's, going to the event in the other ballroom. A quick Internet search gave him the info he needed. It had been a private party thrown by Patricia Vaughan to welcome her great-grandchild into society. Elizabeth Vaughan Bowen.

Amazing how Elle had gotten Alex to agree to take her to that event. Huge hold she had on him. Judging by what Nico had dug up on social media, this chick was involved in a thousand things although he hadn't seen any picture of Alex on her profiles. The Bowens, though, were splattered all over them.

Now he just had to figure out where she was.

Where Elle Cooper wasn't, was at her place or at Rosita's, which was under surveillance. Too many military guys around for it to be a coincidence. It was not going to be possible to get to her as long as this bunch were on high alert. Not to mention Alex Ayala was with her. Nico had personally checked Ayala's background when Exxum had started dealing with him; after all, his job was to foresee the unexpected, and everything had added up. Except for the fact that high-profile career criminals did not protect federal witnesses.

Nico drove to Elle's neighborhood and parked several streets over. People were too nosy in that area.

Sneaking into the house was a piece of cake. There were door squealers but they had been dismantled.

He moved methodically through the house. It didn't look like they had run away or had taken anything with them. The fridge was full; suitcases were still in the closet. There were several bedrooms in the house, but only one seemed to have been used. So Alex, or whoever he was, was screwing this chick.

Elle's laptop didn't provide any big clues until he checked the e-mails. She'd deleted them, but apparently she didn't know enough about computers to erase them permanently, because he retrieved a rather big bunch of them, which confirmed Alex was a covert operative of some sort and totally in love with her. Any respectable agent with half a brain would have severed this relationship long ago. Deleted the e-mail account. Instead, Alex, or the "Borg," as Elle called him, had allowed this to continue. Which also explained how come Elle was roaming around instead of hiding in a hole.

On his way to the kitchen, he picked up the mail from the floor. Bills, catalogs, nothing worth his time, until he came upon a big, heavy envelope from a photography studio. He opened it and studied the pictures. They were from a christening. Cute kid. Then, in between the shots, he spotted a very interesting one. It was of Elle and Alex holding the baby, and the photographer had inserted a band of some sort on the bottom which read: *Me with my godparents.*

Godparents. How interesting. So Alex had been roped into being a godfather, which meant he'd had to sign his name. Catholics were funny that way. They loved bureaucracy.

When he made it to the kitchen, he noticed a calendar on the fridge door full of notes and appointments. Busy chick.

There was this upcoming event circled in red with lots of exclamation marks and hearts.

He might not know yet who Alex was or his whereabouts, but he had a pretty good hunch where he was going to be.

He grabbed his cell and pulled up his boss's details.

"You found her?" a voice greeted him.

"No, but I got something better."

CHAPTER SIXTEEN

Jack turned into the service area and parked near James's black pickup.

James stepped out of it, and so did Cole and Max. Shit, Jack knew where this was headed.

"Three of you to bring a duffel?" he asked as he approached.

James handed him the bag. "We're going with you."

"No, you are not."

"Try stopping us," Max answered with a deceptively easy smile. He felt Elle behind him.

"Hi, guys." She greeted each of them with a big hug.

"The part about you waiting in the truck?" Jack grumbled to her.

"Not changing in the back of your truck. And I need to see what a real chocolate bar tastes like." She smiled at him, her hand out. "Money, sweetie? Or does a kidnappee have to pay her own way too? I wouldn't mind if it wasn't for the fact that I don't have a penny with me. Next time you kidnap me make sure I have my purse."

Smart-ass.

Jack gave her a bill and watched as she sauntered away after taking the bag from him.

"Sweetie?" James asked, lifting his eyebrows.

Jack did his best to ignore him. "The more of us, the more conspicuous we are. If someone is watching, we'll be spotted."

"We know how to blend. This isn't our first rodeo," Cole said.

Jack looked at the three men in front of him. Blend? Yeah, right.

"Besides," Cole continued, "if someone is watching, you're better off with us around."

"Face it; you need eyes on her. You need backup. We are it," James stated. "Deal with it."

"This is too dangerous, for Elle and for you. You don't have to get involved."

The Bowens were an easy connection to Elle. And they were too visible. Anyone digging into her life would find them right away.

"We are already involved. How long do you think it will be until Maldonado figures out he can get to her through us? How long until he'll think of using Tate and Christy and Annie and the kids for leverage? We need her safe, and she's family."

"We are going, regardless," Cole added. "You know it's better if we are all on the same page than running in disconnected teams."

True. They would be more effective as a single unit.

"Where are the women?" Jack asked.

"They are at Annie's grandmother having a sleepover," James explained. "Kyra and Alexa joined them, which means Mike and Wata are there. They are as safe as it gets. So what's the plan?"

"From the security point of view, this event is a nightmare, so we get through it as fast as possible. In and out."

James studied him, a smirk on his face. "I never thought I'd see the day when a woman would lead you by your cock."

"She's not leading me by my cock. We have a deal."

"Since when do you need to make deals to get your way with women?"

Since the happiness of said woman mattered to him. But he kept his trap shut. James could read him well enough without all the explanations. "After this, she's going into hiding until this shit is resolved."

"You got her to agree to that?"

"We have a deal."

"You going into hiding too?" James handed everyone earbuds. Those were among James's latest toys.

Jack shook his head.

"Who's going to make sure she stays put if you aren't around?"

Cole asked. "Because we don't intimidate her in the slightest."

No shit. "I reached out to Kai. He will contact his family." Jack had thought about it long and hard. Because of their meeting at the fund-raiser, when Maldonado found out who Elle was he'd figure out that Alex Ayala didn't exist. Jack needed to stash Elle with someone that couldn't be traced back to him. So all his contacts were out. The Bowens and their resources too.

"Oh boy," James muttered.

Cole turned to his brother, confused. "What?"

"You know the global holding company Shinoda? The one whose assets in the US were frozen for a while but the FBI couldn't link it to the Yakuza? It's run by his family. And it's not linked to the Yakuza; it *is* the fucking Yakuza."

"Oh boy," Cole repeated James's words.

Max grimaced. "She'll lose all her fingers just in the first day."

"If Kai agrees to go into hiding with her to keep her company, she might be more accommodating," James offered, looking intently at Jack.

That was a possibility he couldn't even consider without seeing red. But her security was at risk and Kai and his people were more than capable.

At that moment Elle came out dressed in a two-piece black costume, the jacket trimmed with yellow and red flames and a hood with two red horns on it. She had a red scarf around her neck.

"Ready. You changing?" she asked Jack, pulling on her sunglasses and then handing him some clothes. "We are running kind of late. We won't make it to prep."

"You bet we won't." It was madness enough that he was agreeing to this; the last thing they needed was to spend extra time prepping. Then he remembered her question. "Changing?"

"Yes. Into Jonah's outfit. I suppose it will fit you. You want to shadow me; you'll have to wear it. You have to blend."

Man, he'd known he was going to regret this. And what the hell was that long thing hanging from the ass of the pants? A red tail? Shit.

When he came out of the men's restroom, he threw a glare at the group waiting for him. "First one that laughs, I shoot." The Bowens had the grace to hold on until they got into James's pickup before exploding in laughter.

"You assholes, cut it out. I can hear you through the earpiece," he muttered, but it didn't help jack shit.

"Let them laugh," Elle said. "They're jealous. You're the best devil in the world. The one with the longest tail too. On account of his height and strength, Jonah always held the biggest pitchfork, the one with sixteen firecrackers on it. You're going to look fantastic."

The electronics were good, because the Bowens heard her and broke into more fits of laughter.

Once again, he thanked God for the tinted windows. They were in a rural area. If they got pulled over by the cops dressed like this, they were going into the hole.

They rode for fifteen minutes, while Elle painted her face black and red to the sounds of *Grease*. Jesus Christ, was this record always on one radio station or another?

"What is with these songs?"

"They're fantastic. I've been trying to convince the flash-mob guys to do the one of Travolta on top of the car, 'Greased Lightning', but they outvote me every time. I even have the choreography ready."

Jack had no clue what she was talking about, but decided to keep his mouth shut.

"Love the movie. Don't you?"

"Haven't seen it."

She gaped at him. "You didn't? We need to remedy that. It's a must. No self-respecting rockabilly can miss it."

That he was no rockabilly and couldn't give a flying fuck about that movie, she didn't seem to care.

When they arrived at Little Italy, Jack parked as close as possible to their destination and got out of the truck. "This is…" Jack said, looking around.

"Nuts," Cole finished.

Exactly.

Traffic had been blocked from the main street leading to the square, but it was not clear of people. It was brimming with activity, security fences nowhere to be seen.

There were dozens dressed like Elle. He was going to need to paint a big red dot on her back not to lose her. On the bright side, no one else would be able to spot her either.

"Do you have any idea how dangerous this is?" Jack demanded, looking at some children picking up their small pitchforks. "These are explosives; you have kids handling those?"

He handed an earbud to her. She frowned but put it on. "Don't worry. They dance mainly under us in circles while we hold the big pitchforks. They get the smallest charges and they don't handle them. You see those guys there?" She pointed at a group near a cart full of firecrackers. "Every ten devils have a cart that walks near us in the parade, recharging the pitchforks when they go out. In a corner at the square there's already set a big stash of fire charges for when we all come together for the final show."

Oh well, that surely changed everything. Crazy people.

"This is fun," Max said with a whistle, obviously totally disagreeing. "How come I didn't know about this? We ditch the devil outfits, turn them into green shamrocks and St. Patrick's will never be the same."

"As an explosives expert, I have to object to being here," Cole said, approaching. "There shouldn't be any civilians around, much less without protective gear. And only trained personnel should have access to the fire charges."

Jack couldn't agree more.

"That would be *soo* much fun for the public," Elle said, rolling her eyes. "The idea is for them to participate."

"The idea is for them to make it home in one piece and not missing an eye," Cole muttered.

Elle went on tiptoe and kissed him on the cheek. "You worry too much, bro. People come ready. Most are covered. If they get too hot, they scream 'water,' and buckets full of water are thrown on them from the balconies."

Cole didn't look reassured in the least. "I'm sure that's very effective when you're in flames."

"Cool," Max interjected.

"Come on, let's take position," James said to Cole, shaking his head, "before this wacko joins the parade."

At that moment the devils carrying the big-assed drums started to bang on them.

"That's the signal. Let's go," she said pulling at Jack. "Our team is there."

Even though she had her sunglasses on, the scarf over her mouth, and the hood covering half her face, they all recognized her.

"Ready to light up the night?" she screamed over the

thunderous sound of the drums, picking up her fork.

All of them cheered and then turned to Jack.

"This is…" She faltered.

"I'm her man," Jack interrupted.

A guy she'd introduced as Raul stared at her, his eyes big.

"Yes, and I'm his pet. He plans to return me to the kennel as soon as he tires of me."

By the look on Raul's face, he wasn't sure they were serious or not. "Oh, okay. I guess. As long as he doesn't have you neutered. Or put to sleep."

When Raul got busy charging the others' pitchforks, Jack hooked his finger through the loop of her belt, brought her to him, and spoke in her ear. "You like it in the kennel, pet. Free to play. No owner to obey."

"Have you ever considered I might like to have an owner to disobey?"

He studied her. "I'm not the kind of owner who likes to be disobeyed."

She pursed her lips mockingly. "Oh, I see, I don't deserve your collar." Before he could answer, she pushed on belligerently, "Actually, if you need to put a collar on me, then I'm the wrong pet for you. And you are definitely the wrong owner to obey."

Her pitchfork had been loaded, Raul lit the charges and there she went.

"Your turn," Raul said, handing him a pitchfork.

Right.

Elle had not been totally truthful. It was not only the more daring spectators going to dance with them, but the devils were charging the public too. Not to mention the dragon and the phoenix spitting fire. And the drums hammering at his ears and the people yelling and the water flying from the windows.

In the middle of all that mayhem, he noticed his cell vibrating. It was a message from Mullen.

Donald Solis, Marlene's supervisor, is missing. Last seen leaving a bar with a blond guy matching Grabar's description. His hotel room in Hawaii has strong evidence of foul play, blood spatter on the walls consistent with a throat being slit. Body nowhere to be seen, but plenty of state parks and plantations nearby to dispose of it.

Fuck, game over.

"We're pulling the plug," Jack spoke into the earbud.

"Maldonado knows about Elle. You copy, pet?"

But she didn't answer.

He searched for Elle, who'd gone a bit ahead, spotting her near a kid who was crying desperately in his mother's arms. She smiled at him, said something, and then pulled down her hood and her scarf, uncovering her face.

Fuck, no, no, no.

He tried to rush to her, but there were people under him, so he couldn't let the pitchfork go, and that fucking dragon got in front of him, blocking his way. The last he saw was Elle turning the corner before he lost sight of her.

"Anyone have eyes on the target?" he yelled. "Max? She should be coming your way. You see her?"

No answer either.

"Fuck," came from James. "Max's down."

* * * *

Elle twirled over herself, fire flying all over. Her earbud had gone careening several twirls ago, but she didn't have the time to fish it out of her hood right now. She'd attempt rescue when she went for recharging. Besides, she was half-deaf already from the fireworks and the drums.

The last cracker from her pitchfork blew out. Time to go for a replacement. But before that, she had something else to do. She moved toward the kid crying in front of her. She forgot always how scary the whole event looked like to small children.

"Hey," she said pulling down her hood and the scarf. "This is just a costume, buddy. Nothing else. Don't cry."

The kid looked at her, his tiny arms tightly hugging his mother's neck. Finding out she was not a demon seemed to reassure him and, sniffing, he let out a shaky smile.

As she was turning around, she bumped into someone. She lifted her gaze to apologize and the words froze in her throat.

Intent, mocking eyes stared back at her.

"Miss Cooper, we do meet in the strangest places," Maldonado said. "I decided to come personally and make sure all goes smoothly. You tend to slip through everybody's fingers."

Elle tried to backtrack, but the crowd kept pushing at her. Then she realized it wasn't the crowd, but four huge men who were flanking her. All the Krav Maga self-defense classes she'd taken on how to fight in small places and she'd forgotten the basics: don't let them into your space.

She nailed one in the nose and another in the groin, but she was badly outnumbered and the third guy punched her in the face, sending her to the ground. The blistering pain blurred her sight, leaving her disoriented, fighting not to black out. Strong arms restrained her immediately, yanking her up, and when the man with the bleeding nose was going to retaliate, Maldonado stopped him. "Not here."

She thrashed feebly, but it was useless. No one was paying attention. She couldn't see Jack, or any of the Bowens. Heck, she had trouble seeing anything. The phoenix had been charged and was ramming people and spitting fire and creating havoc. Everyone was being pushed over and as far as she could tell, not a single soul noticed they were dragging her away.

* * * *

Jack fought his way through the crowd, and, when he made it around the corner, he saw Maldonado, followed by Nico and four of his henchmen flanking Elle. The feeling of relief soon turned into fury.

He wasn't going to reach them in time. Too many people in between them. The wackos pushing the dragon started lunging forward, opening a path, so Jack jumped on its back until it was near Elle and then threw himself at her assailants, who, caught by surprise, released her.

"Run," Jack yelled at her as he fought two of Maldonado's men. She hesitated, looking disoriented and overwhelmed—in shock probably—so he pushed her away from Nico and Maldonado. "I said *run*."

He incapacitated one of the thugs and engaged another, but he was unable to stop all of them from going after Elle again, until suddenly James and Cole appeared, coming to his rescue. Jack caught up with one of the men after her and watched, relieved, as the crowd swallowed her before Nico or any of the other henchmen could grab her. Maldonado rushed ahead, trying to get into a car. Jack reached for him, but Nico intercepted him.

He fought the Russian off, losing precious seconds while

Maldonado got into the car. Fuck, the bastard was getting away.

Jack couldn't fire his gun; he didn't have a clear shot and there were too many civilians in the crossfire, but Nico didn't have that problem. He pointed at Jack and pulled the trigger. The bullet missed him, hitting the car that was speeding away. The driver lost control and the vehicle crashed into the stash of explosives on the square, a huge ball of fire lighting up the night, the sound deafening. The expansive soundwave left him disoriented for a long second, but he shook it away and managed to get on his feet. By then Nico was nowhere to be seen.

"Jack, you copy?" he heard from the earbud.

It was James.

"Yes. Max and Cole?"

"Fine."

"James," he called out, fighting to make himself heard among the screams, "where is Elle? Do you see her?"

"No, I don't," came the voice of his friend.

Fuck, where was she?

"Elle?" he yelled, frantic. He had to find her. He hadn't seen her being forced into the car with Maldonado, but he'd lost sight of her. Maybe she'd been run over, or got caught in the explosion. His mind was going crazy with possibilities, his pulse racing, his heart about to come out of his chest. The iceman was fucking panicking.

Then he spotted her, standing shakily amid the smoke and the debris, looking around as if she couldn't make sense of what was going on. The breath he didn't know he'd been holding rushed out of him in a whoosh and before he could order his body to move, he was already with her, enveloping her tiny body in his arms. Thank fucking God. Alive.

"You okay, pet?" he whispered to her. The paint on her face had gotten smudged and was a mess. Between that and the black smoke, he couldn't see if she was injured.

She said nothing, just nodded, hugging him tight, her nails digging into him.

He didn't let her go either. Not while the paramedics were attending to her. Not after the cops showed up and started questioning them. And when they wanted to take her in for a statement, he'd put his foot down. He gave them his cell number and told them he was taking her home. They didn't argue. Neither did she.

CHAPTER SEVENTEEN

Jack had taken her to what she assumed was his place. Too shocked to manage the shower on her own, he'd stepped in with her, washing her face, the water running black and red from the paint. Swearing at the bruises on her face. Then he'd put her into a humongous bathtub in the corner, windows in the walls along both sides affording a fantastic view. Unfortunately, Elle was too overwhelmed to appreciate it.

"How did they find me?" she mumbled, leaning her head on his chest. The water was very hot and Jack was sitting behind her, keeping her in his arms.

"Donald. He's dead."

"Oh God." He'd told her he was going to be traveling the whole month, so she hadn't thought about warning him, not that she would have been able to, seeing as he always liked to be incommunicado. Still, guilt churned in her gut. "How did he…?"

"Die? Badly, we assume. The body hasn't been recovered yet. Once they got your name it was only a matter of time before they'd figure out where you would be. You, my little pet, are too predictable."

Then it dawned on her. "If they found out who I am, then they know Alex Ayala is—"

"A cover," he finished, nodding. "Not too many arms dealers moonlighting as federal witness protectors, I'm afraid."

She was so sorry she'd messed that up for him. She had always been very careful not to mention his name or publish any of his pictures.

Her breath caught in her throat. "Jack, your sister—"

"Already taken care of. I called while the paramedics were with you."

"Good." Elle couldn't recall it, but to be fair, she couldn't recall much of what happened after the explosion. It was all a blur of smoke, screams, and debris.

Her only point of reference, her anchor, had been Jack.

Relief had flooded her when she heard the Bowen men talking around her. The thought that something could have happened to them made her chest hurt.

"Sorry I ruined that for you."

"Don't sweat it. This was bound to happen at some point. Too visible attending all those Bowen events."

"Now what?"

"Now we wait for the DNA results on the charred bodies in the car. If Maldonado is still alive, you go into hiding as we agreed."

His tone was stern. Sterner than necessary.

"Of course I'll go. I gave you my word. I don't go back on my word." She'd put enough people at risk already. If it came down to that, she'd go into hiding. Testify and face the consequences, whatever those might be. Time to grow up. "For what it's worth, though, I saw Maldonado getting into the car." The second Jack had started tearing into Maldonado's men, the big boss had decided to cut his losses and had bolted.

"So did I," Jack stated, "but we are not taking any more risks."

There was something in the air. A heaviness. The realization that however it played today, whether she had to go into hiding or this nightmare was over, her time with Jack was up. And she so didn't want to give him up.

She pushed that thought aside. Didn't want to go there.

"You were right. It was stupid not to go into hiding in the first place. I almost got you killed. And the Bowens. Max's skull is split, for Christ's sake." And it could have been so much worse. Aside from the three bodies in the car, there had been no casualties, just property damage. The crowd had been a bit behind and away from the big stationary cart full of explosives for the final presentation at the square. Five minutes later, it would have been packed with revelers. She didn't want to ponder on how many would have lost their lives because of her stubbornness.

"Don't worry about Max. He's hardheaded."

"The Diablos were so important to Jonah, and I stood him up so many times in that last year. I didn't want to let Tate down by bailing on her again and dumping the restaurant on her. Instead I put everyone in jeopardy. Maldonado was probably at Rosita's and at the house."

Jack tightened his embrace. "You did what you thought was the right thing to do."

She turned around to face him. "I was wrong and stubborn and unnecessarily difficult. Sorry I gave you such a hard time. I didn't mean to."

"Oh yes, you meant it," he said smirking, the laugh lines around his eyes softening his otherwise harsh demeanor.

"Okay, sometimes I did," she conceded. "It's ingrained in me to defy authority types."

"Let's get out of the water," he said, hoisting her up.

He took her to bed after drying her. Wrapped her in a fluffy quilt and engulfed her in his arms. She snuggled against him, burying her face in his neck. Her hair was going to be a mess when she woke up, but she didn't care.

She must have fallen asleep for a while. How long, she didn't know.

When she woke up, she propped herself on her elbow and studied him. Even sleeping he looked…severe. Alert. Bone-deep weariness marring his expression.

She caressed his face, the dark stubble raspy under her fingertips.

"What are you doing?" he asked, not opening his eyes.

"Soothing you."

His inquisitive eyes opened this time. "I already told you once I don't need soothing."

"Yes you do," she said, smoothing the worry lines from his forehead. "You also need to be taken care of. You deserve it."

The way his muscles tensed at her words showed his disagreement, but she didn't care. She nuzzled his scars, kissed them, feeling the tension rolling off him.

"You want me to fuck you?" he asked.

She snorted softly. "You're such a romantic."

"Do you?" he insisted.

She lifted her gaze to his and nodded.

"Open your legs for me. I want to eat you out first."

She did, slowly, enjoying the way he was staring at her, his huge cock twitching.

By the time he lifted his head from her crotch, she was gooey and shivering in the aftermath of her second orgasm. As he placed his mouth on her pussy again, she grabbed his hair and pulled. "No more. You promised to fuck me." She wanted to come with him, not alone.

"How do you want it?"

His question threw her off. "You taking requests now?"

His lips tilted into a slow smile. God, the bastard was handsome. Even while growling at her as he'd done wearing the Diablos outfit, he'd been gorgeous. Gloriously naked with his mouth shiny from her juices, his hard cock leaking precum, asking her how she wanted him? Just out of this world.

"Wiseass."

"Thanks, I do my best."

In spite of his visibly throbbing erection, he didn't charge at her. "Your call."

Elle knew very well what she wanted. "I want to ride you."

Never breaking eye contact, he lay on the bed and she straddled him.

"Wow, I get to be on top. Be still my heart," she joked, which earned her a spank. "I thought now that we're on your home turf, you'd go all macho and try using some of your heavy-duty hardware on me."

"You can't take me on," he stated, the cocksureness in his tone grating on her.

Elle stared at him defiantly. "Oh, but I can." As a matter of fact, and although she would burn in hell before admitting it, the last time she'd taken him on had resulted in an earthshattering orgasm. Tied, blindfolded. At his mercy, yet made powerful by his need.

Jack straightened up and looked her in the eye. "Can you?" Then he leaned toward the nightstand and fished something from the drawer. "Butt plug. I want you wearing it while I'm fucking you."

He didn't ask, didn't push, just waited, the question in his face.

She went for nonchalant. "I'm not sticking anything up my ass that has been in your other lovers'."

"It's brand-new. I bought it for you."

"Really? When?" she asked, taken aback.

"The first time I saw you."

"What made you think you'd get me in your bed, let alone agree to wear that? Wishful thinking?"

He shrugged morosely. "One can always dream."

Dream. That was the first time he'd admitted something like that.

"I'll wear the butt plug, but it will be me fucking your cock." His length jerked and got even bigger. "You'll get to experience what I learned after two years of twerking," she said to break the tension filling the air.

He said nothing, his gaze boring holes in her.

"How do we do this?" she asked in a whisper, spellbound by his eyes.

She moved to unstraddle him, but he stopped her. "Stay. I want to watch you."

Okay. Because she wasn't feeling self-conscious and out of her depth enough.

Dazzled and inexplicably aroused, she stared while Jack, without dislodging her from his lap, got some lube and spread it on the butt plug, and then put a dollop on the tip of his fingers.

"Give me your mouth," he ordered, without moving to get it.

She leaned and kissed him, her rear clenching as Jack's finger, cool from the lube, nudged against her back entrance.

"Relax, pet. Let me in." He didn't force his way in, he just stayed at the door, massaging her rosette in tight circles, little by little lubing her up, stoking her need until she was the one pushing against his hand, panting on his mouth, wanting more. Jeez, that was good. Her ass was spasming, her pussy creaming, her achy nipples incredibly sensitive every time they rasped against Jack's chest, which was with every one of her choppy breaths.

"Such a perfect ass," he growled, his eyes intense, as a second finger breached her. Slowly. Stretching the sensitive ring of muscles and her inner walls.

He withdrew and suddenly she felt something bigger and colder against her behind, pressing inside her, the butt plug getting wider the more he drove it in. She tensed.

"Don't fight me," Jack whispered against her mouth, and then nipped at her lips, teasing her, all while relentlessly pushing that damn device into her, awakening nerve endings she had no clue she had.

"I don't think I can," she whimpered a second before the tapered end lodged in place.

"Oh, but you can," he replied with a devilish grin, his hands splayed on her ass cheeks, rubbing them, which made the butt plug move and jiggle inside her. "You can take me on, remember?"

That had been prior to having this huge thing up her ass, tormenting her. "Jack—"

"Mouth," he said, reading her. "I'll take care of you."

He was a phenomenal kisser, but she doubted he could make her forget how uncomfortably full she felt. He worked his magic though, whispering against her lips how beautiful she was, how much he wanted her, while with one hand he caressed her clit and with the other played with her ass cheeks. In no time she was dripping wet, panting and holding onto his shoulders for dear life. Fighting for breath. Needing him inside her.

He redoubled his efforts on her hypersensitive clit. "Look what you do to me, pet. I'm so fucking hard I'm hurting. Leaking all over you. Dying to have you. And feel your sweet pussy wrapped around my cock."

Her release totally blindsided her, hitting her like a freight train. Her ass clenched around the plug while her pussy spasmed around emptiness.

"So beautiful," Jack grumbled, his erection jerking against her as she whimpered and shuddered, immersed in her orgasm.

"I'm aching so much," she said when she could speak. "I need you in my pussy."

He lay down, nudging the crown against her folds. "Take my cock."

She sat on him slowly, relishing the feel of his shaft spreading her inner lips. But that was as far as it would go. He was big enough without that thing stretching her ass. She wanted him so much, she pushed aside the discomfort.

He grabbed her by her hips. "Slowly, pet."

"I don't want slowly," she complained, frustrated when she couldn't move down on him. "And I'm in charge."

"Tough shit," he grunted. "I'm not down with hurting you."

"One would think you're one of those kinky, lots of extreme

hardware, chains kind of guy."

"I don't normally need those. Since I met you, I've begun to consider the virtues of roping. And caning."

"You wouldn't cane me," she whispered frozen, shocked at his choice of words. Caning? Really? What was she, a horse that needed breaking?

His eyes softened. "No, I wouldn't. I'd fuck you until you can't see straight. Give you that little bit of pain, the intensity you seem to like with your pleasure. Fuck your ass if you ever let me. Restrain you and make you come like crazy, but I would never hurt you."

Good, they understood each other.

Relishing his groans and curses, she took him inside her, her body little by little accepting him until his pubic hair was deliciously pressing against her open, bare folds. She remained still, trembling. Fighting to accommodate him. Her ass stretched to the max, her pussy too.

"Now," he said with a teasing smirk so uncharacteristic of him that jolted her, "what was that you were saying about the virtues of twerking? So far I don't see anything unusual."

Oh he hadn't dared her, had he?

Elle took her time with him, riding him slowly and fast, mixing it up, her hips swirling around, something that seemed to work for Jack, whose body was gleaming with sweat.

"You are killing me," he spat, tense as a bow. "So fucking hot."

"Don't come yet," she said against his lips, breathing through her own need.

"Stop fucking me so good then," he let out, repeating the words that she'd said to him once upon a time.

She clenched her inner muscles around him so hard that she almost sent herself over. "Huge payoff if you don't come."

He stilled her and she watched as he fought to control his body and managed to suppress his need to come.

"That's my Borg," she said.

"Smart-ass," he grunted, surging in hard and fast, ripping a gasp out of her.

For a guy who was giving her the reins, he was mighty bossy. Then again, this was Jack. He was always bossy. That he hadn't knocked her on her back by now and taken over was an accomplishment.

She wrested control back and got him and herself to the brink of release twice more; then she couldn't tease him anymore because she was thrashing and quivering.

He grabbed her hips, trapping her arms at her sides, and decreed, "We're both coming, now."

It might have been the authoritative tone of his voice, or the huge cock pulsing against her womb, or the butt plug torturing her ass, or the way he was restraining her movements, but she melted right away. Staring into his eyes as he lost it too sent her even higher.

"I see the virtues of twerking," she heard him mumble afterward.

She laughed softly. "Told you. Every evil has its flip side. Same goes for the ass thingy."

"You liked it," he said, slowly pulling the sex toy out of her, sending new ripples of pleasure all over her tingly body.

She shrugged, not ready to admit this had been one of the best lovemaking of her life. The guy was already too full of himself; he didn't need any encouragement.

Elle stayed on top of him until their breathing was back to normal, and even after.

"Let me go clean myself. I know you get your Neanderthal kicks out of seeing all your cum dripping from the women you fuck, but honest to God, falling asleep with that sticky goo on me is frigging uncomfortable."

When she came back from the bathroom, Jack was still in bed, in the same position she'd left him. His eyes were trained on her, his pose cocky and arrogant, but she didn't feel intimidated or unsure. She boldly lay on top of him and he engulfed her in his arms.

"For the record, I don't get my Neanderthal kicks from seeing my cum dripping from any woman," he said, that raspy voice of his abrading her senses. "I get them from seeing it on you. Just you."

"Not sure if I should be flattered or insulted."

He snorted. Yeah, she reckoned in his world that was a high form of compliment. Nuts.

Jack's cell beeped, and he reached for it.

Elle couldn't make out the conversation on the other end, and Jack's responses didn't give her too many clues, seeing as they consisted of "Speaking, go," "Right," and "Okay." He even hung up without a measly "Bye."

She lifted her head to him.

"Preliminary DNA results are in. Forensics confirm one of the bodies from the car is Maldonado. Dental records match too."

Her heart skipped a beat. "Really? Is it over?"

He nodded. "It's over, pet."

Her breath whooshed out of her, relief blanketing her.

She'd thought once the nightmare was over, she was going to dance and scream from joy, but she was still too numb, so she snuggled closer to him and closed her eyes.

They stayed like that for a long while, both quiet. She liked hearing his steady heartbeat. Strong. Rhythmic. Dependable.

"So this is your place."

"This is my place," he repeated.

"Aren't you afraid I'll stalk you now that I know where you live?"

"I'm counting on the shock of the explosion to make your memory fuzzy."

She laughed softly. "Damn, you're funny, Borg."

"I don't think I've been accused of that before. Besides," he continued, "your house was too exposed. The cabin too far away. A hotel too impersonal. You needed rest."

"What do you mean my house is too exposed? You think they will come after me even with Maldonado dead?"

"I don't think so. No narco's empire is built on blind trust and loyalty. Once the king is down, the fights will start to crown a new king, and that one won't give a rat's ass what happened to the last one. Heck, he'd probably be thankful to you for it, but I didn't want to risk it, because if Maldonado had been alive, he'd have gone there to search for you. As it is now, with him dead, you're off the hook. Attending the Diablos event and unhooding for that crying kid wasn't the most brilliant of ideas, but I'll grant you it worked out pretty well. Now you don't need to testify. You're free," he continued. "You don't have to put up with me anymore."

The air got so thick, she had difficulty breathing.

Going for light, she shrugged. "Putting up with you had its perks."

Jack's laughter rumbled through her body.

She lifted her head to him. Yes, the whole nightmare with Maldonado was over, she was free from that, but did she want to be free of Jack?

"About that." She cleared her throat. She wasn't sure how to say this. She wasn't used to having to spell it out for guys. The intense way he was staring at her wasn't helping either.

But they'd been through so much together. She'd seen the good, the bad, and the ugly of him. And he'd sure as hell gotten closely acquainted with all her sides. She'd told him things she hadn't opened up about with anybody else, not even her sister. Yes, they had their sticking points, but what worthwhile relationship didn't? She couldn't quite believe she was using the words "Jack" and "relationship" in the same sentence, but there it was.

She wanted to reach out for him because it felt right, even if she might get her hand chopped off, so she caressed his cheek. "From one to ten, how bad was it to be around me?"

A smile flashed on his otherwise severe face. "Let's recap: you've yelled at me and accused me of being married to my sister, you ditched me to go to work, disposed of my tracking bugs. You got me dressed up like a devil, tail included. I almost beat the shit out of everybody in the gym and had a heart attack during your twerking class. Actually, you've given me several heart attacks. You made me lose all my marbles and fuck you in a public parking lot—"

"And a boxing ring," she added.

"True. You had me drive all over Boston to make it to a flash mob in the middle of a busy intersection. You shortened my life span by fifteen years, at the very least. So from one to ten, ten being the worst? Twelve, pet. Being involved with you has been a twelve."

She grimaced. "That bad?"

"Yeah. It was that fucking bad because it was that fucking good."

What the hell did that mean? Whatever. In for a penny, in for a pound. "Who says we have to stop seeing each other?"

He snorted. "Common sense? This was just a temporary arrangement."

"I know, but circumstances change, right?"

"Nothing has changed," he said, the lightness suddenly disappearing from his tone.

"For me it has." Elle tried to ignore his forbidding stare and the silence and forged ahead. "I know I'm not exactly what you're searching for, but let's face it, you won't find it in this century," she said with a smile. "And I am a way better option: I do exist. I'm real. Not to mention you also need some work, you know, in the human interface department, which I'm ready to take on."

Her attempts at joking didn't get her anywhere. His face was inscrutable.

For some reason, she felt unsure for the first time around Jack, and, pulling at the sheet, she covered herself.

"I can drive you a bit crazy, and you press so many of my buttons you make me see red, but we haven't killed each other. The good trumps the bad." There she went, taking the huge leap of faith. Hoping he'd catch her. "I don't believe I'm saying this, but I really like you and I think we have something worth pursuing here. It's undeniable that the chemistry between us is off the charts. I enjoy spending time with you, in a weirdly masochistic sort of way, but I do. And I'd say you do too. Now that we don't have all that life-and-death stuff hanging over our heads, we could give this a go. See where it takes us. Start light and do normal things normal people do. I know a little Italian restaurant that could take a short-notice reservation for dinner tomorrow. What do you say?"

"We agreed there was no future for this."

"Walking away from each other is probably the smartest thing to do, but I don't want to. I really, really don't want to."

"I do," he said curtly.

O-kay.

There, her hand chopped off.

Her whole head, actually.

Something compelled her to keep talking. "Do you feel anything for me?"

His grim expression didn't bode well. "Do you really want an answer to that?"

"Yes, I think I do." She deserved more than a brushoff. She deserved the words. Or so she thought. As soon as he opened his mouth, she realized her mistake.

"Not enough."

"I don't believe you."

"Do you think I'm the sort of guy who would waste time lying?"

He had a point there.

"What do you want me to say?" he continued. "That I enjoyed fucking you, but this is as far as I'm willing to go? Is that what you want to hear?"

He didn't blink while delivering the blow. His voice didn't waver, not even once. Not even a little.

"I see." For once in her life, she was out of words. Her throat clogged. Poor Elle, moping like a kicked puppy because a man didn't want anything to do with her. Fighting not to lose her composure, she smiled. "Well, there it is then. I think I'm going to go now."

Holding the sheet in front of her and doing her damnedest to keep her smile in place, she gathered her clothes and moved to the bathroom to dress and piece together her shattered dignity. That's what she got for sticking her neck out. Stupid, stupid, stupid.

It didn't work. Her dignity was beyond salvation. But losing it and storming out of there wouldn't work. Jack would throw her over his shoulder and take her home. Talk about lost dignity. The spoiled rotten little girl throwing a tantrum because the grown-up hadn't wanted to give in to her.

By the time she left the bathroom, Jack was dressed too.

The fifteen-minute drive to her house lasted an eternity, the silence frigging uncomfortable, weighing a ton. Although it didn't seem to bother him in the least. It was business as usual for The Borg. At least he didn't give her the it's-not-you-it's-me line.

The Bowens appeared at the front door when they pulled into the driveway, their chattering and fussing over her a welcome distraction from the tension in the car.

"You not coming in?" James asked as they walked to the porch.

He shook his head.

They noticed something was not right. Well, Tate did, because she pushed her husband and Cole inside and said, "We'll give you some privacy."

"No need," Elle said, but they'd left, leaving Jack and Elle alone.

Elle's gaze drifted away from him. She was fidgeting. "I guess this is good-bye. Thank you for all that you did for me. I really appreciate it."

He nodded curtly. "I'll send someone to pick up my things."

"I'll give them to James."

Oh, look at them. How very polite. She felt like gagging. Or screaming at the top of her lungs. Shaking the living shit out of him and his imperturbable calm.

"Jack?" she called out. "Not giving us a chance is a mistake. I never thought I'd say this to you, but you're a coward. And you are the one who can't take me on."

His gaze was forbidding. "Pet…"

"Don't sweat it, I get it. Wrong pet," she finished.

He didn't deny it; he said nothing. After holding her gaze for a second, he turned around and left, never looking back.

CHAPTER EIGHTEEN

"You fucked up, bro," Ronnie said. "Royally."

"Watch it, kiddo."

"I'm watching it," she said, sprawled on the chair near him. "I have a great view of the roadkill."

Come on, he'd never been the life of the party. He couldn't be so much worse than usual. "Not forcing my company on anyone. You're more than welcome to leave." That was actually why he'd escaped Boston and gone to the cabin, to be left alone. No such luck.

"I saw you together," Ronnie insisted. "You had something there."

Jack flinched at those words. Elle had uttered them too. "Sure we did, a recipe for disaster," he muttered after downing half his beer.

It had killed him to walk out on her, but he'd done it. And he would do it again, in a heartbeat, because it was the right thing to do. The reasonable thing to do.

The only thing to do.

What seemed unreasonable to him was why, after ten days, he was still having trouble swallowing it. He never wallowed over past decisions. He always moved on without as much as a backward glance. Not this time.

For one, because he hadn't been ready for that conversation. He hadn't expected Elle to bring up the subject so boldly. He would have thought she'd be ecstatic to get rid of him. Instead, she'd basically said she wanted to be with him. No one voluntarily, except for Ronnie, had ever wanted to spend time with him. And if he got real, Ronnie didn't count, seeing as she was his little sister and was more or less forced to put up with him. He was too controlling, too unbending. Too grating. Too abrasive. And too set in his own ways to make any adjustments.

"No recipe for disaster, just life. Messy, unplanned, full of surprises. Just a regular life," Ronnie stated with a sigh. "And what the heck was that crap about looking for an Amish wife?"

"I never said an Amish wife. That was Elle's choice of words."

"I guess you gave her the bull about wanting a wifey wife. Someone to make a home for you and your kids yada, yada, yada."

"It's not bull." He didn't want to spend all his life running after his woman. He wanted peace of mind, thank you very much.

"It so is," Ronnie countered. "You might want that—or believe you want that—but what you need is Elle. You need someone who will stand her ground and won't give in to you. Keep you on your toes and make things interesting. You need someone who is your equal and is not scared to go nose-to-nose with you."

"She would drive me crazy. We would not be good together."

"You kidding? You were great together. I know what this is all about; you're terrified. She got too close to you and surprise, surprise, she didn't want to send you packing, so you ran at the first opportunity."

"She's not in danger any more. She doesn't need me."

It had been a piss-poor idea to bring Elle to his apartment in Boston, because now he had the visual of her around his place, wearing his T-shirts, sitting on his sofa. Haunting him and making his cock hard and his heart hurt.

The cabin wasn't better, but at least here he could be left in peace. Well, that was before his sister had gotten her hands on the GPS coordinates and had decided to pay a visit.

"So you dumped her and left her on her own?"

"I didn't leave her on her own. I have a guy keeping an eye on her."

One of the charred bodies had been confirmed to be Maldonado's and he doubted that anyone in Maldonado's organization would bother to go after Elle, but still, leaving her totally unguarded didn't sit right with him. Her comings and goings had to be restricted and monitored, at least for some time. He was counting on the Bowens for the restricting and Simon, one of his associates, for the monitoring.

He'd been using his contacts to get a feel for the situation and it was pretty calm. Maldonado's empire wasn't crumbling; there had been a couple of scuffles and some guys had gotten killed, but they were just middlemen. Nico, the Russian second in command, seemed to have everything under control.

So far, Jack had refused to read the reports on Elle from Simon, the hired hand. If he started down that stalking road, he would never resurface again. He couldn't justify to himself that level of stalkerism, no way, no how.

Besides, Simon was a very competent man Jack had worked with on several assignments. Worried that she would eat Simon alive, Jack had issued him strict instructions on how to deal with Elle, but surprisingly enough, Elle hadn't given him much shit, ignoring his presence most of the time. It looked like all that had been needed to get her to behave was to hurt her.

"Of course, because keeping an eye on her is something you can't do yourself, right?" Ronnie asked belligerently, taking him out of his reverie.

No, that was something he couldn't do by himself. He was unable to be around her without getting emotionally invested. He'd proved that repeatedly during their time together, running after her and allowing her to do things she shouldn't have been allowed to. Not to mention he missed her so fucking much he physically hurt. Seeing her would worsen this stupid juvenile state of his. And yet, all she would have to do would be to misbehave in a big way and he knew, deep inside him, he would take over from Simon and go to her. And although she must have figured that out, she hadn't done it. She was keeping a low profile—well, as low as possible for someone like Elle.

"What would you have me do, Ronnie? Play house with her?"

"Do you have feelings for her?" his sister demanded.

"That's beside the point. I—"

"I'll take that as a yes," Ronnie interrupted. "So, yeah, I expect my big brother to man up, act mature, and play house with the woman he has feelings for and who makes him smile like crazy. What do you have to lose?"

What did he have to lose? Not much really, just his heart, his sanity. His whole self. Small potatoes.

Elle had been right; he was being a coward, but someone had to maintain a cool head around here.

Did he have feelings for her? Fuck yeah. Had had those since the very first day he'd laid eyes on her and she's smiled at him defiantly. Feelings were fleeting, though, not important. They could burn up the sheets, true, but what about outside the bedroom? Could he compromise on what he'd wanted all his life?

"Do you remember when I was little and you lectured me about doing the hard thing? This time you took the easy way out, so it's my turn to call you out on your shit."

"Leaving her was the hard thing," he replied curtly.

He hadn't seen Elle that quiet or still in his truck. Ever. She hadn't fiddled with the radio or chatted. She hadn't looked mad either; there had been a tinge of disappointment in her eyes, but her smile was firmly in place, her chin up.

Ronnie shook her head. "No, bro. It was the easiest, safest thing to do. For your heart."

"She makes me smile, but she makes me crazy too."

"That's the way it's supposed to be."

"Not for me it's not."

Ronnie snorted drily. "Not for you? What are you, a different species of human or what? Because the nickname Borg is just a jab, you know that, right?"

He ignored the sarcasm. "You just want me occupied with Elle so that I won't be on your case twenty-four-seven," he stated, trying to change the subject.

Ronnie laughed. "You've been on my case since the day I was born. I would actually miss it if you weren't. You look utterly miserable. And for a guy with fewer facial expressions than an over-Botoxed Hollywood star, that's saying a lot."

Yes, his poker face was suffering big-time.

"I've had enough of party girls for a lifetime," he grumbled.

"Jack, our mother wasn't a party girl. She was an egocentric, self-absorbed, entitled, piece-of-shit addict who couldn't stand herself if she wasn't high and who made everyone else's existence miserable because of it. She went missing for months at a time, but she was home too and then she was just as bad, or have you forgotten? The complete opposite of Mom wouldn't be a Pilgrim wife," Ronnie said with a smile. "It would be a supportive, caring one who would love her family, spend time with them, and be there for them no matter what. Being outgoing and outspoken doesn't diminish any of those characteristics. You need a strong woman, sure of herself and her self-worth to get that."

Jack stared at his little sister, dumbfounded. "Where did that come from?"

She laughed. "All those shrink sessions you forced me to attend are finally paying off."

He heard the rumble of the motors before he saw the pickup making its way up the steep hill. It was James. Fuck.

Ronnie blinked at him innocently.

"Can you explain to me how they found this place?" James had been there once but not even he could have remembered the way back.

"I might have given him the GPS coordinates accidentally."

Right. Accidentally.

The motor stopped and Max, Cole, and James stepped out. A full house. Fucking fantastic.

Jack turned to Ronnie, then to the newcomers. "Does anyone understand the concept of a secret hideout, or privacy for that matter?"

Nobody bothered to answer.

"We drove around in circles for ages so you're safe. No one followed us."

"Anybody else coming?" Jack asked, looking at the group in front of him. "Your women? The whole of Alden? The Boston Philharmonic?"

"Christy is working. Tate and Annie wanted to come, but they didn't want to leave Lizzie and Jonah and we were afraid crying kids would send you over the edge," James said with a smirk. "Aunt Maggie might come later with some extra food although she's a disaster with GPS coordinates and is bound to end up in Alaska. The Boston Philharmonic couldn't make it; they have a rehearsal."

"We brought some basics," Cole said, holding a twelve-pack in one hand and some food in the other. "We all heard about your chewy protein bars and MREs. We had enough of that in the military. You got company?" he asked glancing at Ronnie and frowning.

Jack could read the guy perfectly. Cole thought Elle had been replaced and was ready to kick his ass for it.

"This is my sister, Veronica. James you know," he told her while she nodded to him. "The one that looks like he is going to bite my head off is Cole, James's oldest brother, and the one with the Mohawk is Max, the youngest." Then, after the introductions, Jack added, "You shouldn't be here."

"We've given you enough time to come around. You haven't," James stated.

"And that didn't clue you in?"

"Oh yeah it did. That you needed an intervention."

"And a bash on the head," Cole added.

He could use a good, old-fashioned bare-knuckle fight. "Who wants the first shot at me?"

James waved him off. "Later, man. First let's find out how big the fish in that river of yours are."

"We brought rods," Max explained, reaching into the back of the pickup. "We figured you get your catches by paralyzing them with your asinine stare, but we aren't that advanced."

Ronnie's laughter crackled in the air. "I would love to stay to watch this, but now that you all are here, I'm out. I have a bar to run."

Jesus Christ, what was he, on suicide watch?

"Don't make me come get you from here again," she whispered to him after kissing him.

They watched Ronnie drive away, and as Jack was going to shoo the other men away, one of the bastards handed him an ice-cold beer and started setting camp on his front yard, by the river.

"Don't bother. We're not going anywhere," James warned.

"You do know I have plenty of guns up here, right?"

"Come on, man," Max said. "You wouldn't shoot at us."

Really? Because Jack wasn't that sure.

"Fishing is therapeutic."

"And hunting was out," Cole added. "We didn't want to give you a reason to shoot us and then claim it was an accident."

Clever men.

They drank beer and fished. They didn't catch squat but with the way Max talked nonstop and Cole growled at him and James laughed at both of them, the fish heard them miles away.

"You are not going to read me the riot act?" Jack asked James while Max and Cole were busy bantering.

His longtime friend took a slug of his beer. "Nope."

"How very evolved of you."

James snorted. "Tomorrow that band that Elle follows around is jamming at their usual bar. She will be at the club."

He knew. He had the calendar of hers engraved in his brain. Fucking photographic memory.

"Get your stubborn ass there."

"What for?" Jack asked.

"Do I have to spell it out for you? You're gone for her. Hook, line, and sinker. Be a man and go to her. Fix whatever the hell you fucked up."

"You couldn't text me that instead of coming?"

James gave him a *duh* look. Okay, so maybe he hadn't been answering his phone, but there was a damn good reason for that. He hadn't wanted to talk to any of them. Not that the assholes had taken the hint.

"How's she doing?" he found himself asking.

"She's her old self, smiling and making jokes."

"I see." Why the fuck would he have to go talk to her then? She'd gotten over him fast enough.

"She's faking it, you dumbass," James said, reading his silence pretty well.

"How you figure?"

"Please. She hasn't mentioned you, not once. Not even to make fun of you. In what fucking universe is this normal Elle behavior?"

Elle wasn't the touchy-feely type, so yeah, avoiding the subject if it bothered her would be more her style. She didn't like to talk about her feelings or open up, yet she'd done that for him. And he'd slammed that door in her face. But what was he supposed to do?

"She misses you," James continued. "You might as well come back and face the music. You can't hide here forever."

"Of course I can't, you bastard, because you've given the GPS coordinates to everyone but the pope." Jack would have to abandon camp and find himself another stronghold. "Besides, Maldonado is dead; she doesn't need me anymore."

"If the witness had been anyone else but Elle you would have let the Feds stash her in some shitty safe house and forgotten about her. Or went along with Mullen's plan and forced her into being a snitch for you, never caring what would happen to her after that.

This thing with Elle might have started because of Maldonado, but it goes beyond that. The sooner you come to terms with that, the better."

"You've been talking with Ronnie? You sound like her."

"Baby sisters are smart," James said with a nod.

"And speaking of baby sisters… Did you make any headway in finding yours?"

James shook his head. "Everything is sealed."

"Pass me the info you have. Let's see what I can do."

At that moment they heard Max say to Cole, "You know what they do in Shanghai? There's these swimming pools open twenty-four seven full of shrimp where you can fish anytime. I hear gangsters go there at four o'clock in the morning to relax and chat after work. Do you think we can find one of those in Boston? Or maybe we could make our own. Jack, do you have a hot tub?"

Man. He was so going for the guns.

* * * *

He was not going to the bar, Jack repeated to himself while driving back to Boston. He was not. He was heading straight to his place, grabbing some essentials, and disappearing. Figure out how blown his cover was. Maybe create a new one. Something. Anything. He knew what he was doing among thugs and drug dealers. Feelings? Women? Total gibberish to him.

Lack of sleep wasn't helping either. The Bowens had stayed until late. He would have thought the absence of TV and comfy chairs—oh, and a hot tub to stash shrimp—would have discouraged them, but no dice. They'd fished and grilled their measly catch. Thank God they'd brought some steaks because those men were shitty fishermen. Aunt Maggie and the extra food never arrived, so he wasn't clear on the status of the sweet old lady.

As he was musing, he realized he was fiddling with the radio of his car. Bloody hell. What the hell was he doing? Losing his mind, apparently.

He'd always been very careful not to get emotionally involved with any of his hookups, and this whole Elle thing had blindsided him. He'd really expected once he'd fucked her that the fire in his gut would have disappeared, but it hadn't. It was burning hotter. He popped an antacid. Not that it would help squat, considering the burning was more along the lines of his chest. Whatever. He could live with that. He was used to pain and discomfort. Sadly, it wasn't only that; he'd been positive that being with her would prove to him how much he would hate her life. It hadn't. Elle did a thousand things a day, but she always had time for the important stuff. She partied, true, yet despite how tired she was, she got up to babysit Jonah or visit with Tate. She ran herself ragged for others' benefit. To help them and make them happy.

He turned onto his street, though he couldn't bring himself to park. His apartment had nothing that he wanted, so he decided to drive around to clear his head.

Jack wouldn't be caught dead saying this, but he loved her life. It was full of color and fun and people. Yes, she drove him crazy. At the same time he'd never felt more alive than with her. Making love or fighting or just sitting in silence.

Was Ronnie right? Was he taking the easy way out? Was he scared? He stilled at the thought. Scared? Fuck, no. He was terrified. Of giving in to this and making the biggest mistake of his life and of not giving in to this and making the biggest mistake of his life.

Not sure how it happened, he found himself in front of the bar where Elle's favorite band was jamming. He had no clue what he was doing there. Well, he did; he wanted to see her. Just for a second. See her smile. Get his fix. That was all. No talking. Because he didn't have anything to say to her, did he?

Fuck, shit, he did.

Furious with himself, Jack stepped out of the truck and stalked to the bar. He must have looked scary, because the crowd at the entrance parted for him and the bouncer let him in right away. Good; standing in line with all those groupies would have been the last fucking blow to his male dignity. The place was packed, again. He lifted his glance to the stage; no Elle. There was that at least. Making a scene and throwing her over his shoulder wouldn't have made that upcoming talk easier. The music and the pulsing lights were going to give him the mother of all headaches, but whatever. He pushed his way through the crowd. It shouldn't be too difficult to find her; how many women could be there with glow-in-the-dark tattoos, right?

* * * *

Elle straightened the black dress in the bathroom of the bar, took her lipstick from her purse, and reapplied it. She should have picked another outfit, one that wouldn't remind her of Jack, or smell like him, really. But what would have been the use? He'd been gone almost two weeks, and she could still smell him in the house. On her. Ronnie visiting Rosita's had just been the icing on the cake.

The need to ask about Jack had been overwhelming, but she hadn't caved. It hadn't stopped Ronnie from sharing, though. It seemed like the ass was playing Unabomber up at that cabin of his. Scared, probably, that if he remained in his apartment, Elle would go harass him. Ha! Like she hadn't crawled enough already. The sky would fall before she'd lower herself for him to stomp all over her feelings again.

Lost in her reveries, she opened the bathroom door and all but stumbled into a man's chest.

Strong arms steadied her while a whiff of very expensive cologne filled her nostrils.

"Sorry," she said absentmindedly, lifting her gaze to his face.

It was dim and her eyes were still adjusting to the darkness but she would recognize Mr. Asshole anywhere in the world. Apparently, he recognized her too.

"You following me now?" he asked.

A snort escaped her. "Not likely. You can let me go now."

Aston Biggs didn't release her. "You know, I had a flight from hell last time."

"How unfortunate. I won't say it twice. Let go."

He did, but he was still blocking her way. He took a step forward, his drunk eyes narrowed on her. "I see now what's happening here. If you're into me, you don't have to resort to those nasty tricks to catch my attention. All you have to do is ask. Nicely."

Oh God. "Which powerful hallucinogen are you on?"

"You are not hard to look at," the asshole continued, ignoring her words. "I could be convinced to grant you some of my time."

"Move," she demanded, running out of patience.

He grabbed her again. "Playing hard to get?"

That was it. She was going to smash his balls and deal with the fallout and the lawsuits and whatnot later.

She was wrenching away when suddenly someone punched Mr.

Asshole's face and a voice she didn't recognize said, "Disappear. Ms. Cooper and I have things to discuss."

* * * *

Jack was losing his goddamned patience. Although he towered over 95 percent of the people around him, this joint had two levels and numerous private sitting areas. It was going to take a century to find Elle. He had a tail on her, didn't he? Time to use it.

While reaching for his cell to call Simon, he spotted him in a far corner, scrambling to his feet and rubbing the back of his head.

"What happened?" Jack asked after making it to him.

Simon looked at his hand, blood smeared all over his palm. He squinted, trying to get his bearings.

"Elle did that to you?"

Simon shook his head. "She headed for the bathroom. Some suspicious guy intercepted her as she left, started harassing her and trying to corner her, so I decided to intervene, but on my way there was a brawl and I was hit."

Jack's blood froze. "Which guy?" He'd given Simon detailed files about Maldonado's people.

"Didn't recognize him."

Pushing people left and right, he got to the women's room. Some irate ladies screamed at him but he didn't give a fuck.

"Elle?" he yelled, flinging open the doors of the stalls.

Nothing.

He ran back out and scanned the surroundings. The band was playing some popular song that had everyone singing and bouncing, those damn pulses of light hindering his sight. In all that mayhem, he thought he saw a glimpse of what looked to him like her leg tattoo, shiny white, flanked by men and about to go through the front door.

He burst into movement, but when he made it out of the bar, there was no sign of Elle anywhere.

Then he remembered all the bugs he'd had on her. She'd disposed of some of those in one of her defiant stunts, but he'd planted more in her clothes and accessories. Would she have any on? Blood roaring in his ears so fucking badly that he was sure that people around could hear his heartbeat, he rushed to his truck. From the hidden compartment at the back, he took his computer and turned the tracking program on. Praying to all the gods he knew, all of those he'd stopped praying to as soon as his mother had started beating the shit out of him regularly, that something would fire on the screen, a small bleep. Just one. All he needed was one. And there it was, a green dot, blinking and moving slowly but surely away from the bar, going south down Pasadena Street. Fuck, he felt like crying. No time for that. He broke into a run toward a group of people and tackled one of them.

"What the fuck, man?"

"Where did you get this purse?" Jack demanded.

"It was on the ground," he said, scrambling up. "I didn't steal it."

Shit. "Did you see who dropped it? Which direction she went?" The man shook his head.

Jack searched around in desperation. He'd lost her.

CHAPTER NINETEEN

"Look at the photos again," Jack snarled. "Are you sure none of these men hit you?"

He was so losing patience with this asshole. He'd found Biggs at the door of the club, blood running down his nose, yelling left and right at the bouncer how he'd been assaulted while trying to fend off someone he had a restraining order against.

That had been all that Jack had needed to drag him aside.

How he'd gotten access to the club's security tapes was beyond him; he'd never been the picture of diplomacy, but when he'd approached the club's personnel, claiming one of their patrons had been kidnapped, he'd been like an out-of-control eighteen-wheeler, bulldozing over anybody in his way.

"I already told you. It's none of these," Biggs answered affronted. "Why are you keeping me here in this claustrophobic room?"

Jack had gone through the data and pics gathered by Simon, on the premise that whoever had wanted to snatch her must have kept an eye on her and probably got caught in some of the shots that Simon had taken, but no luck. He'd even shown them to Biggs but the asshole hadn't recognized anyone.

According to all his contacts, Maldonado's people had gone back to Miami and were keeping a low profile, but nevertheless Jack had pulled some pictures from his laptop and forced Biggs to look at them.

Nico Grabar, all of Maldonado's bodyguards and security detail personnel. The middlemen too. None of them had been the one with whom Elle had left the club. Not that the world was short of scumbags ready to accept a contract hit for a big cartel.

He'd studied the security video, desperate to get a glimpse of Elle and whoever had her, refusing to think about the endless possibilities. That road would lead nowhere very fast and he would lose his mind. More than he was losing it already.

He'd spotted her walking out of the club, a bit wobbly, wearing the same dress she'd had on the day of the damn fund-raiser, being escorted out of the bar by two guys who must have known where the cameras were because their faces were not visible.

"Go through the photos again," Jack ordered.

"I told you—"

Jack didn't want to hear the same shit. "Think. Do you remember anything about the men who took her? Anything."

"I saw them from the back, leaving with the woman. I only care about the one who attacked me. And I don't understand why you keep saying they took her. Look at her," Biggs smirked, pointing at one of the screens, where the tape was frozen over the image of Elle exiting the club flanked by the two men. "She obviously left with them voluntarily. If they are even snuggling, for God's sake. They are probably now screwing her brains out in some hotel room."

No. Jack knew Elle better than that.

"That bitch—"

Next thing Jack knew, he was holding the asshole by the throat against the wall. He was whimpering and thrashing, the chair where he'd been sitting tipped on the floor.

"Don't fucking dare talk about her like that."

Whatever Biggs said in response was all gibberish, seeing as he could barely draw a breath.

Through his murderous haze, Jack heard Simon's voice. "Put him down. He's not worth it."

No, he wasn't. Beating the shit out of him wouldn't help Elle. Jack released him, and Biggs crumpled to the floor, gasping for air.

One of the security guards came in with a cup of coffee and a bunch of newspapers. Biggs was sputtering something about lawsuits and abuse of authority.

"Sit," the guard said, as he left the coffee and the papers on the table. "And let's try to remain calm. Here, have something to read while we sort this out." Then he turned to Jack. "Are you sure she was kidnapped?"

Jack stared at the image in the screen. Trying to tamp down his fury. "She didn't leave voluntarily."

"That's the man who assaulted me," Biggs suddenly said, pointing at the newspaper on the table.

All the muscles in Jack's body tensed. "What?" In between the sore throat and the bashed nose, the guy sounded a bit weird.

Biggs tapped on one of the newspapers. It was a picture of the fund-raiser for abandoned dogs.

"Isn't that David Exxum and his bodyguard?" Simon asked. "What does he want with Elle?"

Realization froze his insides. Man, he'd been so stupid. "Not with her. With me. Exxum is after me. She just got caught in the middle."

The only way to contact Alex Ayala was through the Internet. He accessed the chat room, entered his password. There it was, a message for him.

Your life for hers. You have 24 hours, then she dies. After her, it will be her family.

* * * *

The brightness blinded her the second Elle tried opening her eyes, a sharp stab of pain making her brain throb. Ouch. Mega, super-duper hangover, although for the life of her she couldn't recall drinking last night. Squinting, she slowly scouted her surroundings. Where the heck was she? Then the events of last night rushed over her like a frigging tsunami swallowing her, her breath catching, her heart thumping in her throat. While Mr. Asshole had gotten punched, she'd been stabbed in the arm with a needle and two men she hadn't recognized had grabbed her. She'd wanted to yell and wrestle, but she couldn't. Her body hadn't been obeying her, a terrifying feeling of falling deep into the rabbit hole had spread over her as they'd taken her out of the bar and she'd been able to do nothing to stop them. Oh God, the ache in her head intensified, but she swatted it away. Last she remembered, she'd been forced into a car. Then a blank slate. She reached for her arm. Yeah, the needle mark was there. She'd been drugged. The fact that she was still wearing the black dress and her shoes were strapped to her feet gave her a small measure of relief.

She scrambled up and tried the door. Locked. Ignoring her wobbliness, her dizziness, and the blinding sun, she rushed to the window. She had to get out, but one look sank her spirits. There was water as far as her eye could see. A small beach on her right, a pier with a couple of boats on the left.

As she heard the door unlock, she turned, hugging herself.

Exxum walked in. "You're finally awake."

Elle had thousands of questions but the first that plopped out of her mouth was, "Where am I?"

"You're my guest at one of my private retreats on the North Shore. My security detail was nice enough to get you for me."

"I'm not too savvy on proper etiquette in high circles, but I'm positive drugging your prospective guests is a big no-no."

Exxum smiled. "I don't usually have to resort to such extreme measures. It was a shot of something to make you more agreeable. I apologize for the inconvenience."

"Apology not accepted. I would like to leave. Now."

"I'm afraid that's not possible."

Of course not. "What do you want from me?"

"From you nothing, but the man I know as Alex Ayala doesn't seem to be what he appears, and I'd like to have a chat with him. In the last six months several of my business deals have gone belly-up inexplicably. Everything has started to make sense.

"Ayala had passed all of my security filters, which are many, with flying colors. He'd brokered several high-profile transactions for me and now, because of him, I have some disgruntled clients, not famous for their coolheadedness or reasonability, thinking I've cheated them out of their guns. He's cost me a lot of money, directly and indirectly. And a lot of the headaches. To say we have a score to settle is understatement. You are a means to an end. So, you see, I don't want anything from you per se."

"I do," she heard a voice say.

The sun was behind the man on the door, so she couldn't see him properly, but as he stepped in, she realized who that was. Maldonado. Alive and well, looking tanned and relaxed, as a matter of fact.

God, this was getting worse and worse.

"I thought you were…"

"Dead? Sorry to disappoint."

"I saw you getting into the car and—"

"You saw my cousin getting into the car. If we could have gotten you, it wouldn't have been necessary, but since your friend intervened, we had to go with plan B. And well, it was my cousin's fault that Aalto died and I'm in this mess, so it just stands to reason that he should pay the consequences. I already had his dental records swapped with mine some time ago. Why would anyone keep useless relatives around, right? Especially one who resembled me so much. I needed you and everyone who saw the incident to be convinced it was me. Ayala wouldn't have backed off otherwise."

Elle frowned. It had not been just dental records that had identified the body. "DNA confirmed it was you."

"Law-enforcement agencies should do their homework better and screen their candidates more thoroughly. People with gambling issues should not be allowed to handle forensic evidence; some unscrupulous thug could use their secrets to encourage them to forge false forensic statements. You have been a very bad girl. You impersonated Mrs. Cabrera and, to add to your stupidity, you went to the cops."

Donald had given them her name; it was useless to lie at this point so she kept quiet.

"Why don't you make things easier for yourself and tell us Alex Ayala's real name?" Exxum asked. "We could bring our...grievances straight to him."

Elle tried to play it cool. "What do you mean, what's his real name? I know him only as Alex Ayala. I'm as much in the dark as you."

Maldonado didn't seem fooled. "He fought my men to get to you. I've read the info Exxum has on him. Alex Ayala does not fight for a woman, much less for a witness under federal protection. Someone undercover does."

She forced her throat to work, her mind racing. She needed a way out and she needed to be damn convincing. For Jack's sake and for hers. "I'm not a witness under federal protection."

"You dispatched my flight. You went to the cops."

"Yes, and yes, but I know there's no future testifying against somebody like you. What I want is to make a deal. My silence can be bought."

Maldonado barked out a laugh. "You are misrepresenting the situation. I don't have to buy your silence. Dead people tend to keep their traps shut."

"Dead people might have a safe deposit box whose contents are sent to the FBI once said people kick the bucket," she said, doing her damnedest to squish the trembling on her voice.

"If I had a penny for every time I heard someone say that, I'd be richer than I am, which, considering the margin of profit in my line of work, is saying a lot," he sneered. "You're bluffing. So cute, and so pointless in the grand scheme of things. Where do we find Alex?"

She remained furiously silent.

"You don't have to tell us anything, true, but we are trying to do you a favor," Exxum explained with a sigh. "We don't need it. As soon as he hears you're missing, he'll come to us."

"You overestimate my influence on him."

Maldonado walked to her. "You got him to forget common sense and remain in the open. He'll come searching for you, and we'll kill two birds with one stone."

"Why didn't you shoot me at the Baile de Diablos? You knew I was the witness. You could have killed me. End of the problem."

"No, dear. Not end of the problem. It would have made matters worse. Obviously you mean a hell of a lot to Mr. Ayala. If I killed you, I'd have to worry about him forever. I have enough enemies already. I don't need one as formidable as him. And things have been too hot for me lately, with all the law-enforcement agencies in the US sniffing up my ass. Pretending to be dead and then kidnapping you would solve all of that.

"Men like Alex don't commit to women. Loving someone is like catching a frightening disease that makes you forget your priorities and self-preservation instincts. He wouldn't allow it to go on for long, so I knew once he perceived the danger to be over, he would walk out on you, and there it would be my opening to get you. And once I had you, he would willingly come to me. After I'm rid of you two, I might remain dead. Check myself into a clinic in Brazil, get a new face and then travel to Spain and dip my toes into the counterfeiting business in Europe. Much less dangerous for one's health, not to mention how ridiculous European punishments are. A slap on the wrist, if anything."

"You're wasting your time. He will not come for me. He

dumped me."

"Maybe, but as soon as he's told you are a prisoner, he'll agree to our terms."

"Which are?"

"Him in exchange for you."

"You'll be waiting for a long time then. He will not agree."

Oh God, she needed to find a way out. Jack would come for her; he was that kind of man, and no matter how good he was, no one could beat an army.

"You better pray he does, little girl. Things can become rather unpleasant for you otherwise, right, Nico?" he asked, turning to the blond man that had entered the room after Maldonado and had stayed guarding it, his arms crossed over his chest.

He gave Elle a cocky once-over, the icy glint in his eyes all but stopping her heart. "I can get the info from her, no problem. She has more spunk, so she'd be more fun than her supervisor was, but that won't put us closer to Alex, or bring him here. And working her would entail quite a lot of damage. I believe he will come for her. He fought hard to protect her that day at the Diablos. My face can attest to that. I'm actually looking forward to meeting him again. I have my own score to settle with that bastard."

Maldonado closed in on her. Everything in her screamed to back down, but she stayed in place, her chin up. "True, such a pretty girl. It would be a pity to damage her looks. She won't make us so much money then."

She tried to control her body and not break into shivers, not sure whether she managed it. "You won't make any money out of me, because you'll have to beat me to death first."

"We'll see. Once we have you hooked on our stuff, you'll do anything for your next high. Anything. Anybody. As many times as we want. When your looks give out, we'll harvest your insides. Women are like pigs; nothing goes to waste."

"My associate is very eager," Exxum said. "Please think of our offer and act before it expires. Work with us and we might be able to find a satisfactory resolution for everyone, one that doesn't include your early demise. In the meanwhile make use of the facilities. Take a relaxing bath," he said pointing at the adjoining bathroom. "Enjoy yourself. Nobody says this has to be unpleasant."

"Not until the real unpleasantness begins anyway," Maldonado added, a promise on his smirking face.

* * * *

"You are not making that appointment, are you?" James asked while Jack loaded guns and clips in a bag.

"I don't have many options." As per the instructions on the message Jack had received, he was supposed to be at a convenience store off exit 44, off I-95, alone and unarmed.

"It's a trap," Cole muttered, adding to the gloomy atmosphere in Jack's apartment. "For all we know they might murder you on sight."

"I know." Jack would not think twice about exchanging his life for hers, but Exxum wouldn't honor that deal. He would kill both of them, just to make a point. "We'll just have to pray you can shadow those motherfuckers to their hideout and to Elle. Make yourself useful now that you're here."

If Jack had his say, the Bowens wouldn't be there, but as always where this crowd was concerned, he'd had no option whatsoever.

"What about contacting the cops?" Max said. "Tell them Exxum is keeping her against her will."

Jack shook his head. He knew her well enough to notice she hadn't been herself, but she hadn't been wrestling on the tape. Going to the police and trying to explain she hadn't left with the bodyguards of the richer-than-God bachelor voluntarily was going to be impossible. Like claiming the Golden Boy was selling guns instead of sending humanitarian help. Exxum wasn't a big narco police were dying to get their hands on like Maldonado had been. Exxum was untouchable.

There was another fund-raiser in two days in Boston, so Exxum would stay close by. According to Jack's intel, he had several properties around Massachusetts, four of them isolated enough to grant the privacy to serve his purposes; what they didn't have was the time to check all of them out. And his informants were coming up empty.

Making that appointment at the convenience store off exit 44 and beating the shit out of whoever appeared was an option too, although Cole was right and they might not know where Elle was.

Ronnie entered the room, not even flinching at all the guns on display. "So, how are you planning to get Elle back?"

Good question. He'd been racking his brain, trying to figure that out.

"You'll find her. Let me bring you guys something to eat."

Then it hit him like a ton of bricks. "You're a genius, baby girl. I know how to find Elle. We'll follow the greens."

"You mean the money?" James asked, looking confused.

"No, we follow the veggies," Jack said, getting to his computer.

The Bowen men looked at each other as if Jack had lost his mind.

"What veggies?" Max asked carefully.

Jack couldn't believe he'd been so dumb as to overlook the obvious. "Exxum is a strict vegan and gets fresh veggies and exotic fruits delivered every day, wherever he is." He'd seen this firsthand in his interactions with him. Granted, they'd been always in Florida and the Caribbean, so his supplier must be different, but the man was a stickler for habit. "There aren't so many companies that deal with such exclusive, highly perishable products in Boston. Cloudberries are a favorite of his, which only grow in the Scandinavian Arctic uplands in August, yet he gets them fresh all year around. Arctic bramble too."

A quick Google search gave him several names, one of which rang a bell right away.

"This, Luxury Delights Inc. That's the catering company that Exxum mentioned during the fund-raiser. We track the deliveries of exotic fruits for tomorrow, we find the bastard."

James wasn't convinced. "What if he has a hankering for something more normal, like an apple or a watermelon?"

"Exxum doesn't eat normal apples." They had to be Sekai Ichi ones. Handpicked and perfect and washed in honey. If the bastard ate watermelon, it was the exclusive Densuke variety, with only a hundred units available per year worldwide.

One look at Luxury Delights Inc.'s products and he knew they were on the right path. Gokusen bananas, Ruby Roman grapes the size of ping-pong balls. Queen strawberries. Yubari King melons, which were given "hats" to prevent sunburn. Square watermelons shipped straight from Japan.

"Ten thousand dollars for a freaking pineapple?" Max asked, all but choking.

"They come from England," Ronnie explained, reading from the screen. "From the Lost Gardens of Heligan. They are grown under straw, manure, and horse urine."

"Jesus Christ," Cole mumbled. "Give me a steak any day of the week, please."

"How are we going to track their deliveries?" James asked. "It can't be many, with these exorbitant prices, but still."

"We hack their e-mail or their website," Cole suggested. "It might take some time but I'm sure Christy can do it. Or we can break into their office after hours. Maybe find one of their regular drivers and get the info out of him."

Rolling her eyes, Ronnie grabbed the cell and punched in the number on the computer. "Hello, I'm calling from Mr. Exxum's office. No, no, everything was great with today's delivery," she hurried to appease the person in the other end of the line. Bingo. Luxury Delights had delivered to Exxum's. "I want to confirm the time and address for tomorrow's delivery. Mr. Exxum has a very tight schedule and I would hate for him to miss…" There was a pause and then Ronnie continued, "nine o'clock, Pricklewood, twenty-five, you say? Yes, all correct. Thank you." Ronnie terminated the call and then turned to her brother. "There. Problem solved."

Jack released the breath he was holding and hugged her. "Love you, baby girl. You're awesome."

"I know. Go do your thing. Be safe. Bring Elle back," Ronnie said while he grabbed all the info he had on the old Victorian mansion in Pricklewood and placed it on top of the pile.

"I will." And God protect the motherfucker if Elle had been harmed in any way, because as long as Jack was alive, there would be nowhere in the world for Exxum to hide.

* * * *

"This place is a fortress," Jack heard James mutter as he watched from their vantage point in the forest. The stronghold had already seemed unassailable enough while they were studying the blueprints and satellite surveillance pictures. Now, with a small army guarding it and cameras and motion detectors all over, it looked worse.

It was dark and they were wearing night-vision goggles, the pinpricks of lights indicating human beings sparkling around the perimeter. They could not take the compound with a full frontal attack. He would never make it to Elle on time. Sneaking in using a distraction was a better option.

Jack froze as he recognized one of the boats by the pier. The whole operation has just gotten infinitely more complicated. They would be confronting not only Exxum's men but the Cali cartel. "That's Maldonado's boat."

And that man coming off it was Joaquín Maldonado, alive and kicking.

Fuck.

"Isn't that—" James started.

"Maldonado." Which meant rescuing Elle was more urgent than ever. She was in even more danger than he'd thought. Exxum didn't need her dead. Maldonado did.

Max and Cole cursed over the earpieces.

"I'm going in with you," James said through the earpiece.

"No. We stick to the plan." They were going to fly drones to set off motion detectors while Jack sneaked inside and got Elle out. All the guest rooms in that old Victorian house were upstairs, on the east wing. There was a basement and other bedrooms on the main floor, but Jack knew Exxum; he had an ego the size of Alaska and he considered himself a gentleman. Elle would be in the poshest bedroom, with the best view. "You are my backup. I need you out here when the shit hits the fan. Use flash grenades to cover our escape. And avoid opening fire if it can be helped. Everyone in position?"

"Just for the record," Cole stated, "we have a Hollywood punk flying drones in the middle of the forest to set off the motion detectors and distract the guards while our best sniper sneaks in to plant explosives and save the girl, and the explosives expert stays behind covering his back with a sniper rifle. Does anyone else see a slight problem with this plan?"

Jack heard James and Max softly chuckling.

"We are about to assault the private property of one of the Forbes richest," Cole continued. "I hope Max's grandmother-in-law has a good lawyer."

"You can all go back home," Jack grunted.

Cole's dry snort came loud and clear from the earpiece. "Don't give us shit. What we should do is all go in with you."

"No."

"T-1000 wants to go in alone," James said.

That was right. He was not risking the Bowens more than he already had. He didn't want them in that house. Heck, he didn't want them anywhere in the vicinity.

They were outnumbered and outgunned. About to engage in a nonsanctioned, very illegal operation against an apparently outstanding citizen. Jack couldn't care less about the consequences he would face afterward, should he manage to live though this, but he cared about Elle and he cared about the Bowens.

Contacting the cops and waiting for them was not an option. As soon as Maldonado saw the authorities coming, he'd dispose of Elle. If the police were called once they had opened fire, the Bowens could be charged with trespassing on private property and committing God only knew how many felonies; but they hadn't agreed to stay behind and he couldn't get Elle out alone.

A second after the motion detectors went off, Jack breached the perimeter and disappeared into the dark. Showtime.

* * * *

Elle paced up and down in the room, from one end to the other, furiously trying to come up with a plan that would involve getting out of there alive and in one piece, preferably before irreparable emotional damage occurred. Or the involuntary donation of several of her organs, whichever came first.

She had no way to tell time, but the sun had set since Maldonado and Exxum had left several hours ago, locked her in, and posted two guards by her door. She'd heard them talk, joke even. They spoke Spanish, so she didn't understand them. Not sure that was a good or a bad thing; she was already scared enough about what was to come.

Elle had no illusions about her chances of making it out of there alive. Giving them Jack's identity was not an option, not that it would save her either. And no way in hell was she turning Jack over, which would lead them to Ronnie too. No, she had to get out of there. Whatever these guys had in store for her, she didn't doubt they could break her.

She was by the bathroom wearing a groove in the floor, when an old iron on the shelf caught her attention. Maybe she'd take Exxum up on his idea to get a bath. She turned the sink faucet on full force, then leaned over the tub and did the same.

Taking on two trained guards was out of the question, but maybe she could level the field a bit. Get an edge. She had water and she had electricity; she should be able to electrocute them, right?

As the sink and the tub overflowed with water, she grabbed the appliance and broke the plastic casing, exposing the wires inside, then plugged it in and climbed onto the toilet seat, hoping the wiring at the house was old enough and that the automatic cutoff wouldn't be triggered.

Leave it to her to get kidnapped in the most impractical outfit. Her heels were a huge liability; she could trip and fall face-first into the water and electrocute herself. The dress was restraining and too frigging long, so she reached down and, ripping at the seam, tore off a length of fabric. Then she took off the shoes, and thought twice about tossing them, opting to keep them. If the electricity didn't do enough damage, she could stab them with the heels.

The water was already well on its way into the bedroom, soaking everything in its path. She turned on the iron and, standing on the toilet seat, waited. From up there, she couldn't see the front door, but she could hear if it opened. That would have to suffice; she'd wait three seconds and then drop the device into the tub and hope she didn't lose her equilibrium and fall in too. On the plus side, that would save her from the bleak future Maldonado had painted for her.

After a while she heard the door being unlocked and her breath caught. Showtime. Ears madly roaring, she counted while hearing the splashing sounds of steps in water, and then she let the electrical device drop into the tub, praying to all the gods she knew that the material the toilet seat was made from was not a conductor.

She closed her eyes tight and waited for what felt like an eternity before unplugging the iron. A burning smell reached her. Not a single sound was coming from the other room; the guards must have been down, and she had to hurry or the water would reach the stairs and start dripping, alerting somebody. Somebody she couldn't electrocute again because the iron was broken and this kind of dumb luck only worked once in a lifetime.

Carefully she lowered one leg to the floor and dipped her toes into the water. No electric shock. Good. Hastily she fished the busted appliance from the tub, lifted her skirt the best she could, and exited the bathroom, stopping at the sight of the man sprawled on the floor, facing down. His broad frame wasn't moving, but she kicked him for good measure. As he flinched and grunted, she realized he looked familiar. Dread started churning in her gut. She turned his face to her. Oh God, she'd electrocuted Jack.

CHAPTER TWENTY

Jesus fucking Christ, Elle had fried him. He shook his head, trying to snap out of it and regain his bearings, but the lethargy didn't go away. And he had James's fretting voice asking for a status update in his ear.

"Found her," he muttered. "Heading out." Well, as soon as he could get his shit together and scramble to his feet.

"Oh God, Borg, are you okay?"

He wasn't sure; he hadn't been roasted before. "What the fuck were you doing?" he grumbled, struggling up.

"Rescuing myself, of course, like in *Shrek the Third.*"

"Shh… What?"

"You don't know Shrek? Of course not," she said rolling her eyes. "I was rescuing myself. What did you think, that I would be here lying around and waiting for someone to do it? You okay? Did I hurt you?"

He cursed. He was soaking wet too.

"Sorry for frying you. On the plus side, you won't need to get a perm, ever."

She wasn't making a lick of sense. "What?"

"Kidding. What are you doing here?"

"What am I doing here? I came to get you." Her look of disbelief said it all. "You thought I wouldn't?"

"Last time we met you couldn't wait to be rid of me so no, I wasn't holding my breath for you to appear, not to mention you didn't know where I was." Then she frowned. "Wait. I'm wearing the dress from the fund-raiser. It's bugged, isn't it?" she asked sounding irate and happy at the same time.

"The purse was, but you dropped it at the bar."

If she gave him any shit for the bug, he was going to gag her. She didn't. She threw herself at him, hugging him so hard it almost hurt to breathe.

"You came for me," she whispered, as if to herself.

"Haven't you realized it yet, pet? I'd run into hell for you."

"No, I hadn't. You walked out on me and stayed away from the Bowens, after telling me off and all but insulting me."

Stayed away from the Bowens? Right. That was an impossibility. Those assholes wouldn't let him.

"I didn't insult you. I said the sex was great."

"Right, fantastic way to make me feel cheap when I was offering you my heart." Her smile was all teeth. "Can't convey in words how glad I am the sex was up to standards. You weren't bad yourself. Your pillow talk is shitty, but we all know talking is not your forte."

"We don't have time to hash this out now, pet, but we will. As soon as we get out of here we'll have a serious conversation."

"Who says I'm interested now, Borg?" she muttered.

He grabbed her and pushed her against him, planting his lips on hers. "I say so. I'll talk and you'll listen. And we'll figure this out. Now let's go so you can scream at me properly."

"The guards—"

"Down," he said.

It had been easier than he'd thought to sneak in, busy as security had been with the distraction at the other end of the compound. Dropping the two thugs who had been posted at her door had been a piece of cake.

"I rigged two cars. If we run into trouble, I'll detonate them and we'll use the diversion to escape. James, Cole, and Max are outside, ready to cover us." He hoped to God it wouldn't come to that. Cole had been right; opening fire on the private property of a rich guy, with an army of ex-military at his disposal and an army of lawyers, was going to be a bitch.

"Jack, wait," Elle said pulling at him. "Maldonado is alive. I forgot to tell you, with the excitement of frying you and all."

"I saw the boat in the marina. Did he or Exxum hurt you?"

"Not yet."

"Let's keep it that way. Do you know how to shoot?" he asked, handing her a gun.

"Does it work like a paintball gun?"

"Basically."

"Then we're good."

"Let's go."

He stuffed the guards into the room and locked them in. The hallway was deserted. So far so good.

"Where are we going?"

"Downstairs to the kitchen." He'd gotten in through the service door. With a bit of luck they could take the same route without encountering resistance. "James, are we clear?" he whispered.

"Lots of movement on the first floor west side" came through the earpiece.

"Understood. Heading out."

They made it to the first floor. Jack heard the guns being cocked a second before a voice said, "Look what the cat dragged in."

Exxum's security detail. Fuck.

There were eight men in front of them, guns at the ready.

"Drop your weapons," one of Exxum's men said. "Now! Hands where I can see them."

Jack spoke calmly. "Do as they say, doll."

The word "doll" did the trick, and Elle's attention snapped away from them and centered on Jack. Good, he needed her on her toes.

He threw the gun to the floor and then lifted his hands, pushing his forearm against the wall, clicking on the detonator on his wrist. Their location was perfect; they were wall-to-wall with the cars parked up front.

She must have realized what he was doing right before the explosion blasted her mind and her senses, leaving her disoriented only for a second. With smoke and broken glass flying all over, Jack burst into action and started dropping guys. This he could do with his eyes closed. This was his comfort zone. That's what he'd been doing all his life, only now he had someone with him whom he cared for more than he could say, so half his attention was on her.

In the middle of the mayhem a man grabbed her, but she

managed to punch him in the throat, getting him to stagger back. That was his girl.

She never saw the guy coming from behind until he knocked her down. She seemed to shake it off, but by then one of the bastards was pointing a gun at her.

Jack lunged for her, knocking her on the floor as the sound of the shot rang in his ears and pain tore through him.

* * * *

"I knew you'd enjoy my present," Exxum said, raising his glass.

Maldonado sat in the magnificent library, sipping a one-hundred-year-old whiskey with Exxum. He had more money than this entitled little brat and could afford hundreds of bottles of better whiskey yet they didn't taste this good. There was something about old money. It bought respectability, never mind how corrupt and ruthless the methods of getting that wealth were. Him? He'd started as a smuggler, and regardless of his present status or possessions, all these high society types looked down on him. He could feel it. Scorn.

"I appreciate it." He could have snatched the bitch by himself, but this little punk had to show him he could get to her first. Marking from the beginning who was the boss. This asshole had no clue whom he was dealing with. No clue whatsoever. Still, Maldonado was to benefit greatly from this business, so he could put up with moneybags for a while.

"Take some more," Exxum encouraged, pointing at the tray with some weird-looking berries. "They come straight from Norway. One hundred percent organic. Handpicked. Best of the best. Great for relieving stress."

Maldonado shook his head and sipped more of the whiskey.

The drink was good, unlike the food. Jesus, if he had to eat any more shit with a name he couldn't pronounce and a taste he couldn't decipher, he was going to shoot himself. Fucking seeds-munching, soy-pumping vegetarians. Vegans. Whatever the hell they were.

"Did you enjoy the meal? The black truffle seitan tasted like exquisite filet mignon. My cook is superb. I stole him from the most exclusive restaurant in Japan. He could make even a cleaning cloth taste like meat."

So that was the name of that vile thing. Seitan. Fitting.

If it wouldn't have been a huge slap in the face, Maldonado would have stayed on his boat to eat supper.

"Giving up meat is so rewarding," Exxum continued. "Animal protein is very dangerous. Straight correlation to all sorts of cancer."

Maldonado stifled a snort. Dangers of eating meat? Ha. Obviously this ass had no clue the shitstorm that a tiny olive could create. He could attest to that. His life had gone down the drain because of it.

"I don't know. I prefer my meat bloody and coming from an animal."

"It'll grow on you," Exxum assured him. "It's an acquired taste. It takes a bit to get used to such exquisiteness."

Maldonado drew in a calming breath. Some day he would show this snotty little brat who had exquisite taste, just not now. Now he needed his contacts. And more specifically his customs-cleared containers bringing Maldonado's product into the US without risk of detection.

"Farming and ranching is so destructive for the planet. The number one reason for the decimation of the sea and the atmosphere. All the means of transport put together wouldn't make it even close to the damage ranching causes. And the uncivilizedness of eating other animals is just barbaric. Unmoral."

Blah, blah, blah. So much preaching was giving him indigestion. Or it was the seitan?

"Many would say we are the morally dubious ones. Worrying about animals and ignoring humans."

Exxum scowled. "Animals are noble. Humans are an infestation, so as far as I'm concerned, providing the means to kill each other is just speeding the process of humanity's self-destruction and saving the Earth a bit faster."

An answer for everything. "Should we discuss numbers?" Maldonado asked, changing the subject. He had no desire to enter into a moral debate or spend more time than necessary with the likes of Exxum.

"If we must, then—"

A huge explosion drowned out the end of that sentence, the black sky outside lighting up with two blasts of fire, the sounds of gunshots following.

Nico dove for Maldonado, covering him, his gun drawn. Exxum's security chief did the same with his boss while everyone in the room drew their weapons, his men pointing at Exxum's and the other way around.

"What is the meaning of this?" Maldonado asked. They already had that minor scare when some animal had tripped the motion detector a while back.

"I don't know," Exxum said. "It looks like we're under attack. Order your men to lower their weapons."

Right, like he was giving that order any time soon. "You said this location was secure."

"Status," Exxum's security chief barked, communicating with someone through his earpiece. Then he turned to his boss. "We have visitors, sir."

* * * *

Oh God, Jack was hurt. Badly hurt. Elle wasn't sure if he'd been shot in his stomach or he'd punctured a lung or what. He was trying, but he couldn't stand up straight, and he was bleeding profusely from his side.

"We are under heavy fire," one of the armed guards said.

Only then did Elle realize what she was hearing was gunshots.

"How many are there outside?" the one that seemed in charge asked, smacking Jack.

Jack remained silent.

"Tell them to stand down," he insisted, pointing the gun at him.

"Fuck off," was Jack's response.

"We need them alive. Boss says to bring them to him," another said.

They were led into the library, where Joaquín Maldonado and David Exxum stood, surrounded by heavily armed guards. A blistering pain was splitting her skull from where she'd been hit, but she ignored it. She needed all her wits about her.

"How thoughtful of you to come by and save us the trouble of picking you up," Exxum stated, and after frowning at Jack, he asked, looking around, "Who shot him?"

The man who had pulled the trigger took a step forward. "They resisted and—"

The gunshot deafened Elle, who watched the lifeless body of

the guard slide on the floor.

"Shooting Mr. Ayala should have been my pleasure. Now, where were we?" He returned the gun to his bodyguard and addressed Jack. "I trust all this fuss outside is your doing, right?"

"I suggest you cut your losses and flee. Police are on the way," Jack said.

Maldonado laughed. "Bullshit. You trust them less than we do. You would never leave your woman's security in their hands. If you proved anything since you took her away from protective custody, it's this. Alex Ayala is—was, I mean, ruthlessly efficient. This," he said, pointing at her, "is a big fuckup, my friend."

"You teaming up?" Jack asked, looking at Maldonado and then at Exxum.

"Exploring new business ventures," Maldonado said.

"Did you neutralize the shooters?" Exxum asked one of his men.

"We are closing in on them, but the situation is not contained at the moment."

With disgust written all over his face, Exxum turned to Jack. "All this for that little whore? You broke your cover for her? You should have known better. Not that I'm unhappy about it. I look forward to not having my shipments intercepted." He punched Jack in the face. "You know how much your interference has cost me?"

"Your grievance is with me. You got me. Let her go," Jack said as he spit blood. "She walks out of here and the attack stops. Nobody will retaliate. I guarantee it."

"Sir, we need to leave," Exxum's security chief insisted. "The boat is ready. We have to get you to safety."

"One would think having a compound and an army would do that. Dispose of them both," Exxum said, gesturing at Jack and Elle. "I would have wanted to make this more enjoyable, and far longer, but now that you are dying, I don't see the point."

"I'll take care of that," Maldonado offered.

"Fine. Make them disappear. For good. I don't want anything linking me to this mess."

"My pleasure."

Exxum walked out, taking his men with him. Maldonado, the one they called Nico, and a handful of what Elle presumed were Maldonado's men remained.

Jack could hardly stand, and he was so damn white, his side oozing blood, yet he took a step forward, trying to keep her behind him.

Elle was desperate for a plan, but she was coming up empty. She had no weapons, Jack could barely move, and there were a dozen armed men in the room. Whatever James and his brothers were doing, they were not going to make it on time.

"Let her go. There are people who care about her. They will not stop if you kill her. Everyone shooting at you now is here for her. Not for me."

"I don't plan on killing her just yet. You, I'm afraid, have run out of time." Maldonado grabbed Elle by the hair and pulled her away from Jack. "I want you to die knowing you couldn't save her. On your knees," he ordered.

When he didn't obey, Nico punched him in the stomach and Jack fell on his knees, doubling over from the pain and spitting more blood.

"Jack," Elle yelled, attempting to wrench away but failing.

Maldonado smiled. "You know how the saying goes: you live by the sword…"

Maldonado nodded at Nico, who pointed the gun at Jack's head and said, "You die by the Russian."

"No!" Elle screamed.

Nico didn't waver, his face scarily blank. He pressed the barrel to Jack's forehead, cocked the gun, and then, suddenly, he turned, shooting Maldonado in the face, his brains splattering all over Elle.

Before she could react, Nico had killed two more of Maldonado's security detail.

Maldonado's lifeless body fell on the floor, his limp hand letting go of Elle's hair. She scrambled to her feet and rushed to Jack.

"Your cover was impressive" Nico said. "Not even my handler knew who Alex Ayala really was. You should have refrained from godparenting though. It just took a phone call to the diocese to access the church records and find out Jack Copeland was registered as Jonah Bowen's godfather.

"Exxum is making his escape through the water while his men hold the attack off," Nico finished, lowering his gun. "You are free to go. If you can make it through their fire, you live."

"Why?" Jack choked out.

"I'm to take over Maldonado's organization by any means

necessary, but I'm not into the habit of killing innocent people if I can spare them."

Elle looked into the Russian's ice-cold eyes. Still. Impenetrable. "And Donald?"

"Not dead." Then Nico signaled to the other men and started leaving. Before crossing the door, he turned to Elle, "Your man is dying. Tick tock, lady."

That snapped her out of it.

She hauled him up but he crumpled to the floor. "Jack!"

"Go," he let out, choking on blood, his chest spasming, his eyes glassy. His face clammy and so damn white.

"In your dreams. On your feet, soldier," she yelled, lifting him back up, but they didn't get too far before his legs gave way.

"I said go. You can't carry me."

"Watch me," she bit out. She wasn't losing him. She was getting him help, now.

Grabbing him by the shoulders, she began dragging him, the blood oozing from him leaving a bright trail on the otherwise pristine white marble tile. She needed to get outside to the Bowens. Away from danger.

She made it to the front door. Bullets were flying everywhere and she couldn't feel her arms. She tripped over a body on the floor, slipping on the blood pooling around it, and fell down. She got up and tried pulling Jack, but she couldn't.

Defeated, she started crying. "Don't die," she pleaded between sobs, her hands on his chest, attempting to stop the bleeding.

"Elle, listen. Sorry I wa—"

"Shh," she interrupted him. "Save your strength. You'll tell me later."

He was choking, barely able to talk. A wheezing sound coming with every word. "Love you, pet."

"No, no, no," she repeated, tears blurring her sight. "Don't dare die. Don't you dare leave me," she ordered, jerking him, but he didn't react.

She started administering CPR, yelling at him, "Breathe, dammit. Breathe. Don't you leave me." He wasn't responding, wasn't breathing, his eyes glassy and empty while she continued pumping his heart.

She could barely make out what she was doing over her tears but somehow saw James running toward her. Max and Cole too.

Sirens were flashing. They were talking, their mouths moving, but she couldn't hear a word, much less understand what they were saying. Screams were echoing in her head, so loud. Gut-wrenching, soul-ripping screams. Her screams.

CHAPTER TWENTY-ONE

Four weeks later

Jack sat in his truck. In front of Rosita's. Again.

Jesus Christ. Two days out of the hospital and he'd spent the majority of his time here, hoping to steal a glance at her.

He'd been told he'd missed a huge mess and that they'd avoided jail by a hair. As a matter of fact, he'd been under arrest and twenty-four-hour surveillance the whole month he'd been in intensive care, a couple of uniforms at his door day and night. Where the fuck they thought he was going to run when he was totally out of it, he had no clue.

Ultimately, it had been thanks to Elle's testimony, the incriminating evidence that was found in the house, and Jack's contacts that they had been saved from doing time. Charges had been dropped and brought against Exxum. Not that it looked like they were going to stick. Not even after finding several of his containers full to the brim with dope, presumably from Maldonado, and others running guns.

Rich people got away with a lot of shit.

The scumbag even managed to get an airtight alibi for the night Jack and the Bowens had stormed his property. He'd been in Boston and had no idea what was going on at Pricklewood. He had witnesses too.

They told Jack that Elle had been adamant about getting in to see him at the hospital. She hadn't cared about the rules, or the police. There had been no way to keep her out. Or so they'd told him.

She'd stayed with him every day while he was in critical condition. Then, the second his status had been updated from dying to conscious piece of shit in a boatload of pain, Elle had disappeared. Which sucked ass, because she was the only person he would have wanted to talk to, yet he was stuck being debriefed and questioned by the feds and several other government agencies, with Ronnie and the Bowens fussing over him. All of them carefully tiptoeing around mentioning Elle. After a couple of days, he'd stopped asking where she was and demanded his laptop. He knew how to contact her.

It hadn't worked.

Elle knew where he lived, where his bar was. Heck, he'd been all but chained to a hospital bed for weeks, staring at the fucking ceiling, yet she hadn't come to him or answered a single one of the many e-mails he'd sent her. He'd created profiles on all the major social media sites and messaged her. Nada. A monumental fuck-off if he ever got one, not that he could let that stand. If she wanted to dump him, she would have to tell him straight to his face.

He still had the keys to her place and he had no qualms about a little home invasion, but at this time of night she was at the restaurant, and waiting until her shift ended wasn't an option.

He glanced at Rosita's windows.

There she was. Elle. His pet.

She was so beautiful. She'd cut her hair short, which made her even more beautiful if that were possible, her features on display without the mane of hair taking any attention from them. So starkly gorgeous in her simplicity. Just a black pencil skirt and a white blouse. No heavy makeup, just some lip gloss on her luscious mouth.

Jack missed her so fucking badly. Her sweet smiles and her sarcastic comebacks. The way she always found an opening to touch him. How she soothed him with just a glance. He missed everything. Every-fucking-thing.

He took a deep breath and stepped out of the car. He couldn't live without her. Time to man up and bite the bullet.

As luck would have it, Rosita's was full, and not only with patrons. All the Bowens were there, kiddies included. Whatever.

That wouldn't derail him. Nothing would derail him.

Elle was at the back and didn't see him coming in. James and Max did, and they walked to him.

"You sure you want to do this here?" James asked.

Sure? Not in the least. Nevertheless, he nodded curtly. He didn't have any other option; he wasn't leaving without talking to her.

Tate hurried to him and hugged him. "Go to her," she whispered. "Before she sees you and bolts."

Right. Very reassuring.

* * * *

Elle was taking Mrs. Copernicus's order when she noticed the old lady was looking behind her, waving and smiling. Elle turned and froze.

Oh God. Jack was in front of her. The need to envelop him in her arms and kiss him was so strong, she had to fist her hands and lock her legs to stop herself from jumping at him.

"I need to talk to you, pet," Jack said, his voice husky.

She glanced around. "I'm working."

Jack didn't move a muscle. "I'll wait as long as I have to. Or talk in front of them. Don't care."

The patrons didn't seem to mind either. Mrs. Copernicus, as a matter of fact, had turned around and was snacking on the bread sticks as if she were watching a movie.

"Go. I'm taking over," Tate told her, realizing they were going to need privacy.

Jack and Elle stepped to the side.

He looked good; a bit skinnier and paler than his normal self, but she guessed that was what a hole in your insides and four weeks in a hospital did to you.

"You okay?" she whispered.

Jack nodded. "I was released the day before yesterday."

"I know." She'd been fighting herself not to go to him.

"You didn't come to visit. Didn't answer my e-mails," he said, his tone dripping with bitterness.

She latched on to the last part. The first part she didn't even want to delve into. "What e-mails? I haven't been checking them." She'd been trying to wean herself off the Internet, so she'd kept away from her laptop. "Have you been writing me?"

He nodded, yet he remained silent.

She was dying to ask about that, but she stopped herself. "I've reduced my cyberactivities."

"So I heard," he answered. "I've decided to reduce my activities too."

That caught her by surprise. "Really? Because you didn't have many to begin with."

"The life-threatening ones."

"Your schedule is wide open, then." He shrugged, looking uncomfortable. Her attempt at joking had backfired and the following silence was so heavy she couldn't breathe. "Was there something you wanted?"

He drew a deep breath and locked eyes with her. "I fucked up when I walked out on you. You were right. I was being a coward. I'm here to correct my mistake."

"I appreciate you saving me, but you might have been right; we aren't a good fit. You'd better go."

"Not going anywhere. I know I fucked up, but you're going to forgive me and I'm going to stay here until you do. And afterward I'm not going anywhere either."

There it was, the obey-me-or-else Jack she knew. It figured being near death hadn't mellowed him. She crossed her arms over her chest, her chin up defiantly. "Really? And why is that?"

"Because you're the one."

"Not the one. You were very clear about that. I offered you my heart and you stomped all over it. I'm the same person you rejected. I haven't changed. Well, I have; you taught me something very important, that it doesn't pay to love someone. You let them in, they break your heart."

Before she could react or fully comprehend what was happening, Jack enveloped her in his arms and took her mouth.

God, he felt so good, and she'd missed him so much. Elle fought the overwhelming need to give in to the kiss.

"I'm still mad at you," she said the second she managed to break away. "We are in the middle of an argument. What are you doing?"

"Continue to be mad, pet. I'm kissing you."

"Why? To shut me up?"

"No. You said you loved me. I couldn't stop myself. I need you.

I need to be as deep inside you as I can. As close to you as humanly possible. I guess fucking you now is out of the question."

She blinked, her stomach dropping, and tried to backtrack. "I didn't say I love you." Her tone wasn't too convincing, she knew, but she found it difficult to lie to him. And she loved him, so much. Her heart had broken when she'd left the hospital, but telling him that wouldn't heal her wounds. It would make her more vulnerable than she already was. And she'd never made herself as vulnerable as with Jack. Ever.

"Yes you did, pet. And you can't take it back. I won't let you, because I love you too."

"You do?" she asked, her eyes welling, her voice breaking.

He nodded and spoke against her lips. "I've been in love with you since the very first moment I laid eyes on you. Just too fucking stubborn to admit it to myself. I was pretty out of it, but I recall telling it to you then, before you know…"

He didn't finish the sentence. Didn't have to.

"You were dying. I thought you were delirious." Heck, she'd been delirious too.

He cupped her face. Brushed her lips with his thumb. "I was not going to die without telling you."

Tears rolling down, she hugged him, so damn hard her arms hurt. "I love you too, Borg."

She felt the tremors going through his body at her words.

"Why did you leave me at the hospital?" he whispered against her lips.

"You'd made it clear that you didn't want anything to do with me."

"At Exxum's, I told you I'd go to hell and back for you."

Elle shrugged, uneasy. "I figured that's what all the heroic types do for everyone."

Jack let out a soft snort. "No, pet, they don't do that for everyone. Nor get a hole in their stomachs."

"You talking about the ulcer I allegedly gave you, or the bullet?"

Jack barked out a laugh, tightening his embrace. "Both." She caressed his scratchy beard and spoke with a barely-there voice. He deserved the truth. "I left the hospital because I didn't want to be pushy."

"You are pushy."

"You don't like pushy," she said, feeling awkwardly

embarrassed.

He kissed her softly. "I love your kind of pushy, pet. Never doubt that. For the record, we aren't a good fit."

She froze at his words. "No?"

"No. We are a fucking perfect one."

Jack took her into his arms and kissed her long and deep. At some point, she heard the patrons at Rosita's clapping and whistling, but she didn't care. Her Borg was home.

* * * *

Jack would have trailed after Elle like a puppy the whole night, gladly, but Tate took pity on him and pushed them out of Rosita's.

Not a word was uttered as they walked to Jack's truck, or all the way to Elle's house.

Once they had a closed door between them and the rest of the world, he cupped her face, kissing her, feeling more complete and at peace than he'd felt in the last four weeks. Heck, in his whole life probably. "I want you."

Her eyes said yes, but her expression was hesitant. "You're injured."

Jack cracked a smile. "Not badly enough, pet."

"I want to see it."

"Why? You've seen it before."

"No, you dork. I don't mean your cock."

She grabbed his T-shirt, bunched it up, and with trembling fingers, proceed to caress the angry red scar on his side, her eyes welling.

Jack put his hand on top of hers. "It doesn't hurt, pet." Which wasn't totally true, but in comparison with the pain he'd endured without her in his life, this little scar was nothing.

She glanced at him, her voice quivering. "I'm so sorry that the biggest scar on your body is related to me. All the other wounds seem insignificant."

"This is the most important of all of them," he corrected her. "This I wouldn't trade for anything. This says I saved the woman I love. I know I'm not the easiest man to be around, but I love you with all my heart. No one will ever love you more than I do. I'd give my life for you."

"You almost did that," she whispered, tears rolling down her cheeks.

"And I'd do it again. In a heartbeat. I'm sorry I wasn't brave enough to take you on and I walked away from you. Honestly, it all but destroyed me. And every time I think that it almost got you killed, I feel furious with myself." If he'd admitted his feelings to her and himself, neither Exxum nor Maldonado would have ever gotten within a hundred feet of Elle, much less kidnap her and threaten her life.

Elle hugged him tight, speaking against his chest. "That wasn't your fault. You saved me."

As far as he was concerned, she'd saved him.

"You cut your hair," he mumbled after a long silence.

"Yes, I hated how it had hindered my movements," she replied, lowering her gaze. "Plus I decided I needed a change. Why? You don't like it?"

Her sudden confrontational tone brought a smile to his face. Fuck, he'd missed her. Her wit. Her warmth. Her smart-ass attitude. "I love it."

"Good. You said some pretty hurtful things when you left me. Not to mention that you left me."

Jack flinched at the pain in her eyes. "Fucking sorry, pet."

Her voice was barely there. "Don't do it again. Please."

"I won't."

He kissed her, slowly. Reverently. Relishing every one of her shivers, and lifting her into his arms, he took her to the bed. Time to love his woman.

* * * *

Elle sat on the porch stairs and read the e-mails that Jack had sent her, furiously wiping the fat tears rolling down her eyes.

Good morning, pet. I woke up at the hospital, without you. You've been here. I can still smell you. And I remember going in and out of consciousness and seeing you. There was no e-mail from you, so I decided to write to you. I miss you. A lot. Where are you?

She scrolled through the e-mails. There were dozens of them, which, considering they hadn't seen each other in four weeks, was a lot.

I finally got to see that damn movie, Grease. *Apparently the same principle applies to the TV and the radio: given enough channel-hopping, you are bound to find one where that movie is on. I still don't get the fascination with it, and I'll probably refuse to watch it ever again, but I did watch.*

She noticed over her sniffling that the front door had opened. She didn't have to turn to know who that was. She could feel his gravitational force, pulling at her. And that sexy scent of his inebriating her.

Jack sat behind her on the stairs, engulfing her with his warm body and planting a kiss on the top of her head. "What are you doing out here?"

Elle shrugged. She'd started reading the e-mails in the living room, but soon she realized the waterworks were unavoidable, and not wanting to wake Jack up, she'd escaped outside.

"You're crying. They're that bad?"

"No, of course not, Borg," she said, irate. "They are wonderful. You wrote to me every day."

"Yes. I think there are several occasions when I wrote twice in the same day. I didn't know what to do with myself without you."

They stayed together on those stairs for a long while, hugging. Going through the e-mails together.

"I love you, pet," he whispered.

Elle kissed him softly. "Love you too. Your morning-after skills have improved, Borg."

Jack chuckled. "So it seems."

"I told you I didn't need all those niceties to let you fuck me and I meant it. I still do."

"I know, but you deserve them. I won't start calling you princess or doll or anything like that though. You are and always will be my pet."

Fair enough.

"Now what?" Elle asked finally. It was his move. This was the proverbial morning after.

He answered right away. "Now we move in together."

"You at my place? Mrs. Copernicus will be thrilled to get someone like you for her neighborhood-watch group, but I don't see you in suburbia."

Jack shrugged. "I can deal with that; it doesn't bother me."

"What if I say I'm not ready to shack up with you?"

"Get ready pretty soon, because I'm waking up to you every day from now on. Every fucking day. Your choice where. You could move to my apartment."

"The one you only allowed me to go to while I was in shock so I would forget where it was afterward?"

He reached into the pocket of his jeans and handed her a key. "This is for you, pet." The key ring attached was engraved. *To Elle.*

She cocked her eyebrow but took it. "Pretty sure you were going to win me back, weren't you?"

"I wasn't going to let the best thing that has ever happened to me slip through my fingers."

Elle cupped his face. "I love you like crazy, Borg, but you know I will never bake you bread, right?"

Jack laughed. "I know. I'll survive."

"Or sew you underwear."

"We'll make do with Target."

"And I will always be a smart-ass."

He brushed his lips against hers. "I'm totally counting on that."

CHAPTER TWENTY-TWO

"You are in so much shit, dude," James said with a snort to Jack as they watched Elle and Ronnie laugh and twirl on the dance floor.

"Brother-in-law to you, asshole," Jack corrected with a grunt.

James turned to him, looking surprised. "You marrying her?"

"Damn right I am. Why? Didn't you think I would?"

"What do I think? That you're so far gone for her you can't see which way is up. Another thing is, how the hell are you going to get her to agree to marry you?"

True. He wasn't that big of a prize. Still, he wasn't letting go of her. Couldn't.

"Although you've been shacking up for a while now and so far you aren't missing important body parts," James continued. "None that I can see, anyways. You might have a shot there."

They'd been living together for a couple of months, moving back and forth from his place to hers, mainly because they couldn't decide where to settle. That is, *she* couldn't decide where to settle. He'd live in a fucking cardboard box as long as she was with him.

"Did you give any thought to my offer?" James asked.

"I'm not the easiest of employees."

James snorted. "Hell of an understatement. Besides, your calendar is wide open, right?"

Jack nodded.

"I heard Exxum had a mishap," James added. "Had a weird

allergic reaction to some exotic berry and kicked the bucket."

"Yeah, I heard that too." The police had gotten involved with the kidnapping, but it had looked like he was going to get away with it. After all, he hadn't been at the club and he'd made sure his bodyguard lawyered up right away.

"I thought you wanted to send him to jail," James reprimanded him. "Do it the standard way."

"That was before he dared to go after Elle. I gave the police a shot. It didn't work."

"Any news about Nico?"

Jack shook his head. "Last I heard, Mullen had been told by his superior that Nico had interceded for us, showing proof of Maldonado's involvement in Aalto's death and the trail of murders after his." According to his contacts, Nico was running the Cali cartel.

"Who is he working for?"

"I don't know," Jack admitted, and then changed the subject, handing his friend an envelope. "Got something for you."

"What is it?"

"Your sister."

James froze. "Fuck, man. You found her?"

Jack nodded. Unsealing closed adoption records was a bit tricky, what with having to go to court and all that shit. Not to mention that the judges tended to agree only if the adopted child made the petition; so he'd gone another route and now owed Mullen and his contacts a huge debt, but whatever.

James was still, staring at the envelope.

"Aren't you going to open it?"

"I'll get Cole and Max first. Thank you," he said.

"Don't mention it. Just keep it in mind when I'm being difficult on the job."

James clapped him on his back, and taking the envelope, headed to where Cole and Max were sitting.

Leaning on the counter, Jack watched as Elle navigated her way through the crowd toward him and was intercepted by a guy who had been looking at her while she was dancing.

He came closer to say something in her ear, placing his hand on her arm. She smiled but took a step back, pulling herself away from his touch, shaking her head, keeping her distance.

Jack felt like rushing to her and flooring the mofo, but he

forced himself to remain still.

Soon enough Elle got rid of the asshole and approached, hooking her finger through his belt loop and pulling. "Come dance with me, Borg."

The music had changed into a ballad. He didn't budge and she frowned, turning back to him. Fuck, she was so cute. And he loved her so much. Jack cupped her neck and brought her to him for a long, wet kiss.

"Please?" she whispered against his lips.

This time, when she pulled the belt loop, he trailed after her to the dance floor. There was nothing he could deny her. Absolutely nothing. Whatever she wanted, he'd give it to her. Fucking horrifying, yet he couldn't stop smiling. Nuts.

He engulfed her in his arms, her body melting into his.

"Having fun?" he asked into her ear as they danced.

"I'll still party with the girls and go out occasionally."

He knew. But he could take it.

Elle cupped his face and looked him straight in the eye. "I will always come home to you and I will never cheat on you."

"I know. I trust you."

And he did. Totally.

The music stopped and Jack looked at his watch: 00:00

"Happy birthday, pet," he whispered into her ear. "Enjoy your present."

* * * *

The place wasn't too full, but she didn't realize a group of people dressed in long trench coats and covering their faces with hats had appeared until they were all over the place. *What the hell?*

Suddenly she heard *"Well, this car could be systematic."* *Boom* and the bunch that had situated themselves around the dance floor shucked off their coats.

"Hydromatic," came from the speakers. *Boom* and the hats went flying, their faces down.

"Automatic."

Boom, and the group lifted their arms and their heads.

Oh God, it was her flash mob. Dressed in black and leather. Her breath caught in her throat.

"Why, it could be greased lightning!"

Elle couldn't stop laughing. That was her song, the one she always wanted to dance to but she always got outvoted.

The one she knew the steps to by heart.

Without thinking twice, she joined them while everyone cheered and sang.

She caught on very fast and in no time she was dancing and laughing, throwing her arm up and pointing from left to right, her only regret that she didn't have leather pants on.

By the end of the song everyone was applauding and whistling.

Elle hugged the flash mobbers closest to her and then searched for Jack. The moment she spotted him, she threw herself into his arms.

"Thank you so much," she said, showering him with kisses while he chuckled. "Who would have guessed you actually listen to me when I talk."

"I always listen, pet."

"How did you get them to agree to this?"

He shrugged, sheepishly. "I just asked. Believe it or not, people have trouble saying no to me. I intimidate them."

She burst into laughter. "You don't say."

* * * *

"I think Max has a point about the Jacuzzi, don't you think?" Elle said, standing on the porch of the cabin.

Jack came out and leaned against the doorjamb, his arms crossed over his chest. "You mean for fishing shrimp?"

Elle laughed. "Don't know about that, but a hot, bubbly Jacuzzi out on the deck facing the forest and the lake, right there," she said, pointing ahead, "would be so relaxing."

"Since when are you into relaxing?"

"Since my boyfriend fucks me blind every night and I get more cardio than the Duracell bunny."

Jack barked out a laugh.

She'd made huge progress on her promise to slow down. He wouldn't say she was Zen-like, but she was much better. Able to sit down and enjoy doing nothing, just watching nature, which was great news for the state's reforestation. And she was talking more about her brother and father. Had taken him to visit their graves. Marlene's too.

"Come here," he ordered.

She turned to him, that sexy defiance on her gaze. So fucking sexy. "Why?"

"Because I say so."

"Mamma mia che pazenzia." Rolling her eyes, Elle obeyed. "The things I put up with for you."

She came to him and he lifted her chin. "And why is that? Stockholm Syndrome?"

"Nah, I can't blame it on that. I just love you."

"How unfortunate for you," he murmured against her lips and kissed her while hauling her up.

Elle wrapped her legs around his waist. "You better be careful, Borg. Don't you know women transform anything into something mighty? Haven't you learned by now? You give a woman a spermatozoid, she gives you a baby. You give her a house, she'll give you a home. You give her a caress, she'll give you her heart. She multiplies and makes bigger anything that's offered to her. So do not give me any shit or you'll find yourself neck-deep in it. Give me problems and prepare yourself because I'll make your life impossible."

He took her to the sofa—a brand-new sofa that Elle had bought from IKEA and had managed to transport to the cabin with Ronnie's complicity—and sat on it. "Is that your subtle way of telling me you want my kid?"

Elle snorted. "Is that all that you got from what I just said?"

He ignored her. "You start having my babies, we might as well get hitched."

She narrowed her eyes. "Shitty marriage proposal, Borg. Even for someone speech-impaired. Besides, we're in the middle of an argument. You can't propose to me now. There are rules for that kind of thing."

"Says who?" He cupped her face, his thumb caressing her sweet mouth. His voice was low. "You want me on my knees? Because you already have me there. Had me on my knees for a long time. They are scraped bloody, pet. I'm an embarrassment to manhood."

Elle's soft body moved with laughter. "I doubt it very much. I can attest to your excellence."

"This formality is for you. As far as I am concerned, we are already married. This is it, for better or for worse, until death do us part. You want the party and the ceremony, you'll have them, but I don't need them. You're my woman."

"I might want the party and the ceremony," she said, looking him straight in the eye. "But you know what I totally and definitely need? A bachelorette party."

"You'll have that too." He might trail them and shoot at every guy who glanced at her but she'll have her bachelorette party.

"I'm thinking coed," she continued, smirking. "At a paintball range, with me in an old wedding dress and the girls wearing bridesmaids' ones."

"Do the guys have to wear the dresses too? Because that's not going to go down well."

She laughed. "No, you can go in your badass regular outfits. So, you game?"

He nodded. He was game for any-fucking-thing she wanted. Now and forever.

"You haven't properly answered, pet," he whispered.

"You haven't properly asked, Borg."

Smart-ass.

He stared into those big, black, bottomless eyes. "Will you do me the immense honor of marrying me? I know you are way out of my league and that you could do much better, get some happy-go-lucky guy who would coordinate his wardrobe, would never snarl, and would have an extremely busy and fulfilling social life, but I love you, snarling hermit up in the mountains that I am."

She smiled and nodded. "Yes, yes, yes, a thousand times yes."

He reached into the pocket of his jacket and presented her the only valuable thing that had ever meant shit to him. "I didn't get you a diamond engagement ring, pet."

It was Celia's family ring. *"Take it, mijo,"* she had said on her deathbed, forcing him to accept the ring. *"For whenever you find the person you can't breathe without."*

Jack had found her.

"Good, because I'm not the diamond-engagement-ring type."

Jack slid it on her finger. Perfect.

"Jack?"

"Hmm?"

"I prefer the snarling hermit with the cabin up in the mountains. Hands down. He's much more fun to tease. The happy-go-lucky guy who doesn't snarl and has an extremely busy and fulfilling social life? He tends to be gay."

Man, she was so freaking funny. He had no clue how he'd managed to get her to fall in love with him but he was going to work his butt off every fucking day to make this work.

"Where are we going?" she asked as he lifted her and headed for the kitchen counter where he'd left his duffle bag.

"To get a dildo. I want to see how you use it."

"On me or on you?"

Jack barked a laugh. "Dream on, pet." Then he kissed her and added, "But never lose your kind of pushy. It makes me want to fuck you harder."

"I won't. You know, though, you won't be able to fuck me into submission, right?"

"That doesn't mean I'm ever going to stop trying."

She cupped his face and brushed her lips over his. "That's my Borg."

* * * *

James and Cole stepped out of the car, followed by Max.

They stood in the suburban cul-de-sac, in front of the pink house, not really believing their eyes.

"Are you sure this is the right address?" Cole asked, looking around.

James nodded. "I double-checked. This is where she lives."

Jack's information hadn't been too detailed, but the tracking was sound. The baby who Rachel Bowen had given up for adoption was living there and her name was Morgana.

"Can't be. This is so…"

Max seemed at lost for words. James too.

"Martha fucking Stewart," Cole offered.

True. Matching welcome mat and drapes. Flowers on every windowsill. Cute, perfectly tended garden with a couple of gnomes watching over.

"She's supposed to be a parole officer, not Miss Peggy Sue." James was already half expecting someone dressed like Lucy opening the front door.

"It's the California sun," Max offered, walking toward the porch. "It makes people do weird things."

They knocked but no one answered, so they decided to check the backyard.

The kitchen door was ajar.

"Hello?" Cole said, poking his head in.

The door fell open.

The kitchen was creamy pink, very fifties, but no Lucy was there greeting them. More like an angry version of Lara Croft.

A man who looked rather the worse for wear was lying on the floor, whimpering, badly beaten up, and Lara Croft, aka their lost sister, was standing over him, holding a frigging chainsaw.

"This is not what it looks like," she said, turning to them.

TITLES BY ELLE AYCART

The Bowen series:
More than Meets the Ink
Heavy Issues
Inked Ever After
To the Max
Heavy Secrets
Jacked Up
Hard Limits
* * * *

The OGs Series:
Deep Down
* * * *

Doomsday Preppers:
Sky's the Limit

ELLE AYCART

After a colorful array of jobs all over Europe ranging from translator to chocolatier to travel agent to sushi chef to flight dispatcher, Elle Aycart is certain of one thing and one thing only: aside from writing romances, she has abso-frigging-lutely no clue what she wants to do when she grows up. Not that it stops her from trying all sorts of crazy stuff. While she is probably now thinking of a new profession, her head never stops churning new plots for her romances.

No-spam Newsletter
http://eepurl.com/c9QHLX

Keep in touch with Elle by visiting her at
http://elleaycart.blogspot.com.

Facebook
https://www.facebook.com/elle.aycart

Facebook Author page
https://www.facebook.com/Elle-Aycart-380858418611512/

Bookbub.com
https://www.bookbub.com/authors/elle-aycart

QR newsletter sign-up link:

Made in United States
North Haven, CT
19 November 2022

26967955R00159